Praise for
The Fantastic Novels of Lynn Flewelling

Hidden Warrior

"Stellar high-concept fantasy." —*Mysterious Galaxy*

"A rousing prince-in-hiding adventure, with some unexpectedly satisfying developments for a middle volume in a series." —*Locus*

"A beautiful, compelling, dark tale." —*Booklist*

"A superlative job . . . the world she has built is complex, and the action non-stop. . . . Flewelling handles the gender questions with such skill that the reader really feels Tobin's ambivalence, and gradual change. . . . Recommended highly for anyone seeking a rollicking good read." —*SF Site*

"Satisfying . . . intriguing . . . exploring not merely issues of gender and power but questions of honor as well."
—*Lambda Book Report*

"Lynn Flewelling doesn't disappoint. . . . Questions of obligation and independence have no easy answers for anyone in this maze, adding a welcome depth to the tale." —*Alien Online*

The Bone Doll's Twin

"*The Bone Doll's Twin* is a thoroughly engrossing new fantasy. It got its hooks into me on the first page, and didn't let loose until the last. I am already looking forward to the next installment."
—GEORGE R. R. MARTIN

"Lynn Flewelling's *The Bone Doll's Twin* outshines even the gleaming promise shown in her earlier three books. The story pulled me under and carried me off with it in a relentless tale that examines whether the ends can ever completely justify the means." —ROBIN HOBB

"Fresh and original—and unlike most fantasies that try to put women in traditionally male roles, hers works. I found the world exceptionally well realized and coherent. I think you have a winner here! My congratulations to Lynn. Books like this are too good not to share."   —KATHERINE KURTZ

"*The Bone Doll's Twin* is a great read. Lynn Flewelling has outdone herself with this vibrant tale of dark magic, a hidden child, and the demon ghost that haunts it. She builds a convincing, colorful world with carefully chosen details, and her characters are memorable because their dilemmas are vividly drawn and heartbreakingly believable. This is exactly the kind of fantasy novel that will keep you up long past your bedtime."   —KATE ELLIOTT

"A fascinating read, both intellectual and haunting."
—BARBARA HAMBLY

"A dark and twisting enchantment of a book, a story of deception and loyalty and heroism that will magick its readers along with its characters."   —LOUISE MARLEY

"Lynn Flewelling is one of the best at creating complicated stories peopled by diverse characters, each with his own agenda, and each absolutely believable. This tale of a girl disguised by magic and brought up as a boy is engrossing and compelling as it explores the honorable reasons behind dishonorable deeds—and the dark consequences that follow a single desperate act. Flewelling accompanies her skill at storytelling with an exquisite level of detail that brings her entire world to life. A most satisfying tale for readers already familiar with her Nightrunner series—for others, an excellent introduction to the joys of a Flewelling fantasy."   —SHARON SHINN

"You liked Lynn Flewelling's Nightrunner series? This novel is even better. *The Bone Doll's Twin* is a sharply honed, powerful story where good and evil are as entwined as two children's lives, and salvation carries a very high price. Highly recommended."
—ANNE BISHOP

"An intriguing prequel to Flewelling's splendid Nightrunner series and a solid beginning to a new triad of fantasy from a most generous and skilled fantasist, *The Bone Doll's Twin* will satisfy old fans and capture many new."   —PATRICK O'LEARY

Praise for the Nightrunner Series

Luck in the Shadows

"Memorable characters, an enthralling plot and truly daunting evil . . . The characters spring forth from the page not as well-crafted creations but as people . . . the magic is refreshingly difficult, mysterious, and unpredictable. Lynn Flewelling has eschewed the easy shortcuts of clichéd minor characters and cookie-cutter backdrops to present a unique world. . . . I commend this one to your attention."   —ROBIN HOBB

"Part high fantasy and part political intrigue, *Luck in the Shadows* makes a nice change from the usual ruck of contemporary sword-and-sorcery. I especially enjoyed Lynn Flewelling's obvious affection for her characters. At unexpected moments she reveals a well-honed gift for the macabre."   —STEPHEN R. DONALDSON

"A new star is rising in the fantasy firmament. . . . I am awed by the scope of the intricate world . . . it teems with magic and bustles with realistic people and spine-chilling amounts of skullduggery."   —DAVE DUNCAN

"A splendid read, filled with magic, mystery, adventure, and taut suspense. Lynn Flewelling, bravo! Nicely done."
—DENNIS L. MCKIERNAN

"An engrossing and entertaining debut . . . full of magic, intrigues, and fascinating characters. Witty and charming, it's the kind of book you settle down with when you want a long, satisfying read."   —MICHAEL A. STACKPOLE

"Exceptionally well done and entertaining."   —*Locus*

"Lynn Flewelling has written a terrific first novel, a thrilling introduction to this series. . . . Highly recommended."   —*Starlog*

Stalking Darkness

"Flewelling is . . . bringing vigor back to the traditional fantasy form. In this highly engaging adventure novel, the most powerful magic is conjured out of friendship and loyalty. The author has a gift for creating characters you genuinely care about."

—TERRI WINDLING,
The Years's Best Fantasy and Horror,
Eleventh Annual Collection

"Events move forward in this second adventure . . . it's up to four companions to stop Mardus's schemes. Things get very violent and there's also a strong emotional undercurrent . . . an amusing twist on the old 'damsel in distress' scenario."   —*Locus*

"While fans . . . will find enough wizardry, necromancy, swords, daggers, and devilishly clever traps here to satisfy the most avid, this book also provides entry to a complete and richly realized world that will please more mainstream readers."

—*Bangor Daily News*

Traitor's Moon

"What most fantasy aspires to *Traitor's Moon* achieves, with fierce craft, wit, and heart. It is a fantasy feast—richly imagined, gracefully wrought, and thrilling to behold. An intoxicating brew of strange and homely, horror and whimsy, lust and blood, intrigue and honor, great battles and greater loves. It is a journey through a world so strange and real you can taste it, with companions so mysterious and memorable you won't forget it. Lynn Flewelling is a fine teller of tales who delivers all she promises, cuts no corners, and leaves us dazzled, moved, and hungry for more. *Traitor's Moon* is a wonderful book."   —PATRICK O'LEARY

Also by Lynn Flewelling

Luck in the Shadows
Stalking Darkness
Traitor's Moon
AND
The Bone Doll's Twin
Hidden Warrior

The Oracle's Queen

Lynn Flewelling

BANTAM BOOKS
New York Toronto
London Sydney Auckland

THE ORACLE'S QUEEN
A Bantam Spectra Book / July 2006

Published by Bantam Dell
A Division of Random House, Inc.
New York, New York

This is a work of fiction. Names, characters, places, and incidents
either are the product of the author's imagination or are used
fictitiously. Any resemblance to actual persons, living or dead,
events, or locales is entirely coincidental.

Bantam Books, the rooster colophon, Spectra, and the portrayal
of a boxed "s" are trademarks of Random House, Inc.

ISBN-13: 978-0-553-58345-8
ISBN-10: 0-553-58345-X

Printed in the United States of America
Published simultaneously in Canada

www.bantamdell.com

OPM 10 9 8 7 6 5 4 3 2 1

For Patricia York
August 14, 1949–May 21, 2005

Wish you were here to see how this one ended.
Thanks for always reminding me "it's not the
number of breaths we take, but the number of
moments that take our breath away."

Catch you later, my good, dear friend.

Acknowledgments

Thanks, first and foremost to Dr. Doug, my main Muse and best friend. Also to Pat York, Anne Groell, Lucienne Diver, Matthew and Timothy Flewelling, Nancy Jeffers, Dr. Meghan Cope, and Bonnie Blanch for all their helpful feedback and patience, and to all the readers who've given me such great support over the years.

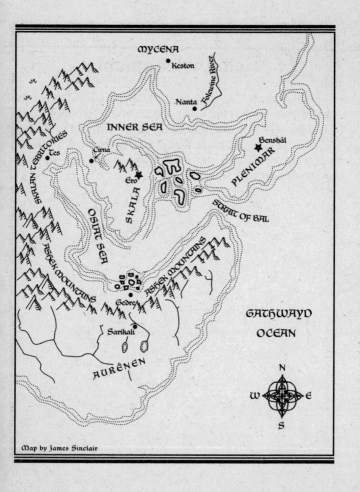

Map by James Sinclair

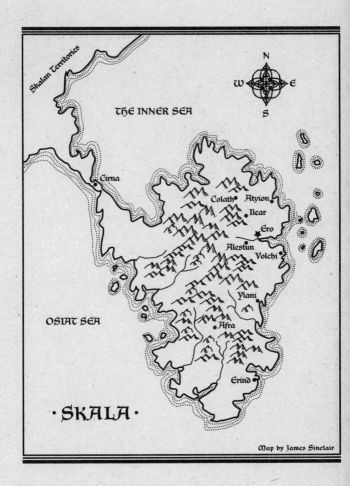

N
W   E
S

Skalan Territories

THE INNER SEA

Cirna

Colath
Atyion

Ilear

Ero

Alestun

Volchi

Ylani

OSIAT SEA

Asra

Erind

· SKALA ·

Map by James Sinclair

Chapter 1

The cold night breeze shifted, blowing stinging smoke from old Teolin's campfire into Mahti's eyes. The young witch blinked it away, but remained squatting motionless, his bearskin cloak pulled around him like a little hut. It was bad luck to fidget during this last crucial step of the making.

The old witch hummed happily as he heated his knife again and again, using the tip and edge to incise the rings of dark, intricate patterns that now covered most of the long wooden tube. Teolin was ancient. His wrinkled brown skin hung on his skinny frame like old cloth and his bones showed through. The witch marks on his face and body were hard to read, distorted by the ravages of time. His hair hung over his shoulders in a thin tangle of yellowed strands. Years of making had left his blunt, knobby fingers stained black, but they were as nimble as ever.

Mahti's last *oo'lu* had cracked one cold night this past midwinter, after he'd played out an elder's gallstones. It had taken months of searching to find the right kind of bildi branch to make a new one. Bildi trees weren't scarce, but you had to find a sapling trunk or large branch that had been ant-hollowed, and the right size to give a good tone. "High as your chin, and four fingers broad"; so he'd been taught and so it was.

He'd found plenty of flawed branches in the hills around his village: knotted ones, cracked ones, others with holes eaten out through the side. The large black ants that followed the rising sap through the heartwood were industrious but undiscerning craftsmen.

He'd finally found one, and cut his horn stave from it. But it was bad luck for a witch to make his own instrument, even if he had the skill. Each must be earned and given from the hand of another. So he'd strapped it to his back over his bearskin cloak and snowshoed for three days and nights to bring it to Teolin.

The old man was the best oo'lu maker in the eastern hills. Witch men had been coming to him for three generations and he turned away more than he accepted.

It took weeks to make an oo'lu. During this time it was Mahti's job to chop wood, cook food, and generally make himself useful while Teolin worked.

Teolin first stripped the bark and used live coals to burn out the last of the ants' leavings. When the stave was fully hollowed he went out of earshot to test the tone. Satisfied, he and Mahti rested and traded spells for a week while the hollow branch hung drying in the rafters near the smoke hole of Teolin's hut.

It dried without warping or cracking. Teolin sawed the ends square and rubbed beeswax into the wood until it gleamed. Then they'd waited two more days for the full moon.

Tonight was the sit-still.

That afternoon Mahti had scraped away the snow in front of the hut and dragged out an old lion skin for Teolin to sit on. He laid a large fire, with more wood stacked within easy reach, and hunkered down to tend it.

Teolin sat down wrapped in his moth-eaten bearskin and set to work. Using a heated iron knife, he etched the rings of magic onto the wood. Mahti watched with rapt attention as he fed the fire, marveling at how the designs seemed to flow from the tip of the blade, like ink onto deerskin. He wondered if it would come so easily to him, when the time came for him to make oo'lus for others?

Now the Mother's full white face was high overhead and Mahti's ankles ached from squatting, but the oo'lu was nearly done.

When the last of the rings was complete, Teolin dipped the mouth end in a little pot of melted wax, then rolled a softened lump of it into a thin coil and pressed it in a ring to the waxed end of the horn. He squinted across at Mahti, gauging the size of his mouth, and pinched the wax in until the opening was about two thumbs wide.

Satisfied at last, he gave Mahti a toothless grin. "Ready to learn this one's name?"

Mahti's heart beat faster as he stood and stretched the stiffness from his legs. His last oo'lu, Moon Plow, had served him seven years. In that time he'd become a man and a healer. Honoring the Moon Plow mark, he'd planted many fine children in women's bellies at Mother Shek'met's festivals. His sons and daughters were scattered through three valleys and some of the oldest were already showing witch's talent.

When Moon Plow cracked, this cycle of his life ended. He was twenty-three summers old, and his next future was about to be revealed.

Drawing his own knife, he cut his right palm and held it over the mouth of the oo'lu as Teolin held it. A few drops of his blood fell inside it as he sang the claiming spell. The black tracery of witch marks across his face, arms, and chest tickled like spider feet. When he thrust his hand into the fire, he didn't feel the heat of it. Straightening, he moved to the far side of the fire and faced the old man. "I'm ready."

Teolin held the oo'lu upright and chanted the blessing, then tossed it across to Mahti.

He caught it awkwardly in his fire hand, gripping it well below the center. Even hollow, it was a heavy thing. It nearly overbalanced, and if it had fallen, he'd have had to burn it and start all over again. But he managed to hang on to it, gritting his teeth until the witch marks faded completely from sight on his arms. He took the horn in his left hand and inspected it. The shiny black print of his fire hand was branded into the wood.

Teolin took it back and carefully examined how the marks of Mahti's splayed fingers intersected the carved designs. He was a long time at it, humming and sucking his gums.

"What's wrong?" asked Mahti. "Is it a bad luck cycle?"

"This is the Sojourn mark you've made. You better spit for it."

Teolin scratched a circle in the ashes at the edge of the fire with his knife. Mahti took a mouthful of water from the gourd and spat forcefully into the circle, then turned away quickly as Teolin hunkered down to interpret the marks.

The old man sighed. "You'll travel among strangers until this oo'lu cracks. Whether that's good luck or bad, only the Mother knows, and she doesn't feel like telling me tonight. But it's a strong mark you made. You'll travel a long way."

Mahti bowed respectfully. If Teolin said it would be so, then it would be. Best just to accept it. "When do I go? Will I see Lhamila's child born?"

Teolin sucked his gums again, staring down at the spit marks. "Go home by a straight path tomorrow and lay your blessings on her belly. A sign will come. But now, let's hear this fine horn I've made for you!"

Mahti settled his mouth firmly inside the wax mouthpiece. It was still warm and smelled of summer. Closing his eyes, he filled his cheeks with air and blew gently out through loosened lips.

Sojourn's deep voice came to life with his breath. He hardly had to adjust his playing style at all before the rich, steady drone warmed the wood beneath his hands. Gazing up at the white moon, he sent a silent thanks to the Mother. Whatever his new fate was, he knew already that he would do great magic with Sojourn, surpassing all he'd done with Moon Plow.

By the time he finished the claiming song he was light-headed. "It's good!" he gasped. "Are you ready?"

The old man nodded and hobbled back into the hut.

They'd agreed on the payment their first day together. Mahti lit the bear fat lamp and set it by the piled furs of the sleeping platform.

Teolin shrugged off his cloak and undid the ties of his shapeless robe. The elk and bear teeth decorating it clicked softly as he let it fall. He stretched out on his pallet, and Mahti knelt and ran his eyes over the old man's body, feeling compassion tinged with sadness rise in his heart. No one knew how old Teolin was, not even the old witch himself. Time had eaten most of the flesh from his frame. His penis, said to have planted more than five hundred festival seeds, now lay like a shrunken thumb against his hairless sac.

The old man smiled gently. "Do what you can. Neither the Mother nor I ask more than that."

Mahti leaned down, kissed the old man's lined brow, and drew the fusty bearskin up to Teolin's chin to keep him warm. Settling beside the platform, he rested the end of the horn close to the old man's side, closed his eyes, and began the spell song.

With lips and tongue and breath, he altered the drone to a sonorous, rhythmic pulse. The sound filled Mahti's head and chest, making his bones shiver. He gathered the energies and sent them out through Sojourn to Teolin. He could feel the song enter the old man, lifting the strong soul free of the frail, pain-wracked body, letting it drift up through the smoke hole like milkweed fluff. Bathing in the light of a full moon was very healing for a soul. It returned to the body cleansed and gave a clear mind and good health.

Satisfied, Mahti changed the song, tightening his lips to weave in the night croak of a heron, the booming boast of grandfather frog, and the high, reedy chorus of all the little peepers who knew the rain's secrets. With these, he washed the hot sand from the old man's joints and cleansed the little biting spirits from his intestines. Searching deeper, he smelled a shadow in Teolin's chest and followed it to a dark mass in the upper lobe of his liver. The death there was still asleep, curled tight like a child in the womb. This, Mahti could not cleanse away. Some were fated to carry their own deaths. Teolin would understand. For now, at least, there was no pain.

Mahti let his mind wander on through the old man's body, soothing the old fractures in his right heel and left arm, pressing the pus away from the root of a broken molar, dissolving the grit in the old man's bladder and kidneys. For all its wizened appearance, Teolin's penis was still strong. Mahti played the sound of a forest fire into his sac. The old man had a few more festivals in him; let the Mother be served by another generation bearing his fine old blood.

The rest was all old scars, long since healed or accepted. Allowing himself a whim, he played the white owl's call through Teolin's long bones, then droned the soul back down into the old man's flesh.

When he was finished, he was surprised to see pink dawn light shining in through the smoke hole. He was covered in sweat and shaking, but elated. Smoothing his hand down the polished length of the oo'lu, he whispered, "We will do great things, you and I."

Teolin stirred and opened his eyes.

"The owl song tells me you are one hundred and eight years old," Mahti informed him.

The old man chuckled. "Thank you. I'd lost track." He reached out and touched the handprint on the oo'lu. "I caught a vision for you while I slept. I saw the moon, but it was not the Mother's round moon. It was a crescent, sharp as a snake's tooth. I've seen that vision only once before, not too long ago. It was for a witch from Eagle Valley village."

"Did she learn what it meant?"

"I don't know. She went away with some *oreskiri*. I've never heard anything of her return. Her name is Lhel. If you meet her in your travels, give her my greeting. Perhaps she can tell you the meaning."

"Thank you, I'll do that. But you still don't know if my fate is a good one or a bad one?"

"I've never walked Sojourn's path. Perhaps it depends on where your feet take you. Walk bravely in your all travels, honor the Mother, and remember who you are. Do that and you will continue to be a good man, and a fine witch."

Mahti left the old man's clearing at dawn the next day, Teolin's blessing still tingling on his brow.

Plodding over the crusty snow, Sojourn a comforting weight across his shoulders in its sling, he smelled the first hint of spring on the morning air. Later, as the sun rose over the peaks, he heard it in the dripping of water from bare branches.

He knew this trail well. The rhythmic crunch and rasp of his snowshoes lulled him into a light trance and his thoughts drifted. He wondered if he'd plant different kinds of children now than he had under the Moon Plow sign? Then again, if he were to travel far, would he plant any children at all?

He wasn't surprised when the vision came. He often had them at moments like these, tramping alone through the peace of the forest.

The winding path became a river under his feet, and the sinew and bent ash of his snowshoes grew into a little boat that bobbed gently on the current. Instead of the thick forest on the far bank, there was open land, very green and fertile. He knew in the way of visions that this must be the southland, where his people had once lived, before the foreigners and their oreskiri had driven them into the hills.

A woman stood between a tall man and a young girl on that bank, and she waved to Mahti as if she knew him. She was Retha'noi like him, and naked. Dark-skinned and small, her fine, ripe body was covered with witch marks. The fact that she was naked in the vision told him that she was dead, a spirit coming to him with a message.

Greetings, my brother. I am Lhel.

Mahti's eyes widened as he recognized the name. This was the woman Teolin had spoken of, the one who'd gone away with the southlanders on a sojourn of her own. She smiled at him and he smiled back; this was the Mother's will.

She beckoned him to join her but his boat would not move.

He looked more closely at the others with her. They were black-haired, too, but the man's was cut short and the girl's hung in long waves around her shoulders rather than the coarse curls of his people. They were taller, too, and pale as a pair of bones. The young man had an aura of strong magic about him: oreskiri, surely, but with a hint of power Mahti recognized. This witch, Lhel, must have taught him something of their ways. That was troubling, even though Teolin had spoken no ill of her.

The girl did not have magic, but Lhel pointed to the ground at the girl's feet and Mahti saw that she had a double shadow, one male, and one female.

He didn't know how to interpret the vision yet, except that these two were both living people, and southlanders. He was not afraid or angry to see them here in his mountains, though. Maybe it was the way the other witch rested her hands on their shoulders, love so clear in her dark eyes. She looked at Mahti again and made a sign of bequeathing. She was giving these two strangers into his care, but why?

Without thinking, he set the new oo'lu to his lips and played a song he did not recognize.

The vision passed and the forest path returned around him. He was standing in a clearing, still playing that song. He didn't know what it was for; perhaps it was for the southlanders. He would play it for them when they met and see if they knew.

Chapter 2

"It's one thing to accept one's destiny.
It's quite another to live it."

I am Tamír!"
Ki stood beside her in that ruined throne room, the acrid stink of the burning city thick in the air, and watched as his friend declared herself a woman and rightful heir to the throne. Imonus, high priest of Afra, had brought Ghërilain's lost gold stele as proof. It was as big as a door and he could see Tamír reflected in it, crowned by the ancient prophecy engraved there:

> So long as a daughter of Thelátimos'
> line defends and rules, Skala shall
> never be subjugated.

She didn't look much like a queen yet, just a ragged, tired, too-thin girl in battle-stained men's clothing. She hadn't had to strip for the crowd this time, but there was no mistaking the jut of small pointed breasts through the loose linen shirt.

Ki averted his eyes with a vague pang of guilt. The thought of how her body had changed still gave him a sick feeling.

Iya and Arkoniel stood with the priests at the foot of the dais, still in their dirty robes. They'd helped turn the tide of battle, but Ki knew the truth about them now, too. It was their doing, all the lies.

The oath takings and rituals dragged on and on. Ki

scanned the crowd, trying to share in the joy he saw around him, but all he could think of at that moment was how young and thin and brave and worn out Tobin—no, *Tamír*—looked.

He tried the unfamiliar name in his mind again, hoping to make it stick. He'd seen the proof of her sex with his own eyes, but he still could not get his mind around it, or his heart.

I'm just tired.

Had it only been a week since they'd ridden for Atyion at the king's order? Just a week since he'd first learned the truth about Tobin, his dearest friend, his heart's brother?

He blinked away the sudden stinging in his eyes. His friend was not Tobin anymore. There she stood, right in front of him, yet he felt as if Tobin had died.

He glanced sidelong at Tharin, hoping the man hadn't noticed his weakness. Teacher, mentor, second father, he'd slapped Ki when he'd panicked that night on the road to Atyion. Ki had deserved it, and he'd been grateful for the correction. He'd stood fast with Tharin and Lynx a few days later when Tobin had sliced the fragment of Brother's bone, and the witch's magic with it, from his own breast on the steps of Atyion castle, calling down the mystical fire that burned away his male body. Horrified, they'd watched as Tobin bled and burned and somehow lived to strip withered flesh away like a snake shedding last year's outworn skin, leaving in his place this wan, hollow-eyed girl.

The rituals ended at last. Tharin and the newly organized bodyguard closed ranks in front of them. Close by Tamír's side, Ki saw how she wavered a little as she stepped down from the dais. He slipped a discreet hand under her elbow, steadying her.

Tamír pulled her arm away, but gave him a small, tight smile, letting him know it was only pride.

"May we escort you to your old chamber, Highness?" Tharin asked. "You can rest there until arrangements can be made elsewhere."

Tamír gave him a grateful look. "Yes, thank you."

Arkoniel made to follow, but Iya stopped him, and Tamír did not look back or summon them.

The palace corridors were packed with the wounded. The air was rank with the stench of blood. The fish pools set into the floors were stained pink with it. Drysian healers were at work everywhere, overwhelmed by the sheer numbers of those in need of their skills. Tamír looked around sadly as they hurried on, and Ki could guess her thoughts. These soldiers had fought under Erius' banner and fallen for Ero. How many would have fought for her? And how many would serve under her now?

Reaching her old chamber at last, she said, "Keep guard out here, Tharin, please?"

Ki hesitated, thinking she meant to leave him, too, but she dispelled his doubts with a sharp glance and Ki followed her into the ransacked room that had once been their home.

As soon as the door was closed she slumped back against it and let out an unsteady laugh. "Free at last! For now anyway."

That voice still sent a shiver through him. Tobin wasn't yet sixteen, and hadn't lost his high, boyish voice. Still hoarse from battle, Tamír sounded just the same. In the gathering gloom, she even looked like Prince Tobin, with her warrior braids and long black hair falling forward around her face.

"Tob?" The old name still came too easily.

"You can't call me that anymore."

Ki heard the echo of his own confusion in her voice and reached for her hand, but she brushed past him and went to the bed.

Nikides lay as they'd left him, still unconscious. His sandy hair was plastered to his cheeks with sweat and blood, and the bandages around his side were crusted with it, but his breathing was even. Tamír's little page, Baldus, was curled asleep at his feet.

Tamír rested a hand on Nikides' brow.

"How is he?" asked Ki.

"Feverish, but alive."

"Well, that's something."

Of the nineteen original Companions, five were dead for certain, and the rest missing, except for Nik and two squires. Tanil would be lucky to survive the brutal torture he'd suffered at the hands of the Plenimarans. Lynx still seemed recklessly intent on not surviving his fallen lord, Orneus, yet he'd come through every battle without a scratch.

"I hope Lutha and Barieus are still alive," Ki murmured, wondering how their friends would fare without them. He sat down on the floor and ran his fingers back through his tangled hair. It had grown long over the winter. The thin brown braids framing his face hung to his chest. "Where do you suppose Korin went?"

Tamír sank down beside him and shook her head. "I still can't believe he'd abandon the city like that!"

"Everyone says it was Niryn's doing."

"I know, but how could Korin let that bastard sway him like that? He never liked him any more than we did."

Ki said nothing, keeping his bitter thoughts to himself. From the day they'd met, Ki had seen the weakness in the Prince Royal, just as clearly as Tamír had seen the good. It was like a streak of poor alloy in a fine blade, and had already betrayed him twice in battle. Royal or not, Korin was a coward, and that was unforgivable in a warrior—or a king.

Tamír shifted over, leaning against his shoulder. "What do you suppose Korin and the others thought if they've heard news of me?"

"Nik or Tanil can tell us that when they wake up, I guess."

"What would you think, in their place?" she fretted, scratching at a bit of dried blood on the back of one hand.

"How do you suppose it will sound to anyone who wasn't there to see?"

Before he could answer that, Arkoniel slipped in without knocking. Unshaven, one arm in a sling, he looked more beggar than wizard.

Ki could hardly bear to look at him. Arkoniel had been their teacher and their friend, or so they thought. But he'd lied to them all these years. Even knowing the reason, Ki wasn't yet sure he could forgive him for that.

Arkoniel must have read his thoughts or his face; the sudden sadness in his eyes betrayed him. "Duke Illardi has offered his villa as a headquarters. The grounds have strong walls and there's been no plague in that ward. It's a safer place for you than here. The fires are still spreading."

"Tell him I accept his offer," Tamír replied without looking up. "I want Nik with me, and Tanil, too. He's at the camp we overran yesterday."

"Of course."

"And we should save what we can of the royal library and archives before the fire spreads."

"Already seen to," Arkoniel assured her. "Tharin's placed a guard on the Royal Tomb, as well, but I'm afraid there was some looting."

"Seems I'm always saddled with caring for the dead." Tamír rose and walked out onto the broad balcony that overlooked the palace gardens and the city beyond. Ki and Arkoniel followed.

This part of the Old Palace was hardly touched by the destruction outside. Snowdrops and banks of white narcissus glowed in the failing daylight. Beyond the walls, smoke hung heavy over the city, lit from below by flames.

Tamír gazed up at the red-stained sky. "One of the last things my uncle said to me before we rode for Atyion was that if Ero is lost, Skala is lost. What do you think, Arkoniel? Was he right? Were we too late?"

"No. It's a terrible blow, certainly, but Ero is only one city among many. Skala is wherever you are. The queen is the land. I know things look grim to you right now, but births are seldom easy and never clean. Rest a bit before we ride. Oh, and Iya's spoken to some of the women in your guard. Ahra or Una can stay with you tonight."

"Ki is still my squire."

The wizard hesitated, then said quietly, "I don't think that's advisable, do you?"

Tamír rounded on him, pent-up fury blazing in those dark eyes. Even Ki took a step back in the face of it.

"It *is* advisable because I *say* it is! Consider that my first official proclamation as your queen-to-be. Or am I just a wizard's puppet after all, like my uncle?"

Arkoniel looked stricken as he pressed a hand to his heart and bowed. "No, never that. I swear on my life."

"I'll remember you said that," Tamír snapped. "And you remember this. I accept my duty to Skala, the gods, my line, and my people. But right now, I warn you—" A quaver crept into her voice. "Don't cross me in this. Ki stays with me. Now just—go away!"

"As you wish, Highness." The wizard quickly retreated, but not without a sad look in Ki's direction.

Ki pretended not to notice. *You put her here. You can damn well suffer the consequences along with the rest of us!*

"Prince Tobin?" Baldus stood in the doorway, rubbing his eyes. Tamír's valet, Molay, had hidden the child in a trunk during the final attack. When Tamír and Ki had found him afterward, he was too exhausted and terrified to notice the change in her. He looked around in confusion. "Where's the princess you were talking to, Lord Ki?"

Tamír went to the child and took his hand. "Look at me, Baldus. Look closely."

The boy's brown eyes widened. "Highness, are you bewitched?"

"I was. Now I'm not."

Baldus nodded uncertainly. "An enchanted princess, like in the bard's tales?"

Tamír managed a pained smile. "Something like that.
We need to get you someplace safe."

Chin trembling, the child fell to his knees, clutching
her hand and kissing it. "I'll always serve you, Princess
Tobin. Please don't send me away!"

"Of course I won't, if you want to stay." Tamír pulled
him to his feet and hugged him. "I need every loyal man I
can find. But you must call me Princess Tamír now."

"Yes, Princess Tamír." The child clung to her. "Where's
Molay?"

"I don't know."

Ki doubted they'd see him again on this side of
Bilairy's gate. "Get some sleep, Tamír. I'll keep watch." To
his surprise, she didn't argue. Stretching out beside Nikides
on the bare mattress, she turned on her side and surrendered at last to exhaustion.

Ki pulled up a chair and sat with his sword unsheathed
across his knees. He was her squire and he would do his
duty, but he studied that shadowed face with the heavy
heart of a friend.

Darkness had fallen when Tharin came in with a lamp. Ki
blinked in the sudden light. Tamír sat up at once, reaching
for her sword.

"Everything's ready, Tamír." Tharin stepped aside to
make way for the litter bearers who'd come for Nikides.
Lynx followed, carrying Tamír's discarded armor.

"I've assembled an escort for you in the front court and
Manies has gone for your horses," said Tharin. "You'd best
wear your armor. The streets are far from secure."

Ki took the Aurënfaie hauberk from the other squire.
Lynx understood. This was Ki's responsibility, and his
honor.

He helped Tamír put on the supple mail hauberk, then
buckled on the breastplate for her. These pieces, as well as
what Ki, Lynx, and Tharin wore, had all come from the
Atyion armory. Wrestling with the unfamiliar buckles, he

wondered what had become of the armor they'd left behind in Ero that night. *Lost with everything else,* Ki thought with regret. His had been a gift from Tobin, one of her own designs.

Tamír, he thought, catching himself. Damnation! How long before that came naturally?

The rest of the royal guard was mounted and waiting for them in the courtyard. Beyond the wall, the Palatine was as bright as day from the fires still burning there. The hot breeze was against them, and ash had drifted over everything like a grey killing frost.

There were at least a hundred riders assembled, many of whom held torches to light the way. Most of the horses had shorn manes, Ki noted. Mourning for the king, perhaps, or lost comrades. The few remaining men from the Alestun guard were at the forefront, still keeping together as a group. Aladar and Kadmen saluted him and he returned it with a heavy heart; too many missing faces there.

Lady Una was there, too, with Iya, Arkoniel, and the ragtag collection of wizards Iya had gathered. The rest were soldiers still wearing the baldric of Atyion, Captain Grannia and her women foremost among them.

Lord Jorvai and Lord Kyman, Tamír's first allies among the nobles, waited with sizable contingents of their own riders.

Left-handed Manies hoisted Tamír's tattered banner aloft. It still showed the blended coat of arms of her parents, Ero and Atyion together. A long black ribbon was tied to the top of the staff, out of respect for the dead king.

"You should ride under the royal banner now," said Tharin.

"I haven't been crowned yet, have I? Besides, Korin took that with him, too." She leaned closer, whispering, "So many? It's less than three miles to Illardi's house."

"As I said, the streets are still dangerous. A lot of Erius' men have refused to join us. They could still be out there somewhere, planning who knows what."

Tamír settled her sword on her hip and went down the steps to the tall black horse a man still wearing Erius' colors was holding for her.

"Keep your eyes open and stay close to her," Tharin muttered as he and Ki followed.

"I will!" Ki shot back under his breath. What did Tharin think he was going to do, go woolgathering as if they were out for a hunt?

As Ki swung up onto his borrowed horse, he saw that Tamír had drawn her dagger. Her horse's mane had not been shorn. She grasped a hank of the coarse black hair and cut it free, then singed it in a nearby torch. It was a symbolic act, but a worthy one. "For my kin," she said, loud enough for all to hear. "And for all who died bravely for Skala."

From the corner of his eye, Ki caught Iya smiling and shaking her head.

Ki and Tamír rode at the center of the column, shielded on all sides by arméd riders and wizards. Jorvai took the forward position, and Kyman and his men the rear guard. Tharin rode with Tamír, and the two wizards flanked them. Baldus clung wide-eyed behind Arkoniel, a small bundle clutched in one hand.

With much of the Palatine still in flames, the usual route to the gate was impassable. Tamír and her column crossed the ruined park to a small secondary gate behind the ravaged drysian grove.

This way took them past the Royal Tomb. Tamír glanced up at the scorched ruins of the portico. Ranks of priests and soldiers stood guard there, but most of the royal effigies were gone.

"Did the Plenimarans knock down the statues?"

Iya chuckled. "No, the defenders on the Palatine dropped them on the enemies' heads."

"I never went back," Tamír murmured.

"Highness?"

Ki understood. The night they'd first come to Ero, Tamír had taken her father's ashes down into the royal crypt and seen her mother's preserved corpse. That had been the only time she'd ventured into the catacombs, avoiding them even on Mourning Night and the other holy days. Ki figured that after living with Brother all these years, she'd had her fill of the dead.

And where's he now? he wondered. There'd been no sign of the demon since the unbinding ceremony. All the bits of bone from the doll had burned away with the magic. Perhaps Tamír was finally free of him, as Lhel had promised.

And he's free, too. Ki still recalled the look of agony on Brother's face in those final moments. Despite all the fear and pain he'd caused over the years, and the harm he'd tried to do, Ki hoped that the angry spirit had passed the gate at last, for everyone's sake.

Chapter 3

The city outside the Palatine was in chaos, the air filled with angry cries and the sound of weeping. The rain had lessened, but ragged clouds still hung low over the city. Fires still raged in some of the wards, and an endless stream of refugees choked the streets. Soldiers stood guard outside the gates, trying to keep people from returning to salvage or loot.

Tamír looked around at these people—*her* people. Most of them had no idea who was passing them tonight. What would they think if they saw her abandoning the capital?

"By the Flame, I'm tired of sneaking about in the dark," she muttered, and Ki nodded.

Smoldering foundations and lurking freebooters weren't the worst of the dangers in the ruined city. Hundreds of bodies, the victims of battle and plague, lay rotting in the streets, breeding more disease. Most of the Scavengers who tended to such things were dead themselves.

Tamír's guard doused their torches once they were free of the city, not wanting to serve as targets for any lurking enemy archers. The north high road was crowded with a dark, seething line of people, horses, and carts of every description stretching away into the night.

Have I already failed? she wondered again.

If the Lightbearer wanted a queen so badly, then why had the Immortal chosen such a dark moment to reveal her? She'd put the question to the Afran priest earlier, but Imonus' maddeningly serene smile had been her only answer. The priests and wizards were delighted with this turn of events, despite all the suffering that came with it.

And yet the sight of all these homeless people left her feeling very small and tired. How was she to help them all? The burden of this new role, and all the uncertainty that came with it, bore down on her like a great weight.

"Don't worry," Tharin said quietly. "Things will look better in the morning. The clouds are breaking up. I can see the stars already. See that group over there?" He pointed up at a constellation. "The Dragon. I take that as a good omen, don't you?"

Tamír managed a wan smile; the Dragon was one of Illior's signs. She'd been a devotee of Sakor all her life; now every sign and omen seemed to come from the Lightbearer. As if in answer to her thoughts, an owl hooted loudly somewhere off to their right.

Imonus caught her eye. "Another good omen, Highness. When you hear the Lightbearer's bird, you salute the god." He showed her how, touching three fingers to his forehead between his brows.

Tamír copied the gesture. Ki and Tharin followed suit, then other riders around them who'd heard and seen.

Is it because they've accepted Illior's hand in all this, or because they'll follow anything I do?

She'd always been in Korin's shadow at court and seen how everyone went along with whatever he did. If that was to be the case, she vowed to set a better example than he had.

Duke Illardi and his mounted escort met them on the road. Tamír and the Companions had guested with him often, during the hot days of summer. He was a pleasant, greying fellow, who'd always reminded her a bit of Tharin.

"Greetings, Highness," he said, covering his heart with his fist as he bowed from the saddle. "Delighted as I am to offer you hospitality once again, I regret the circumstances."

"So do I, your grace. I'm told you're willing to swear fealty to me, and support my claim to the throne?"

"I am, Highness. We're an Illioran house and always have been. I think you'll find a good many others around the country who will be glad to see the Lightbearer's prophecy upheld at last."

"And plenty who won't," Lord Jorvai put in as they set off again. "The Sakor factions who enjoyed the king's favor won't so readily see his son displaced. Some have already left the city on account of him."

"Will it be civil war, then?" Illardi asked.

The question sent a chill through Tamír. Forgetting her resentment for a moment, she turned to Iya. "Will Korin fight me for the crown?"

"With Niryn still alive and dripping poison in his ear? Yes, I'd say it's likely."

"Skalans fighting Skalans? I can't believe that's what the Lightbearer wants of me!"

They reached Duke Illardi's estate without challenge. Large beacon fires burned along the tops of the walls, illuminating the archers stationed there.

Beyond lay a pleasant, rambling stone villa set on a promontory overlooking the sea. The Plenimarans had attacked as they passed; black-fletched arrows still littered the bailey yard and gardens, but the gates had not been breached.

Tamír and the others dismounted at the main entrance to the house. Two pillars carved with Illior's Eye flanked the doorway and a crescent moon decorated the lintel. When they'd visited here in Erius' time, Sakor's Flame had been painted there. Tamír hoped Illardi didn't change his loyalties too quickly, or too often.

He'd always been a kind host to the Companions, however, and he seemed sincere now as he bowed and said, "All that is mine is yours, Highness. I've ordered a bath and food prepared. Perhaps you'd prefer to take them in your chambers?"

"I would, thank you." Tamír had suffered through enough formalities for one day.

He led her to a set of rooms on a terrace facing the sea. Baldus clung to her hand, and Ki and Tharin followed. In addition to the main bedchamber there was a sitting room, dressing room, and antechambers for her guard. In the heat of summer these rooms had been pleasantly cool. Now they were dank despite the candles and hearth fires burning there.

"I'll leave you to rest and refresh yourself, Highness," said Illardi. "My servants will bring you anything you require."

"I'll see the men settled in," said Tharin, discreetly withdrawing to leave her alone with Ki. "Come, Baldus."

Baldus looked panicked and Tamír nodded to him. "You'll attend me."

The child gave her a grateful look as he scampered to join them.

Despite the damp, the hangings were warmly colorful, and the bedsheets were clean and smelled of sunshine and wind.

Baldus looked around the unfamiliar chamber. "What do I do, my lady? I've never attended a girl before."

"I have no idea. Help me off with these boots, for starters."

She sat down on the edge of the bed and chuckled as the boy struggled with her boots. "I think we could fit your whole family in this bed, Ki."

He dropped into a chair and grinned. "And the dogs, too."

Baldus gave the boot a final yank and tumbled back, his already dirty tunic covered in mud.

Tamír regarded her filthy sock and the rest of her stained clothing with a wry smile. "I don't look much like a lady, do I?"

"I don't imagine Queen Ghërilain looked much different, after her great battles," said Ki, as Baldus wrestled off her other boot.

"I stink, too."

"You're not the only one."

Ki's hair hung in dirty tangles around his haggard, unshaven face, and the tunic over his hauberk was filthy. They both reeked of blood and battle.

Baldus hurried over to the washstand and poured water into the basin. Tamír washed her face and hands. The water was cool and scented with rose petals, but by the time she was done it was stained the color of rust. Baldus emptied the basin out the window and poured fresh for Ki.

"Maybe he shouldn't do that," Ki warned. "It might not look right to people, him waiting on your squire, too."

"People can go hang," Tamír snorted. "Wash your damn hands."

Trestle tables were brought to the terrace. Tamír and her people ate with the duke and his two young sons, Lorin and Etrin. Ki had played with them on their previous visits and found them to be good, solid sorts, and smart.

Lorin was a tall, quiet boy a few years younger than Tamír. His brother, who was of an age with Baldus, stared at her wide-eyed throughout the meal, as if expecting her to change form again before his eyes.

Baldus staunchly carried out his duties here, too, until Tamír coaxed him into sharing her bench, and made him eat a few morsels from her portion.

As soon as the meal was done servants cleared away the dishes and Illardi spread out charts of the harbor to assess the damage.

"The Plenimarans knew their job. While the land forces attacked the shoreline, their sailors cast burning pitch on every vessel they could reach and cut the mooring lines. I'm afraid all your warships are at the bottom of the harbor now, or burning on the far reach. Only a few small carracks escaped. Twenty-seven enemy vessels were captured."

"Any word of how many ships escaped?" Tamír asked.

"The lookouts at Great Head claim no more than ten."

"Enough to carry home word of their defeat," Jorvai noted.

"Enough to carry word of Ero's weakness, too," Iya warned. "We cannot afford to be taken by surprise again. I have several of my wizards watching the sea, but without knowing where to look, they may not find them. Tell the lookouts to be vigilant, especially in foul weather."

Illardi and the others left at last. A large bathing tub had been carried in and filled as they dined and Ki eyed it enviously. They'd lived in the saddle for days.

"Baldus, go into the corridor and keep watch with the guards for a while," said Tamír. She flopped down on the bed and nodded toward the tub. "You want first go?"

"No, you go on—That is—" A week ago Ki wouldn't have thought twice about it. Now he could feel his face going warm. "I should step out—shouldn't I?"

It seemed a logical enough conclusion, but Tamír suddenly looked close to tears. "Do I disgust you that much?"

"What? No!" he exclaimed, astonished both by the sudden change of mood and that she'd jump to such a harsh conclusion. "How can you think that?"

She slumped forward with her face in her hands. "Because that's how I feel. Ever since Atyion, I've felt like I'm trapped in a bad dream and can't wake up. Nothing feels right! I have this empty feeling in my trousers—" Ki saw color rise in her cheeks, too. "And these?" She glared down at the hard little points under the dirty linen of her shirt. "They ache like fire!"

Ki found himself looking anywhere but at her. "My sisters said the same when they ripened. It passes as they grow."

"Grow?" She looked horrified at the prospect. "But you want to know the worst of it?"

She pulled the shirt off over her head, leaving herself naked from the waist up except for her parents' rings on a chain around her neck. Ki hastily averted his eyes again.

"That. You can't even look at me, can you? Every day since Atyion I've seen you flinch and turn away."

"It's not like that." Ki faced her squarely. He'd seen naked women enough growing up. She didn't look any different than one of his sisters, apart from the mottled bruise on her shoulder where she'd been struck during the first attack on the city. It had faded to a green-and-yellow blotch, stippled at the center with the purpled imprint of the chain mail that had stopped the arrow. "It's—Damn it, I can't explain it. Fact is, you don't look all that different than you did before."

"Lying doesn't help, Ki." She hunched in on herself, arms crossed over her tiny breasts. "Illior is cruel. You wouldn't touch me when I was a boy and now that I'm a girl, you can't even look at me." She stood and stripped her breeches off, angrily kicking them aside. "You know a hell of a lot more about girl's bodies than I do. Tell me, do I look like a boy or a girl now?"

Ki shuddered inwardly. It wasn't that there was anything wrong with what he saw. The dark sprinkling of hair covering her cunny looked the same as any girl's. No, it was knowing what used to be there that made his belly clench.

"Well?" She was still angry, but a tear rolled down her cheek.

The sight of it made his heart ache; he knew how much it took to make her cry. "Well, you're still skinny, and your ass has always been kind of flat. But lots of young girls are like that. You're not so old yet to be— ripening." He stopped and swallowed hard. "That is, if you—"

"Bleed with the moon?" She didn't look away, but her

face went a darker shade of scarlet. "I did, sort of, before the change. Lhel gave me herbs that stopped it, mostly. But I suppose I will now. So now you know it all. These past couple years, you were sleeping with a boy who bled!"

"Damn, Tob!" This was too much. Ki sank into a chair and put his head in his hands. "That's what I can't fathom. The not knowing!"

She shrugged miserably and reached for the dressing gown someone had left across the end of the bed. It was a lady's gown, velvet trimmed with silver lace and embroidery. Tamír wrapped herself in it and huddled against the bolsters.

Ki looked up and blinked in surprise. "There now, that makes a difference."

"What?" Tamír muttered.

"It makes you look more—girlish." This earned him a dark glare.

Determined to make things right between them, he looked around and spied an ivory comb on the dressing table. This must have been a lady's room, or else Illardi's duchess had taken pains to equip it properly. There were pots with fancy lids and little odds and ends he couldn't guess the use of.

Taking up the comb, he sat down next to her on the bed and forced a grin. "If I'm to be your tiring woman, Highness, can I fix your hair?"

That got him an even blacker look, but after a moment she turned her back to him. He knelt behind her and began working at the tangles, taking it in sections like Nari used to.

"Don't think I don't know what you're up to."

"What am I up to?"

"Currying the skittish horse?"

"Well, it needs doing. You're all full of knots."

He worked in silence for a while. Tamír had thick hair, and it was almost as black as Alben's, but it wasn't as straight as his. When he was done, it fell in thick waves down her back.

Gradually her shoulders relaxed and she sighed. "This isn't my fault, you know? I didn't choose this."

"I know that."

She looked back over her shoulder. With their faces mere inches apart, he found himself lost for an instant in those sad blue eyes. The color reminded him of the Osiat, the way it looked on a clear day from the headlands at Cirna.

"Then what is it?" she demanded. "It feels so different between us now. I hate it!"

Caught off guard, Ki let his mouth run away with him and spoke the truth. "Me, too. I guess I just miss Tobin."

She turned around and gripped him by the shoulders. "I *am* Tobin!"

He tried to look away, to hide the tears stinging his eyes, but she held him.

"Please, Ki, I need *you* to be the same!"

Ashamed of his own weakness, he pried her hands from his shoulders and held them tightly between his own. "I'm sorry. I didn't mean it like that. But now, you're—"

"Just a girl?"

"No. You're to be queen, Tamír. You are already, by right." She tried to pull away, but he held on. "A queen this grass knight can't sleep close with on cold winter nights, or swim with, or wrestle—"

"Why not?"

It was Ki who pulled away this time, unable to bear the hurt in her eyes. "It wouldn't be proper! Damn it, if you're to be queen, you have to act the part, don't you? You're still a warrior, but you're a woman, too—or a girl, anyway. And boys and girls? They just don't do all that. Not nobles, anyway," he added, blushing. He'd made do with servant girls, just like everyone else, but he'd never felt ashamed of that until now.

Tamír sat back, lips set in a grim line, but he could see

the corners trembling. "Fine. Leave me, then, while I bathe."

"I'll go see how Nik and Tanil are doing. I won't be long."

"Take your time."

Ki headed for the door. She didn't call him back, just sat there glaring a hole in the bed. Ki slipped out and set the latch softly, his heart in turmoil, then turned to find Tharin and Una watching him expectantly.

"She's—uh—going to bathe," Ki mumbled. "I'll be back."

Ducking his head, he brushed past them. As he strode away, it felt like a door of a different sort had slammed shut between them, with him on the outside.

Tamír fought back more tears as she undressed and slid into the tub. She ducked under the water and briskly rubbed the soap over her hair, but she couldn't escape her thoughts.

She'd always been odd, even as Tobin, but Ki had always understood and accepted her. Now it seemed he could only see the stranger she'd become—a homely, scrawny girl he was too embarrassed to look at. She slid a finger through the ring that had been her mother's, gazing down at the profiles of her parents. Her mother had been beautiful, even after she'd gone mad.

Maybe if I looked more like her? she wondered glumly. Not much chance of that.

She wanted to be angry with Ki, but this sumptuous room suddenly felt too lonely without him. Her gaze strayed to the large bed. She'd seldom slept alone. First there'd been Nari, her nurse, then Ki. She tried to imagine replacing him with Una and cringed, remembering that embarrassing kiss the girl had given her, believing Tobin was just a shy, backward boy. There'd been little time to speak with her since the change, but thanks to Tharin and his organizing, it would be hard to avoid her now.

"Bilairy's balls!" she groaned. "What am I going to do?"

Survive, Sister. Live for both of us.

Tamír sat up so abruptly water sloshed over the side onto the floor. Brother stood before her, a faint but unmistakable shape untouched by the fire or candle glow.

"What are you doing here? I thought—I thought you'd gone on."

It was hard to look at him now—the image of the young man she thought she'd be. He was as pale as ever, his eyes as flat and black, but otherwise he looked as he would have in life, right down to a faint tracing of dark hair on his upper lip. Suddenly shy under that unblinking gaze, she wrapped her arms around her knees.

His hard, whispery voice invaded her mind. *You will live, Sister. For both of us. You will rule, for both of us. You owe me a life, Sister.*

"How do I repay a debt like that?"

He just stared.

"Why are you still here?" she demanded. "Lhel said you'd be free when I cut out the piece of your bone. The rest of you burned up with the doll. There was nothing left, not even ash."

The unavenged dead do not rest.

"Unavenged? You were stillborn. They told me."

They lied. Learn the truth, Sister. He hissed the last word like a curse.

"Can you find Lhel for me? I need her!"

The demon shook his head and the hint of a smile on his dead lips sent a chill through her. The bond of skin and bone was sundered. Tamír could no longer command him. The realization frightened her.

"Are you here to kill me?" she whispered.

Those black eyes went darker still and his smile was poisonous. *How many times I wanted to!*

He advanced, passing through the side of the tub to kneel before her in the water, face inches from her. The water went achingly cold, like the river below the keep in spring. The demon grasped her bare shoulders and his cold fingers bit into her flesh, feeling all too solid. *See? I am no helpless shade. I could reach into your chest and squeeze your heart as I did to the fat one who called himself your guardian.*

She was truly terrified now, more than she ever had been with him. "What do you want, demon?"

Your pledge, Sister. Avenge my death.

Dreadful realization penetrated the haze of fear. "Who was it? Lhel? Iya?" She swallowed hard. "Father?"

The murdered cannot speak the name of their killers, Sister. You must learn that for yourself.

"Damn you!"

Brother was still smiling as he slowly faded away.

The door flew open and Tharin and Una burst in, swords drawn.

"What's wrong?" asked Tharin.

"Nothing," Tamír said quickly. "I'm fine, just—just thinking out loud."

Tharin nodded to Una and she retreated and closed the door. Tharin swept a suspicious eye around the room as he sheathed his sword.

"I'm almost done here," she told him, hugging her knees to her chest. "I told Ki he could use the water when I'm done but it's gone cold."

Brother had stolen the last of the heat. *No, don't think of him right now, and what he'd hinted at.* She'd had too much to bear already, without looking for murderers among what was left of her circle of trusted friends. She clung to the fact that Tharin had not been anywhere near her mother that night. But Iya had, and Arkoniel. Perhaps there had been someone else? It was too painful to contemplate.

"That's a long face." Tharin helped her from the tub and wrapped her in a large flannel, rubbing her hair with a corner of it.

Tamír dried herself and put on the robe again, not looking at him as she let the flannel drop.

When she was dressed, he urged her into bed and pulled the comforter up around her, then sat down and took her hand. "That's better."

His kind, knowing look undid her. She threw her arms around his neck and hid her face against his chest, not caring that he still stank of blood and smoke. "I'm glad you're still with me!"

He rubbed her back. "As long as I draw breath."

"I'm going to make you a prince of the realm when I'm queen."

Tharin chuckled. "Bad enough you've made me a lord. Leave well enough alone."

He stroked a wet strand of hair back from her cheek and gave one braid a tug. "You're worried about Ki."

Tamír nodded. It was half the truth, anyway.

"He didn't look any happier than you when he left." She felt him sigh. "You're determined to keep him by you, aren't you?"

"You think I'm wrong?"

"No, but you might consider the boy's feelings."

"I'd be happy to, if he'd tell me what they are! He treats me like I'm someone else now."

"Well, like it or not, you are."

"No!"

Tharin patted her shoulder. "Maybe just who you were, then, with more added on."

"Tits, you mean?"

"You call those little flea bites tits?" He laughed at her outraged look. "Yes, your body's changed, and that's something that can't just be pushed aside, especially not by a young man with Ki's hot blood."

Tamír looked away, mortified. "I want him to see me as a girl, to like me that way, but then again, I don't. Oh, Tharin, I'm so confused!"

"You both need time to know your hearts."

"*You* always treat me just the same."

"Well now, it's different with me, isn't it? Boy or girl, you're Rhius' child. But you're not a little one anymore, for me to carry on my shoulder and make toys for. You're my liege and I'm your man. But Ki?" He picked up the discarded flannel and rubbed it over her dripping hair. "I know what your feelings for him have grown to this past year or so. He knows it, too."

"But shouldn't that make it easier?"

He paused in his drying. "How would you feel if you woke up tomorrow and Ki was a girl?"

Tamír blinked up at him through her tangled hair. "It's not the same! That would make things harder between us, like when I was a boy. This way, we can—have each other. If he wants to!"

"First he'll have to stop seeing Tobin every time he looks at you. And that won't be easy because he's still looking so hard to see him."

"I know. Who do you see, Tharin?"

He patted her knee. "I told you. I see my friend's child."

"You really loved my father, didn't you?"

He nodded. "And he loved me."

"But he left you for Mother. Why didn't you stop loving him then?"

"Sometimes love can change its form rather than end. That's what happened with your father."

"But your feelings never changed, did they?"

"No."

She was old enough now to guess at what he was leaving unsaid. "Didn't it hurt?"

She'd never seen the sorrow more clearly in his face, or the sharp edge of anger that came with it when he nodded and replied softly, "Like fire, at first, and for a long time after. But not enough to drive me away, and I can say now that I'm glad. There was a time when I'd have answered differently. I was a grown man by then, and I had my pride."

"Why did you stay?"

"He asked me to."

She'd never heard him say so much before. "I always wondered—"

"What?"

"After Mama got sick and turned against him, were—were you and Father ever lovers again?"

"Certainly not!"

"I'm sorry. That was rude." Still, something in that last response intrigued her—a flash of pride. She wondered what it meant but knew better than to ask. "So what do I do about Ki?"

"Give him time. Ki could never have loved you the way you wanted as Tobin. It just isn't in him. But he suffered over it, and now he's suffering over the loss of who you two were together." He draped the flannel over her shoulder. "Let him heal a while. You can do that for him, can't you?"

She nodded. Of course she could. But that didn't make her feel any better tonight. "Is he out there?"

"He went off by himself, but he'll be back."

"We'll need more hot water for sure, then," Tamír mused. "Should I leave while he bathes?"

Tharin shrugged. "It would be polite to ask."

Chapter 4

The courtyard was filled with soldiers and servants. Ki kept to the shadows and went to the new stone stable, where the wounded were being tended.

Illardi bred fine horses from Aurënfaie stock; his stable was far nicer than the house where Ki had been born, and considerably larger. Inside, Ki could just make out rafters and dressed stone at the edge of the lamplight. It smelled of new wood and fresh straw, but also of blood and wounds, and herbs being burned or brewed on the braziers. Half a dozen drysian healers were at work, wearing bloodstained aprons over their long brown robes.

People lay everywhere on makeshift pallets, looking like bundles of laundry laid out for washing day. Ki picked his way among them, looking for Nikides and Tanil. One of the healers noticed him and came over.

"Lord Kirothieus, are you seeking the Companions?" she asked. "We put them together, over there in that stall at the end."

He found Nikides propped up in a deep bed of new straw. Another figure sat huddled in a far corner of the stall, muffled in several blankets. Even his head was covered.

"Tanil?" When Ki moved closer, the squire let out a soft moan and cowered deeper into the shadows. Ki settled back on his heels. "It's all right. You're safe here."

Tanil said nothing, just curled more tightly in on himself.

"Ki, is that you?" It was a papery whisper.

Ki turned to find Nikides awake and blinking up at him. "Yes. How are you?"

"Better, I think. Where are we?"

"At Duke Illardi's estate."

"Illardi?" Nikides glanced around in confusion. "But I thought— I dreamed I was at the Old Palace. There were people dying around me. I thought I saw you—and Tobin."

"It was no dream. We had you moved here. Lynx is still with us, too, and came through without a damn scratch! I think he and I are the only ones who did. And Una, too. Remember her?"

Nikides brightened at that. "She's alive?"

"Yes. She ran off and joined up with my sister Ahra's riders. She learned her lessons well. She's a blooded warrior already."

"So there are some of us left, after all."

"Yes. What happened with you, Nik?"

Nikides tried to sit up and groaned. "I told them I was never cut out to be a warrior." With Ki's help he managed to prop himself against the wall. "I was with Korin. We were trying to get him away—" He closed his eyes against some painful memory. "I didn't see the archer until it was too late."

"You were lucky. The shaft missed your lung."

Nikides shifted again and caught sight of the huddled figure in the corner. "Who's that?"

"Tanil."

"Thank the Four, we thought you were dead! Tanil? Ki, what's wrong with him?"

"He was captured." Ki leaned closer and lowered his voice. "Tortured, and—well, raped, like they do. We found him planked up against a barn north of the city."

Nikides' eyes widened. "Maker's Mercy!"

"He's in bad shape. Tamír wanted him kept close to you."

"Tamír?"

Ki sighed. "Tobin, that is. You saw her back at the palace, remember? You spoke to her."

"Ah. I thought I'd dreamed that, too."

"No dream. A prophecy fulfilled, or so they say."

"Then Skala has a queen again!" Nikides whispered. "If only Grandfather had lived to see it." He fell silent a moment. "So, how is Tobin? Princess Tamír, I mean."

"She's fine."

"She." Nikides murmured, "It's going to take some getting used to, isn't it? Tell me, how did it happen?"

Ki gave him a quick summary. "It was magic, but not like anything I'd ever heard of before. But I saw her myself, naked as the dawn, and it's no trick. She's Tamír now; Tamír Ariani Ghërilain."

"A good name."

Nikides was taking it very well, Ki thought sourly.

"Amazing, isn't it, that the queen the Illiorans have been whispering about all these years was hiding right in plain sight?"

"Amazing, all right." The bitterness in his voice left Nikides speechless for a moment.

"And Ero?" he asked at last.

"We drove the enemy out, but the city's pretty near ruined." Ki clasped his shoulder. "I'm sorry about your grandfather. I'm told he died defending the palace."

"Yes. I'll miss him, but it was an honorable death."

"What can you tell me about Korin? Do you know where they went?"

"They haven't come back?"

"No. What happened?"

"The enemy had broken through our last defenses. They were everywhere, killing and burning. Master Porion and Captain Melnoth organized the retreat, with what soldiers they had left to cover their escape. I was unlucky, that's all, and got cut off."

"And they just left you?"

"You can't blame Lutha, if that's what you're thinking."

He paused and Ki saw a look of pain in his eyes. "I saw him looking back at me, shouting something. He wanted to go back for me, but of course, he couldn't. His duty was to Korin."

"I would have, Nik. So would Tamír."

Nikides shook his head. "I wouldn't have wanted you to. Duty first, in all things. That's what Master Porion would tell you, too."

Ki kept his arguments to himself for now. Nikides was still too ill to fully appreciate the situation. "Do you know where Korin was headed?"

"No. Niryn just said to get him out of the city. We were trying for the west gate when I lost them."

"The wizard was giving the orders?"

"Korin wouldn't listen to anyone else by then, not even Cal."

The drysian who'd spoken with Ki earlier came back just then and put her ear to Nikides' chest. She looked pleased with what she heard. "You're a lucky fellow, my lord. A few days more and you should be on your feet again, though it will take time to fully heal. I'll send someone over with broth. See that he eats, won't you, Lord Kirothieus?"

"I will." Ki grinned at his friend. "Not that we ever had any trouble getting you to eat."

Nikides made a rude gesture, then looked over at Tanil again. He'd stirred when the drysian came, and appeared to be awake. "Hello, Tanil. I'm glad you're here. Are you hungry?"

Tanil shook his head and the blanket fell back from his face.

"Bilairy's balls!" Nikides gasped softly.

The young squire's face was still badly swollen and discolored from the beating, and his dark hair hung in lank strands around his shoulders. His braids had been cut off, too. Worst of all, though, was his vacant, frightened expression. He hunched in on himself, arms crossed tight across his chest. Livid bruises covered his bare shoulders, and his wrists were wrapped with bloodstained linen. He gave them a confused look, then hid his face against his knees.

"Poor fellow," Nikides whispered sadly.

"And he was one of the lucky ones," Ki replied softly, leaving it unsaid that his captors had been about to gut him when Tamír and her forces showed up. "The wounds in his wrists aren't so bad. The healers say he'll probably have the use of his hands again when they heal."

He spoke lightly, but he and Nikides exchanged a knowing look. Wounds to the body were nothing to a warrior, but to be so dishonored and left crippled? It would have been kinder if the bastards had killed him.

The drysian woman returned with two bowls of strong-smelling broth. Nikides took a sip from his and wrinkled his nose. "Horse meat!"

"Plenty of that about," Ki said, moving slowly and carefully to sit by Tanil. He held out the bowl. "It stinks, but it'll put strength back into you. Come on now, try a little. It's me, see? Nobody's going to hurt you. Nik's here, too."

Tanil regarded them with empty eyes, then a hint of recognition seemed to dawn. He let Ki hold the bowl to his lips and managed a few sips before he gagged and turned his face away.

Nikides gamely downed his portion and put the bowl aside with a grimace of distaste. "You haven't said what happened to you, since you left Ero."

Ki quickly outlined the chaos of the past few days. "Tharin's reorganized the remains of the old Alestun guard, along with Lynx and some of the warriors from Atyion, into a new guard for Tamír," Ki said, all the while coaxing Tanil to drink more of the broth. "We've got Lord Jorvai, and Kyman of Ilear on our side already, and Illardi, and more who swore fealty after the battle. Not everyone is supporting Tamír, though."

"That's to be expected," Nikides said, looking thoughtful. "Well, you can count me in as another loyal man, for whatever it's worth."

"Even over your Companion's oath? She'll send you back to Korin if that's what you want."

"No. I won't say it doesn't hurt, but in my heart I know it's the right thing. Erius broke with the prophecy, and where did that get us? If Illior has made Tobin into a queen, then who am I to argue? So, how can I help?"

Ki clasped his friend's hand and smiled. "Get your strength back and keep an eye on Tanil for me. Well, I better get back. Take care of yourself and do as the healers tell you."

Ki felt a bit better for seeing his friend awake, but returned to the house unsure of his welcome. He felt bad about how things had gone earlier and was anxious to put it right.

Tamír was sitting on the bed reading a letter. She had on a long linen shirt under the dressing gown, and her damp hair hung loose over her shoulders. Baldus was curled up asleep on his pallet by the door.

She looked up as he came in, and he could tell she was trying to gauge his mood, too.

"I just saw Nik and Tanil."

"How are they?"

"Nik's mending. Tanil's not doing so well. His spirit's broken."

"I don't wonder. I'll go see him tomorrow." She gestured casually at the tub. "I had more warm water brought in." She paused, looking uneasy again. "I can go in the sitting room—"

"Whatever you like," Ki answered too quickly. Did she want to stay, or go? He was damned if he could tell. He had the feeling that no matter what he did, it would be wrong. When it came right down to it, though, she'd seen him naked so often that that didn't make a bit of difference. All he wanted right now was hot water and a clean bed. "I don't mind either way."

After all the earlier embarrassment, he'd expected her to leave. Instead, she shrugged and went back to the letter.

Suit yourself, he thought, wondering at this new shift in the wind. He stripped and sank gratefully into the tub. It wasn't very hot, but it was the cleanest water he'd seen in days. Settling back, he went to work with the soap and sponge.

As he washed, he found himself glancing over at Tamír. She was still engrossed in that letter. He ducked his head, rinsing lather from his hair, and looked up to find her still staring down at the parchment. It was only a single sheet. It couldn't be taking her that long to read it.

"What's that you're looking at?" he asked.

She glanced up with a guilty start and colored a little, as if he'd caught her staring. Damn, this was strange!

"A letter from Lady Myna of Tynford, offering fealty," she told him.

"Already? Word travels fast."

She tossed the letter aside and stretched out on her stomach, chin propped on one hand. "I can't stop thinking about Korin. A retreat's one thing, but for him to just run off like that and leave the city open to the enemy? That doesn't seem right."

"I'm sure he had his reasons at the time." *Cowardice, most likely,* he thought, scrubbing at a bloodstain on his left knee.

Tamír stared off at nothing for a moment, brow knitted in thought. "Damn that Niryn! It has to be him, weakening Kor's mind."

"I don't doubt it. But maybe Korin wasn't too hard to sway, either." So much for tact.

Tamír gave him a wry look. "I know, Ki. You were right about him all along, but I still say there's good in him, too. Once we know where he is, I'll call for a parley. There's got to be some way to resolve this, short of war!"

"I admit I don't much like the idea of facing friends on the battlefield. Not even Alben or Mago. Well, maybe Mago."

That earned him a fleeting grin. Ki stood up and reached for the dry flannel by the tub, noting how she averted her eyes. He quickly wrapped the cloth around his waist and looked around for something to put on besides his own filthy clothes.

Someone had laid out clean garments for him, too. The long linen shirt had white silk embroidery around the neck and gathered cuffs. He pulled it over his head, then stood there with the breeches in his hand, unsure what to do next.

He looked up at Tamír again and saw the same confusion. They both wanted this to be simple, like nothing had changed.

She shrugged, not quite looking at him. "Stay?"

"All right." But he pulled on the breeches anyway, then blew out all but one lamp. He returned uncertainly to the bed, wondering if he should sleep on the floor with Baldus. Tamír was under the covers now, with the coverlet pulled up to her nose. He could just see her dark eyes watching him expectantly.

Still uncertain, he wrapped himself in a spare blanket and settled on the far edge of the bed. They lay facing each other, faces half-shadowed in the soft glow of the night lamp. Less than two arms span separated them, but it felt like a mile.

After a moment, Tamír reached out to him. He laced his fingers with hers, glad of the contact. Her fingers were warm and sun-browned from days in the saddle, not soft and pale like the girls he'd bedded. Those hands had trembled, or caressed. Tamír held his hand firm and sure, same as always. It made Ki feel very odd inside, even as he watched her eyes drift shut and her face relax in sleep. With her face pressed into the pillow and her hair spilled across her cheek like that, she looked like Tobin again.

He waited until he was certain she was really asleep, then let go of her hand and rolled on his back, teetering on the edge of the mattress and longing for the nights when they'd so innocently slept warm in each other's arms.

Chapter 5

In the dream she was still Tobin who'd lived at the keep, and the tower door was never locked.

He climbed the stairs to his mother's ruined sitting room at the top and found Brother waiting for him. Hand in hand, the twins climbed onto the ledge of the window that looked west toward the mountains. Between the tips of his boots, Tobin saw the river below, surging black beneath the ice like a great serpent trying to break free.

The grip on his hand tightened; it was his mother with him now, not Brother. Ariani was pale and bloody, but she smiled as she stepped off the ledge, pulling Tobin down with her.

But Tobin didn't fall. He flew up into the sky and far over the mountains to a cliff above the dark Osiat Sea. Looking back over his shoulder he saw the now-familiar hills, and snowy peaks beyond. As always in this dream, the robed man stood off in the distance, waving to him. Would he ever see the man's face?

Then Ki appeared at Tobin's side and took his hand, drawing him to the brink of the cliff to show him the fine harbor that lay below. Tobin could see their faces reflected down there, side by side, like a miniature painted on silver foil.

Tamír had experienced this dream so often now that she knew she was dreaming, and turned all the more eagerly to Ki. Perhaps this time . . .

But as always, she woke with a start before their lips could touch.

Ki lay curled up on the far side of the bed, and opened his eyes as soon as she stirred. "You were restless. Did you sleep at all?"

"Yes. And now I'm starving." She lay there, watching with bittersweet fondness as Ki yawned and stretched and rubbed his eyes. He'd left the front of his shirt unlaced and she could see the little horse charm she'd made him soon after they'd met, still hanging around his neck on its chain. He'd never taken it off since she'd given it to him, not even in the bath. For a fleeting moment it could have been any morning in the old days, the two of them waking up together to face a new day.

The illusion shattered as quickly as her dream had when he got up so quickly and made his way barefoot to the door.

"I'll go find us something to eat," he said, not looking back. "I'll knock before I come back in."

Tamír sighed, guessing he was anxious to give her time to get dressed.

A moment later there was a knock at the door and Lady Una stepped in, still in her mud-stained tunic and boots. She wore a new baldric with the colors of Tamír's guard.

Baldus woke at last and sat up, rubbing his eyes.

"Go find yourself some breakfast," Tamír told the boy.

"Yes, Highness." The boy yawned and gave Una a curious look, his eyes lingering admiringly on her sword. Then he recognized her and made her a hasty bow. "Lady Una!"

Una looked down at the boy, then gave a little cry of surprise. She knelt and took his hand. "You're Lady Erylin's son, aren't you? I bet you know my brother Atmir. He's Duchess Malia's page at court."

"Yes, lady! We have lessons together, and sometimes we play—" Baldus trailed off and his face fell. "Well, we did—before."

"Have you seen him, since the attack?"

He shook his head sadly. "I haven't seen any of my friends since the enemy came."

Una's kind smile couldn't cover her disappointment. "Well, I'm glad you're safe. If I see him, I'll tell him you're looking for him."

"Thank you, my lady." Baldus bowed to Tamír and went out.

Una straightened to attention. "Forgive me, Highness. I didn't mean to be rude. It's just that I've had no word of any of my family."

"No need to apologize. Poor Baldus. He doesn't really understand what's happened. I hope you both find your kin." She paused expectantly. "Why are you here?"

Una began to look uncomfortable. "Lord Tharin thought you might need assistance, Highness."

Suddenly self-conscious to be sitting there in nothing but a woman's nightgown, Tamír found the robe and wrapped herself in it. "Better?"

Una made her another hasty bow. "I'm sorry. I don't know what to say to you, really, or how to act."

"You and everyone else!" Tamír spread her arms. "Well, here I am. Take a good look."

Una blushed. "It's not that. You know, when I threw myself at you and kissed you that time? If I'd known, I'd never have done such a thing."

Tamír still blushed at the memory. "It wasn't your fault. Hell, I didn't know either back then. Believe me, I don't hold it against you. Let's just forget it." She raked a hand absently back through her tangled hair. "Look at you now, a warrior, after all! I guess those sword-fighting lessons were useful, after all."

"It was a good start," said Una, obviously relieved by the change of subject. "Although I think I was the only girl who wasn't there just to make eyes at the boys."

Ki hadn't minded that at all, Tamír recalled. She pushed that thought aside at once. "So, Captain Ahra finished your education?"

"Yes. I remembered Ki's stories about his sister, so I rode for Lord Jorvai's holding the night I ran away and found her. I put all my trust in her, and she promised to make a soldier of me. Her methods weren't quite as refined as yours, though." Una grinned. "I must admit, I was a bit surprised when I met her. She's much—rougher than Ki."

Tamír laughed outright at that. "I've met his whole family, and that's a very forgiving assessment. But tell me, why did you run away like that? There were rumors that you'd been killed by the king, or your father."

"That's not far from the truth. Father was terrified of losing favor with your uncle. He beat me and said I was to be sent off to live with some ancient aunt in the central islands until he could marry me off. So I ran away. All I took was this." She touched her sword hilt. "It was my grandmother's. Mother gave it to me with her blessing when I left. But things are different now, aren't they? Women can be warriors again, even noblewomen."

"Yes, even nobles."

Forgetting her breeches and sword, Una made her a graceful curtsy. "You have my loyalty until death, Highness."

Tamír bowed. "And I accept it. Now tell me honestly, do *you* think I look much like a girl?"

"Well— Perhaps if you combed your hair? And didn't scowl so much?"

Tamír let out an unladylike snort, noting with a twinge of envy that Una really was quite pretty, with her smooth, dark hair and oval face.

Baldus peeked in just then. "It's Mistress Iya, Highness. She wants to come in."

Tamír frowned at the intrusion, but nodded.

Iya wore a gown of fine brown wool and a fancy leather girdle, and her long grey hair was combed loose over her shoulders, making her look younger and less severe than usual. She was carrying what looked like several dresses over one arm.

"Hello, Una. Good morning, Highness. Ki said you were awake. I hope you rested well?"

Tamír shrugged, eyeing the gowns with suspicion.

Iya smiled and held them up. "I've come to help you dress."

"I'm *not* wearing those!"

"I'm afraid you must. There are already enough rumors flying about saying you're only a boy playing at being a girl, without you adding to them. Please, Tamír, you must trust me in this. There's nothing shameful about wearing a dress, is there, Lady Una? It hasn't stopped you being a soldier."

"No, Mistress." Una shot Tamír an apologetic glance.

But there was still too much of Tobin in her for Tamír to give in so easily. "Ki and Tharin will laugh their heads off—and the rest of my guard, too! Damn it, Iya, I've worn breeches all my life. I'll trip on the skirts. I'll turn my ankles in slippers and look a fool!"

"All the more reason for you to get used to them now, before you have a great crowd of nobles and generals to impress. Come now, don't make such a fuss."

"I won't ride in a gown," Tamír warned. "And I sure as hell won't ride sidesaddle! I don't give a damn what anyone says."

"Should a princess use such rough language?" asked Una, trying to stifle a smile and failing.

"One step at a time," said Iya. "Besides, her grandmothers all swore like Scavenger men. Queen Marnil could make generals blush. For today, let's just concentrate on appearances. Duchess Kallia will send her dressmaker to you. In the meantime, she was good enough to lend you some of her eldest daughter's gowns. The two of you are close in size."

Tamír blushed as she took off the nightgown, then felt a perfect fool as Iya and Una helped her into a linen shift and pulled a heavy green satin dress down over her head.

"What do you think of this one, before we lace it up?" asked Iya, turning her to face the mirror.

"I hate it!" Tamír snapped, barely glancing at her reflection.

"I admit that's not a good color for you. Makes you look sallow. But you must wear something, and these are all we have."

Tamír discarded one after another, grudgingly settling at last on a high-necked hunting gown of dark blue wool, mostly because it was plainer than any of the others, shorter in the front, and cut loose for easy movement. The laced sleeves were tied on at the shoulder, letting her move her arms easily. The style also allowed her to wear her boots rather than the soft shoes Iya had brought. When Una had laced it up, it was still loose through the bodice, but not as uncomfortable as she'd expected.

"This goes with it, I believe." Iya handed her a leather girdle embossed with leaves and flowers. It fastened with a golden clasp and hung low on her slim hips, with a long gold-tipped end that hung down the front of the gown to her knees. Tamír picked it up, impressed with the workmanship. "This looks like Ylanti work."

"You always did have an eye for fine things." Una pulled out the sword pendant Tamír had made for her a few years earlier. "Are you still making jewelry?"

Tamír looked up, chagrined at being caught liking any part of this ridiculous outfit. "All my tools were lost in Ero."

"You'll find more, I'm sure," said Iya. "You have the gift. You mustn't ignore it. Now Una, see what you can do with that hair. My horse's tail looks better."

Tamír sat fidgeting as Una combed her hair. "Nothing too fancy. I don't want to be fussing with it all the time like—like some girl!"

Una and Iya both chuckled at that.

"There's no reason you can't wear it as you always have," Una told her, deftly replaiting the warrior braids. "All the women soldiers I know wear their hair loose, or in a long braid in back to keep it out of their faces. Let's see how that looks." She plaited Tamír's hair back into a thick braid, then took a bit of red leather thong from her belt pouch. "See, no ribbons. And I promise not to make a bow, either. There. Have a look."

Tamír faced the mirror again and was rather surprised at what she saw. "Hand me my sword belt."

She buckled it on over the girdle, then checked her reflection again. The gown was actually rather flattering, making her look slender rather than skinny and angular. The small side braids and the sword still marked her as a warrior, but she looked less boyish than she had. She made an effort not to scowl. No one would call her a beauty, that was for certain, but her eyes seemed bluer, accented by the gown.

"I've been saving something for you. Your father entrusted it to me, years ago." Iya produced a thin golden circlet from the folds of her robe and presented it to Tamír. It was beautiful, and very simple, just a band of gold engraved with a stylized wave pattern. "That's Aurënfaie work. It was your mother's."

Tamír started to put it on, but Una stopped her. "No, it won't look right with your hair back. Let me."

She undid the large braid and combed the hair out with her fingers. Then she lifted the top layer and drew it up through the circlet before settling the ring around Tamír's brow. She let the hair fall back over it, so that only the section of the band across Tamír's brow showed. She smoothed the small braids back into place. "There! Now people will know you're a princess."

Tamír pulled the gold chain from around her neck and broke it, slipping off the two rings. She placed her father's heavy black signet on her right forefinger, and the amethyst portrait ring on her left ring finger, where it fit perfectly. When she studied her reflection again, her expression was softer, almost wondering. This time, a girl was looking back at her, even if she did still feel like a boy in a dress.

Iya stood just behind her, one hand covering her mouth and a suspicious brightness in her eyes. "Oh, my dear girl, look at you—the true warrior queen returned at last. Una, call in Ki and Tharin, and Arkoniel, too, if he's out there."

Tamír stood nervously by the mirror as the men came in, with Baldus on their heels.

"You look pretty!" the little boy exclaimed.

"Thank you." Tamír glared at Tharin and Ki, daring them to laugh.

"The lad's right," Tharin said, coming to her and turning her this way and that. "By the Flame! What do you say, Ki? Our girl polishes up well, doesn't she?"

Ki had been staring at her all this time, not saying a word. At last he gave her a doubtful nod. "Better."

"Better?" Tamír's heart sank a little and she hated herself for it. Not in a dress for an hour yet and she was already acting like those girls at court!

"No, really," Ki said quickly. "You're much prettier with your hair fixed and all. That dress suits you, too. I bet you could fight in it if you had to."

Tamír drew her sword and made a swift series of thrusts and feints. The skirts swirled around her legs, and she caught the hem with her bootheel once or twice. "It needs to be shorter."

"You'll start a new fashion," Tharin said, grinning.

Una laughed. "Or a scandal!"

"Yes, it might be better if you put on breeches to fight," mused Iya. "Failing that, though, if you're caught off guard, try this." She swept up the right side of her long skirt and tucked the hem into her girdle. "It's easier to run like this, too."

Tamír groaned, imagining a life hampered by gowns.

"Come along, Highness. Your court awaits," Iya told her. "Let them see their queen and spread the word."

Chapter 6

Tamír's first official audience was held in the villa court-yard. Flanked by her friends and new guard, she entered the winter-brown gardens to find a restless crowd of warriors, wizards, and frightened guild masters awaiting her, anxious for news.

She looked around, searching out familiar faces, and spotted Nikides slumped in an armchair near the fountain, talking with Lynx and Iya.

"I didn't expect to see you up and around yet," she exclaimed, oblivious to all the eyes following her as she strode over to give him an awkward hug.

"Healer's orders," he rasped. His round, unshaven face was parchment pale, but his eyes were shining with wonder as he stared at her.

She took his hand. "I'm so sorry about your grandfather. We could do with his counsel now."

He nodded sadly. "He would have served you, and so will I." He looked more closely at her. "You really *are* a girl. By the Light, I wanted to believe it, but it didn't seem possible. I hope you'll make me your court historian. I believe there are going to be wondrous things to record."

"The post is yours. But I'm also in need of Companions. I'd like you and Lynx to be the first, along with Ki, of course."

Nikides laughed. "Are you sure you want me? You already know what a poor swordsman I am."

"You have other talents." She turned to Lynx. His dark eyes were still haunted, even when he smiled. "What about you?"

"Be Lord Nikides' squire, you mean? Lord Tharin did suggest it."

"No. You're my friend, and you've stood by me. I'm raising you to full Companion. You'll both have to find squires of your own."

Lynx blinked at her in surprise. "I'm honored, Highness, and you have my loyalty always! But you do know my father was only a knight? I'm a second son, with no holdings of my own."

Tamír faced the assembly, hand on her sword hilt. "You all heard that, I suppose? Well, listen well. Loyal men and women who serve me well will be judged on their merits, not by their birth. There's not a noble in Skala whose ancestors were born with circlets on their heads. If it is Illior's will that I rule Skala, then I want it known that I look to people's hearts and acts, not their birth. Nikides, you can record that as one of my first decrees if you like."

She couldn't tell if he was coughing or laughing as he bowed to her from his chair. "I shall make a note of it, Highness."

"Let it be known that anyone I choose to elevate will be accorded as much respect as a noble of six generations. By the same token, I won't think twice about taking away the title and holdings of those who prove themselves unworthy."

She caught warning looks from Tharin and Iya, but most of the crowd cheered.

She turned to Una next. "What do you say, Lady Una? Will you join our ranks too?"

Una fell to one knee and offered her sword. "With all my heart, Highness!"

"That's settled, then."

Lynx knelt, too, and she drew her sword again and touched him on the shoulder. "I name you Lord—Wait, what's your real name?"

Nikides seemed about to supply that bit of information,

but Lynx stopped him with a sharp glance. "I've been called Lynx for so long, it feels like my true name. I'd remain so, if that's acceptable."

"As you like," said Tamír. "I name you Lord Lynx, with lands and holdings to be determined later. Lady Una, I also accept your fealty. Your first charge as my Companions is to take good care of my royal chronicler. And yourselves," she added with a warning look at Lynx.

Lynx gave her a guilty nod. "Bilairy doesn't seem to want me yet, Highness."

"Good. I can't spare you."

With that settled, she took the chair that had been set out for her and turned her attention to the assembled nobles. "My friends, I thank all of you for what you've done. I'll be honest with you, as well. I don't know exactly what's going to happen next. It seems I must go against my cousin, and anyone who upholds Korin's claim to the throne. I do not want a civil war, but it could come to that. If any of you has had second thoughts about backing me, you're free to go. No one will stop you. But go now."

Silence greeted this offer, and no one moved. After a moment Lord Jorvai came forward and knelt before her, offering his sword. "I swore fealty to you on the battlefield, Highness, but I do so again before these witnesses. Accept Colath as your sworn ally."

"And Illear," Kyman said.

One by one, all the others reasserted their oaths. No one left.

Tamír stood and raised her hand to them. "I don't hold the Sword of Ghërilain, or wear the crown, but with the authority of Illior and before these witnesses, I accept your fealty, confirm your holdings, and count you as my dear friends. I will never forget the sight of your banners coming to my aid when I needed you most."

*   *   *

When she'd finished with the oaths, Tamír turned to the guild masters and mistresses who'd been waiting nervously for her attention. One after the other, men and women wearing the insignias of their offices knelt and pledged the loyalty of their guilds. Butchers, smiths, carters, bakers, masons—it seemed an endless stream, but Tamír was glad for a chance to mark the leaders of the city's common classes.

Finally, with the sun almost at midday, she came to Iya and the wizards.

"Your valor during the battle will not be forgotten. My lords and good people, I ask you to honor these brave wizards."

The throng bowed or cheered with varying degrees of enthusiasm. In spite of all the wizards had done, she knew that Niryn and his Harriers had left a bad taste in the mouths of many—one that made them regard all wizards with a degree of suspicion. In fact, the free wizards of Skala had always had a mixed reputation. For every grave and serious wizard like Iya, or kindly one like Arkoniel, there were a hundred ha'penny cheats and market fair conjurers. And there were those who, like Niryn, attached themselves to the rich and powerful for their own ends. While Tamír had her own reasons for mistrust, she owed a great deal already to the nineteen wizards Iya presented.

Some wore robes, but most were dressed like merchants or minor nobles. Others looked like humble travelers, and at least half of them bore wounds from the battle. She was glad to see the fair-haired young mind-clouder, Eyoli, among them. He'd helped her reach Atyion during the battle and nearly lost his life in the process.

Two of the wizards presented, Dylias and Zagur, looked as old as Iya. Kiriar and a very pretty woman introduced as Elisera of Almak, appeared to be Arkoniel's age, although Tamír knew enough of wizards to realize

that their true ages were as hard to guess as any
Aurënfaie's.

The last woman presented was by far the most intriguing. Grey-eyed Saruel of Khatme was Aurënfaie, and wore
the elaborate red-and-black headcloth, or *sen'gai,* and the
black robes of her people. The fine black facial tattoos and
jewelry that also distinguished that clan made her age difficult to guess at, and since Aurënfaie aged even more
slowly than Skalan wizard-born, the guess would probably
have been wrong.

Tamír's friend, Arengil of Gedre, had taught her something of his people's ways. "May Aura be with you in the
light, Saruel of Khatme," she said, placing her hand over
her heart and bowing.

Saruel solemnly returned the gesture, her head tilted a
bit to the left, as if she had trouble hearing. "And in the
darkness, Tamír ä Ariani Agnalain of Skala."

"I thought all the 'faie left Ero when the Harriers began
burning wizards and priests?"

"I was one of those who shared the vision given to
Mistress Iya. Aura Illustri, known to you as Illior Lightbearer,
smiles upon you. Your uncle committed great evils upon
your land and spat in the face of our god. You are the light
sent to drive away the darkness spread by the Usurper and
his dark wizards. It is my duty, and my great honor, to support you in whatever way I can."

"I welcome your aid and your wisdom." Such pledges
were never lightly made to outsiders—*Tirfaie,* as the
Aurënfaie called short-lived humankind. "Mistress Iya, how
should I reward you and your people for your service?"

"We are not tradesmen or mercenaries, come to present a bill, Highness. You know of my vision about you,
yet you don't know the extent of what I've done to bring
that vision to fruition.

"While you grew, Arkoniel and I traveled this land,
seeking out others who'd had been granted so much as
a glimpse of that same vision. Some of them stand here

before you now. Others await word to join us and aid you. Not all of them are powerful, but the Lightbearer has called them nonetheless, to protect you, the queen who must be.

"I tell you now, before all these witnesses, that we were not charged by the Lightbearer simply to help you to this point, then walk away—"

"That's the same sort of talk we heard from that traitor Niryn, when he gathered his gang together," Kyman interrupted. "He claimed they were serving the throne, too. I mean no disrespect to you, Mistress, or any of your friends, nor do I discount what you've done. But I'm not the only Skalan who's a bit skittish, seeing too many of your kind together in one place again." He turned and bowed deeply to Tamír. "Forgive my plain speech, Highness, but it's the truth."

"I know better than you what Niryn did, my lord. Mistress Iya, what is it you're proposing?"

"I understand the fears Niryn and his ilk have bred," she replied calmly. "My 'kind' and I know still better than you, Highness, or anyone else here, the evil the Harriers practiced."

She reached into a fold of her gown and held up a large silver brooch inset with the copper flame of Sakor. "The Harriers imposed these on us." The others held up brooches of their own, all except Arkoniel and Eyoli. Numbers were stamped on the back of each, a different one for each wizard. Iya's was marked 222.

"They listed us in their ledgers like cattle." Iya tossed the brooch on the pavement at her feet. The other wizards did the same, making a small, glittering pile. "Every free wizard in Ero was made to wear one of these," she went on bitterly. "Those who resisted burned. Wizards who'd sworn to aid you were among them, Highness. I felt the flames as they died. Niryn meant to teach us our place, teach us to fear, but instead, he made me remember something.

"Most wizards are solitary by nature, it's true, but in the time of your ancestor and the Great War, many of us came together with the queen and fought against the Plenimarans and their necromancers. The great chroniclers of that age credit them with stemming the tide of war.

"Niryn and his white-robed murderers reminded me what wizards can accomplish by joining forces. If the Harriers could create such power for evil, then isn't great good also possible? I swear to you by our most sacred oath, Highness—by Illior's Light and by my hands, heart, and eyes—that the wizards who stand before you today seek to forge a union for the good of Skala, as in the days of your ancestor, and to support you, Illior's chosen one. We have no greater desire than that. With your permission, we would demonstrate our good faith and the power of unity before these witnesses."

"Go ahead."

Iya and the others formed a circle around the cast-off brooches. Iya raised her hands over them and the metal melted into a steaming puddle. Dylias waved a hand and the metal formed into a perfect sphere. At Kiriar's command it floated up to eye level. Zagur made a sigil on the air with a polished wooden wand and the sphere flattened to a disk, forming itself into a silver mirror. Saruel stepped forward and wove a pattern on the air and the edges were transformed into a delicate frame of Aurënfaie floral tracery. Finally, Arkoniel cast a spell on the air, opening a small black portal. The mirror disappeared into it and dropped out of thin air into Tamír's hands. The metal was still warm.

She held it up, admiring the exquisite workmanship. The intertwined copper leaves and vines that framed it were as good as anything she'd seen in a silversmith's stall.

"It's lovely!" She handed it to Ki to see, and it passed from hand to hand around the courtyard.

"I'm glad it pleases you, Highness. Please accept this as a gift of the Third Orëska," said Iya.

"The what?" asked Illardi.

"Orëska is an Aurënfaie word meaning mage-born," Iya explained. "Their magic passed by blood to our people, the free wizards, or Second Orëska. We are different in our powers than the 'faie, and often not as powerful. But now we mean to make a new kind of magic and a new way of practicing it, as you have just seen. Thus, we are a new, third sort."

"And your Third Orëska will serve Skala?" asked Kyman.

"Yes, my lord. It is Illior's will."

"And you want nothing in return?" Kyman still looked skeptical.

"We ask only for the queen's trust, my lord, and a safe place to nurture and teach the wizard-born."

Tamír heard a few snorts and mutterings from the crowd but she ignored them, thinking of the orphans Arkoniel had already gathered and protected—just like he and Iya had protected her. "You will have it, as long as I have your loyalty.

"Now, we must turn our thoughts to Ero. Duke Illardi, what do you have to report?"

"The winter crops were not much damaged by the Plenimarans, but the grain stores were lost. If the spring crops aren't planted, you risk starvation by winter. At the moment, however, it's shelter and disease that most concern me. If the people scatter away to other cities, they may carry illness with them. But you can't expect them to live on the plain in tents forever, either. Some sort of succor must be given, or you'll have a rebellion on your hands before you've even begun."

"Of course, they must be helped."

"And they must know their help comes from you, Highness," said Tharin. "Atyion has ample stores to draw from. Send for food, clothing, and lumber. Those the drysians deem healthy could be allowed to go there, or wherever they have kin. The rest must be looked after here."

Tamír nodded. "Send word to my steward there at once. Lady Lytia knows best what to do. I've also decided to make Atyion my new capital. It's defensible and has the resources to supply and house an army. With the treasury at Ero lost, I've little to work with here.

"Now, regarding Korin. I need to know where he is and if he can be reasoned with. I need to know how many wizards Niryn has with him, too. As long as old Fox Beard is with my cousin, I believe he'll be a poisonous influence. Jorvai, Kyman, I want you to organize scouting parties. Make arrangements among your best riders and report back to me this afternoon. Thank you all again for your support."

The audience had gone well enough, but speaking for so long had left Tamír tired and off-balance. As a young prince, she'd been groomed for leadership, but she still felt far more at home on the battlefield with a sword in her hand. These people were not asking her simply to win a battle, but decide the fate of the land.

All that, and learn to walk in skirts, she amended sourly as the assembly broke up. It was quite enough for one morning.

She caught Ki by the elbow and drew him away with her. "Come on, I need to walk."

"You did well," he exclaimed softly, falling in beside her.

"I hope so." She made her way up to the wall walk overlooking the harbor and the distant citadel. The long hem of her dress was a hazard on the ladder. She caught her foot and nearly fell on top of him.

"Damnation! Give me a moment." She braced her feet on the rungs and pulled up the edge of the skirt and undergown, tucking the hems into her leather girdle the way Iya had shown her. It worked rather well. By the time she reached the top of the ladder, she already had an idea for a special sort of brooch for the purpose. Her fingers itched for a stylus and tablet.

The sentries on duty bowed respectfully as they passed. She and Ki paced the wall for a while, then stopped at an empty embrasure and leaned on the parapet, watching the gulls circling over the waves. The day was clear, the water green and silver in the afternoon light. If she only looked east, the world seemed clean and free. Behind her, the city still smoldered, a blackened ruin, and the beaches were littered with broken ships.

"All that you said about advancing men on merit, and loyalty being rewarded? They could tell you meant it," Ki said at last. "You had the heart of every warrior in that yard! I saw Iya whispering to Arkoniel, too. I bet even she was impressed."

Tamír frowned out at the sea.

Ki rested a hand on her shoulder. "I know you're still angry at her about all that's happened, and the way they lied to you. But I've been thinking it over and I see why they did all that.

"I'm mad at them, too," he went on. "Well, mostly Arkoniel, since he was the one we knew best. Only . . . Well, I've been thinking. Don't you suppose maybe it was hard on him, too? I see the way he watches you, and how proud he looks sometimes, but sad, too. Maybe you ought to give him another chance?"

Tamír gave him a grudging shrug. Anxious to change the subject, she tugged at the skirt of her gown. "So you don't think I look like a complete fool in this?"

"Well, I'm still getting used to it," Ki admitted.

"And I have to squat to piss," she muttered.

"Does it hurt? Where your cock and balls came off, I mean? I damn near fainted when that happened."

Tamír shuddered at the memory. "No, it doesn't hurt, but I can't let myself think much on it. I just feel—empty there. I don't mind the tits half so much as that. It's like I'm one of those poor bastards the Plenimarans castrated!"

Ki grimaced and leaned in beside her, resting his shoulder against hers. She leaned gratefully into him. For a moment they just stood there, watching the gulls.

After a moment he cleared his throat and said without looking at her, "Illior might have taken that away, but you've got a girl's—parts in their place, right? It's not like you're a eunuch or anything."

"I guess so."

He raised an eyebrow at her. "You *guess* so?"

"I haven't exactly explored," she confessed miserably. "Every time I think of it, I feel sick."

Ki fell silent and when she was finally able to look at him, she found he'd blushed scarlet right up to his ears. "What?"

He shook his head and leaned over the parapet, still not looking at her.

"Come on, Ki! I can tell when you've got something to say."

"It's not my place."

"That's the first time I've ever heard that from you. What is it?"

"Well—if you are a proper girl *there,* then—" He broke off, reddening even more.

"Bilairy's balls, Ki, just come out with it!"

He groaned. "Well, if you are a true girl, then you haven't really lost anything. For fuc—for fun, I mean. Girls tell me they enjoy it just as much as men do."

Tamír couldn't look at him either, knowing he was talking about girls he'd bedded.

"That's what all my father's women and my older sisters always claimed, anyway, that women are more randy than men," he added quickly. "Maybe not the first time or two, but after that? All the ones I know claim to like doing it."

"I guess you'd know about that," Tamír replied.

Ki was quiet for a moment, then sighed. "You never did any of that, did you?"

"No. I didn't fancy girls."

Ki nodded and returned to his contemplation of the sea. They both knew whom she had fancied.

Chapter 7

Lutha sat alone, far down the long table from Korin and the others, among soldiers and minor lords he didn't know, men who had drifted into Cirna looking for a king to serve. They knew who Lutha was, though, and eyed him curiously over their wine, no doubt wondering what he was doing so far from his rightful place. They probably thought he was in disgrace and they weren't far off.

Shame and resentment smoldered in Lutha's heart as he watched Korin and the older Companions laughing with Niryn while Caliel, ignored, stared glumly into his mazer. Lutha had joined the Companions when he was eight years old and served Korin loyally every day since. So had Cal. Now Korin hardly spoke to either of them. And all because, their first morning here, Caliel had suggested that a Companion go back to Ero to learn the truth about Tobin and Lutha had agreed.

There had always been rumors about Tobin—the madness in his family, the demon ghost, and of course, the gossip about him and Ki. Neither Lutha nor Caliel knew what to make of this latest business, though. They'd swum naked with Tobin too many times to believe he'd been a girl in boy's clothes. Now Lutha was torn between wondering if Tobin had somehow gone mad overnight, or if he'd just suddenly turned traitor and liar. Lutha couldn't imagine the Tobin *he* knew doing either, much less Ki going along with such a farce. No, something very strange indeed was going on.

Tired of the sidelong glances of his tablemates, Lutha wanted nothing more than to steal off to his room with

Barieus or Caliel and a skin of wine, but Caliel wouldn't leave Korin's side and Barieus currently had his hands full, trying to fill the serving duties of his fellow squires who'd fallen at Ero.

So few of us left, he thought, taking another sip of wine to ease the sudden tightness in his throat. He missed Nikides most of all. He'd been Lutha's first friend at court, and now he was dead. Barieus had taken it hard, too, and was also quietly pining for Lynx, for whom he had a bit of a fancy.

If Korin missed them, too, he showed it by drinking more than ever at night and Niryn only seemed to encourage such behavior. With Caliel under a cloud and Tanil gone, there was no one left to curb Korin. Master Porion was as disapproving as ever, but there was little he could say, given his rank. Korin was no longer the old swordsman's student, but his king.

It was a strange and cheerless court they kept here. Korin claimed to be the rightful king of Skala, and had even had himself crowned by a trembling priest, but they lived like exiles on this lonely, windswept stretch of the isthmus.

The fortress yards still stank of blood and fire. The garrison, still loyal to Tobin, had tried to resist, but Erius had made Niryn Protector here, and he'd had his Red Hawk Guard at the ready. They cut down the Cirna men and opened the gates to Korin. The sight of all those Skalans dead by Skalan hands had turned Lutha's stomach the night they'd ridden in. There were women among the dead, too, and even a little page who couldn't have been more than six. Someone had run him through. What sort of warrior killed a page?

Cirna was a formidable defensive position, though, one of the most critical in the land. It stood at the narrowest point on the land bridge connecting the Skalan peninsula to the rich farmland territory to the north. A man with a good strong arm could throw a stone into the Osiat Sea from the western wall; from the eastern wall an archer could shoot an arrow into the Inner Sea.

That also meant, however, that whichever way the wind came from, it carried the damp and salt and left it on every surface. The bedsheets were clammy and every door in the place was warped, their hinges stiff and loud with rust. No matter how many times Lutha licked his lips, he always tasted salt. Even the great hall was perpetually dank and cold, despite the hearth fires and torches that burned there day and night.

Korin was bantering drunkenly with Alben now, reaching around Niryn to tug at a lock of the young lord's prized long black hair. Alben laughed and pushed him away. Korin swayed on the bench, jostling Caliel's arm and spilling his wine. Alben lurched back into Urmanis, sitting beside him. Urmanis swore and pushed him back. Alben lost his balance and tumbled backward off the bench amidst much laughter. Even Old Fox Beard joined in. The wizard was especially thick with those two now, and had tried to court Caliel, but Caliel kept his distance from the man.

Lutha had never cared much for Alben or Urmanis. They were arrogant and could be mean bastards when they chose, which was often enough. They'd always gone along with all Korin's whims, no matter how base, and they were in high favor these days.

Poor Caliel was another matter. He still had his place at the table, but something was very wrong between him and Korin. Dark-eyed, golden-haired Cal had always been the sun to Korin's moody clouds, the one among them who, together with Tanil, could cajole him out of a vicious prank or get him to bed before he poisoned himself completely with wine. Korin seldom listened to him anymore.

Korin was better in daylight, perhaps because he stayed sober then. Still dressed in mourning, he greeted the worried nobles flocking to his court, accompanied by the remaining Companions and Porion. He wore his grief with a dignity beyond his years. In less than a year's time he'd lost wife, child, father, and capital. Men who hadn't seen him hesitate in battle were drawn in by his flashing eyes and ready smile. They saw his father in him: strong, hearty, and charming. Nobles old enough to be Korin's grandfather knelt with tears in their eyes to kiss his ring and touch the hilt of the great sword at his belt. At times like that Lutha could almost forget his own doubts.

Late at night, in the privacy of his own hall, however, Korin drank more heavily than ever and that grim, haunted look returned. It was the same look he'd had after their first raid, and when he'd gotten them all cornered in Ero. When Korin was drunk, the fear showed through. And Niryn was always there at the young king's elbow, whispering.

"Advising him," Old Fox Beard called the bile he fed Korin.

Niryn usually kept out of sight during the day, and Lutha kept as far from the man as he could at any hour. He'd felt the wizard's gaze on him too often. Anyone could see that Niryn meant for Korin to take up where his father had left off, but Lutha was smart enough to keep such thoughts to himself.

A few lords and officers who'd dared speak their minds had already been hanged in the bailey yard, including a handsome and popular young captain named Faren, from Duke Wethring's regiment. His bloated corpse still hung in the yard, twisting slowly in the unrelenting breeze with a placard around its neck. It bore a single epithet scrawled in large letters: *Traitor.*

Only Caliel still dared stand up to the wizard, and Lutha feared for him. Others might feel the same, and Lutha knew of those who did, but Caliel was too hot-blooded and loyal to hold his tongue. He braved the warning signs and Korin's occasional bouts of drunken abuse and stayed by his friend, even when it seemed he was not wanted.

*   *   *

You're going to land yourself in the dungeon, or worse," Lutha warned him one night as they huddled together in a sheltered corner of the windswept battlements.

Caliel leaned down and put his mouth close to Lutha's ear. "I can't just stand by and watch that creature steal his soul."

It sent a chill through him that even here, alone, Caliel wouldn't speak Niryn's name aloud.

In addition to the few surviving Harrier wizards and his "grey-back" Guard, Niryn had Moriel. Moriel the Toad. Moriel looked more like a white rat with his pale hair and long sharp nose, but he had the cold, hungry heart of a toad. He'd lurked around court ever since his first patron, Lord Orun, had tried to put him in Ki's place as squire.

Neither Tobin nor Korin would have anything to do with him, but he'd somehow managed to attach himself to Niryn after Orun's death, and now it seemed there was no getting rid of the little shit short of poisoning his soup. He was called the wizard's secretary, and though he seemed to be perpetually at the man's side like a bleached, moist-eyed shadow, he was still up to his old tricks. He had sharp eyes and long ears and a nasty habit of turning up where he was least expected. It was whispered among the common soldiers that it had been on Moriel's evidence that Captain Faren had been hanged.

Lutha caught sight of him now, approaching along the wall walk. Caliel snorted softly, then leaned on the parapet, as if he and Lutha were simply taking in the view.

Moriel came abreast of them and paused, as if expecting a greeting. Caliel turned his back coldly, and Lutha did the same.

"Pardon me," Moriel murmured in that oily, insinuating tone he'd picked up from his time in Lord Orun's house. "I didn't mean to intrude on a lovers' tryst."

Caliel watched him walk out of sight, then muttered, "Filthy little ass-licker. One of these days I'll find an excuse to slit his throat."

Lutha elbowed him, nodding at a white-robed figure ghosting across the misty yard just below. It was impossible to tell if it was Niryn or one of his remaining wizards, but it was safest to assume that all of them were spies.

Caliel stayed silent until the wizard was out of sight. Lutha noticed how he rubbed absently at the golden ring on his right forefinger. It was the hawk ring Tobin had made for him. Caliel still wore it, even now, just as Lutha still wore the horse charm Tobin had made for him.

"This isn't the Skala I was raised to fight for," Caliel muttered.

Lutha waited for him to add, "This isn't the Korin I know," but Caliel just nodded to him and walked away.

Not yet ready to face his damp bed, Lutha lingered behind. The moon was struggling out from behind the clouds, silvering the sea fog rising over the Osiat. Somewhere out there, beyond the scattered islands, lay Aurënen, and Gedre. He wondered if their friend Arengil was awake there, looking north and wondering about them.

Lutha still cringed at the memory of the day Erius had caught them giving sword lessons to the girls on the Old Palace roof. Arengil had been sent home in disgrace and Una had disappeared. Lutha wondered if he'd ever see them again. No one handled hawks better than Arengil.

As he started for the stairs, a flash of movement on the tower balcony caught his eye. Lamps still glowed through the windows there, and he could make out a lone figure looking down at him—Nalia, Consort of Skala. Without thinking, he waved. He thought he saw her return the gesture before she disappeared inside.

"Good night, Highness," he whispered. By rights, she was a princess, but in fact she was little better than a prisoner.

Lutha had spoken with the young woman only once before, the day of her hasty marriage to Korin. Lady Nalia was not pretty, it was true, her plain features marred by a mottled red birthmark that covered one cheek. But she was well-spoken and gracious, and there was a sad pride in her bearing that had pulled at Lutha's heartstrings. No one knew where Niryn had found a girl of the blood, but Korin and the priests seemed satisfied of her lineage.

Something wasn't right, though. Clearly she'd married under duress, and since then she wasn't allowed out of her tower except for the occasional brief, heavily guarded walk on the battlements at night. She didn't join them for meals, or go for rides or hunts, like a noblewoman should. Niryn claimed that it wasn't safe for her to go out, that she was too precious as the last true female heir of the blood, and that the times were too uncertain.

"Doesn't it seem a bit odd that she can't even come down to the hall for supper?" Lutha had asked Caliel. "If she's not safe there, then things are worse than anyone's letting on!"

"It's not that," muttered Caliel. "He can't stand the sight of her, poor thing."

Lutha's heart ached for her. If she'd been stupid, or petty like Korin's first wife, then he might have been able to forget her in that tower. As it was, he found himself fretting for her, especially when he caught glimpses of her at her window or on her balcony, gazing longingly at the sea.

He sighed and headed back to his room, hoping Barieus had the bed warmed up for him.

Chapter 8

Nalia flinched back from the low parapet and stole a guilty look at Tomara, who sat knitting in the chair by the open door behind her. She hadn't noticed the young man on the walls below until he'd waved.

She hadn't been looking for anyone. She'd been staring down into the paved yard below the tower, gauging yet again whether or not she'd die at once if she jumped. It would be such a simple matter. The parapet was low, hardly up to her waist. She could stand on it, or simply climb over and let go. She didn't think Tomara was strong enough to stop her.

A moment's courage and she would be free from this dishonorable captivity.

If Lord Lutha hadn't startled her, she might have managed it tonight. Instead, his brief, friendly gesture had sent her shrinking back from the edge, worrying that Tomara had noticed her impulsive response.

But she just looked up from her handiwork and smiled. "It's a chilly night, my lady. Close the door and I'll make us some tea."

Nalia sat at the small writing desk and watched as Tomara set about preparing the pot, but her thoughts strayed back to Lutha's kind gesture. She pressed a hand to her breast, blinking back tears. *How could something as simple as a wave to a stranger in the night make my heart race like this?* Perhaps because it had been the closest thing to simple human kindness she'd known in the weeks since this nightmare had descended?

If I had the courage to go back out and do as I planned,

*would he still be there to see? Would he be sad that I was
dead? Would anyone?*

She doubted it. Korin, and the few servants and guards
she was allowed to see—even Niryn—they all called her
Consort now, but she was nothing but a prisoner, a pawn
in their game. How could such a thing have happened?

She'd been so happy, growing up in Ilear. But Niryn—
the man she'd called guardian, and then lover—he had betrayed her with breathtaking cruelty, and now he expected
her thanks.

"It's safer here, my darling," he told her, when he'd
first brought her to this awful, lonely place. Nalia had
hated it the moment she'd set eyes on it, but she'd tried to
be brave. After all, Niryn had promised he could come to
her more often.

But he hadn't, and a few months later madness took
the garrison. One faction of soldiers, the ones with the red
hawks on their grey tabards, attacked the Cirna guard. The
sounds that came to her window from the yards that night
had been horrifying. She'd cowered in her chamber with
her nurse and little page, thinking the world was ending.

Niryn had come that night, but not to save her. With
no warning or explanation he'd ushered in an unkempt,
hollow-eyed young stranger who stank of blood and sweat
and wine.

Niryn, who'd played with her as a child and taught her
the joys of the bedchamber and made her forget her own
flawed reflection—that monster had simply smiled and
said, "Lady Nalia, allow me to present your new husband."

She'd fainted dead away.

When she'd come around again she was lying on her
bed and Prince Korin was sitting there, watching her. He
must not have realized she was awake at first, because she
caught the look of revulsion on his face just before it disappeared. He, all bloody and stinking, the invader of her
chamber, looking at *her* that way!

They were alone, and she cried out and cowered back from him, thinking he meant to rape her.

To his credit, Korin had been kind. "I've never forced a woman in my life," he told her. He was handsome under all that grime, she couldn't help noting, and so very earnest. "You are of royal blood, a kinswoman. I have no wish to dishonor you."

"Then what do you want?" she asked faintly, pulling the coverlet up to her chin over her shift.

He'd looked a bit confused at that. Perhaps he thought Niryn's cold introduction was explanation enough. "My father, the king, is dead. I am king now." He took her hand in his dirty one and tried to smile, but it was a sickly attempt. His gaze kept straying to the livid mark that ran like spilled wine from her mouth to her shoulder. "I need a consort. You will bear the heirs of Skala."

Nalia had laughed in his face. All she could think to say was, "And Niryn has no objection?" Some part of her poor, addled mind could not yet grasp that her lover, her protector, had betrayed her.

Korin had frowned at that. "Lord Niryn was guided by prophecy to protect and hide you so that you could fulfill this destiny."

But he was my lover! He's had me to his bed countless times! She tried to throw the words in his face, thinking it the only way to save herself from such disgrace. But nothing came out, not so much as a whisper. An icy numbness took her lips, then spread down her throat, on down to engulf her heart and belly, and pooled at last between her legs, where it changed to a brief, hot tingle, like a lover's parting kiss. She gasped and blushed, but the silence held. Some magic had been laid on her. But how? And by whom?

Mistaking her intent, Korin raised her hand to his lips. His silky black moustache tickled against her skin so differently than Niryn's coppery beard. "We will be properly married, lady. I'll come to you with a priest tomorrow."

"Tomorrow?" Nalia said. Her voice was hers again, though faint. "So soon?"

"These are uncertain times. Later, when things are more settled, perhaps we can have a proper wedding feast. For now, it only matters that our child be legitimate."

Our child. So she was to be nothing but a royal brood-mare. For the first time in her young life, Nalia felt the beginnings of true anger.

Your friend Niryn has been in my bed more times than I can count! How she longed to shout it, but again the icy coldness stopped her lips and her breath with it. She pressed a hand to her useless mouth as tears of frustration and fear rolled down her cheeks.

Korin noticed her distress and to his credit, she saw genuine concern in those dark eyes. "Please don't cry, lady. I know this is all very sudden." Then he spoiled it again, when he stood to go and added, "It's not my choice, either. But we must think of Skala."

Alone again, she'd pulled the covers over her head and sobbed. She had no family, no protectors, no friend to turn to.

She wept long into the night, and fell asleep on the sodden pillow. When she woke at dawn, she found she was still alone and had no tears left.

She went to the east window, watching the sky brighten over the Inner Sea. Men with red hawks on their breasts patrolled the walls below, while the true birds rode the morning breeze in freedom beyond.

I've never been free, she realized. It had all been an illusion and she'd been such a contented fool. The anger she'd felt last night returned, stronger now. If she had no one to look to for help, then she must look after herself. She was not a child, after all. And she was done being a fool.

Vena and Alin hadn't been allowed to come back yet, so she dressed herself and went to the writing desk. If she could not speak the truth to the prince, then she would write him a letter.

But whoever had bespelled her had been very clever. Her hand froze above the page and the ink in the quill went dry at each attempt. With a frightened cry, Nalia threw the pen down and backed away from the table. Niryn had entertained her with tales of great magic ever since she was a child, but she'd never witnessed anything more powerful than a festival conjurer's tricks. This felt more like a curse. She tried to speak the words again, alone here in the stillness of her room. *King Korin, I am not a virgin.* But the words would not come. She thought again of that strange sensation that had overtaken her the first time she'd tried to confess the truth to him, the way it had coursed down through her body.

"Oh Dalna!" she whispered, sinking to her knees. With trembling fingers, she reached beneath her shift, then let out a frightened sob. "Maker's Mercy!"

She was cursed indeed, and a virgin again. That had been the first time she'd thought of the balcony, and the long drop below.

Her nurse and page never returned. Instead, wrinkled old Tomara was sent up to serve her and keep her company.

"Where are my own servants?" Nalia demanded angrily.

"I don't know anything about any other servants, Highness," the old woman replied. "I was fetched up from the village and told I was to wait on a great lady. I haven't done since my mistress passed some years ago, but I can still mend and braid. Come now, let me brush out your pretty hair for you, won't you?"

Tomara was gentle and neat-handed, and there was nothing in her manner to dislike, but Nalia missed her own servants. She suffered through her toilet, then took her place by the window, trying to see what was going on below. She could see riders milling about and hear them on the road beyond the walls.

"Do you know what's happened?" she asked at last, with no one else to talk to.

"Ero's fallen, and a traitor is trying to claim the throne, Highness," Tomara told her, looking up from a piece of embroidery. It appeared to be a bridal veil.

"Do you know who Lord Niryn is?"

"Why, he's the king's wizard, lady!"

"Wizard?" For a moment Nalia thought her heart had stopped beating. A wizard. And one powerful enough to serve a king.

"Oh, yes! He saved King Korin's life at Ero and got him away before the Plenimarans could capture him."

Nalia considered this, putting it together with the disheveled man who'd come to her last night. *He ran away, this new king of mine. He lost the city and ran away. And I'm the best he can do for a wife!*

The bitter thought was balm on her wounded heart. It gave her the strength not to scream and throw herself at Niryn when he came to her later that morning, to escort her to the priest.

She had no proper wedding dress. She'd put on the best gown she owned, and the hastily stitched veil Tomara had made for her. She didn't even have a proper wreath. Tomara brought her a simple circlet of braided wheat.

There were no gaily attired attendants or musicians, either. Men with swords escorted her to the great hall. The midday light streaming in through the few narrow windows only made the shadows deeper. As her eyes adjusted to the gloom she saw that the wedding guests were all soldiers and servants. The priest of Dalna stood by the hearth, and with him were a handful of young nobles, the Companions.

With no father to speak for her, Nalia was given over by Niryn, and had no choice but to obey. When the blessings had been said and Korin took a jeweled ring from his own finger and slid it loosely on her own, she found she was a wife, and Princess Consort of Skala.

Afterward, as they sat over a meager feast, she was introduced to the Companions. Lord Caliel was tall and fair, with a kind, rather sad face. Lord Lutha was hardly more than a boy, gangly and a bit on the homely side, but with such a ready smile that she found herself smiling back and taking his hand. His squire, a brown-eyed boy named Barieus, had the same kind look about him. The two others, Lord Alben and Lord Urmanis, were more what she'd expected; proud and handsome, and doing little to disguise their disdain for her plain looks. Even their squires were rude.

Finally, Korin presented his swordmaster, a grizzled old warrior named Porion. The man was pleasant and respectful, but hardly more than a common soldier, yet Korin treated him with the utmost respect. Taken all together, with Niryn's wizards, too, it was an odd assembly that surrounded her young husband. Nalia pondered this as she picked listlessly at her roast lamb.

When the meal was over she was left to herself in the tower again, until nightfall. Tomara had found oils and perfume somewhere in this awful place. She prepared Nalia for her marriage bed, then slipped away.

Nalia lay rigid as a corpse. She had no illusions and knew her duty. When the door opened at last, however, it was not Korin but Niryn who entered and came to stand over her bed.

"You!" she hissed, shrinking back against the bolsters. "You viper! You betrayer!"

Niryn smiled and sat down on the edge of the bed. "Now, now. Is that any way to speak to your benefactor, my dear?"

"Benefactor? How can you say that? If I had a dagger I would plunge it into your heart, so that you might feel a fraction of the pain you've caused me!"

His red beard caught the candle's glow as he shook his

head. There was a time when she'd found that color beautiful. "I saved your life, Nalia, when you would have died in the king's purges. Your mother and all her kin were killed, but I protected and nurtured you, and now I've seen you made Consort. Your children will rule Skala. How is that a betrayal?"

"I loved you! I trusted you! How could you let me think you were my lover when you never meant to keep me?" She was crying, and hated herself for her weakness.

Niryn reached out and caught one of her tears with a fingertip. He held it up to the candlelight, admiring it like a rare jewel. "I must confess a bit of weakness on my part. You were such a dear, affectionate little thing. If Korin had found himself a suitable bride, who knows? I might even have kept you for myself."

Once again, anger burned away the tears. "You dare speak of me as if I'm some hound or horse you acquired! Is that really all I was to you?"

"No, Nalia." His voice was tender as he leaned forward and cupped her cheek, and in spite of herself, she leaned a little into that familiar caress. "You are the future, my dear little bird. Mine. Skala's. Through you, with Korin's seed, I will bring peace and order back to the world."

Nalia stared at him in disbelief as he rose to go. "And you knew all this, when you found me orphaned as a babe? How?"

Niryn smiled, and something in it chilled her heart. "I am a great wizard, my dear, and touched by the gods. I was shown this many times, in visions. It is your fate, your destiny."

"A wizard!" she threw after him as he went to the door. "Tell me, was it you who bespelled me and made me a virgin again?"

This time his smile was answer enough.

A little while later Korin came to her, stinking of wine the way he had that first night, but clean this time. He stripped naked without so much as looking at her, revealing a fine young body but a lagging arousal. He hesitated by the bed, then blew out the candle and climbed on top of her between the sheets. He didn't even bother to kiss her before pulling up her nightdress and rubbing his soft member between her legs to make himself hard. He found her breasts and stroked them, then fumbled between her legs, trying clumsily to pleasure her a little and get her ready.

Nalia was grateful for the darkness, so that her new husband would not see the shamed, angry tears streaming down her cheeks. She bit her lip and held her breath, not wanting to betray herself as she resisted memories of sweeter lovemaking, now tainted forever.

Nalia cried out when her false maidenhead was torn, but she doubted he noticed or cared. Her new husband seemed in a greater hurry than she was herself to be done with the act, and when he spewed inside her, it was with another woman's name on his lips: *Aliya*. She thought he might be weeping when it was over, but he'd rolled off and left her before she could be certain.

And so ended the wedding night of the Consort of Skala.

The memory still burned her with shame and anger but Nalia could take comfort in the fact that so far, she had refused her captors the one thing they wanted from her. Her moon blood had come and gone. Her womb remained empty.

Chapter 9

Despite her best intentions, Tamír lost hope of leaving for Atyion anytime soon. There was still too much to do in Ero.

The sporadic spring rains held on. The footpaths between rows of hastily built shacks and tents were often more channels than byways. There'd been no time to establish wards. Nobles unlucky enough to have no estate to retreat to found themselves cheek by jowl with tradesmen's families or half-starved beggars who'd found their way here, hoping for the queen's generosity.

Tamír was on her feet or in the saddle from dawn until dusk, when she wasn't holding court. Meals were often a bit of bread and meat passed to her while she worked.

The conditions had one advantage; so far, no one had tried to make her wear a dress outside of Illardi's house. Out here she was free to stride around in boots and breeches.

The first supplies from Atyion arrived at last, in a caravan led by Lady Syra, whom Lytia had appointed as her understeward.

Tamír rode out to meet her as the caravan reached the settlement.

"Highness!" Syra curtsied, then presented her with the manifest. "I've brought canvas, blankets, ale, flour, salted mutton, dried fish, cheese, dry beans, firewood, and herbs for healing. More is on the way. Lady Lytia has organized temporary accommodations in the town and castle yards for those you send for shelter there."

"Thank you. I knew she'd arrange things properly." Tamír took a sealed document from the sleeve of her tunic and handed it to her. "I'm deeding the hundred acres of fallow ground between the north wall and the sea for an expansion of the town. People can build and settle there, and pay rent to the castle. See that she gets this."

"I will, Highness. But does this mean you've decided not to rebuild Ero?"

"The drysians say the wells and earth are too badly tainted. It will take more than a year to clear. And the priests all claim it's cursed ground. I'm being advised to burn what's left, to purify the land. Skala must have a new capital, a stronger one. For now, it will be Atyion."

"Now if we could just make you go there," muttered Ki, and some of the other Companions chuckled.

A crowd was already gathering as word of supplies spread among the shacks. Tamír saw gratitude in the faces of some, but also greed, anger, impatience, and despair. There were still nearly eight thousand of them on the plain, not counting the soldiers, and there had been too many incidents of violence. Her bailiffs came before her daily to present reports of theft, rapes, and other crimes. The laws were still in force and she'd ordered more hangings than she cared to think about, but it was an impossible situation.

And this was only a temporary respite, she reminded herself. What winter crops had escaped the blight would soon be rotting in the fields if they weren't gathered, and most of the spring crops had not been sown. By winter they must all have a harvest and a proper roof over their heads or more would perish.

Exhausting as this all was, Tamír was glad to be so busy all day long. It gave her an excuse to avoid the wizards and kept her mind off what the nights held.

Brother left her alone by day, but in the darkness the

angry spirit invaded her room or her dreams, demanding justice.

To make matters worse, after a few awkward nights together with little sleep for either of them, Ki had taken to sleeping in the dressing room of her bedchamber. He'd said nothing, just quietly made the change. Now and then he also asked leave to go riding on his own after the evening meal. He'd never needed to be apart from her before. She wondered if he was looking for a girl—a real girl, she amended bitterly—to tumble.

Ki went out of his way to treat her as he always had, but something was irrevocably changed between them and there was no use pretending otherwise. When he disappeared into that little side room each night he left the door open between them, but he might as well have been in Atyion.

Tonight was no different. He'd seemed happy enough as he joined her and the other Companions for a game of bakshi, but when it broke up a few hours later he made some excuse and left. Lynx slipped out after him, as he sometimes did. Tamír longed to ask him where Ki went, but pride kept her silent.

"It's not as if I'm his wife," she growled, striding back to her own room.

"What was that, Highness?" asked Una, who'd been closer behind her than she'd thought.

"Nothing," Tamír snapped, embarrassed.

Baldus had prepared her room for the night. He looked expectantly behind her as Tamír came in. *Looking for Ki,* she thought.

Una helped Tamír off with her circlet and boots, and Baldus hung her sword belt on the rack with her armor.

"Thank you. I can manage the rest myself."

But Una lingered a moment, looking like she had something to say.

Tamír raised an eyebrow. "Well? What is it?"

Una hesitated, shooting a glance at the boy. Coming closer, she lowered her voice. "Ki? He's not off to see a lover, you know."

Tamír turned away quickly to hide her flaming cheeks. "How do you know?"

"I overheard Tharin trying to tease it out of him the other day. Ki was rather angry at Tharin for suggesting it."

"Is it so obvious? Are all my Companions talking about me now?" Tamír asked miserably.

"No. I just thought it might ease your heart a little, to know the truth."

Tamír sank down on the bed with a groan and rested her face in her hands. "I'm no good at this, being a girl."

"Of course you are. You're just not used to it yet. Once you marry and start having children—"

"Children? Bilairy's balls!" Tamír tried to imagine herself with a big belly and cringed.

Una laughed. "A queen doesn't just fight wars and give speeches. You'll need an heir or two." She paused. "You do know about how—"

"Good night, Una!" Tamír said firmly, cheeks aflame again.

Una laughed softly. "Good night."

Tamír would almost have welcomed a visit from Brother just then. Better that than sitting here alone with such thoughts. Sending Baldus to his pallet, she changed into her dressing gown and settled by the fire with a mazer of wine.

Of course a queen must have children. If she died without issue, the land would be torn by chaos as rival factions strove to establish a new line of succession. All the same, when she tried to imagine coupling with Ki—or anyone for that matter—it made her feel very strange.

Of course she knew how sex went. And it had been Ki who'd first explained it to her, that day in the meadow with his forked stick people and blunt, country language. She wanted to laugh at the irony now.

She finished off the wine and felt the warmth of it spread. That, and the sound of the waves below her window lulled her, and she let her mind drift. As she began to doze, something Lhel had once told her came back. She'd spoken of a special power in a woman's body, in the ebb and flow of blood that followed the moon.

Tamír had started bleeding again yesterday and spent a good deal of time since cursing the inescapable tyranny of rags and blood and the random pains that cramped her belly. It was one more cruel joke of fate, like having to squat to piss. But Una's offhand words held truth. There was a purpose behind it all.

The thought of a great round belly pushing out the front of her tunic was still disturbing, nonetheless.

Baldus stirred on his bed, whimpering softly in his sleep. She went and drew the blanket up around the boy's shoulders, then stood gazing down at his sleeping face, so soft and innocent in sleep. What must it be like, she wondered, to look at a child of your own? Would it have her blue eyes?

Or brown?

"Damnation!" she muttered, going for more wine.

Ki's borrowed horse shied as a gust of damp breeze scooped a cloud of acrid smoke up from a blackened foundation just inside the remains of the north gate. Beside him, Lynx tightened the reins of his own mount, nervously scanning the dark square they were presently patrolling.

"Easy, there." Ki rubbed his horse's neck to calm him, then adjusted the vinegar-soaked cloth tied over his mouth and nose. Everyone who ventured into the ruins had to wear them, to fend off disease. Ki knew he was taking a pointless risk, coming here. He claimed to be helping hunt down looters, and he'd killed a few, but in truth, he was drawn back time and again, looking for familiar places. When he came upon them, though—inns, theaters, and taverns they'd frequented with Korin—it only made the ache in his heart worse.

The smell of vinegar was rank, but better than the reek that still lurked in the streets and alleys. Foul humors and the stench of rotting flesh and burnt buildings mingled with the night mists in a cloying miasma.

They rode for nearly an hour without meeting another living person. Lynx kept his sword drawn, and above his mask his eyes darted ceaselessly, scanning for danger.

There were still too many corpses lying about. The few Scavengers left were kept busy day and night, carting away the now-putrid bodies to the burning grounds. They were bloated and black, and many had been cruelly torn up by hungry dogs, pigs, or ravens. Ki's horse shied again as a huge rat darted across a nearby alley with what looked like a child's hand in its mouth.

The fires had burned fiercely, and even after almost two weeks, smoldering pockets of coals remained beneath the ruins, deadly traps for looters or unlucky householders seeking to salvage what they could. Up on the Palatine, broken black stonework loomed against the stars, marking where the great palaces and fine houses had once stood. It was a lonely place, but it suited Ki's mood these past weeks.

"We should head back," Lynx murmured at last, plucking at the rag across his face. "I don't know why you keep coming here. It's depressing."

"Go on back. I didn't ask you to come." Ki nudged his horse into a walk.

Lynx followed. "You haven't slept in days, Ki."

"I sleep."

He looked around and realized they'd come out in the theater ward. The once-familiar neighborhood looked like the landscape of a bad dream. Ki felt as much a ghost here as Brother himself. *But better this than tossing on that lonely cot,* he thought bitterly.

It was easier during the day. Tamír still resisted wearing women's garb much of the time, and there were moments when Ki could pretend to see Tobin. When he let himself sleep, he dreamed of Tobin's sad eyes lost in a stranger's face.

So instead, he settled for stolen naps and rode down his dreams here at night. Lynx had taken to coming with him uninvited. He didn't know if Tamír had sent him to keep an eye on him, or if he'd simply taken it upon himself to keep watch over him. Maybe it was habit, from his days as a squire. Whatever the case, Ki hadn't been able to shake him off these past few nights. Not that Lynx wasn't a decent companion. He said little and left Ki to the dark thoughts that continued to plague him, no matter how hard he tried to keep them at bay.

How could I not have known, all those years? How could Tobin have kept such a secret from me?

Those two questions still burned at the edges of his soul, though it would have shamed him to voice them. It was Tobin who'd suffered the most. She'd carried the burden of that secret alone, to protect them all. Arkoniel had made that very clear.

Everyone else, even Tharin, had accepted it readily enough. Only Lynx seemed to understand. Ki saw it there now as he glanced over at his silent friend. In a way, they'd both lost their lords.

*T*amír was still awake when Ki stole in. He thought she was asleep, and she stayed quiet under the quilts, studying his face in the faint light of the night lamp as he crossed to the dressing room. He looked tired, and sad in a way that she never saw during the day. She was tempted to call out to him, invite him into the too-big bed. It wasn't right that Ki should suffer for his constancy. But before she could gather her courage, or master her discomfort over the wet rag tied between her thighs, he was already gone. She heard the sound of him undressing, and the creak of bed ropes.

She turned over and watched the way the light of his

candle made the shadows in the doorway dance. She wondered if he was lying there, sleepless as she was, watching them, too?

*T*he next morning she watched Ki yawn over his breakfast, looking uncommonly pale and tired. When the meal was finished she gathered her courage and drew him aside.

"Would you rather I had Una take your place at night?" she asked.

Ki looked genuinely surprised. "No, of course not!"

"But you're not sleeping! You won't be much good to me exhausted. What's wrong?"

He just shrugged and gave her a smile. "Uneasy dreams. I'll be happier when you're settled at Atyion, that's all."

"Are you sure?"

She waited, giving him the chance to say more. She wished with all her heart that he would, even if she didn't want to hear what he might say, but he just smiled and clapped her on the shoulder and they both left their true thoughts unsaid.

Chapter 10

Niryn stood on the battlements, enjoying the damp night air. Korin had gone up to Nalia's tower again. As he watched, the light there was extinguished.

"Labor well, my king," Niryn whispered.

He'd removed the blighting spell from Korin; the boy would father no monsters on Nalia. It was time at last, the time of Niryn's choosing, for an heir of Skala to be conceived.

"My lord?" Moriel appeared at his elbow, stealthy as always. "You look pleased about something."

"I am, dear boy." This lad was proving useful, as well. For all his faults, that odious pederast, Orun, had groomed Muriel well, to sneak and spy and sell his loyalty. Niryn could well afford it, and knew better than to trust him too far. No, he had spells around young Moriel for that, and the boy would do well not to cross him.

"Have you been keeping an eye on that new lord for me? The one who rode in yesterday?"

"Duke Orman. Yes, my lord. He seems quite taken with the king. But Duke Syrus was complaining again, about how Korin shows no sign of marching on the usurper."

Moriel never referred to Tobin by name. There was bad blood there, and Tobin wasn't the only Companion against whom Moriel harbored a grudge. "How is Lord Lutha faring?"

"Sullen, and hanging about Lord Caliel, as usual. I caught them whispering together on the battlements again tonight. They don't much like the way things are right now. They think you've led King Korin astray."

"I'm quite aware of that. What I need from you is proof of treason. Solid proof. Korin will not act on anything less."

The boy looked crestfallen. "Everyone has retired. Is there anything else I can do for you, my lord?"

"No, you may go to bed. Oh, and Moriel?"

The boy paused, his pale, harelike face uncertain.

"You are proving most valuable. I depend on you, you know."

Moriel brightened noticeably. "Thank you. Good night, my lord."

Well, well, Niryn thought, watching him go. *It seems you do have a heart to win. I thought Orun crushed that out of you long ago. How very useful.*

Niryn returned to his enjoyment of the night. The sky was clear, and the stars were so bright they turned the dark sky a deep indigo.

The men he passed on guard greeted him respectfully. Many of them were his own Guard, and those who weren't had the good sense to show him proper courtesy. Niryn had touched the minds of the various captains, and found most of them fertile ground, well sown with doubts and fears for him to manipulate. Even Master Porion's had been surprisingly easy to slip into; his own stolid sense of duty to Korin did Niryn's work for him. There was no need to meddle there.

Niryn's own master, Kandin, had taught him that the greatest talent of wizards of Niryn's sort lay in their ability to see into lesser men's hearts and prey on the weaknesses there. Korin's flaws had been an open door to him, despite his burning dislike for the wizard. Niryn had simply bided his time, waiting for the seasons to turn. He took his first careful steps in the last year of the old king's life, when Korin had already led himself astray with doubt, drink, and drabs.

In the days after the old king's death, when the prince

was lost and foundering, Niryn seized the advantage and wormed his way just as securely into the heart of the boy as he had his father.

Erius had not been so easy. The king had been an honorable man, and a strong one. Only when the madness began to eat away at his mind did Niryn find a foothold there.

Korin, on the other hand, had always been weak and full of fears. Niryn used magic on the boy, but lately a few carefully chosen words and skillful flattery worked just as well. His beloved cousin's betrayal could not have been better timed.

Looking around the dark fortress, Niryn savored a swell of pride. This was *his* doing, just as the burning of the Illiorans and the banishing of countless headstrong nobles had been his work. He especially enjoyed bringing highborn lords and ladies down into the dust. He enjoyed being feared and cared not one whit how many hated him. Their hatred was the hallmark of his success.

Niryn had not been born a nobleman. He was the only child of two palace servants. During his early days at court, certain people who'd considered themselves his betters had been anxious not to let him forget that, but once he'd caught favor with the king they'd soon learned not to cross the soft-spoken wizard. He took no direct action against them, of course, but Erius had been quick to show his displeasure. Some of Niryn's early detractors now found themselves without title or lands—many of the latter having been since given to Niryn himself.

Niryn did not regret his lowly birth; quite the opposite, in fact. Those early years had left an indelible mark on him and taught him some valuable lessons about how the world worked.

His father had been a simple, taciturn man who'd married above himself. Born to a family of tanners, his marriage had allowed him to leave behind that malodorous trade and become one of Queen Agnalain's gardeners. His mother had been a chambermaid in the Old Palace, often working in the rooms of the queen before Agnalain went mad.

His parents lived in a tiny thatch-roofed cottage by the north gate. Each day his mother woke him while the stars were still out and they set off with his father up the long, steep road to the Palatine. They left their own humble quarter in darkness, and he could see the sky brightening as they ascended the steep streets. The houses grew larger and grander, the higher you went, and once inside the Palatine itself, it was like a great, magical garden. Elegant villas clustered around the walls and ringed the dark bulk of the Old Palace. There had been only one, back then, and it had been a lively place, filled with color and courtiers and good smells; it didn't fall into disrepair until Erius had left it behind, after his mother's death. The young prince could not abide the place after that, fearing his mother's mad, vengeful ghost would come after him in the night. Years later, when Niryn had gained the young king's trust and access to his inner thoughts, he learned why. Erius had killed his mother, smothering the mad old woman with a cushion after he learned that she'd signed an order for his own execution and that of her infant daughter, having decided they were both conspiring against her.

But when Niryn was a child, the Old Palace was still a wondrous place, with fine tapestries on the walls of the rooms and hallways, and fancy patterns of colored stone on the floor. Some of the corridors even had long, narrow pools, filled with flowering water plants and darting silver-and-red fish, set into the floors. One of the understewards had taken a liking to the red-haired boy and let him give crumbs to the fish. He was also taken with the palace guards. They were all tall, and wore rich red tabards, with handsome swords at their hip. Niryn secretly wished he might grow up to be a guard so he could carry a sword like that and stand watching the fish all day.

He often saw Queen Agnalain, a gaunt, pale woman with hard blue eyes, who strode like a man in her fine gowns and always seemed to have a group of handsome young men around her. Sometimes she had the young prince with her, too, a boy a bit older than Niryn. Erius, he was called, and he had curly black hair and laughing black eyes and his own pack of playmates called the Royal Companions. Niryn envied him, not for his fine clothes or even his title, but for those friends. Niryn didn't have time to play, and no one to play with if he had.

He sometimes went in with his mother very early in the morning to bring the queen the ale and black bread she broke her fast with each day. Soldier's food, his mother called it, disapproving. Niryn didn't see why it wasn't a proper breakfast for a queen. She sometimes gave him the crusts the queen didn't eat and he liked it very much; it was dense and moist, rich with salt and black syrup; much nicer than the thin oatcakes the cooks gave him to eat.

"That sort of food might be good enough on the battle-field, maybe, when she was still a warrior!" his mother sniffed, as if the great queen disappointed her.

She got the same look on her face at the way there was often a young lord in the queen's bed in the morning. Niryn never saw the same one twice. His mother didn't approve of this, either, but she never said a word, and cuffed him on the ear when he asked if they were all the queen's husbands.

During the day the corridors teemed with men and women in wonderful clothes and glittering jewels, but he and his mother had to turn and face the wall as they passed. They were not allowed to speak to their betters or attract any attention. A servant's duty was to be invisible as air, his mother told him, and the child soon learned to do just that. And that was just how the lords and ladies treated him, and his mother and all the host of other servants who moved among them, carrying the nobles' dirty linen and night soil buckets.

The queen had noticed him once, though, when his mother didn't pull him back in time to avoid her notice. Agnalain loomed over him and bent down for a closer look. She smelled of flowers and leather.

"You have a fox's coat. Are you a little fox?" she chuckled, running her fingers gently through his red curls. Her voice was hoarse, but kind, and those dark blue eyes wrinkled up at the corners when she smiled. He'd never gotten a smile like that from his own mother.

"And such eyes!" said the queen. "You'll do great things, with eyes like that. What do you want to do when you're all grown up?"

Encouraged by her kindly manner, he'd pointed shyly at a nearby guard. "I want to be one of them and carry a sword!"

Queen Agnalain laughed. "Would you now? Would you cut off the heads of all the traitors who creep in to murder me?"

"Yes, Majesty, every one," he replied at once. "And I'll feed the fish, too."

When Niryn was big enough to carry a watering can, his visits inside the palace came to an end. His father took him to work in the gardens. The great lords and ladies treated the gardeners as if they were invisible, too, but his father did the same with them. He cared nothing for people, and was shy and backward even with Niryn's sharp-tongued mother. Niryn had really never paid the man much mind, but he discovered now that his father was full of secret knowledge.

He was not patient or any less taciturn, but he taught the boy how to tell a flower seedling from a weed sprout, how to bind an espaliered fruit tree into a pleasing shape against a wall, how to spot disease, and when to thin a bed or prune a bush to make it flourish. Niryn missed the fish, but discovered that he had a talent for such things and a child's ready interest. He especially liked using the big bronze shears to cut away dead branches and wayward shoots.

There was still no time to play or make friends. Instead, he came to love seeing the garden change through the seasons. Some plants died without constant tending, while weeds thrived and spread if you didn't fight them every day.

No one realized Niryn was wizard-born until he was ten years old. One day several of Erius' Companions decided to amuse themselves by throwing stones at the gardener's boy.

Niryn was pruning a rose arbor at the time and tried his best to ignore them. Invisible. He must remain invisible, even when it was perfectly apparent that the sneering young lords could see him very well and had excellent aim. Even if they'd been peasants like him, he wouldn't have fought back. He didn't know how.

He'd endured taunts and teasing from them before, but had always ducked his head and looked away, pretending he wasn't there. Deep down, though, something dark stirred, but he'd been too well trained to his station to acknowledge anything like anger toward his betters.

But this was different. Today they weren't just taunting him. He kept at his pruning, carefully lifting the suckers away and trying not to let the long thorns pierce his fingers. His father was just beyond the arbor, weeding a flower bed. Niryn saw him glance over, then go back to his work. There was nothing he could do for Niryn.

Stones pattered around the boy, striking his feet and bouncing off the wooden trellis next to his head. It scared him, for they were trained to be warriors and could probably hurt him badly if they wanted to. It made him feel small and helpless, but something else stirred again, deep down in his soul, and this time it was much stronger.

"Hey, gardener's boy!" one of his tormentors called out. "You make a good target."

A stone followed the taunt, striking him between the shoulders. Niryn hissed in pain and his fingers tightened on the rose cane he'd been trimming. Thorns pierced his fingers, drawing blood. He kept his head down, biting his lip.

"He didn't even feel it!" one of the other boys laughed. "Hey, you, what are you? An ox with a thick hide?"

Niryn bit his lip harder. *Stay invisible.*

"Let's see if he feels this."

Another stone struck him on the back of the thigh, just below his tunic. It was a sharp one and it stung. He ignored it, nipping a stray shoot with the shears, but now his heart was pounding in a way he'd never felt before.

"Told you. Just like an ox, stupid and thick!"

Another stone hit him in the back, and another.

"Turn around, little red ox. We need your face for a target!"

A stone hit him in the back of the head, hard enough to make him drop his shears. Unable to help himself, he reached back and felt the stinging place where the stone had hit him. His fingers came away smeared with blood.

"That got him! Hit him again, harder, and see if he'll turn."

Niryn could see his father, still pretending he didn't know what was happening to his son. It came to Niryn, then, what the real gulf between commoner and noble was. Niryn had been taught to respect his betters, but he'd never fully appreciated until now that the respect was not returned. These boys knew they had power over him and delighted in using it.

A larger stone hit him on the arm as he bent to retrieve the shears.

"Turn around, red ox! Let's hear you bellow!"

"Throw another one!"

Something larger hit him in the head, hard enough to

daze him. Niryn dropped the shears again and fell to his knees. He wasn't quite certain what happened after that, until he opened his eyes and found himself lying under the arbor he'd been tending, watching unnatural blue flames devouring the carefully tended vines.

His father did come then, dragging Niryn away from the scorching blaze.

"What've you done, boy?" he whispered, more alarmed than Niryn had ever seen the man. "What in the name of the Maker did you do?"

Niryn sat up slowly and looked around. A small crowd was gathering, servants and nobles alike, while others ran for water. The three boys who'd been tormenting him were gone.

Water had no effect on the blue fire. It continued to burn until the arbor was reduced to ash.

Guardsmen came with the water carriers and their captain demanded to know what had happened. Niryn couldn't answer them because he had no idea. His father remained dumb, as usual. At last a broad-shouldered man pushed through the crowd, dragging one of Niryn's attackers by the ear. The young lord cringed beside him.

"I understand this young rascal was using you for target practice," the soldier said to Niryn, still holding the boy almost up on his toes.

Even in such an embarrassing position, the boy was looking daggers at Niryn, letting him know what his fate would be if he told.

"Come on now, lad, find your tongue," the man demanded. He wasn't angry with Niryn, it seemed, just impatient to complete an unpleasant task. "I'm Porion, swordmaster to the Royal Companions and I'm responsible for the behavior of the boys. Is he one of them who hurt you?"

Niryn's father caught his eye, silently warning Niryn to keep silent, stay invisible.

"I don't know. I had my back to 'em," Niryn mumbled, staring down at his dirty clogs.

"You sure about that, lad?" Master Porion demanded sternly. "I had it from some of his fellows that he was one of them."

He could feel Master Porion's eyes on him, but he kept his head down and saw the young lord's fine bootheels settle in the grass as the older man released him.

"All right then, Nylus, you get back to the practice yard where you belong. And don't think I won't keep an eye on you!" Porion barked. The young lord gave Niryn a last, triumphant smirk and strode away.

Porion remained a moment, staring pensively at the ruined arbor. "Word is you did this, lad. That the truth?"

Niryn shrugged. How could he? He didn't even have a flint.

Porion turned to his father, who'd been lingering nearby. "He's your boy?"

"Aye, sir," his father mumbled, unhappy not to be invisible to this man.

"Any wizard blood in your family?"

"None that I know of, sir."

"Well, you'd better get him to a proper wizard who can judge, and soon, before he does something worse than a little fire."

Porion's face grew sterner still as he glanced back at Niryn. "I don't want him on the Palatine again. That's the queen's law. An unschooled wizard-born is too dangerous. Go on, take him away and get him seen to, before he hurts someone."

Niryn looked up in disbelief. The other boy had gotten away with hurting him, and now *he* was to be punished? Throwing caution to the wind, he fell at Master Porion's feet. "Please, sir, don't send me off! I'll work hard and not make any more trouble, I swear by the Maker!"

Porion pointed to the ruined arbor. "Didn't mean to do that, either, did you?"

"I told you, I couldn't—!"

Suddenly his father's broad hand closed over his shoulder, yanking him to his feet. "I'll take charge of him, sir," he told Porion. Gripping Niryn's thin arm, he marched his son like a criminal out of the gardens and away from the palace.

His mother beat him for losing his position and the small pay that went with it. "You've shamed the family!" she railed, bringing the belt down across his thin shoulders. "We'll all go hungry now, without the extra silver you brought home."

His father stayed her hand at last and carried the sobbing boy up to his cot.

For the first time in Niryn's life, his father sat by his bed, looking down at him with something like actual interest.

"You don't remember nothing, son? Are you telling me the truth?"

"No, Dad, nothing, until I seen the arbor burning."

His father sighed. "Well, you done it, putting yourself out of a position. Wizard-born?" He shook his head and Niryn's heart sank. Everyone knew what happened to those of their station unlucky enough to be born with a touch of wild power.

Niryn didn't sleep at all that night, caught up in dire imaginings. His family would starve, and he'd be set out on the road to be marked and stoned, all because of what those young lords called fun! How he wished he had spoken up when he had the chance. His face burned at the thought of his own fruitless obedience.

That thought took root, watered with shame at how he'd let a single look from the guilty one silence him. If he'd spoken up, maybe they wouldn't have cast him out! If those three boys hadn't used him for their sport, or if his father had made them stop, or if Niryn had moved or turned sooner or tried to fight back—

If, if, if. It ate at him and he felt the dark feeling well up again. In the darkness, he felt his hands tingling and when he held them up, there were blue sparks dancing between his fingers like sheet lightning. It scared him and he thrust them into the water jug by his bed, fearing he'd set the bedclothes on fire.

The sparks stopped and nothing bad happened. And as his fear subsided, he began to feel something new, something else he'd never felt before.

It was hope.

He spent the next few days wandering the marketplaces, trying to catch the attention of the conjurers who plied their trade there, selling charms and doing fancy spells. None of them were interested in a gardener's boy in homespun clothes. They laughed him away from their little booths.

He'd begun to think he might indeed have to starve or take to the road, when a stranger showed up at the cottage door while his parents were away at their work.

He was a stooped, ancient-looking man with long dirty whiskers, but he was dressed in a very fine robe. It was white, with silver embroidery around the neck and sleeves.

"Are you the gardener's boy who can make fire?" the old man asked, staring hard into Niryn's eyes.

"Yes," Niryn replied, guessing what the old man was.

"Can you do it for me now, boy?" he demanded.

Niryn faltered. "No, sir. Only when I'm angry."

The old man smiled and brushed past Niryn without an invitation. Looking around the spare, humble room, he shook his head, still smiling to himself. "Just so. Had your fill of 'em and lashed out, did you? That's how it comes to some. That's how it came to me. Felt good, I expect? Lucky for you that you didn't set them on fire, or you'd not be sitting here now. There's lots of wild seeds like yourself, that get themselves stoned or burned."

He lowered himself into Niryn's father's chair by the hearth. "Come, boy," he said, gesturing for Niryn to stand before him. He placed a gnarled hand on Niryn's head and bowed his own for a moment. Niryn felt a strange tingle run down through his body.

"Oh, yes! Power, and ambition, too," the old man murmured. "I can make something of you. Something strong. Would you like to be strong, boy, and not let young whelps like that take advantage of you ever again?"

Niryn nodded and the old man leaned forward, eyes glowing like a cat's in the dim light of the cottage. "A quick answer. I can see your heart in those red eyes of yours; you've had a taste of what wizardry is, and you liked it, didn't you?"

Niryn wasn't certain that was true. It had scared him, but under this stranger's knowing gaze, he felt that tingle again, even though the man had withdrawn his hand. "Did someone tell you what happened?"

"Wizards have an ear for rumor, lad. I've been waiting for a child like you, these many years."

Niryn's pinched, parched young heart swelled. It was the closest thing to praise he'd ever known, save for one time; he'd never forgotten the way Queen Agnalain had looked at him that day and how she said she thought he'd do great things. She'd seen something in him, and this wizard did, too, when all the rest wanted to cast him out like some rabid dog.

"Oh yes, I see it in those eyes," the wizard murmured. "You have wit, and anger, too. You'll enjoy what I have to teach you."

"What is that?" Niryn blurted out.

The old man's eyes narrowed, but he was still smiling. "Power, my boy. The uses of it and the taking of it."

He stayed until Niryn's parents came home, and made his offer. They gave Niryn over to the old man, accepting a purse of coins without even asking his name or where he would take their only child.

Niryn felt nothing. No pain. No sorrow. He looked at the two of them, so shabby compared to the old man in his robes. He saw how they feared the stranger but didn't dare show it. Perhaps they wanted to be invisible now, too. But Niryn didn't. He'd never felt more visible in the world than that night when he walked away from his home forever, at the side of his new master.

Master Kandin was right about Niryn. The talents that had lain dormant in him were like a bed of banked coals. All it took was a bit of coaxing and they leaped to burn with an intensity that surprised even his mentor. Master Kandin found Niryn an apt pupil and a kindred spirit. They both understood ambition, and Niryn found he lacked nothing of that.

Through the years of his apprenticeship, Niryn never forgot his time at the palace. He never forgot how it felt to be nothing in the eyes of another or the way the old queen had spoken to him. Those two elements combined in the crucible of his ambition. Kandin honed him like a blade and, when his mentor was done, Niryn was ready to return to court and make a place for himself. The lessons of his childhood were not forgotten, either. He still knew how to seem invisible to those from whom he wished to hide his power and purposes.

He'd missed his chance with Queen Agnalain. Erius had put his mother out of the way before Niryn could establish himself, and taken his young sister's rightful place on the throne.

Niryn, now a respectable young wizard and loyal Skalan, had gone to pay his respects to the girl one day at the pretty little house her brother had installed her in on the palace grounds. By rights she should have been queen, and there was already muttering in the city about prophecies and the will of Illior. Niryn put no stock in priests, considering them nothing but skilled charlatans, but he wasn't above putting their game to his own uses. A queen would be best.

The lessons he'd learned among the roses and flower

beds came back to him then. The royal family was a garden in its own way, one that needed proper tending.

Ariani, the child of one of her mother's many lovers, was the rootstock of the throne. As the only daughter of the queen, her claim was strong, perhaps strong enough to overthrow that of her brother, when she was old enough and carefully groomed and supported. Niryn had no doubt he could nurture a faction on her behalf. Sadly, he found the stock to be diseased. Ariani was very pretty and very intelligent, but the fatal weakness was in her already. She would suffer her mother's fate, and earlier. It might have made her easier to control, but the people still had dark memories of her mother's mad ways. No, Ariani would not do.

That decided, he insinuated himself into Erius' court. The young king welcomed wizards at his feasts.

The young king was made of stronger stuff than his sister. Handsome and virile, strong in body and mind, Erius had already won the hearts of the people with a string of impressive victories against the Plenimarans. As weary of war as they were of royal madness, the Skalans turned a deaf ear to dusty prophecies and ignored the grumblings of the Illiorans. Erius was beloved.

Fortunately for Niryn, the king also had a strain of his mother's weakness in him, but just enough to make him malleable. Like his father's espaliered fruit trees, Niryn would trim and prune the young king's pliant mind, bending it to the pattern that best suited his use. The process took time and patience, but Niryn had a great deal of both.

Niryn bided his time, finding other wizards he could use and forming the Harriers and their guard, ostensibly to serve the king. Niryn chose carefully, taking in only those he could be sure of.

With Erius he prepared the ground, discrediting any who stood in his way, most especially Illiorans, and gently coaxing the king into killing any female of the blood who might challenge his hold on the throne.

Erius grew more malleable as his mind became less stable, just as Niryn had foreseen, but there were always unforeseen events to contend with. Erius had five children, and the eldest daughter had shown great promise, but plague struck the household, killing all of the children save one, the youngest and a boy. Korin.

Niryn had a vision then, of a young queen, one of his own choosing, who would be the perfect rose of his garden. It was a true vision, too, that came to him in a dream. Like many wizards, he paid little more than lip service to their patron deity, the Lightbearer. Offerings and the drugged sacred smoke of the temples had nothing to do with their power. That came with the blood of their birth; a tenuous red tie back to whatever Aurënfaie wanderer had slept with some ancestor and given the capricious magic to their line. Nonetheless, he found himself offering up a rare prayer of gratitude when he woke from that dream. He had not seen the girl's face, but he knew without question that he'd been shown the future queen who, with his careful guidance, would redeem the land.

Prince Korin would not have been the child Niryn would have chosen to breed his future queen from. There'd been other girls, and one of them would have made his task easier, letting the disaffected have their queen and their prophecy again. Even he could not discount the years of famine and illness that had blighted Erius' reign. A girl would be best, but like any good gardener, Niryn must work with the shoots that matured.

It was about this same time that he found Nalia. He'd gone with his Harriers to dispatch her mother, a distant country cousin of the queen, with royal blood in her veins and that of her twin babes. One girl child had been comely, like her father. The other had inherited her mother's disfigurement. Something like a vision stayed Niryn's hand over the marked child; this was the next seedling for his garden. She would bear daughters of her own, if left to grow and properly tended. He secreted her away, making her first his ward and then, when the humor took him, his concubine. Wizard-born, he had no seed to plant in that fertile womb.

Korin was not a stupid boy, or an ignoble one, not at first. He instinctively distrusted Niryn from an early age. But he was weak-spirited. The wars kept the king away, and Korin and his Companions were left to run wild.

Niryn lent only the occasional small encouragement here and there. Some of the Companions were quite helpful, albeit unwittingly, as they led Korin into the wine houses and brothels of the city. Niryn began more rigorous tending when Korin began to spread his seed about. It was an easy matter, with his wizards and spies now well established, to put any royal bastards out of the way. Princess Aliya had been a regrettable pruning. The girl was healthy, and intelligent, too, but lacked the usual sort of flaw that he could exploit. No, she would in time prove to be a dangerous weed in his garden, strengthened by the prince's love.

By the time Erius died, Korin was a dissipated young rake and a drunkard. The death of his pretty wife and the horror of the misshapen fruits of her womb left him broken and lost, and ripe for the first harvest.

Niryn broke from his pleasant reverie and looked up at the darkened tower again. There, high above this sheltered haven, the seed of the next season was being planted.

Chapter 11

After a lifetime as a free wizard, wandering where she chose, Iya now found herself not only with an untried, and at times unwilling young queen on her hands, but a pack of her own kind who needed organizing, as well. The Third Orëska had been a noble concept; now she and Arkoniel were faced with finding out whether or not their wizards could actually work together.

Tamír had kept her word and insisted from the start that Iya's wizards be made welcome in Illardi's house, despite the grumbling from some of the lords and generals. In return, they found ways to make themselves useful, making small useful charms like firechips and roof wards. Iya, Saruel, and Dylias all knew a bit of healing and helped where they could, with the drysians' blessings.

Arkoniel's own little group of wizards had arrived at the end of Lithion. Iya had been touched by the joy with which he'd greeted them. He'd truly missed them, especially a green-eyed boy of nine named Wythnir, whom he'd taken as his first pupil. He was a frail little thing, and shy, but Iya sensed the strong potential in him. She exchanged an approving look with Arkoniel, who was positively beaming.

Busy as Tamír was, she ordered a special banquet for them in her chambers with the other wizards and Companions that night, and Arkoniel proudly presented them.

The old ones, Lyan, Vornus, Iya's friend Cerana, and a gruff, scowling, common-looking fellow named Kaulin were the first to bow to Tamír with their hands to their hearts.

"You are the queen that was foreseen, indeed," Lyan said, speaking for them all. "By our hands, hearts, and eyes, we will gladly serve you, and Skala."

The younger ones came forward next, a noble-looking pair in tattered finery, named Melissandra and Lord Malkanus, and a plain young fellow named Hain. He was about Arkoniel's age and had the same aura of banked power about him.

The children came forward last, and Iya saw Tamír's eyes light up as they were presented. Ethni was close to Tamír's age, with only the faintest trace of magic about her. The twin girls, Ylina and Rala, weren't much stronger, nor was little Danil. Wythnir shone among them like a jewel in a handful of river stones. This was the sort of child Iya had imagined, all those years ago when they first spoke of gathering wizards, but Arkoniel seemed delighted with all of them, regardless of their ability.

"Welcome, all of you," said Tamír. "Arkoniel has told me good things about you, and your studies. I'm glad to see you here."

"I understand you spent some time at our old home," Ki added. He shot Arkoniel a grin. "I hope you didn't find it too dreary there?"

"Oh no!" Rala said at once. "Cook makes the best cakes and mince tarts."

Ki pulled a comical stricken face. "You're right. Now I'm homesick."

The children laughed at that, and it set the tone for the evening. Most of the older wizards seemed quite fond of the children and had them demonstrate their little tricks for the other guests after supper. It was mostly colored lights and bird calling, but Wythnir made a dish of hazelnuts fly about the room like a swarm of bees.

Iya's wizards were quick to welcome the newcomers, too, and she and Arkoniel exchanged a happy look. Thirty-three wizards, counting themselves, plus a handful of new-comers who'd straggled in; it was a good start.

After they had the children settled in their new rooms, Arkoniel walked with her on the walls.

"Can you imagine it?" he'd said to her, eyes shining. "The children have made such tremendous progress, with only a few minor wizards for teachers. Think what they'll learn from these powerful ones you've gathered! Oh, some of them don't have the talent to be more than healers or charm makers, I know, but a few may grow to be great."

"Especially that boy you've taken on, eh?"

Arkoniel's face glowed with affection and pride. "Yes, Wythnir will be great."

Iya said nothing, recalling how she'd thought the same of all her early pupils. Wythnir was certainly brighter than the others, but she knew from long experience that disap-pointment was as likely as success with one so young, even those who seemed promising.

More important than any single apprentice or wizard was the memory of the vision she'd had all those years ago: Arkoniel an old, wise man in a great house of wizards, with a different child by his side. She'd passed the vision on to him, and she sensed it taking hold ever more strongly, now that he'd had a small taste of success.

And Arkoniel loved children. That had come as some-thing of a surprise to Iya, who had no use at all for ordi-nary ones, and rarely considered wizard-born as anything more than potential apprentices. She'd loved her own stu-dents, as much as she was capable of loving anyone, but knowing that each one would leave her and go their own way eventually, it didn't do to get overly attached. Perhaps Arkoniel would come to understand that in time, but for now, he was seeing that shining palace, full of life and learning. It showed in his eyes, and Iya knew better than to stand in the way of Illior's will. Arkoniel was fated for a dif-ferent path than the one she and her predecessors had trodden.

He still carried the cursed bowl, too, and guarded it well. Perhaps he was fated to find a safe place for it. That was on the knees of the gods, too. Iya had no regrets, and new challenges to face.

Dylias and the Ero wizards had some experience at unity, having banded together to protect themselves from the Harriers. Iya would have been happy to leave the demands of leadership to him, but everyone seemed determined to defer to her.

"The Oracle gave the vision to you," Arkoniel laughingly reminded her when she grumbled in the days that followed. It seemed someone was always coming to her with some question of magic, and there were always children underfoot. "You are Tamír's protector. Naturally they look to you."

"Protector, eh?" Iya muttered. "She still hardly speaks to me."

"She's better with me now, but there's still a wariness there. Do you think she's guessed at the truth?"

"No, and we must put her off as long as we can, Arkoniel. She cannot have any distractions now and she still needs us. Perhaps she'll never ask. It would be better so."

With Dylias' help, they kept watch as best they could across the sea toward Plenimar. Others stayed near Tamír by turns, ready to protect her from any threat. This had to be done discreetly, with so many of Tamír's new allies openly distrustful of their kind.

Iya was equally distrustful of many of them, these nobles and warriors. Eyoli was recovered from his wounds and had already proven his worth. The young mind-clouder could walk into any encampment and move about freely, virtually unnoticed, listening and watching. Coupled with Arkoniel's strange new blood spell and Tharin's long memory for loyalties and intrigues, Iya judged Tamír to be as well guarded as could be managed.

She also found a sound ally in the Oracle's high priest, Imonus. The man had stayed on all this time and showed no signs of leaving. He and the two others who'd come with him, Lain and Porteon, spent their days tending the makeshift Temple of the Stele, as it was called now. People came every day to see it, and to hear from the high priest's own lips that their new queen was indeed Illior's chosen one.

Imonus had gathered the surviving Illioran priests from Ero and counseled them to set up makeshift temples in the camps. He and his own priests established the largest of these, setting up the golden stele and offering braziers under a canopy in the courtyard of Illardi's estate, just inside the gates. Anyone coming to see Tamír had to pass it and be reminded by the prophecy of her right to rule.

Imonus spoke with the authority of the Lightbearer, and the devout believed. They left small offerings of flowers and coins in the baskets at the foot of the great tablet and touched it for luck. Destitute as most of them were, people nonetheless found food to bring to the priests, placing wizened apples and chunks of bread in the covered baskets. Then they cast their wax votives and feathers onto the ornate bronze braziers, rescued from some temple in Ero. These burned night and day, filling the air with the scent of the Illiorans' pungent incense and the acrid undertone of burned feathers. Imonus and his brethren were always there, tending the fires, bestowing blessings, interpreting dreams, and offering hope.

Iya approached most priests with certain skepticism. She'd seen too many of them profit from false promises and false prophecies. But Imonus was honest, and devoted to Tamír.

"Our daughter of Thelátimos is strong," he remarked as he and Iya sat together in the great hall after the evening meal. "She's well-spoken and I see how she lifts the hearts of those she talks to."

"Yes, I've noticed that. Perhaps she had a touch of Illior's inspiration?"

"More than a touch," Imonus said. "She believes more in building than power. This will be both a blessing and a burden to her."

"Is that a prophecy?" asked Iya, raising an eyebrow at him over her mazer.

He just smiled.

Chapter 12

As the sunnier days of Nythin lengthened across the land and the roads dried, Tamír discovered that the news of the destruction of Ero and her own transformation had not always traveled in tandem. Confused emissaries were still arriving from distant holdings. Some came with belated replies to the war summons sent out by King Erius, expecting to find the king still on the throne. Others came looking for word of the miraculously transformed princess. A few brave souls carried terse missives frankly denouncing her as a sham.

It was from these newcomers that they heard rumors that Korin was at Cirna and building up an army there.

"That means we're cut off from the nobles in the territories north of there, except by sea," Tharin noted.

"And we still don't have enough ships to matter," Illardi added. New keels were being laid down at boatyards from Volchi to Erind, but not all of those ports had declared for the new queen. Even if they had, it took time to build ships of that size.

"Well, at least we know where he is," said Ki.

Arkoniel and Iya tried to verify this, using the wizard eye and window spells, but to no avail.

"You can't see into the fortress at all?" Tamír asked in disbelief.

"Whenever I try, it feels as if someone is sticking knives in my eyes," Arkoniel told her. "Niryn has thrown up some sort of protection around the entire fortress."

"Did he catch you trying to peek?"

"Perhaps, but we've been very careful," Iya said. "He'd know to guard against such magic."

"Is Niryn stronger than you?"

"It's not such a difficult sort of ward. The Harriers were powerful in their way, and there are at least four of them left besides Niryn. It won't do to underestimate them. We only saw them at work, burning wizards. We don't know what else they're capable of," Iya warned. "You've seen what our little band can do when we put our heads together, after only a few months. Niryn has had years to explore and test the powers of his own people. I suspect they are still a force to be reckoned with, even diminished as they are."

"What can we do, then?"

"Send more scouts," Arkoniel suggested.

For now, that seemed to be her only option, and she did so and returned to learning how to rule.

She spent each morning holding court in the makeshift throne room they'd made of Illardi's hall, sitting on the canopied dais, attended by Illardi, Tharin, her Companions, and a few of Iya's wizards.

It still felt odd, sitting in the place of honor, but everyone else treated her like she was already queen. The arrangements for the displaced and incoming lords and warriors still took up much of her attention. There were endless needs to be addressed, disputes to be heard. Fights broke out and the whole camp was placed under military tribunal. The citizens were growing impatient with their situation. The miracle of their new queen was old news now; they were hungry and dirty and wanted more than the promises of their priests that life would improve.

Hundreds who'd been judged healthy by the drysians had already been allowed to leave. Some went to Atyion. Others had family in other cities. But there were still over a thousand left in the encampment and even with supplies from Atyion and other towns, careful rationing was necessary, which made for short tempers.

Some of those left were too sick to move, many had nowhere to go; but most still wanted to return to the city and try to rebuild or reclaim what they could, despite warnings about tainted water and cursed ground. Day after day, they appeared before Tamír, cajoling, begging, and complaining.

Worse yet, the lords who'd come to join her were growing restless. Tamír had made it quite clear that she was in no hurry to precipitate a civil war, especially since she'd had no word from Korin yet. All her generals and advisors insisted that her cousin's continued silence had to be taken as a bad sign, and in her heart, she suspected they were right.

Bored warriors were a danger to all. There were fights between rival factions, murders, rapes, and pilfering. She left the disciplining of the culprits to the nobles they answered to, but knew she either had to use them or send them home.

"Work parties," Tharin advised. "Most of them are yeomen and farmers when they're at home. Put them to work and keep them out of trouble!"

Most of her nobles had been amenable to the idea, and so she had a sizable force to work the fields and carry on with the cleansing of the city.

It was exhausting and discouraging work, trying to keep order. Tamír wasn't trained for this and felt the weight of it all as a personal responsibility.

"If I'm to be the queen that saves them, then why doesn't the Lightbearer show me how?" she complained to Imonus.

"There has not been one report of plague," the priest pointed out.

That didn't put bread in anyone's mouth, as far as she could tell.

She was not without help, however. Duke Illardi had

experience in such matters and vetted many of the suppli-
cants for her. He was well respected and better versed in
the ways of court than her warlords. Soon he was acting as
her unofficial chancellor.

Nikides was proving invaluable, as well. He'd learned
firsthand about matters of court protocol from his illustri-
ous grandfather. Tactful, deeply knowledgeable in history
and court procedures, and wise beyond his years, he
quickly earned respect even from the older country lords.

Tamír kept the two of them by her at all audiences and
they guided her when necessary.

It was during this time, too, that Tamír saw a different
side of Tharin. She'd always known him as a steady and
fair-minded man, a staunch warrior and friend. Now she
discovered shrewdness in him, born of years at her father's
side at court and on the battlefield. He had never sought to
lead, but he was a good judge of character and had a long
memory. Thanks to her father's power and influence at
court, there were few among the higher nobles whom
Tharin had not met at one time or another.

One morning a young knight appeared with a message
from Duke Ursaris of Raven Tor. The duke had arrived the
previous day, with a force of five hundred riders and men-
at-arms, but had not yet come to pay his respects.

Tharin knew Ursaris from their days in Mycena and
privately expressed his distrust to Tamír. "He's a staunch
Sakoran, and owes your uncle both his title and his lands,
which were seized from a lord who maintained his allegiance to Ariani after Erius took the throne."

The duke's messenger shifted nervously until Tamír
took notice of him, then bowed low, looking like a man
with a distasteful duty to perform. "I am Sir Tomas, and
I bring greetings from his grace, Duke Ursaris, son of
Melandir, to—" He swallowed uneasily. "To Prince Tobin
of Ero."

Tharin caught Tamír's eye and lifted one eyebrow

slightly. She acknowledged the caution with a slight nod and gave the young man a stern look. "You may tell your lord that I am Tobin no longer. If he wishes parley with me, he can come himself and greet me by my proper name."

"You may also tell your lord that in the future if he wishes to spy out the situation, he should not send a known cat's-paw under the honorable banner of a herald," added Tharin, glowering down at the startled fellow.

"I am a knight, Lord Tharin!"

"Then you've come up in the world by quite a mark. I remember a camp runner with a talent for picking pockets and telling clever lies. I remember you, *Sir* Tomas, and your master, too."

"So do I," old Jorvai growled from the back of the audience chamber, where he'd been playing dice with some of the other lords. He came forward, dropping a hand to his sword hilt. "And like Lord Tharin here, I have a good memory for faces and reputations. Ursaris always wanted his bread buttered on both sides."

Tamír held up a hand to stay them. "If your master wishes to support me, then tell him he is welcome in my court. If not, he should be gone by morning or I'll consider him my enemy." It was no idle threat and the man knew it.

"I will report your reply, Highness." He bowed and hurried out.

Tamír and her guard rode out by Beggar's Bridge to see what Ursaris would do. By sundown he'd decamped and marched west, taking his warriors with him.

"Good riddance!" Ki called after them, rising in the saddle and waving his middle finger at their retreating backs. "You cowards!"

"He's not, you know," Tharin said. "Ursaris is a good leader and his men are brave."

"They didn't believe the truth about me," said Tamír.

"I doubt it mattered one way or the other to him,"

Tharin replied. "He's made up his mind to back Korin." He leaned over and clasped her shoulder. "He won't be the only one, you know."

Tamír sighed, watching Ursaris' banners dwindle in the sunset light and dust. "I know. Do you think that Korin has lost people to my side, too?"

Tharin waved a hand around at the spreading cluster of tents and corrals on the plain. "There they are, and more coming every day."

Tamír nodded, but still wondered how many warriors Korin was gathering, with the Sword of Ghërilain and his father's name?

Such thoughts made her all the more grateful for the familiar faces around her.

Not all of them were as they had been, however.

Tanil's wounds had healed, but his mind was still unhinged. Tamír and Ki visited the squire every day, in the room he now shared with Lynx. He slept a great deal and spent most of his waking hours staring out the window at the sea. The others even had to remind him to eat. His once-lively brown eyes were dull now, his hair lank and dirty around his shoulders, except for the two small tufts of unevenly shorn hair at his temples, where the enemy had cut off his braids. It was a mark of shame for a warrior. Quirion had been made to cut off his own, when he was banished from the Companions for cowardice. Now Tanil would have to prove himself worthy again, before he would be allowed to plait in new ones.

Tamír doubted he cared. The only person he would willingly talk to was Lynx, and he said very little to him. Lynx often sat quietly with him when he wasn't needed elsewhere, concerned that he might do himself harm.

"Bad enough what those Plenimaran bastards did to him, and then left him alive with the shame of it, but he feels he failed Korin, too," Lynx confided to Tamír and the others. "His mind wanders and he wants to go looking for him, thinking Korin fell in battle. Other times he thinks he hears Korin calling for him. I have to set a guard on his door when I'm not there."

"How did Korin take it, losing him?" Ki asked Nikides.

"Hard. You know how close they were."

"But he didn't go back to look for the body, to give his friend proper rites?"

Nikides shrugged. "There wasn't time. The citadel was overrun right after that and Lord Niryn convinced Korin to flee."

"I'd have found a way," Ki muttered, exchanging a look with Tamír. "I'd have made sure one way or the other."

One rainy afternoon a few days later another familiar face appeared at her court.

Tamír was presiding over a dispute between two displaced millers over the ownership of a small, undamaged granary outside the city walls. She'd watched her uncle at this many times, but found it just as boring to adjudicate as to watch. She was doing her best not to yawn in their faces when Ki leaned down and touched her shoulder.

"Look there!" He pointed into the crowd of petitioners that ringed the hall and she caught sight of a head of golden hair. Leaving Nikides to sort out the millers, she hurried across the hall to greet her father's liegeman, Lord Nyanis. She hadn't seen him since the day he accompanied her father's ashes home from that last battle. His welcoming smile now swept that memory away with happier ones and she embraced him warmly. He was one of the few lords she'd known, growing up at the keep, and she'd always liked him. Even as she embraced him, however, she remembered that he and Lord Solari had once been friends, as well as her father's warlords.

"So here you are!" he laughed, hugging her like he had when she was a child at the keep. "And Ki, too. By the Four, look how the pair of you have grown! And fine warriors, too, by all reports. Forgive me for not coming sooner. I was still in Mycena when word of the Plenimaran raid reached me, and the spring storms on that coast forced us to march back."

Tamír pulled back. "Have you heard about Solari?"

Nyanis' smile faded. "Yes. I always told him his ambition would be the ruin of him, but I had no idea he'd throw in with the likes of Niryn. I'd seen nothing of him since your poor father's passing. If I'd known, I'd have tried to reason with him and do more to protect you. As it is, I do have news for you, though it's not good. I've had word from Solari's eldest son, Nevus, on my way here. The fool wanted me to help him oppose you and take Atyion."

"I hope you told him no?" Tamír said, grinning.

Nyanis chuckled. "Your father was my liege, and I'll pledge my sword to you, if you'll have me."

"Gladly."

He looked her up and down; she'd come to expect such scrutiny from those who'd known her before the change, and recognized the wonder mixed with disbelief.

"So this was Rhius' great secret? I spoke with Tharin on my way in. He says I'm to call you Tamír now. Or should it be Majesty?"

"Highness, for now. It's important that I follow the laws and rituals."

"That would include getting back the queen's sword."

"Yes."

"Then I will see it in your hand, Highness." Nyanis knelt and presented his sword to her, right there in the bustle of servants and milling plaintiffs. "In the meantime, I repeat the pledge of my heart and my sword to the scion of Atyion. I will see the crown of Skala on your brow and the Sword of Ghërilain in your hand. I will gladly give my life for that, Princess Tamír." He stood and sheathed his sword. "Let me present some other allies I brought to you."

Arkoniel happened by as she was greeting the knights and lords. "Lord Nyanis! I'd not heard of your arrival."

"Wizard!" He clasped hands with Arkoniel. "Still minding your charges, I see. Were you ever able to teach either of them to write properly?"

"One of my greatest accomplishments," Arkoniel replied, smiling.

Taking a bitty of the red. That's what Lhel had called the spell when she first taught it to Arkoniel. Away from prying eyes, he pressed the tiny drop of Nyanis' blood from beneath the sharpened corner of his little finger's nail and spread it over the pad of his thumb, then spoke the words she'd taught him. Like Tamír, he wanted to trust the man, but Solari had been a harsh lesson. He felt the tingle of the magic working, and then relief when no hint of evil intent came to him from the blood.

He'd used this spell often, and had already found a few lords who weren't to be trusted. Satisfied about Nyanis, he returned to the audience chamber, looking for more newcomers to greet.

Chapter 13

Mahti's first vision for this journey had been a river, and so it seemed, though his feet never left dry land. The trails he was drawn along led him east and north for the next two turnings of the moon.

For the first weeks he traveled through valleys he knew, following each one down from the peaks like the spring melt trickling down in little streams to swell the larger ones at the bottom, where the villages lay. He met with those he'd healed and those he'd bedded, and learned the names of children he'd fathered. Some begged him to stay, but the old ones who knew how to read the marks on his oo'lu gave him gifts of food that could be lightly carried and sang parting-forever songs when he moved on.

He soon left the valleys he knew, but Mahti was not lonely, for the ghost witch Lhel was often with him. She came into his dreams at night, telling him of the girl she'd shown him in that first vision. Her name was Tamír, and she'd been a boy until recently, sharing a body with her dead brother. Lhel had made that magic, with the Mother's blessing, but she'd died before she could see the girl completely into womanhood. This, and the unhappy ghost of the boy, kept her own spirit earthbound. Like many witches, Lhel was at ease in spirit. That she stayed for love rather than for vengeance had made her a *pagathi'shesh,* a guardian spirit, rather than a *noro'shesh,* like the girl's twin.

Lhel showed him that spirit, too, and he was fearsome, bound to Lhel and to his sister by rage. Playing his vision song, Mahti saw the spirit cords that bound them all together. They were very strong.

"I watch over her, but I wait for him," Lhel confided, lying next to Mahti on his pallet in the darkness under an oak. "I will guide him on when he is ready to let go."

"He hates you," Mahti pointed out.

"As he must, but I love him," she replied, resting her cold head on Mahti's shoulder and wrapping her cold arms around him.

Lhel had been a beautiful woman, with her thick hair and ripe body. The marks of the goddess covered her skin like twig shadows on snow and her power still clung around her like a scent. She inflamed Mahti's flesh as if she'd been a living woman. Because she was a pagath-i'shesh, he lay with her like a living woman under each full moon, but only then. By the full light of the Mother's face they might make more guardian spirits together, who could be incarnated as great witches later on. Any other night risked making the souls of murderers and thieves. But she often lay with him, even without coupling, and he wished he'd known her in life.

She was also his guide, and in his dreams showed him rocks and trees to look for to keep him on the path he'd chosen. She told him of other people around the girl who had been a boy, showed him faces: a boy with brown, laughing eyes; a fair-haired southland warrior filled with love and sadness; the young oreskiri he'd seen in the first vision, who was filled with pain; and an old woman oreskiri with a face like flint. He would know the girl by these people, Lhel said.

The way grew harsher as he pushed ever east and north, and so did the people who lived there. They were still his own kind, but they lived too close to the southlanders to be generous or welcoming to a stranger heading in that direction. They showed him scant courtesy, just enough not to offend the Mother, and sent him on his way with silence and suspicious looks.

On and on he went, and the mountains shrank to hills. The Retha'noi villages grew smaller and meaner and farther between, then there were no villages at all, just the occasional camp of hunters or a lone witch.

Another two days and the hills gave way to forest and spring rushed up to meet him, even though at home he knew people would still be breaking ice on the water buckets in the morning. Here the grass was green and lusher than any meadow he'd known. The flowers were different, and even the birds. He knew from the old tales that he had at last reached the outlying lands of the south-landers.

The first ones he met were a family of wandering traders who'd had dealings with the Retha'noi and greeted him with respect in his own language. The patriarch's name was Irman and he welcomed Mahti into their tent like kin and sat him at his side by the fire.

When they'd washed their hands and eaten together with his wife and sons and all their wives and children, Irman asked after hill people Mahti might know, then asked the nature of his journey.

"I'm seeking a girl who was once a boy," Mahti told him.

Irman chuckled at that. "Can't be many of those about. Where is she?"

"South."

"South's a big place in Skala. From where you're sitting, it's just about all south from here. Go north and you'll soon find yourself in the Inner Sea."

"That is why I must go south," Mahti replied agreeably.

Irman shook his head. "South. All right then. Your kind has a way of getting where you need to go. You carry a fine oo'lu, too, I see, so you must be a witch."

The man said it with respect, but Mahti caught an undercurrent of fear. "You people distrust my sort of magic, I'm told."

"Like poison and necromancy. I don't think you'll get very far if people know what you are. I've seen some of the good you folk can work, but most Skalans would burn you without a second thought."

Mahti considered this. Lhel had said nothing of such dangers.

"Do you speak Skalan?" Irman asked.

"Yes, I have learned it from a boy," Mahti answered in that language. "Our people are learning it from traders, like you, so know to protect ourselves. I am told to say I am from Zengat, to fool them."

At least that's what he thought he said. Irman and the others stared at him for a moment, then burst out laughing.

"I am not saying the words?" he tried again.

"You're getting a few of them, here and there," Irman replied, wiping his eyes. "People will take you for simpleminded rather than Zengati, talking like that. And the Zengat aren't exactly loved in Skala, either."

So it would be harder than he thought, making his way in a place where no one liked or understood him. "If you will teach me to speak better, I will heal your ills and make good charms for you," he said in his own language. He pointed over at one of Irman's women with a big belly. "I will play blessings for the child."

The young woman glared at him, muttering something in her own tongue.

Irman growled something at her, then gave Mahti an apologetic look. "Don't mind Lia. She's from the towns and doesn't understand your folk the way we hill people do. I'll take your healing on my animals, if you swear to me by your moon goddess you mean no harm."

"By the Mother, I swear I work only good," Mahti promised, pressing a hand to his heart and gripping his oo'lu.

He stayed three days in the forest with Irman and his clan, practicing his Skalan and laughing at himself and his people who'd thought they knew the language. In return, he healed a spavined ox and played the worms out of

Irman's goats. It scared his hosts a little, when the witch marks showed on his skin as he called his power, but Irman let him heal a rotten tooth all the same, then asked him to play over his old wife, who had a lump in her belly.

The old woman lay shivering on a blanket under the moon, while her whole clan looked on with a mix of wonder and concern. Mahti gently felt the swelling and found it hot and angry. This called for a deep healing, like the one he'd done for Teolin.

He drew Irman aside and tried to explain about playing the spirit out of the body in order to work there without disturbing it.

The man rubbed his cheek where Mahti had driven out the bad tooth. At last he nodded. "You do what you can for her."

Mahti settled down beside her and rested the end of the oo'lu near her hip. "You sleep now, woman," he said, using his newly learned Skalan. "Good sleep. I make you not sick. You give me—" He didn't know the right word for it. He needed her agreement.

"I give you leave," the woman whispered. "It won't hurt none, will it?"

"No pain," he assured her.

He droned her to sleep and called her spirit up to bathe in the moonlight, then set to work exploring her abdomen. To his relief it was only an abscessed ovary. A bad one, to be sure, but he soon cooled the hot humors and drew them away. It would take a few days and some cleansing herbs to finish the job, but when he played her back and bade her open her eyes, she pressed a hand to her side and smiled.

"Oh yes, that's much easier! Irman, he is a good healer. Why do folks tell such tales of them?"

"We can make harm," Mahti admitted. "Bad witches, too, but also those who fight the southlanders." He gave the others an apologetic little bow. "Not friends, but those who kill us to take away our land."

"Is it true, your people used to live all the way to the eastern sea?" one of Irman's grandsons asked.

Mahti nodded sadly. The old ones still sang of sacred places by that salt water—rock shrines and sacred springs and groves that had gone untended for generations. The Retha'noi still had their hills and mountain valleys because the Skalans didn't want them yet.

On the fourth morning he prepared to take his leave. He'd dreamed of Lhel again the night before and she was impatient for him to move on, but to the north again, not south.

Irman gave him food and clothes to help him move better along his journey. Their tunics and trousers fit closer than his loose shirt and leggings, and they weren't sewn with any charms. Mahti sewed some on the inside of the tunic, and kept his elk and bear tooth necklace and bracelets. He accepted a Skalan knife, too, and hid his own in a cloth bag with the food they'd given him.

"What about your horn?" Irman asked as Mahti fitted it into its cloth sling. Mahti just winked. It was easy enough to make people not see it if he chose.

"Now can I tell that I am Zengat?" he asked, grinning.

"Better than saying what you are, I guess," Irman said. "Are you sure you have to do this 'sojourn' of yours? You'd be better off heading home."

"The goddess will help me." He didn't tell him about Lhel. Southlanders didn't understand the dead.

He walked south until he was out of their sight, then turned north all that day and the next, and the forest grew thinner. He could see over the tops of the trees in places, to an endless expanse of flatland. It was green, and dotted with forests and lakes. He hurried on, anxious to see what it was like to walk in such a place, with the sky so wide overhead.

He went on like this for three days, when his feet brought him to a wide river. There were many villages and farms, and herds of cattle and horses.

He could not swim, so he waited for darkness to look for a way across the water. The moon rose full and white in a clear sky, so bright his shadow showed sharp and black on the dew-laden grass.

He had almost reached the river when he met a new group of southlanders. He'd just left the safety of a small wood and was striding across the moon-bright meadow when suddenly he heard voices. Three men ran out of the dark wood and made straight for him. Mahti dropped his traveling sack and pulled the oo'lu from its sling, holding it loosely in one hand.

The men came on, letting out cries that were probably intended to frighten him. Mahti's fingers tightened on the smooth wood of the oo'lu, but he was smiling.

The men drew swords as they came close. They smelled dirty and their clothes were ragged.

"You!" the tallest one hailed him roughly. "I can smell the food in your bag from here. Hand it over."

"I need my food," Mahti replied.

"Bilairy's balls, where you from, talking like you got a mouthful of stones?"

It took Mahti a moment to puzzle out what the man was asking. "Zengat."

"Fuck me, a Zengat, way down here all by his self!" one of the others exclaimed, stepping closer.

"You not fight me," Mahti warned. "I wish not to harm any."

"Well ain't that sweet?" the tall one growled, closing in. "And what you going to 'harm' us with? That walking stick? I don't see no sword on your belt, friend."

Mahti cocked his head, curious. "You call me 'friend' but voice and sword say 'enemy.' Go away, you. I will go my own way in peace."

They were almost close enough to strike. Mahti sighed. He'd given fair warning. Raising the oo'lu to his lips, he blew a catamount cry at them. His attackers sprang back in surprise, as he'd hoped.

"Balls, what were that?" the third one said. He sounded much younger than the other two.

"You go," Mahti warned again. "I kill you if you don't."

"That ain't no Zengat," the leader growled. "We got us a filthy little hill witch here. That's one of them fancy bull-roarers. Cut his throat before he gets up to mischief!"

Before they could attack Mahti began the drone of the bees. They stopped again, and this time they dropped their weapons and grabbed their heads in pain. The young one fell to his knees, screaming.

Mahti played louder, watching the other two fall writhing to the ground. The blood that burst from their ears and noses looked black in the moonlight. If they were innocent men, the magic would not hurt them so. Only the guilty with murder in their hearts and blood on their hands reacted like this. Mahti played on, louder and stronger until all three stopped thrashing and crying out and lay still in the grass. He changed to the song he'd used to lift the souls out of the bodies of Teolin and Irman's old wife, and played over the body of the leader. This time, however, he ended it with a sharp raven's croak that severed the thin thread of spirit that tethered the soul to the body. He did the same with the man in the hat, but let the boy live. He was young enough that perhaps this life hadn't been his choice.

The spirits of the two dead men flittered around the bodies like angry bats. Mahti left them to find whatever afterlife southlanders had and continued on his way without a backward glance.

Chapter 14

The weather around the isthmus was always unpredictable, but even here, summer finally arrived with warmer days and softer winds. The coarse grass above the cliffs came to life, looking like a strip of green velvet stretched between the blue and silver seas on either side. Small flowers carpeted the waysides and even grew from the cracks in the stonework along the walls and in the courtyards.

Riding along the cliffs with Korin and the Companions, Lutha tried to find hope in the new season. Rumors still came thick and fast from the south, carried by the shaken warlords and nobles.

A sprawling encampment was slowly spreading over the flat ground before the fortress, nearly five thousand men in all. It wasn't only cavalry and foot, either. Fifteen stout ships under the command of Duke Morus of Black Stag Harbor rode at anchor in Cirna harbor. By all reports, Tobin had only the few that had survived the Plenimaran raid.

Korin found seasoned generals among the newcomers, including Morus, whom he'd declared admiral; Lord Nevus, the eldest son of Duke Solari; and eager, fierce Lord Ursaris of Raven Tor, said to have some of the finest horsemen in the northern territories. Ursaris had arrived only recently, but had quickly found a place of honor at the king's table. More than once, Lutha had seen the man speaking with Niryn and put it down to the wizard's influence. All the generals seemed to be cozy with the man.

At night the long tables in the great hall were filled

with grim-faced lords who drank Korin's health and swore by Sakor to take Ero back for her rightful king.

Passing these same men on the corridors or in the castle yards, however, Lutha caught snatches of muttered arguments and heated debates. It was no secret that the treasury at Ero had been lost. There was talk that their young king had not distinguished himself in battle. Many scoffed at that, but even Korin's defenders had begun to wonder why he still made no move to march against the pretender.

Men stopped talking and guiltily looked away when they saw Lutha's baldric, but he overheard enough to concern him. A few nobles had slipped away in the night, but most stayed, professing loyalty to the memory of Korin's father.

There were rumors aplenty about Tobin, or Tamír, as he was calling himself now, in addition to the reports brought back by Niryn's spies, but they were confused and hard to credit. But one rumor that did seem to run consistent was that the Oracle at Afra had sent her own priests to bless this changeling queen.

There was also talk of a huge golden tablet with a spell on it. One spy who actually saw the thing reported that it was the golden stele of Ghërilain, which had once stood in the Old Palace. This was immediately denounced by Niryn as a forgery. Everyone knew that the great tablet had been destroyed.

"Illiorans, treasonous priests and rogue wizards: that's who would foist a sham queen on you!" Niryn told any doubters. Each night at the feast table he found reason to rail against the rebel faction. "Traitors, all of them. And treason cannot be tolerated. Lowborn or highborn, they must be seen for what they are, a threat to the peace of Skala. Like snakes in long grass, they have lain in wait. Now they're slithering out to bite at what they think are weak heels."

"What do you make of it, then, Lord Niryn?" a grizzled

lord named Tyman challenged one night as they sat drinking in the great hall. "Can a wizard change a boy into a girl?"

"Without the aid of a sharp knife and four strong men to hold him, you mean?" the wizard replied with a sly grin.

That got a good laugh from the assembly. Lutha was sitting by Caliel, though, and felt his friend shudder at the joke. He felt a bit sick himself.

Suddenly he felt eyes on him and looked up to see that cur Moriel watching him again, no doubt storing up things to tattle to his master later on. Lutha had had more than his usual ration of wine. With a snort of contempt, he threw his mazer at the nosy little whoreson's head. Moriel ducked it and scuttled away into the crowd.

"If you mean by magical means, however, then I must disappoint you," Niryn went on. "There is no spell in Orëska magic that could do such a thing. It would take nothing short of necromancy to effect such a transformation."

"Necromancy? In Skala?" Caliel asked dryly. "I thought you and your Harriers had rooted out that sort of thing long since. Don't tell me you missed a few?"

Niryn smiled down the table at him. "Necromancy is always a threat, my lord, and we must be vigilant against it."

"But why would the Oracle's own priest throw in with necromancers?" Caliel persisted.

"We have no proof that this is so," Niryn replied sharply. "When we march on Ero and capture these traitors, I'm certain you will find that it is all a tissue of lies."

"*If* we march," someone down the table from Lutha muttered.

"An Illioran plot," Korin muttered over the rim of his cup, his voice a bit slurred. "They hounded and cursed my father to his grave. They betrayed the city to the Plenimarans!"

"What?" exclaimed Ursaris.

Lutha exchanged a surprised look with Caliel. It was the first they'd heard of such a plot.

Korin nodded darkly. "I have my spies and my sources."

Lutha and Caliel exchanged another discreet look at that; Lord Niryn was in charge of the king's spies, and all information came to Korin from him.

"All of you who were in the city—You saw their crescent marks appearing everywhere for months before the attack," Korin went on, addressing the general company. "You heard them speaking treason against my father on every corner, saying he brought plague and famine on the land by wearing the crown. My father, with all his victories! The man who healed the land like a kind father after the ravages of his mad mother!" Korin brought his wine cup down hard on the table in front of him, so hard that the dregs splashed up the front of his tunic. His dark eyes flashed and his voice shook. "My father was a good man, a hero of Skala! Ariani was nothing but a child and the enemy was at the gates. Would you have had a child on the throne then? Where would we be now, eh?" He was on his feet now, nearly shouting. "And she turned out as mad as her mother, didn't she? And now Tobin?" He paused, chest heaving.

Lutha watched with growing alarm; this was how King Erius had acted when the fit came on.

"I always thought he was out for himself, from the day he showed up in Ero," Alben drawled, chiming in as usual to support any slander against Tobin. "You were good to him, Korin, better than a brother, and here's how he repays you."

Korin slumped back into his chair, looking rather dazed. "Mad. He's gone mad!"

"How do we know for certain?" Caliel asked. "With all respect, Lord Niryn, I don't know these spies of yours. I don't know how reliable they are as observers. And I doubt any of them know Tobin as we did."

A more ominous silence fell over the table as Niryn turned to Caliel again. "You doubt the king's judgment in this matter, Lord Caliel?"

Caliel tensed, sensing his misstep, and Lutha saw him look to Korin for support. Korin concentrated on paring an apple, as if he was paying the conversation no mind.

The other lords and warriors watched this exchange like a pack of wolves, gauging who the strong ones were and whom they could pick off later. Caliel wasn't coming off well. Even Alben and Urmanis were carefully keeping their own counsel.

Lutha was ashamed of his own silence. Before he could think what to say, however, Cal caught his eye and shook his head, warning him off. Lutha unhappily complied.

"I'm only saying that we're a long way from Ero here," Caliel went on, speaking to Korin as if no one else was in the room.

Korin just went on with his apple, cutting a slice and dipping it in his wine.

"We'll know the truth of it when we've captured Prince Tobin and all his traitors!" said young Nevus. "We're ready to follow our true king, aren't we?" he cried, and was greeted with a cheer.

"We'll celebrate the summer solstice on the Palatine!" someone else shouted.

"Aye, Majesty, give the word! We can be there by week's end," Master Porion said.

Korin smiled and pressed his fist to his heart in acknowledgment, but he didn't stand to announce a campaign.

Looking around, Lutha felt the same current of impatience he'd sensed before, unspoken behind all the shouting and pounding of wine cups.

The company broke up soon after, leaving Korin's allies to find their way back to their drafty tents or sleep drunk in the hall on benches and tabletops. Lutha trailed after Caliel, hoping to speak with him, but he just shook his head and retreated alone to his own room.

Disheartened, Lutha was on his way back to his chamber with Barieus when they were waylaid by the other Companions and drawn into Urmanis' chamber.

"What's gotten into Cal?" Alben demanded. "Why is he turning his back on Korin now, when he needs him most?"

"Turning *his* back?" Lutha looked in disbelief from him to Urmanis. "Haven't you been paying the least bit of attention? I know you never liked Tobin, but are you ready to let Niryn play Lord Chancellor and high priest and Sakor only knows what else like this? You know what Korin can be like, and with all that's happened, he's worse than ever—"

The Companions had always spoken honestly among themselves, lord and squire alike, even to Korin. So neither Lutha nor Barieus was prepared when the others drew their daggers and backed them into the corner farthest from the door.

"You two swore an oath!" Alben growled. "You are the King's Companions and your loyalty is to *him*. Not to Cal or Tobin or any priest. Isn't that so?"

Barieus moved to cover Lutha.

"You know we're loyal!" Lutha gasped, less shocked by the naked gleam of steel than the doubt in his fellow Companions' eyes. "Damn it, so is Cal! We're just worried for Korin, that's all! He hasn't been himself for ages, and he's drinking so much—and—"

And Niryn is on him like a bad fever, Lutha thought, but something in the others' eyes stopped the words from coming out his mouth. Lutha might not be the quickest wit in Skala, but his instincts were good and telling him now that speaking ill of Niryn to anyone was unwise.

"Sheathe your blades unless you mean to use them," he said instead, trying to make light of it. "Bilairy's balls, Alben, are you calling *me* a traitor now?"

The others slowly put away their knives and Lutha heard Barieus let out a faint, pent-up breath.

Urmanis gave him a chagrined smile and ruffled Lutha's hair. "These are uncertain times, little brother. You should think before you open that foolish mouth of yours. I feel bad about how things are between Korin and Caliel, too, but don't let your heart blind you to your duty. Korin isn't the one who's betrayed Skala. Tobin has."

Lutha shook his hand off and pushed past him to the door. "I'm as loyal as you, and so is Cal," he threw back over his shoulder. "You've no right to accuse us, just for speaking honestly! Korin doesn't need lackeys and slaves, like some Plenimaran Overlord. He needs warriors. Skalan warriors! Don't you forget what we are."

By the time he'd made it out the door he was shaking and doubly glad of Barieus close behind him. He was so angry he had to spit three times to ward off drawing bad luck for it.

"What's going on?" Barieus asked as soon as they were safely behind their own door. "How can they just sit there in that hall, watching Fox Beard insult Caliel like that?"

"I don't know. And then they have the gall to question *my* loyalty, right to my face?" Lutha spat again and paced the narrow room. "Maybe they're all going mad as old Agnalain herself! I'll tell you one thing, though. If Korin doesn't make up his mind which way he's going to jump soon, those cheers won't be so loud."

Niryn saw better than Lutha the impatience among the warriors. The young king felt it, too, and would have led them out tomorrow, but for Niryn's subtle intervention. The wizard realized the risk, putting off the fight, but he was not ready to slip Korin's leash just yet.

Nalia's tiring woman, Tomara, had taken fondly to her new mistress, but she was still Niryn's willing informant. When she came to Niryn's room the previous night, it had been with a long face.

"Her moon flow's come again," she said, holding out the bloodstained linen for proof.

Frowning, Niryn went to one of the large, locked chests that lined his chamber and sorted through the bags of herbs stored there. Selecting three, he mixed dried leaves and blossoms in a basin and carefully packed them in a linen bag.

"Make her teas with this and see that she drinks them. She will kindle."

"Of course she will, young and strong as she is," the old woman assured him. "And the young king so attentive, too!" She gave the wizard a wink. "The sheets bear witness to that."

Niryn smiled and gave her a sester.

Sitting by his window later, gazing up at Nalia's tower, he murmured, "You must kindle for me, my girl." He was not worried, only impatient. He'd foreseen an heir born to the stock of Erius. It would be so.

Chapter 15

Captain Ahra's scouting party returned early one rain-soaked morning near the end of Gorathan with more news of Korin's position at Cirna. Most of the northern lords had declared for Korin, and trade from that area had stopped.

Ahra came directly to the audience chamber, still in her armor and muddy boots. She dropped to one knee before Tamír, left hand on her sword hilt, and raised her right fist to her heart. "Prince Korin has a sizable force gathered, perhaps five thousand men, and twenty ships. I have a list of the nobles who've declared for him."

"Is Lord Niryn still with him?"

"Yes, and everyone is scared to death of the bastard and the handful of wizards he has left. Your loyal garrison there was slaughtered, and his grey-back Guard put in their place."

"Any news of the Companions?" Ki asked.

"Lord Caliel and Lord Alben were seen, and there are said to be others, but I wasn't able to learn who or how many. Master Porion is with them. Korin isn't showing himself much outside the keep."

Tamír exchanged a worried glance with Ki and Nikides, wondering if Lutha and Barieus had survived.

"Leave it to Alben to scrape through," Ki muttered. "Garol's probably right there beside him, too."

"It's good that Caliel and Master Porion are still with him, though," Nikides mused. "They could always talk sense to him."

"Perhaps, but they'll stand by him, no matter what," Tharin mused.

Tamír nodded and turned back to Ahra. "Anything else to report?"

"Well, Korin wears his father's crown now, and carries Ghërilain's sword. He claims to be king."

"It is not valid. He has not been properly consecrated," said Imonus.

"I guess that didn't stop him," Ahra replied. "He's sent out heralds, calling for the nobles of Skala to join him against you, Highness. Prince Korin claims you're nothing but a mad boy in a dress, the puppet of rogue wizards and priests."

Tamír's hands tightened on the arms of her chair; the words cut her to the quick. She knew she shouldn't be surprised, but it hurt all the same, to have her own fears confirmed.

"Niryn's put that into his head," Nikides offered, though he didn't sound very convinced, either.

"I wouldn't doubt it," said Ahra. "Korin has taken a new wife, too. The Princess Consort Nalia, they call her. I heard her called Nalia the Plain, and Nalia the Marked, too, on account of some birthmark on her face."

Tamír rubbed at the dark pink stain on her left forearm. That was said to denote wisdom. She wondered what this other woman's mark meant.

"Are you sure you heard right?" asked Lynx. "Korin's not the sort to take an ugly girl into his bed."

"Supposedly she's of the royal blood, some degree of cousin. Her mother was Lady Ana, who married Lord Sirin of Darie."

"I remember her," said Iya. "She had a wine stain birthmark on her face, too, and no chin to speak of, but she was intelligent and wellborn enough to find herself a good husband. The Harriers murdered her during the purges. I never heard of any child, though. How old is she said to be?"

"About Prince Korin's age, I believe," replied Ahra.

"Couldn't she be an imposter?" asked Nikides.

"It's possible, of course, but they'd be foolish to try such a sham. The truth is easily learned," said Imonus.

"The truth can be manipulated," said Arkoniel. "Still, it would be foolish to try and pass off a false heir when Korin himself can claim royal blood."

"Niryn must want the added legitimacy of a direct female bloodline," said Iya, frowning. "By the Light, he was playing a long-sighted game. Tamír, if Korin fathers a daughter on her, that child could make a claim to your throne."

"No one has a clearer claim than Princess Tamír!" Kyman objected. "She is the daughter of the rightful heir, and of the unbroken line of Ghërilain. I say the sooner we do away with Korin and this upstart girl the better. Get rid of them both before they breed!"

"Would you have me become my uncle so quickly?" Tamír sighed.

Kyman bowed, but he was glowering through his beard. "I meant no disrespect, but you must understand that the existence of such a child would be a threat."

Iya nodded darkly. "It's true, Tamír."

Looking into Iya's pale, hard eyes, Tamír felt a sudden chill, as if Brother had come up behind her. The demon was nowhere to be seen, but the uneasy sensation lingered. "I am the daughter of Ariani, of Ghërilain's line, and Illior's Chosen. I do not fear any distant cousins or their unborn children."

"You're all jumping at shadows anyway," said Ki. "Korin has never planted a child that lived."

"I pity this Nalia more than I fear her," Tamír said softly. No one else there, not even Ki, had seen what she had, standing beside Korin in that birthing chamber: Aliya screaming in agony on a blood-soaked bed, dying to birth a dead thing with no arms or face. "If Illior means for me to be queen, then I shall be queen; but I've told you already, I won't rule with a kinswoman's blood on my hands."

For once Tamír was glad of her long skirts. They hid the way her knees shook as she stood. "What I declared before the walls of Ero I declare to you all now; anyone who murders kin of mine, any kin, is my enemy!"

Everyone bowed to her. Out of the corner of her eye, Tamír saw Arkoniel and the other wizards doing the same with their hands to their hearts. Iya alone remained unmoved, regarding Tamír with that unblinking gaze that had frightened her as a child. A twinge of that same fear angered her now. It reminded her too much of how she'd felt around Niryn.

Tamír retreated to her chamber after the audience, clearly needing to be alone. Ki and Tharin followed but found the door closed against them.

Tharin drew Ki away from the guards at the door and shook his head. "She's done well, so far, with that honest kind heart of hers, but I saw doubting faces in the crowd tonight. These men are risking everything to follow her, and now we know that Korin already has more than twice her army at his command. She can't afford to let kindness turn to weakness in front of them. Can you talk to her?"

"I'll try. But she's right to say she won't act like her uncle." Ki paused, studying the older man's face closely. "You think she's right in that, don't you?"

Tharin smiled and patted his shoulder. He didn't have to reach down to do that anymore; Ki was as tall as he was. "Of course. But Mistress Iya is probably right about Niryn being even cleverer than we gave him credit for. He didn't just pull this girl out of the air."

"I can't help that. What do I do for Tamír?" Ki asked, looking unhappily back at the closed door.

Tharin squeezed his shoulder. "You've always taken good care of her, as a squire and a friend, and I know you'll stand by her now. Just see that she doesn't worry herself sick over this business."

"Easier said than done," Ki grumbled. "She's stubborn."

"Just like her father."

Ki searched Tharin's face. "Did Duke Rhius have people killed for this, Tharin? Or her mother?"

"Ariani never hurt a soul in her life, except herself and that child. Rhius did what was called for when he had to, but never for his own ends. He served Skala and did whatever needed to be done. We put down a few rebellious lords in our day, and some were got out of the way quietly. But it was for Skala. Help her accept that, won't you?"

"I'll try, but you know I'll stand with her, whatever she decides."

"Just as you should, and so will I. Go on now. You're the only one she wants to see now, I'm sure."

When Ki slipped in, Tamír was sitting by the fire, chin resting on her hand. It was a familiar pose, as was the look of wistfulness he caught before she looked up. Ki had a sudden urge to stride over and hug her. Before he could decide whether to act on the impulse or not, Tamír turned and gave him a wry look.

"I heard you two whispering out there. What was that about?"

"He said to not let you fret too much."

"I see. How are you supposed to do that?"

He grinned. "Get you drunk enough to sleep well for a change? I hear you tossing and muttering all night."

Tamír raised an eyebrow. "That makes two of us, then."

Ki shrugged. "You talk to Brother in your sleep sometimes. He's still around, isn't he?"

"Yes."

"But why? What's keeping him around?"

Tamír just shook her head, but Ki sensed there was

much she wasn't telling him. "He's not done with me, I guess," she replied at last. "Don't worry, I can deal with him."

Ki knew there was more she wasn't saying, but he let it go. "I'm sorry you had to hear all that about Korin. It must have hurt."

She shrugged. "Put yourself in his place. What would you think? If I could only talk to him!"

"I don't think that's going to happen anytime soon."

*T*amír went to bed fretting about Korin, but it was Brother who was waiting in her dreams again, gaunt and covered in blood, his black eyes filled with hatred. He had something in his hands, something terrible he wanted her to see.

"They did this to us, Sister!" he hissed. His hands were bloody, and at first she couldn't understand why. All he held was one of their mother's cloth rag dolls—a boy, with no mouth, just like all the others she'd made during Tamír's childhood. As he thrust it at her, however, she noticed that there was blood on it, too. It was dripping from an open wound in Brother's chest. It was raw, just as it had been in the vision she'd had of him that day at Lhel's tree, during their second binding.

A sudden tearing pain in her own chest stole the breath from her lungs.

"They did this!" Brother snarled. "You! You let them live! My blood is on *your* hands now!"

Looking down, Tamír saw that he was right. Her own hands were sticky with blood and she was holding Lhel's silver blade in one hand and her sharp silver needle in the other.

She woke panting and covered in cold sweat. The night lamp had gone out. The room was in utter darkness but she heard a noise and threw herself back against the bolsters, reaching wildly for the sword belt on her bedpost. Her hands still felt wet, sticky. *Blood?*

"Highness!" Somewhere in the darkness, Baldus sounded terrified.

And there was Brother, a glowing, snarling presence at the end of her bed. He wasn't naked or bloody, but he still held that mouthless doll in one hand, while with the other he pointed at her, silently accusing.

Her fingers brushed the strap of her scabbard, and she cried out again as strong, warm hands closed over hers. "No! Leave me alone!"

"It's me, Tob!"

She jerked in Ki's grasp but he held on, and that was somehow comforting, as comforting as hearing him use her old name. She knew without looking that Brother was gone.

The door flew open behind them and a guard was silhouetted in the lamplight from the corridor, sword drawn. Baldus let out a startled yelp as the door struck him.

"Highness, what's wrong?" Captain Grannia demanded.

Ki dropped Tamír's hand and stepped back from the bed, dressed in nothing but a long shirt. "Just a nightmare. Her Highness is safe."

Tamír could only imagine what this must look like. "A nightmare, as he said," she snapped. "Go back to your post and close the door."

Grannia gave them a last confused look, saluted, and obeyed.

Tamír expected Ki to go back to his cot, but instead, he sat down and pulled her close. Too shaken to object, she sagged against him, glad of his arm around her. She was glad for the darkness so he wouldn't see how it made her blush.

"I think we might have just started a rumor," she muttered.

Ki chuckled. "As if we haven't already."

"Highness?" Baldus whispered. He still sounded scared.

"It's all right," Ki told the child. "The princess just had a very bad dream. Go to sleep."

Tamír's eyes had adjusted to the darkness enough now to make out Ki's form, but she'd have known him anyway. Ki bathed often when he had the chance, but always seemed to smell faintly of horses and leather, fresh air and wine and clean sweat. It was a nice smell, comforting and familiar. Without thinking, she reached up and buried her fingers in the soft hair at the back of his neck and felt his start of surprise.

He hugged her and whispered, "What was that all about?"

"Don't know." She didn't want to think about it any more, not in the dark like this. Baldus was still whimpering, over there by the door. She knew too well what that felt like, to be afraid in the dark.

"Come here," she called to him.

The child climbed onto the bed and curled trembling against her legs. She reached down and made sure he'd brought a blanket with him, and then stroked his hair to comfort him. It felt cool and coarse under her fingers, nothing like Ki's.

"I'm sorry, Highness," the child whispered, voice hitching.

"Sorry for what?"

"For not being brave. I thought I saw a ghost. I thought you saw it, too."

She felt Ki's arm tighten around her. "It was just a bad dream."

Baldus fell asleep quickly and Ki carried him back to his pallet, then returned to the edge of the bed.

"This isn't the first time I've heard you calling out to him in your sleep, Tamír, just the worst. Can't you tell me what's going on? I know he's lurking around. I can feel him sometimes, and I see the way you go still all of a sudden, staring at something no one else can see. If there's anything I can do to help—"

She found his hand and drew him back down beside her. "He's still angry at me about the way he died, but he can't tell me what it is, except that I must avenge him," she whispered.

Ki was quiet for a moment, rubbing a thumb over her knuckles with a soothing rhythm that sent chills up her arm. At last he said, "There's something I never told you."

"About Brother?"

"Yes. I'd forgotten all about it. It happened the day Lord Orun died."

"That was years ago." She'd tried to forget that day, too, when she'd watched Brother kill her abusive guardian with a single touch of his hand.

"That day you went to see him, I stayed behind at your mother's house, remember? I never told you—I never told anyone—but I *saw* Brother that day, while you were gone. That was the first time.

"I was pacing around in Tharin's room, fretting over why Orun wanted me gone and worrying about you being alone with him and all. Then, out of nowhere, Brother just appears and says something like 'Ask Arkoniel.' It scared the piss out of me, but I asked what it was I was supposed to ask the wizard about. He wouldn't say, though, just stared at me with those dead eyes of his and disappeared." He paused. "Then they brought you back half-dead and told us about Orun and I forgot all about it. But now, with him still hanging on this way, it makes me think. Do you suppose Arkoniel knows more about him than he lets on?"

Brother's empty hissing laugh in the darkness was answer enough for both of them.

"If Arkoniel knows something, then Iya must, too," she replied.

"So maybe you should talk to them? I know you're still angry with them, but they have to help you, right?"

Tamír gave a grudging shrug and Ki sighed and settled more comfortably beside her. His breath stirred a strand of hair against her face. "I don't like to admit it, but I guess I'm getting past being mad at Arkoniel. And why would Brother say to talk to him if he didn't know something?"

"Something else they've been lying to me about all my life?" Tamír muttered bitterly.

"I know, but I believe them when they say they wanted to protect you any way they could. Ask him, will you?"

"I guess I'll have to. I just haven't found the right moment, with all that's had to be done. Maybe— Well, maybe I don't want to know."

Ki put his arm around her again and hugged her. "You still care for Arkoniel, don't you?"

Tamír nodded. In the months since the change, she'd begun to remember how it had been before. She was still hurt at the deception the wizards had practiced, but deeper than that ran the memory of what a patient, kind teacher Arkoniel had been. She hadn't welcomed him then, either. He'd been awkward and known nothing of children, but even so, he'd done his best to ease her loneliness. And it had been Arkoniel who'd convinced her father and Iya to bring another child to the keep, a companion for her. Ki.

Sitting here next to him like this, the simple fact of his presence fending off the darkness and fear, she decided that she could forgive Arkoniel a great deal on that account. Whether that forbearance extended to Iya remained to be seen.

"Maybe you don't have to ask them," Ki whispered suddenly. "Maybe you could go to the Oracle's priest instead."

"Imonus?"

"Why not? He speaks for the Oracle, doesn't he? You could at least ask him."

"I suppose so." She was still getting used to the idea that the Lightbearer was her own special patron. "I'll talk to him in the morning."

She reluctantly lay back against the pillows, knowing Ki would leave her and go back to his cot.

He didn't. Instead, he settled against the bolsters beside her and kept a hold on her hand. After a moment she felt him shift, and then the quick, awkward press of his lips against her hair.

"No more bad dreams tonight," he whispered.

Not trusting herself to speak, Tamír just squeezed his hand and rested her cheek against it.

Ki hadn't meant to kiss her. It had been a sudden impulse, and it left him blushing in the dark. Her silence afterward left him even more confused, but she hadn't pushed him away or taken her hand away.

What am I doing? he thought. *What does she want me to do?*

What do I want to do?

Her breath was warm and even against his wrist, her cheek smooth against his fingers. He knew she didn't use scent but he could swear there was a new sweetness rising from her hair, something decidedly unboylike. For an instant, it was just him and any girl, on a bed.

Not just any girl, he reminded himself, but that only increased his confusion. Was she asleep, or waiting for him to get under the covers with her?

As a friend, or as a lover?

Lover. The thought made him go hot and cold all over and his heartbeat quickened.

"Ki?" A sleepy whisper. "Lie down, why don't you? You'll get a crick in your neck."

"I—um—All right." Ki slid down a little.

Her breath was against his cheek now, and one of her braids had shifted to tickle across his hand. He reached to move it with his free hand, but paused a moment, noting how silky it felt between his fingers. He thought of how her fingers had felt against the back of his neck and felt a ghost of that same tingle.

A girl's touch, even with callused fingers.

He turned his head a little and felt her breath against the corner of his mouth. What would it be like, to kiss her mouth?

His heart was beating so hard now it hurt. He turned away, close to panic. Mixed into the confusion was a slight but unmistakable stir of arousal, something he'd never experienced around her before. Not like this.

"Tamír?" he whispered, not even sure what he wanted to say.

His only answer was the gentle sound of her sleeping breath.

Oh hell! he berated himself silently, staring up into the darkness. *What am I going to do?*

Chapter 16

Tamír didn't have any more dreams that night, and woke early the next morning, aware even before she opened her eyes that Ki had stayed with her all night. Her cheek was pressed to his shoulder and she'd shifted in her sleep, letting go of his hand to wrap an arm around his waist. He was still asleep, lying on top of the covers with his head at an awkward angle against the bolsters and one hand clasping her by the elbow.

For one sleepy moment it was like any other morning when they were younger. Then she came fully awake with a start, wondering if it was better to lie still and not wake him or try to get her arm free before he realized what she'd done. Frozen with indecision, she lay there, studying the planes of his sleeping face. His long hair spread across the pillow, strands of it brushing her cheek and hand. His dark lashes looked like fine brushstrokes on parchment against his tanned skin, and a scattering of fine stubble on his chin caught the morning light. His slightly parted lips looked very soft.

So close, she thought, just like that dream she'd had so often, when they almost kissed on the cliffs above that harbor. What would it feel like? It was so tempting, just to lean a little closer and find out.

Before she could find the courage, however, his eyes fluttered open and she flinched back. His hand tightened instinctively on her arm, pinning her where she lay, a breath away. So close.

Ki's eyes widened, then he let go and hastily slid out

from under her arm, only to fall off the edge of the bed with a comical thud.

Just like my dreams, she thought, caught between laughter and hurt at his hasty withdrawal.

"Uh, good morning," he stammered, reddening as she peered down at him.

"You—you didn't look very comfortable—" she began, then stopped, face aflame as she saw how his nightshirt had ridden up to his waist. His exposed cock was half-erect.

She looked away quickly, tempted to burrow back under the covers until she could make sense of her unruly emotions. *It doesn't mean anything. That used to happen to me all the time before—*

Ki hastily pulled down the shirt and gave her a lop-sided grin. "No, I was fine. And you slept! No more night-mares?"

"No, no dreams."

"Well— Good." He still looked embarrassed, even with the grin. It made her feel even worse.

"I'm sorry. I should have sent you back to your own bed."

"I didn't mind," he insisted. "I just— Are you hungry?"

No, I want to kiss you, she thought, annoyed.

It was a relief when he dressed and went off in search of breakfast. She hurried into her clothing, choosing a gown at random from the wardrobe and pulling it hastily over her shift. By the time he came back, she had her feelings under control again, or so she told herself.

They ate their bread and cheese and ale, and then went out together to the canopied temple in the courtyard. Little cloth banners showing Illior's Eye and the crescent moon fluttered from the ropes and poles, some of them hardly more than rags.

One of the Afran priests sat on a low stool under the

awning, anonymous in his voluminous red robe and silver mask. Tamír knew it was Imonus by his long grey hair.

The golden stele caught the morning light like a mirror. There were the prints of many fingers on the smooth surface. People touched it for luck, in prayer, in wonder. Tamír pressed her palm to it, imagining her ancestors doing the same. Perhaps it was some trick of the light, but just for an instant she thought she saw the reflection of another woman, standing just behind her. The face was indistinct, but Tamír could make out a crown and sword.

"Good morning, grandmother," she whispered, wondering which spirit it was this time.

"Only a queen may see a queen there," Imonus said. "It is good that you greet her with such respect. But I think you are no stranger to spirits."

Tamír lowered her hand. "I thought maybe it was just a shadow."

"You know better than that." The man sounded rather amused.

It was unsettling, talking to that expressionless mask. "Can't you take that off? There's no one else around."

"Not while I serve, Highness. Not even for you."

"Oh." She fidgeted a moment under that impassive gaze, then held up the owl feathers she'd brought. "I've come to make an offering and to ask a question. I don't know the proper prayers yet, though."

"Place your offering and ask your question. Illior will hear you."

As Tamír bent to cast the feathers on the brazier, something flew over her shoulder and fell into it, scattering a few coals and sending up a little flurry of sparks. A gnarled little root lay shriveling in the flames. It began to smoke, then caught fire, smelling of earth and resin.

So you are here, she thought.

Brother had left such offerings at the small shrine back at the keep: roots, acorns, dead leaves, dead moles. She looked around but saw no sign of him except for the root.

"Shadows and spirits cling around you," Imonus said softly.

A chill ran up Tamír's spine in spite of the warm sun on the back of her neck. "Do you see my brother?"

Imonus nodded. "He has caused you great pain, and you him. He haunts you still."

"Yes," Tamír whispered. She gave Ki a nervous half smile and went down on one knee before the priest, so she could speak softly. "That's why I came today. He wants something of me, but he speaks in riddles and he lies. Is there some spell you could use?"

"Do you know what it is that he desires?"

"Yes, but not how to give it to him. You serve the Oracle. Can you help me learn more?"

"I am only the servant, as you say. It is time you followed your ancestors, Tamír Ariani Agnalain, and visit Afra for yourself. The Oracle sees farther than any priest."

"That's days away. I have so much to do here, and I have to get my people to Atyion."

"You must go, daughter of Ariani. Every queen has made a pilgrimage there to honor the Lightbearer's gift and seek guidance for her reign."

Tamír tried vainly to stifle her impatience. "Then you can't help me?"

"I did not say that, Highness, only that I could not answer your question. There is another offering you can make. Throw a coin in the basket and I will show you."

Tamír fished a sester from her purse and tossed it in the basket with the other money offerings. Imonus leaned down and took a small cloth packet from a covered pot by his feet. "Kneel before the brazier. Place another feather on the coals with this and bathe your face in the smoke."

Tamír cast her offerings on the coals. The feather caught fire at once and shriveled to cinders. The incense packet burned more slowly, and released a cloud of sweet-smelling smoke. Instead of rising straight up in good omen, however, it rolled off the coals in writhing tendrils like questing fingers.

"What does that mean?" Tamír asked in alarm as they coiled around her.

"It is the Lightbearer's breath, this smoke. Breathe it in, Highness, and you may find your answer."

With some trepidation, Tamír fanned the smoke up into her face and inhaled deeply. It was sweet and strong, but not unpleasant, though it made her a little dizzy.

The smoke enveloped her. There must have been more incense in the packet than she'd thought; it was so thick now it completely obscured the temple and courtyard from sight. She coughed and tried to wave it away from her face. It roiled before her eyes, then parted.

She let out a surprised gasp, for instead of Imonus and the stele, she was looking out across a high mountain pass. A road twisted sharply away before her, hugging the sides of barren stone peaks. In the distance Brother stood in the road under a painted archway, beckoning to her. Just beyond him stood a woman. Tamír was too far away to tell who it was, but somehow she could hear her words, as clearly as if she stood beside her.

"You shall have your answer in Afra, Tamír, Queen of Skala. You must be strong to accept it."

"Come to Afra, if you dare!" Brother taunted.

"Why can't you tell me now!" she called back, but he only laughed.

Tamír felt a strange shift, and just as suddenly she found herself standing by a shallow, vaguely familiar cove at night, with a three-quarter moon rising before her. It painted a glistening white trail across the dark water that seemed to end at her feet.

"Beware, Queen Tamír. Be strong," a voice whispered in her ear, but there was no one there. Waves lapped the sandy shoreline and she heard the low hooting of an owl somewhere nearby.

"Prepare for what?" she whispered thickly, not sure if she spoke aloud or not. "Why are you showing me this?"

Another sound came from far out on the water. It was the splash of oars. There were tall warships riding at anchor out there. Now she could make out scores of longboats being rowed swiftly for the beach.

She watched helplessly as the first boats came to rest on the shingle and armed men climbed out—Plenimaran archers and swordsmen, and squires carrying shields. They passed within arm's length of her but no one seemed to take any notice.

She turned to look for help, but the high ground beyond the beach was empty. However, she caught sight of a familiar headland in the distance and realized where she was. This was the stretch of coast where the enemy had come ashore before. Beyond the rise was the farm where they'd rescued Tanil and the other captives.

Another invasion. They've come back!

The Plenimarans still took no notice of her, but when she tried to run, the stinging white smoke closed in around her again, making it hard to catch her breath. She closed her eyes, choking and coughing, and when she opened them she was on her knees before the brazier, with Ki close beside her, grasping her shoulder.

"Are you sick?" he asked, concerned. "You look terrible."

"The Plenimarans," she whispered hoarsely. "I saw—I saw them coming again, at night—" Ki kept a hand under her arm as she rose and brushed the dust from the front of her skirt. "I saw—I saw a second Plenimaran invasion force. It was night, and they landed up the coast, just like before." She looked at the priest again. "But before that, I saw something else—my brother, and a gateway in the mountains, in the middle of nowhere."

"That's the road to Afra, Highness."

Tamír passed a hand across her eyes as another wave

of dizziness tried to claim her. "There was a woman, too. She kept calling me Queen Tamír."

Imonus touched his fingers to his brow. "Then queen you are, Majesty, with the Sword or without it."

"Listen to him," Ki urged.

"But—"

"All hail Tamír, the true queen, by the Lightbearer's own mouth," Imonus declared.

"Hail Queen Tamír!"

Tamír looked around, still a bit dazed. A small crowd had gathered and were watching her expectantly. "But— that wasn't what I was asking."

"Remember what you were shown," Imonus said gently. "You must go to Afra. But everything in its own time. Right now, you should go and consult with your generals and your wizards."

"And tell them what? That I had a dream?"

"A vision."

"But I don't even know when they're coming."

"You said you saw the moon. What shape was it?"

Tamír thought a moment. "Three-quarters, waxing."

"That would be tonight," said Imonus.

"Tonight!"

"Or a month off," Ki pointed out.

"It could be a year off, for all I could tell. I mean no disrespect, Imonus, but I'm not used to this sort of thing."

The priest laughed behind his mask. "How did the vision feel?"

"Feel? Like I was right there on that beach with them."

"Then give thanks to your patron deity, Majesty, and go consult with your generals at once."

"You don't have much time," Ki murmured, sensing her doubt.

"Visions!" she muttered, just loud enough for his ears. Then she called up to a horn bearer on the wall, "Sound the alarm and assembly. Make sure it reaches the camps."

"A vision. Queen Tamír's had a vision!" The word passed quickly around the yard and beyond.

Arkoniel came running from the house, with Wythnir at his heels. She explained as quickly as she could what she'd seen as they hurried toward the hall, hoping he wouldn't think she'd gone mad.

Arkoniel took her at her word. "We've been using the wizard's eye spell to keep watch over the eastern waters, but it's a very large sea. It's also possible that they are using magic of their own to conceal their approach."

"I don't see what use your magic is, then," she muttered.

Forgotten in the excitement, Wythnir watched his master with wide, solemn eyes, clinging to his tunic with one hand and running to keep up.

Arkoniel put a comforting hand on the child's head. "I know you still distrust it, Tamír, but we've come up with a few new tricks I think you'll find useful."

"What about Brother?" asked Ki. "Do you think you could send him to spy out the situation?"

"I doubt it," Tamír replied. "Even if he did, how could we believe anything he told us? I doubt he cares much what happens to Skala. Gather all my warlords and generals together in the audience hall. We'll make a start Sakor's way."

To her surprise, most of her generals had far less trouble accepting the vision than she did.

"Your grandmother and all those who came before her relied on such visions," Kyman pointed out. "It's only fitting the Lightbearer would speak to you, as well. It's a lucky sign, I'd say."

"You are Illior's Queen," Arkoniel murmured, standing beside her with Ki and the Companions. "They accept it, and so do your friends. Isn't it time you did, as well?"

"What do you say, my friends?" she asked the others.

"It seems Illior means for me to be queen, even without the proper investiture."

"A sword doesn't make a queen," Nyanis replied. "You've been touched by Illior all your life. That's good enough for me."

"And me!" the others agreed.

"Then I am queen," she said, and was surprised by a sudden sense of lightness, as if a burden had been lifted from her shoulders. "How many warriors do we have now?"

"At most two thousand, without counting your reserves in Atyion and those who may join us from the Ero camps," Tharin told her.

"I have several of my captains there, looking for able-bodied fighters," Illardi added.

"I saw at least twenty ships in the vision. How many men do you make that?"

"It depends on what sort of ships they are. Could you tell?" Illardi asked.

"Three masts, I think. As long as our own warships."

"It could be a second attack, or a supply convoy. There's no way of knowing if they've had word of the defeat you dealt the first force."

"A few ships did get away," she reminded him.

"Yes, but we don't know if they ever reached port," Arkoniel put in. "This could be a new assault coming with no word of the fate of the other. Whatever the case, it's best to prepare for the worst."

"Illardi, do you have maps and sea charts of that area?" asked Tharin.

"Of course. I'll fetch them at once."

Tamír turned impatiently to Arkoniel as she waited. "You said you had magic that could help. Couldn't you board one of the ships the same way you caught up with us that night on the road to Atyion?"

Arkoniel considered the idea. "Perhaps, if I could get a clear idea of where one was. But even if I did manage not to end up in the sea instead, it would be impossible to do it quietly. You saw how violent the transition is. Someone would be bound to see me hurtling out of thin air. And I can only cast that sort of magic on myself every few days. It takes a great deal of strength to cast and control. I wouldn't be able to get back to you, even if it all worked."

"I thought you said this Third Orëska of yours is supposed to serve Tamír?" Kyman growled.

Arkoniel gave him a pained smile. "I didn't say I wouldn't serve. I was just pointing out the flaws of that particular spell for such a purpose."

Just then Kiriar came running into the hall. "Lady Iya has found the enemy!"

Ki and the wizards followed as Tamír left Tharin in charge in the audience chamber and hurried upstairs to Iya's chamber. They found her at her window, a crystal wand held loosely in her hands where they rested on the sill. Her eyes were closed, yet she still seemed to be looking out across the sea. Tamír couldn't help doing the same, half-expecting to see sails beyond the mouth of the cove. "Do you see them?" she asked softly.

Iya nodded and opened her eyes. "A glimpse just now. I counted thirty warships, loaded with armed men. I'd guess two thousand men-at-arms, at the very least. They're well west of the islands. They could be here by tonight if they are sailing for Ero. It's too soon to tell."

"I think I know where they're headed—" It still felt very odd saying it. "From the vision. They're landing in the same place they did before."

"Tamír's given me rather a good idea," Arkoniel told her. "How is your Plenimaran these days?"

"Still quite fluent," Iya replied.

"Good. Mine was never very good." Arkoniel gave Tamír a wink. "I think you've seen this spell before, too. I must ask you all to be very quiet now. Sound carries with this one. Iya, where are they?"

"West and south of Little Crowberry Island. Do you remember the oak grove on the point there?"

"Ah, yes." He closed his eyes and pressed his palms together in front of him. His lips moved soundlessly for a moment, then he slowly opened his palms. A tiny circle of light appeared between them, hanging in the air. Tamír and the others moved to look over his shoulder.

"Look through, Tamír," he whispered. "What do you see?"

It was like looking through a knothole in a fence. She leaned closer and caught a glimpse of shimmering blue. There were sounds, too, like rushing water and the cry of seabirds. Without thinking, she moved around him for a better look.

"Don't touch," Arkoniel warned.

He moved his hands and the circle widened to a handbreadth. It was a window, and through it, they could see a bird's-eye view of open sea, with the dark line of a wooded island in the distance. Arkoniel murmured softly and the view shifted dizzyingly. Tamír caught sight of many ships floating like toys far below.

"There they are!" Arkoniel exclaimed softly, sounding a bit surprised and rather pleased with himself. "Found them on the first try, too. We're far enough away to be safe. They can't hear us way up here."

"They can see back through it, and hear too, can't they?"

"Yes, that's why I have to be very careful. We don't want to give ourselves away."

Carefully manipulating the spell, he guided the "window" down to what appeared to be the flagship. Barefoot sailors were busy on deck and in the sheets, but there were other men lounging at the rail and around the deck, men who wore the boots of soldiers. Arkoniel spied a pair who appeared to be officers and carefully brought the narrowed window up behind them. They were talking in low voices. It was difficult to hear them over the rush of waves under the keel and what Tamír could make out was in a language she did not speak.

Iya listened intently for a moment, then shook her head and motioned for Arkoniel to end the spell.

"At the moment the tall one's bragging about some horses he's bought," she said. "It's a good spell though, and a good idea. We will try again in a little while."

"Maybe you should show this to some of our nobles," Ki said. "The ones who were doubting whether wizards would be of use, anyway."

"Yes, perhaps we can change their minds when they see how useful your magic is," Tamír agreed.

"Better not to," Iya replied. "It's a useful spell, and not only against foreign enemies. First and foremost, Tamír, we serve you. It might be best if others did not know that we can watch them like this."

"There's also the danger that someone versed in magic might recognize it as something other than an Orëska-derived spell," Arkoniel added. "You two are used to Lhel and her ways. But you know how most people feel about her kind and their magic."

"They think that it's necromancy," Ki replied.

"Yes, and Tamír can afford no taint of that."

"Have you taught this spell to any of your other wizards here?" Tamír asked.

"No, not this one."

"Do you watch them, too, then?"

"No, for none of them have given me any reason to. Without trust, we can't hope to achieve the sort of unity Iya foresaw. But I would not hesitate to do so if I thought any of them were secretly disloyal. As Iya said, our loyalty is to you, and you alone, even before Skala."

"So only the two of you know this spell?"

"These wizards from Ero still know nothing of Lhel, and for now, that's best," Iya told her.

"Those I gathered at the keep do, though," said Arkoniel. "Lhel was with us for a time."

Tamír nodded, considering all this. "I won't have you using that kind of watching spell on me. Give me your word on that."

Both wizards pressed their hands to their hearts and gave their oaths.

"You have my word as your friend, too," Arkoniel added earnestly. "We will find other ways to watch over you. We always have."

"My secret watchers, eh?"

Iya smiled. "Those who watch on your behalf."

"Very well. Now, what's this magic you're so anxious to show me, Arkoniel?"

"Come down to the courtyard."

"I've spent a great deal of time, pondering how to combine spells to the best offensive advantage," he explained. "I believe I've hit upon a few that will be most effective, and they take only a few of us rather than exhausting all of us at once, as that spell before the gates did."

In the courtyard they found Hain and Saruel waiting next to a burning brazier. The man held a bow, and a space had been cleared and a round wooden target set up for a shooting list.

"You're joining my archers?" Tamír asked, curious.

"No, Majesty," he replied, handing the bow to her, and an arrow with a bit of oil-soaked rag wrapped around the head. "If you would be so kind as to assist us in our demonstration?"

"Fire, that's the key," Arkoniel explained. "Step over here."

He led her away from the target so that she was facing the wooden curtain wall.

Ki looked around. "She's facing away from your target."

Arkoniel's grin widened as he lit the tip of her arrow with a snap of his fingers. "You only think she is. Get ready to draw on my word, Tamír."

He moved a few yards away and wove a pattern on the air with his wand.

A small circle of blackness appeared out of thin air near the tip of his wand. At his silent command, it dilated until it was about two feet across. He stepped back. "At this close range, that should be an easy target for a skilled archer like you. If you would?"

Tamír drew and let fly. The flaming shaft struck the black circle dead center and disappeared into it. The circle winked out of existence, leaving no trace of the arrow behind. It should have been quivering in the wooden wall a few yards away, but it had disappeared without a trace.

"Now, if you'd step back to the target," Arkoniel said.

The burning arrow was embedded dead center in the wooden target, the shaft and fletching already charring black. The thick wood of the target began to smoke as they watched, then burst into flame.

"Saruel added a nice bit of magic to the oil," Arkoniel explained.

"Yes, anything it touches once it is ignited will burn quite intensely," the Khatme woman said. "It is very dangerous, not to be handled carelessly."

"Bilairy's balls!" Ki laughed. "So you can send an arrow anywhere you like, and it will set whatever it hits on fire? That's a neat trick."

Tamír took in the impossible trajectory of the shaft. "How is that possible?"

"It's just the translocation spell. I visualize where I want an object to go and that's where it comes out. A normal flame is snuffed out in the transition, but Saruel's spell makes it strong enough to survive. Well, most of the time, anyway."

"And you are certain it will work against the ships?"

Arkoniel rubbed at his beard, eyeing the burning target. "Reasonably so, based on the tries we've made so far."

"Amazing," Tamír said, genuinely impressed.

"That is his gift," Iya said proudly. "He's already come

up with ideas I'd never have dreamed of. Or anyone else, it seems."

"Even in Aurënen, no one has ever made such a spell as this," said Saruel. "The Lightbearer has touched him with special sight."

"How did my uncle ever dare to turn his back on that immortal?"

"We've seen what comes of that," Iya said. "You are already healing the land and restoring Illior's favor. And you have Sakor's as well. They are the patrons of Skala, and you embody them both. That is no accident."

Chapter 17

There was no time to assemble their full force. Even if there had been, Tamír was unwilling to leave Ero completely open to attack on the strength of a single vision. She sent mounted messengers up and down the coast, raising the alarm and summoning more reinforcements from Atyion. There were three nobles with estates within half a day's ride, but one was already here with his fifty men and the other two had made no effort to acknowledge Tamír's claim to the throne.

She gathered her generals in Illardi's library and consulted his maps.

"It's deep water here where you think they'll arrive, and a long smooth beach for landing," Illardi said, pointing to the area in question. "Lots of room to beach longboats or ferry in horses. They'll most likely rely on swordsmen and archers, and may shoot from the boats as they come in. They're masters at that."

"*If* they come in," said Ki. "If I found myself facing a massed army, I'd withdraw."

"Not if you were a Plenimaran," Tharin pointed out. "Their Overlord is unforgiving if his orders aren't carried out to the fullest, no matter what the cost."

Jorvai nodded. "That's true. In any case, though, the open beach still works to our advantage."

"We can mass our archers to the fore, with the cavalry behind," said Tamír. "Their archers will be scattered and shooting from unsteady boats. No matter how skilled they are, that won't help their aim. For all the history lessons old

Raven gave us, I don't recall one battle where the enemy won the advantage with that kind of assault."

"Don't underestimate them," Tharin warned. "I hate to praise an enemy, but I've fought them all my life and they come by their reputation honestly. They're as fearless as they are brutal."

"Then we'll make certain the tide comes in red with their blood." Tamír turned to the others. "With warriors like you at my back and Illior on our side, how can we fail?"

In the end, she decided on two hundred mounted archers and five hundred more armed riders. Jorvai and Kyman would lead the two wings. She would command the center, with Tharin and her Companions, together with Nyanis and her Atyion companies. Illardi would remain at Ero, to protect the city.

When they'd finished she sent the generals back to their camps but remained in the library with Tharin and her Companions, fanning herself with a folded map. The day had turned out hot.

"So, have you all found squires for yourselves?" she asked. "You'll be needing them."

"We have, Majesty," said Nikides. "I'll send for them and their kin, for the investiture."

Iya had suggested privately that it would be wise to promote the kin of Tamír's allies to the Companions. Tamír had agreed and was pleased to find Illardi, Kyman, and one of Jorvai's knights all waiting solemnly in the sweltering hall. With them stood two boys and a girl, dressed in full armor in spite of the heat.

The first presented was Illardi's eldest son, tall, dark-eyed Lorin. He was a good choice; she'd seen the boy sparring in the practice yard and he had skill. The other two were strangers, but looked steady and strong. They all seemed young, and none of them had earned their braids yet, but she'd been younger than them when she'd joined Korin's Companions.

"Arkoniel had a word with them earlier, too," Tharin whispered to her. "He was pleased."

Not standing on ceremony, she joined them by the hearth. "Companions, present your choices."

Nikides had precedence by birth. "Majesty, I present Lorin, son of the Duke Illardi, and humbly request you accept his service as a squire among the Companions."

"Do you desire to serve in this manner?" she asked the boy. Lorin immediately fell to one knee and presented his blade. "With all my heart!"

"Duke Illardi, do you give permission for the bond?"

"I do, Majesty," Illardi replied proudly.

"Then I accept your son into my service. Rise, Lorin, and join hands with your new lord for the bond."

Lorin clasped hands with Nikides. Duke Illardi unbuckled his sword belt and wrapped the long end around the boys' hands. "Serve well, my son, your lord and your queen."

"I swear by the Four," Lorin vowed solemnly.

"Lord Nikides, I ask that you care for my son as your retainer."

"By the Four, he will be as a brother to me."

Una was the next in rank and presented a sun-browned girl with wild blond hair caught back in an unruly braid. "My queen, I present Hylia, daughter of Sir Moren of Colath. She's one of Ahra's riders, and we've fought together since I joined. I humbly request you accept her service as a squire among the Companions."

Ki grinned. "I'll vouch for her, too. We grew up near each other and used to wrestle every time we met."

The vows were given and Sir Moren gave his daughter a kiss on the brow.

Lynx presented his candidate next, a boy of fourteen named Tyrien, a nephew to Lord Kyman. "His father's dead and his mother is at home, but I speak for him," said

Kyman, resting a hand on the boy's shoulder. Tyrien was a head shorter than Lynx, but wiry-looking and strong, and had a hint of Aurënfaie about him, with his large grey eyes and fair skin.

The ritual was repeated and Tyrien took his place beside Lynx.

"Welcome, my friends," Tamír said to the new squires. "I know you will serve Skala well and be worthy of the title of Royal Companion. These are uncertain times now, and you'll all have a chance to prove yourselves in battle soon. Fight bravely, and I'll put in your braids myself."

As she finished, her gaze came to rest on Ki. At his own insistence, he was still only a squire in name, but she was determined to change that. He was more to her than that, and everyone knew it.

They don't know all of it, though, she thought, remembering her confusion when they'd woken up together that morning. *I don't even understand it completely myself.*

"Majesty?" Imonus approached, holding something covered in a cloth. "I have something for you."

He swept the cloth aside to reveal a fine helm. The steel headpiece, cheek guards, and mail neck curtain were chased with gold, and a simple golden crown encircled the brow.

"Where did you get this?" she asked.

"From the wagons bearing the contents of the royal catacombs, my lady. I do not know which queen it belonged to, but I suspect none of them would begrudge a kinswoman wearing it to battle. The enemy should know that they face a true queen."

Tamír turned it over in her hands, admiring the fine metalwork. The image of Illior's dragon stood rampant in gold on the cheek pieces. "It's beautiful. Thank you."

Imonus bowed. "It will do until the true crown graces your brow."

*　*　*

Baldus was fairly bouncing with excitement when she and Ki reached her room. "Highness, look, look what's arrived and just in time for the battle!"

"She's Majesty now," Ki informed him as Tamír strode over to the bed with a happy gasp.

The seamstresses of Illardi's house had been busy. A new silk tabard was worked beautifully with her arms, and a new banner was spread out across the bed beside it.

Tamír sent Baldus out, wanting a last moment alone with Ki.

His blood was up and his eyes were shining in a way she hadn't seen in weeks. "You're looking forward to this."

"So are you."

She grinned. "It should be a nice change from complaining millers."

"It's going to be a tough fight if the wizards counted right."

"But we're better rested and can meet them in place."

"Old Raven would be proud of you. You were good at your history and warfare lessons." He paused and eyed her closely. "You've got something on your mind besides the battle."

Tamír hesitated, wondering how to broach the issue of Ki's promotion to him. "It came to me during the investitures. I've no business treating you like a squire. You're as dear to me as—" She paused, and felt herself blushing. "As Caliel is to Korin," she finished quickly. "It's not right, after all we've been through together."

Ki's brown eyes narrowed. "No."

"You'd still be—"

"No, Tamír!" He folded his arms, mouth set in a stubborn line. "We've both had enough changes to last us a while. This isn't the time for you to break in some green squire."

"You're as bad as Tharin."

"He stayed your father's man, didn't he? There's no shame in it."

"Of course not, but you deserve more respect. So does he."

"I'm at your side, Tamír. If people don't respect that, then to hell with them. I've never cared what anyone thinks and you know it."

That was a lie, of course. Taunts of "grass knight" and "horse thief's brat" had cut him to the quick, even if he'd been too proud to say so.

Can a queen take her squire for a consort? Blushing again at the unbidden thought, she turned and pretended to admire the new tabard. She'd let Ki have his way for now, but sooner or later she'd see him raised to his proper place. And anyone who wanted to remember him as a grass knight then could go to Bilairy.

Iya and several other wizards had kept on with their watching and sent word that the Plenimarans meant to make landfall exactly where Tamír had foreseen.

The sun was at its zenith and the house was sweltering as Ki helped her on with her padded tunic and Aurënfaie chain mail. Sweating in his own armor, he tugged her burnished cuirass snugly into place, making sure there was the least gap possible on either side. The elegant goldwork on the breastplate caught the light. This armor, like the helm, had been made for a woman warrior and accented the slight curve of her bosom with glinting steel and tracery. She felt rather self-conscious about that. Still, she couldn't resist stealing a sidelong look in the mirror.

Ki laughed as he dropped the silk tabard over her head. "Pretty taken with yourself, ain't you?"

Tamír scowled at her reflection. "Do I look like a queen?"

Ki clapped the new helm on her head. "You do now, except for the Sword."

"I still have a good one." She drew her blade and held it up. It had been her father's.

Ki clasped her shoulder. "He'd be proud of you, and

so would your mother, too, I bet, if she could see you now."

Tamír wished she could believe that. "Let's go," she said. "I want to be well placed when our guests show up."

The Companions and standard-bearers stood ready in the courtyard. Arkoniel, Saruel, and Kiriar were with them. The wizards wore no armor but were dressed for swift riding. The Khatme still wore her long dark gown, but sat astride with her skirts pulled back over tall riding boots.

"How is Iya?" she asked Arkoniel.

"Exhausted."

"You've been using magic, too. Aren't you tired?"

Arkoniel smiled. "I've been at different tasks, and they were not as taxing. I'm ready for battle. We all are."

"My Orëska wing," she said, smiling. "May Sakor join with Illior for your work today."

Lynx was holding her mount. She missed her old horse, Gosi, who'd been missing since Ero fell, but the little palfrey wouldn't have been suited for this sort of work. She rode a tall black Aurënfaie stallion named Midnight now, from her Atyion herds. He was trained for battle: swift, responsive, with no hint of skittishness. She'd seen to it that Ki had a horse of equal mettle, a fine bay named Swift.

She made a last offering at the shrine of the Four and was glad to see the smoke from Sakor's brazier float straight up, an auspicious sign before battle. She also stopped at the stele and burned incense and owl feathers there. The smoke caressed her again, but the Lightbearer had no more visions for her.

She rode out the gate to take her place at the head of the mounted column, and a huge cheer went up from the riders and the other warriors who stood watching. The banners of her lords fluttered above the ranks in a stiff sea breeze, bright against the morning sky.

"Ta-*mír*! Ta-*mír*! Ta-*mír*!" The chant sent a chill up her spine.

She rose in the saddle and saluted them. The cheering swelled as she kicked her mount into a gallop and rode for the head of the column.

A calm certainty settled over her, as it always did at such moments. *This is what I was born for.*

Chapter 18

They reached the cove just before nightfall and Tamír sent out scouts to look for advance forces. On the horizon, she could just make out a few dark shapes.

Arkoniel verified them as enemy ships. "They must mean to come ashore after dark, just as you foresaw."

"Yes." The three-quarter moon was rising behind the ships. It had been much higher in the vision. "I want the riders held back a quarter mile. The archers will lie low along the head of the beach here. Do you know yet if they have wizards with them?"

"I've seen no sign of any," he replied.

"Good."

Tamír rode among the wings, speaking with the captains as they and their warriors shared a cold meal. They wanted no fires to alert the enemy. It was a clear night and even the smallest flame would be visible for miles. Each company of archers along the beach had a fire laid ready, with a cup of firechips to throw on when the time came.

Silence was ordered, for sound carried, too. Tamír stood with her guard, watching and listening.

"There," Saruel whispered at last. "Can you see the glimmer of the sails? They're sailing without lanterns."

Wizards saw better than most in the dark, but Tamír could soon make out the scattered brightness of sails catching the moonlight. Soon they could hear the creak of ropes and the snap of canvas.

The first enemy vessels entered the cove mouth, unaware of the welcome that awaited them, and the first longboats were lowered. The boats were strongly rowed, and skimmed swiftly shoreward.

Tamír and her Companions stood at the center of the beach with bows in hand. Nyanis stood with them, and one of the archer captains. At her signal, Nyanis scattered a few firechips onto the dry wood and flames flared up. In an instant other fires leaped up along the beach. Tamír grinned at Ki as they heard the first shouts of alarm from the approaching boats.

Ki handed her an arrow tipped with a knot of pitch-soaked rag. She nocked the shaft, lit the head, and fired it high into the air. It was too late for the Plenimaran boatmen to retreat. Two hundred Skalan archers had already drawn on Tamír's signal and loosed a deadly, flaming volley at the enemy.

Hundreds of arrows lit the sky, and for a moment the enemy boats cast shadows on the water. Then the shafts found their mark and darkness returned, filled with screams. Another volley was loosed, then another, and a fourth. More shouts and cries of pain echoed across the water.

As Tharin had predicted, however, the Plenimarans were not immediately dismayed. Answering volleys whistled back through the air. Ki and the other Companions threw up their shields around Tamír, catching half a dozen points. Other arrows struck the ground around them, sticking quivering in the sand.

"Arkoniel, now!" she ordered.

The wizard cast a spinning black disk on the air a few yards in front of him, and Lynx and Ki covered Tamír with their shields as she sent a flaming shaft through it. The shaft disappeared and the disk collapsed.

An instant later the sail of a distant ship caught fire. The flames spread with unnatural speed, driven by Saruel's charm.

"It worked!" Arkoniel crowed.

The flames quickly claimed the masts and spread to

the deck below. In the red glare of the flames, they could see sailors abandoning the vessel.

He and the other wizards cast more of the spells, until ten ships were burning. They'd scattered the attacks among the fleet; the wind carried bits of burning sail to other vessels. The harbor was bright with the light of burning ships.

The Plenimarans managed a few more ragged volleys, but they lacked the concentration of the Skalan assault.

"They're turning back!" a lookout called and the cry went down the line.

The Skalan warriors gave their war cries and beat their shields in a deafening roar of defiance. As it died away, however, Tamír heard a horn from their northern flank, signaling an attack there.

"They must have gotten a force ashore up the coast!" Tharin cried. "Companions, guard your queen!"

"Nyanis, hold the longboats with your archers," Tamír ordered. "Companions, to your horses!"

Tamír rallied her cavalry and galloped north to meet the foe there. It was impossible to make out exact numbers in the darkness, but the moon cast enough light to see a sizable force marching quickly to meet them. They clashed half a mile north of the cove, horse against foot, and the battle cries rang out on both sides.

"For Skala and the Four!" Tamír cried, pressing the Skalan cavalry's advantage and riding the Plenimarans down.

Slashing left and right with her sword, she hewed her way through upraised swords and pikes. Midnight reared at her command, lashing out with steel-shod hooves. The Plenimarans' shouts turned to screams under her onslaught and hot blood spurted up her arm and into her face. Battle lust seized her, driving away any thought of pain or fatigue. She was dimly aware of Ki shouting something behind her.

She looked around and spotted her standard waving

over the heads of the massed foot soldiers, and Ki and the others fighting frantically to catch up with her.

Suddenly too many arms were reaching for her, hands grasping and pulling, trying to drag her from the saddle. She laid about with her sword, driving back all she could reach. Midnight snorted and bucked, kicking out at those trying to slash his legs below the barding. Tamír clung on with her thighs and twisted her rein hand in his mane. The high bow of the saddle kept her steady as the horse tried to rear again. She reined him down, concerned that there were too many sharp blades ready to slash at his underbelly. Someone grabbed her by the ankle and tried to yank her down.

Just as she was certain she was going to fall, the man who had her foot suddenly let go and fell away. Righting herself in the saddle, Tamír looked down to see Brother's pale face among the press. Men falling dead without a blow marked his wake as he disappeared again.

Then Ki was with her, screaming with rage as he and Tharin cut down the Plenimarans still clinging to Tamír's legs and harness. Her other Companions soon caught up and cleared a circle around her.

Lynx was struck in the shoulder by a pike and nearly toppled from his saddle, but Tyrien rode the pikeman down. Just beyond them, Una and Hylia were fighting side by side, widening the swath of open ground around Tamír. Kyman and his riders were pushing the enemy back on her right. In the distance she could make out Jorvai's banner waving above the fray.

"Fight through and wheel!" Tamír shouted, brandishing her sword toward the thin line of enemy soldiers that stood between them and the beach.

They cut their way through and turned to crash into the enemy line again. They might be outnumbered, but their horses gave them the advantage and their first charge broke the lines. They swept through the disorganized men like a scythe through a grainfield, cutting them down and trampling them under their horses' hooves.

"They're breaking!" Tharin shouted.

Tamír heard a wild shout of victory and looked to see Nikides—bloody-faced and cheering—brandishing his darkened blade, with young Lorin beside him, grim and equally blooded.

"To me!" Tamír called, rallying them for another pass.

The enemy broke, trying to flee back to the boats they'd come in on. Ships were anchored here, too, and Tamír had no wizards to burn them.

Tamír and her riders rode the fleeing warriors down, driving them into the water, then pulled back and let Kyman's archers finish them off and burn their boats. Some managed to escape, rowing back into the darkness, but behind them the corpses of their fallen comrades littered the sand and rolled in the swell of the incoming tide.

They rode back to the beach where Nyanis' archers stood ready to resume their attack. Tamír dismounted by one of their watch fires.

"The dogs have gone back to their kennels for now," he reported, looking her over. She was covered in blood, and her tabard was stained and torn. "You look like you had a good time."

"A bit too good," Tharin said softly, glowering at her. "You left your guard behind and came close to losing Ki in the bargain."

"Then you'd all better learn to ride faster," she retorted. He was right, of course, but she wasn't about to admit it.

He held her gaze a moment, then pursed his lips and looked away, knowing better than to say more in front of the other nobles.

The wizards joined her by the watch fire and they stood in silence a moment, marveling at their success.

"What do you think they'll do now?" asked Arkoniel. "They still outnumber us, and it's too soon to expect our reinforcements."

Tamír shrugged. "If they come in again, we'll fight them again. They've lost the element of surprise and they know it. I think they'll ask to parley."

As the misty dawn broke over the water, she was proven right. The Plenimaran flagship raised a long white banner. She gave orders for her standard-bearer to answer in kind, then summoned her entire force to mass along the beach in plain sight.

A longboat bearing a smaller version of the parley banner was lowered and rowed ashore. The Plenimaran commander was a black-bearded giant of a man, dressed in ornate black leather and mail. His surcoat bore the device of a noble house. Half a dozen grim-looking men accompanied him, all unarmed.

They splashed from the boat, but the commander left the others at the water's edge and strode without escort up the beach. When he saw Tamír standing there in her crowned helm he hesitated, perhaps surprised not to meet a more formidable foe.

"I am Duke Odonis, General of Plenimar and Admiral of the Overlord's fleet," he announced gruffly in thickly accented Skalan. "With whom do I speak?"

"I am Tamír Ariani Agnalain, Queen of Skala," she replied, removing her helm so that he could see her face better. "You parley with me."

His bushy eyebrows shot up in surprise. "Queen?" he scoffed. "Skala has no queen now. Who are you, little girl?"

Little girl! She was still enough Tobin in her own mind to be doubly offended by the jibe. She drew herself up sternly. "I am Tamír, daughter of the Princess Ariani, daughter of Agnalain. My uncle, the usurper king, cursed of Illior, fell to your first assault on the capital. I stand in his place now, the chosen of Illior Lightbearer. The priests of Afra will bear witness to this."

Odonis was still regarding her with some skepticism.

"You lead this—" He took in the small size of her force and arched an eyebrow at her again. "This raiding party?"

"I do. Do you mean to carry on with your assault? My army and my wizards stand ready to fight you."

"Wizards? Ah, Orëska. Toothless wanderers."

"They are not so toothless," Tamír replied calmly, pointing out at the burning ships. "That's their work. Allow me to convince you."

Arkoniel cast the spell once again and she shot a flaming shaft neatly through it. Across the water, the mainsail of Odonis' ship caught fire.

Odonis no longer looked so smug. "What is this?"

"This is the work of my Orëska, and they will do so to your entire fleet if you do not leave our shores at once."

"You do not fight us in an honorable way!"

"Was it honorable for the commander who came before you to sail out of the teeth of a gale with no challenge and fall on a sleeping city? It was a cowardly attack and he was defeated with all his force, at Illior's will, by Skalan warriors and Skalan wizards. Their ships lie at the bottom of Ero harbor now. The rest of your ships will suffer the same fate if you do not withdraw and go home. Go back to your Overlord and tell him that a daughter of Thelátimos rules again, and Skala is once more under the Lightbearer's protection."

Odonis considered this, then gave her a stiff bow. "I will carry your words."

"I'm not done," Tamír snapped. "I demand reparation for Ero. I will keep ten of your ships. You will surrender them at once and leave them here at anchor."

"Ten!"

"You may take the crew away with you. I have no time to deal with them. Leave the vessels with their stores and take the rest of your ships. Otherwise, I will burn them all out from under you and kill every Plenimaran who makes it to shore."

She had no idea if the exhausted wizards could carry

out her threat, but then, neither did Odonis, and he had little reason to doubt her.

She could see his jaw working through his beard as the man gritted his teeth in frustration. At last he bowed again. "As you say. Ten ships, with stores but no crew."

"You will surrender your banner, as an acknowledgment of your defeat here today. Before these witnesses, I place you under my sacred protection if you will leave my shores now. Land again, and I will leave none of you alive. I suggest you go at once, before I change my mind."

Odonis made her a last grudging bow and walked quickly back to his waiting boat. Tamír's people jeered at his retreat.

Tamír stood watching until he was well away, then sank down wearily on a stone as the night's work caught up with her. "Tharin, pass the word that everyone is to rest a little before we head back. All of you," she added, giving the Companions a meaningful look. Grinning, they spread out around her, lying on their cloaks on the beach.

Ki stretched out beside her, leaning back on his elbows. He still had blood on his face, but a long stalk of wild oat hung from the corner of his mouth and he looked well content with the world.

"That was a nice bit of fighting, Your Majesty, except for you charging off without us," he said, just loud enough for her ears.

"I thought you'd all keep up."

The stalk bobbed against Ki's lip as he sucked on it in silence for a moment. "Now that you're my queen, can I still tell you that I'll kick your ass from here to Alestun if you do that again?"

The last of the day's tension dissolved as she let out a laugh and punched him roughly on the shoulder. "Yes, I think you still can."

Ki grinned up at her. "Well, since you managed to survive it, I guess I'll tell you that I've heard what some of the warriors are saying. They think you're god-touched by Sakor and the Lightbearer, all at once."

"I'm beginning to think so, too." But she hadn't forgotten that glimpse of Brother in the fray, either. It was the second time he'd aided her in battle, and she silently thanked him.

Arkoniel was grateful for the respite. He'd never cast so many spells in such a short space of time before. Even Saruel was pallid beneath her markings as they retired to get their breath.

Glancing back, Arkoniel saw Tamír and Ki sitting together down the beach. The way they were talking and smiling, they looked almost like the two young boys they'd been.

Seasoned by tragedy and battle, and not yet sixteen. But she was not the first queen to take the throne so young, and others had been married and bedded at her age.

And then there was Ki. He'd turn seventeen soon. As the wizard watched, he leaned over to Tamír and said something and they both laughed.

Arkoniel felt another bittersweet tug at his heart as he allowed himself to lightly brush Ki's mind. He loved Tamír with his whole heart, but there was still great confusion there.

Still mindful of his promise, the wizard turned away without touching Tamír's thoughts. Joining Saruel and Kiriar above the beach, he sprawled on the coarse grass there and closed his eyes. Every spell took its toll, but he'd never experienced a sense of depletion like this. What good would they be to Tamír in a real war if a single battle used up all their strength?

The sun was just peaking over the horizon when a horn call roused him from his doze. The wizards rose with a collective groan. Arkoniel gave Saruel his hand and helped her to her feet.

To his surprise, warriors and captains reached out and patted their backs and saluted them as they mounted and joined the others.

"By the Light, that was a neat bit of magicking you lot did!" Jorvai exclaimed.

Tamír gave Arkoniel a genuine smile. "The Third Orëska proved its worth today. We lost less than twoscore. I wonder what it would be like, to settle all disputes so easily," she mused.

Jorvai snorted. "Wouldn't leave us warriors much to do, now would it?"

Arkoniel couldn't imagine magic ever supplanting war, and doubted if it would be a good thing if it did. War gave men like Jorvai purpose.

Chapter 19

Outriders carried the news of their success back to Ero and Tamír returned to find her people lining the roads, waving flowers and bright bits of cloth and chanting her name in an endless roar.

At Illardi's gate she drew her sword and proclaimed, "This victory belongs to Illior, protector of Skala!"

They rode a circuit of the camps and Ero's ruined eastern gate. She poured a soldier's libation there for the spirits of all who'd died in the last battle and again gave thanks to Illior.

They ended at Illardi's courtyard and the soldiers took their leave. The commanders dismounted and followed Tamír into the temple of the stele, where the three masked priests of Afra stood waiting to greet her.

"Tell me, my queen, do you now believe in the visions of the Lightbearer?" Imonus asked.

"I do," she replied, presenting him with the captured Plenimaran banner. "I present this trophy to Illior as a token of my gratitude. The vision was true, and saved many lives. We were not taken unaware this time."

"It is a sign, my queen. The covenant that was broken by Erius has been restored."

"I will uphold it as long as I rule."

Tamír held a victory feast the following night and sent ale and victuals out to the camps. Bonfires burned across the plain well into the night.

Arkoniel was pleased to find himself and Iya at the

head table once again, with the other wizards in places of honor among the nobles.

Tamír entered the hall when all the others were seated. She wore a dark blue velvet gown embroidered with silver, with her sword hanging at her side. The golden circlet shone on her brow, contrasting with her black hair.

"She looks rather pretty, don't you think?" said Iya.

Arkoniel had to agree although she still strode like a man. Ki was at her side, looking older and very noble in his dark velvet tunic. His long hair was drawn back in a braid, with the two thin warrior braids still loose on either side of his face. Arkoniel took a closer look at the other Companions and saw that the others had done the same, except for Nikides, who wore his hair pulled back in a simple queue.

"Tamír's idea, I believe," Iya murmured. "I like it. Signifies a change."

Between the meat and fish courses, Tamír stood and poured the libation to the gods, then toasted her commanders. When the cheering had subsided, she turned to the wizards and saluted them with her mazer.

"My friends," she began, and Arkoniel's heart skipped a beat as those dark eyes lingered on his face longer than the rest. "My friends, once again you have proven your great value and skill. Skala thanks you! No wizard who serves the Third Orëska will lack a roof over his head or food to eat in my city."

As they returned to their meal, Arkoniel leaned over to Iya and whispered, "Do you think we're forgiven at last?"

"I hope so. To protect her, we must remain close to her."

The feast broke up late in the evening, but Arkoniel lingered, hoping for a word with Tamír. She was about to retire but excused herself from the others and drew him across the hall to an unoccupied corner.

"Yes?"

Arkoniel smiled, feeling a little awkward. "I appreciated your kind words tonight. You know that I have given my life to you, but—well, I do hope you can find it in your heart to see me as a friend again."

Tamír was quiet for a moment, then held out her hand. "I'm sorry if I've been cold. It was hard, but now, I do truly see what we can accomplish together. This was meant to be. You and Iya have been faithful guardians."

Blinking back sudden tears, he sank to his knees before her and pressed his lips to her hand. "I will never leave you, my queen."

She chuckled. "Well, I hope you'll leave me to go to bed."

"Of course." Arkoniel rose and bowed.

She turned to go, then paused, an odd look in her eyes—it was a question, with perhaps a hint of doubt. At last she said, "When I go to Afra, you and Iya will come with me, won't you? Since Illior spoke to you there."

"Only to Iya," Arkoniel reminded her.

"You've carried the burden, too. I want you both with me."

"As you wish."

"Good. I'll settle things in Atyion, then a journey." She leaned closer and confided, "I'm actually looking forward to it. I don't mind the fighting and feasting, but holding court is so *boring*! Well, good night."

Arkoniel stifled a laugh as he watched her rejoin the Companions and take her leave.

Tamír took leave of her friends and went to her room with Ki.

"That was a good feast," Ki said, patting his belly happily. "A good feast for a good victory."

"It was," Tamír agreed, but other thoughts had been nagging at her all day. "Can you imagine facing Korin like that?"

"You're still worried about a war with him."

"Aren't you?"

"I guess so, but what can you do? He's made no effort to talk with you, just sat up there in Cirna gathering his army. You don't think he's doing that just to pass the time, do you?"

"But I haven't made any effort to contact him, have I?"

"You're the legitimate queen. It's up to him to come to you."

Tamír let out an exasperated sigh and dropped into a chair. "That's what Illardi and everyone else keeps telling me. But he won't, and as queen, it's up to me to keep the peace, wouldn't you say?"

"Well, yes—"

"So I've made up my mind. I'm going to write to him. Privately, as kin, not an enemy."

"I don't suppose a letter could do much harm," he replied doubtfully. "Or much good either, probably."

"Go and fetch me a herald, will you? I won't be long." She paused, wondering what Iya or her generals would think of her plan. "Be discreet, won't you?"

Ki gave her a wry wink as he went out. "Is that what we call it, now that we're all grown up?"

Tamír went into the day room next to her bedchamber and sat down at the writing desk. Quill in hand, she stared at the blank parchment, searching for the right words. Nikides and Illardi helped her with her correspondence in court matters, but she wanted to speak to Korin from her heart, not in formal court language. The words flowed easily onto the parchment.

To Prince Korin, Beloved Cousin and Brother, I know you've had word of me, Kor, and what has happened. I know how hard it must be to believe, but it's true . . . ,

By the time she finished the words were blurring before her. She wiped her eyes hastily on the sleeve of her gown, not wanting tears to spoil the page and signed it *Your loving cousin and sister, Princess Tamír, who was Tobin.* She didn't realize Ki had come back until she felt a hand on her shoulder.

"I sent Baldus down— Hey, what's wrong?"

She turned and threw her arms around his waist, pressing her face to the soft velvet of his tunic. He held her and after a moment she felt a hand stroke her hair.

"He's not worth this, you know!" he whispered. "He's not worth your little finger!"

She reluctantly released him, then sealed the letter with the expensive blue wax from the desk, pressing the Atyion signet into it. "There. Done."

"I hope you know what you're doing," Ki muttered, patting her shoulder.

Baldus returned with the herald, a young man with a long blond braid that reached nearly to his waist and the sacred silver-capped baton of his office tucked into the belt of his blue tunic.

"Ride to Cirna and deliver this to Prince Korin in private," she told him, giving him the sealed missive. "No one else is to see it, you understand? Destroy it if necessary."

The herald touched the seal to his lips. "You have my oath, by Astellus the Traveler. I will deliver your message within the week, barring mishap on the roads."

"Good. Wait for Prince Korin's reply. I'm leaving for Atyion soon, so bring me his answer there. A safe journey to you."

The herald bowed and strode out.

"Atyion at last, eh?" Ki said, pleased.

"And then Afra," Tamír replied, picking at a drop of wax on the desktop.

"You haven't asked Arkoniel about what Brother said, have you?"

"When would I have had time?" she asked, but knew that was only an excuse. Deep down, something was holding her back, even if it meant Brother's continued anger.

"Well, you should get some rest."

She looked up and found Ki fidgeting nervously as he glanced at the bed.

Does he want to sleep with me again, or is he afraid I'll

ask him to? she wondered. She didn't know which she wanted, either. It had been so easy the other night, when she was upset in the dark. Now it felt more awkward than ever.

"Well— good night," Ki mumbled, and settled the issue by disappearing quickly into the dressing room.

"Good night." Tamír stayed at the desk for some time, idly covering a sheet of parchment with designs and small sketches. She was in no hurry to lie down alone.

Chapter 20

With the first harvests in and planting over, more nobles came to Cirna seeking to pledge themselves to
the new king. Lutha eagerly searched each band of newcomers for familiar faces. There weren't many.

Heralds arrived daily, but some of these messages
were cool in tone and evasive about support. Others
seemed to be sounding out the new king, weighing his influence against Tobin's claim. They asked the same questions as the nobles who'd been cooling their heels here
since spring: Why hadn't he marched to reclaim his capital?
Why did he remain at such a distant holding when the land
needed him? Why had there been no royal progress? Some
sent offers of their daughter's hands, not knowing the king
had already taken a wife.

Korin and the others were returning from an early-
morning ride on the south road when Lutha spotted a rider
coming on at a hard gallop.

"Look there," he said, pointing.

"A messenger," said Lord Niryn, shading his eyes.

The entourage reined in, and Captain Melnoth rode
out with a few men to intercept him.

The man didn't slow his horse until he was almost
upon them. Reining in his lathered horse, he called out, "I
bring news for King Korin!"

"Come," Korin ordered.

This was one of Niryn's men. "I was spying at Ero,
Majesty. There has been another Plenimaran raid. They attacked north of the city, and Prince Tobin defeated them."

"Did you witness the battle, Lenis?" asked Niryn.

"Yes, my lord. They have powerful wizards at court there, using some sort of fire spells."

"What about my cousin?" Korin demanded, twisting the reins in his hands. "Is he still passing himself off as a girl?"

"Yes, Majesty. I caught a glimpse of her—ah, him, as he rode out."

"And?" Korin demanded.

The man smirked. "He makes a very homely girl, Majesty."

Most of the company laughed at that, but Caliel and Lutha exchanged concerned looks. This meant another feather in Tobin's cap. His Illioran supporters would certainly see it as another sign of the god's favor. Korin's supporters here might, as well. They were growing increasingly restless, baffled by Korin's refusal to move.

"Shall I carry word on to the fortress, Majesty?" the messenger asked nervously.

Korin looked to Niryn before he replied.

The wizard shrugged. "There's little hope of keeping this sort of news from traveling."

Korin waved the man on.

"Damnation!" Alben exclaimed. "Lord Niryn, do you hear that? Another damn victory for Tobin, while we're languishing up here, doing nothing!"

"No doubt it was only a small raid, my lord," Niryn replied calmly. "Such things always grow in the telling."

"That doesn't matter," Alben retorted.

"He's right, you know," Lutha burst out. "*We* should be down there, holding off the enemy."

"Hold your tongue," Korin ordered. "I say when we go or stay. You'll do well to remember that, all of you!"

Even so, Korin was seething as they rode back to the fortress. Whatever his reasons for staying here, Korin was as frustrated as the rest of them.

*   *   *

The news of the victory was met with all the resentment and frustration Lutha felt himself. That night in the great hall, and for many thereafter, there were dark looks and guarded grumbling. Warriors who'd fled the city with Korin burned anew with the shame. Could it be, Lutha heard men whispering, that there was something to this talk of prophecy?

Yet no one dared question the king.

Lutha marked the days off on the calendar stick and saw Ki's birthday come and go. He and Caliel raised a wine cup to him that night and wondered if he'd celebrated it this year. Korin's name day had been a forced, dreary affair.

Things had not improved between Korin and Caliel. Cal still sat at Korin's right hand, but where once all the Companions had often accompanied Korin to his chambers at night, now only Alben and Urmanis seemed welcome. Moriel the Toad was always lurking about where he was least wanted, too, and Korin seemed to have warmed to him, as well, and often included him in his private drinking circle, at least on the nights when Korin did not go straight to Nalia in her tower.

They saw a bit more of the young consort these days. She came down to supper at the high table now and then, when Korin ate privately with his Companions.

She and Korin still seemed ill at ease with each other, Lutha noted. Korin had been a loving and attentive husband to Aliya, but it was increasingly apparent that he felt no such affection for his new wife. Nalia was quiet, but did attempt a bit of polite conversation with whoever was sitting next to her. A few times she'd noticed Lutha staring at her and smiled shyly.

She often came out walking in the bailey yard or along the walls on the long evenings, always heavily guarded. Lutha and the other Companions served as escorts, but

Niryn was always there, making it difficult to speak with her. Korin was conspicuously absent on these occasions.

Even without conversation, Lutha felt an increasing sympathy for her. He was homely himself, but he was sure that didn't matter as much in a warrior as in a consort. Nalia was not beautiful, it was true, but her voice was pretty enough to make him wonder what she sounded like if she ever had the occasion to laugh. She had a lady's dignity about her that he admired, but her eyes were so sad it broke his heart.

It must be hard on her, too, having the entire fortress whispering about whether she was pregnant yet or not. Korin still made nightly visits to her tower, but Lutha had seen Korin's face more than once as he approached the tower door; he didn't have the look of a happy bridegroom. It was no secret that he seldom passed more than an hour or two there, and returned to his own bed to sleep.

All in all, it seemed an odd way to treat a wife, homely or not. Korin had treated his whores better, back in Ero.

"Perhaps it's Aliya's memory that keeps him from treating Nalia better," Barieus suggested one night as they all sat together over wine in one of the cheerless guardrooms.

"Aliya was beautiful, and he chose her for love," Alben reminded him. "This one? I'd keep her shut away, too, if she were mine."

"That's an unmanly sentiment, even from you," Caliel growled. The stress of their situation had frayed the regard between them.

"Well, you don't think he chose her on his own, for love or romance, now do you?" Alben shot back. "She's a girl of the blood, one of the last left of a breeding age, as far as anyone knows. That's what Niryn told me."

"Getting pretty thick with him, aren't you?" Lutha muttered into his wine.

"You speak of her like she's a prize bitch in his kennel," Caliel retorted.

Alben shrugged. "What do you think Kor's doing up there with her at night, reading her poetry?"

"Shut your filthy mouth, you heartless bastard!" Lutha yelled. "That's the Consort you're speaking so lightly of. She's a lady of the blood!"

"And you're her champion?" Alben threw down his cup and jumped to his feet, hot for a fight.

Caliel quickly got between them. "Stop it, both of you! The penalty for brawling still stands, and I don't want to be the one having to carry it out!"

Alben angrily yanked his arm free of Caliel's grasp.

"Where is her family?" Urmanis wondered drunkenly over his cups. "For that matter, where did she come from and how do we know she is what they claim?"

That gave everyone pause. After a moment Alben slumped back down in his chair and snatched his squire's wine cup. Draining it, he wiped his mouth and muttered, "I'm not going to be the one to ask Korin about it. You go ahead, if you care so much. Bilairy's balls, Lutha, anyone would think she was your wife, the way you go on about her! I wouldn't let Korin catch you making long eyes at her."

"You bastard!" Lutha was on his feet again, reddening at the accusation. Caliel and Barieus both got hold of him this time. Alben laughed as they pulled him from the room before he could defend his honor.

Sitting by the balcony door in her shift, trying to catch a breath of morning breeze, Nalia looked down at the red stain in her lap and smiled. She didn't mind the discomfort and mess of her moon flow; it meant a welcome respite from her husband's cold attentions.

Korin still came to her almost every night, and she never refused him, though she still sometimes wept after he'd gone. He was never cruel or coarse, but neither was he passionate. Their congress was merely duty, a task to be carried out as quickly and efficiently as possible. She got no pleasure from it, and wondered if he did, beyond the physical release. Had he been cruel, she might have found the courage finally to make that leap from the balcony. As it was, she'd grown resigned.

She had known affection with Niryn, and passion, and she had mistakenly imagined herself his beloved.

Life was nothing like that with Korin. When he was sober he would take time before their coupling to drink with her and tell her something of his day. It was all speculation about weaponry and marches, and bored her terribly.

Sometimes he asked about her day, though, and she'd dared hint at the empty hours. He'd surprised her, letting her come downstairs to dine more often. He still refused to let her outside the fortress to ride or walk along the cliffs, claiming it wasn't safe, but little comforts began to arrive.

She had stacks of books now, baskets of needlework and painting supplies, even a cage of cheerful yellow birds. Korin also sent gifts of perfumes and cosmetics, but these felt more like unspoken taunts. Her mirror had never lied to her and she'd long since made peace with her reflection. Did this man think that a little paint would change the way she looked? It hurt that it mattered enough for him to send such things, just as it still hurt that he would only come to her bed after the lamps had been put out. Niryn had never made her feel ugly.

Niryn. It still felt as if her heart would tear itself in two, whenever she thought of him. She could not escape him; he was there at table, and often walked with her, speaking lightly of inconsequential things, as if they were mere acquaintances. She realized now that he enjoyed this game between them, knowing that she could never speak the truth to Korin, even if she'd dared.

Oh, but how she longed to! She dreamed of it sometimes, screaming out the truth, so that Korin would mete out his wrath on her seducer. The Korin in her dreams was a warmer, kinder man than the waking reality. She often wished he were not so handsome and coolly attentive. She couldn't quite bring herself to hate him as she did Niryn, but she could not love him, either.

She dressed and returned to her chair. "Tomara, tell my husband my moon blood has come again."

The woman examined the stained linen and Nalia could see the woman counting silently on her fingers. "Aye, lady. Such a pity!"

"Why do you say that?"

"Why, you've not kindled, and him trying so hard!"

Nalia was shocked at the hint of reproof. "You make it sound as if I'm to blame. Haven't I endured his efforts without complaint?"

"Of course you have, my lady. But he's fathered children on other women before you."

"Others?" Nalia said faintly. She'd never considered that.

Tomara patted her hand. "There are women whose wombs are stony, my lady, and can't sprout their husband's seed, no matter how many times he plants it. If you prove barren, then what shall our young king do for an heir?" She shook her head and set about tidying up the room.

A stony womb? Nalia pressed her fingers to her lips, not wanting to betray the sudden hope she felt. Niryn's seed had never grown in her, either! If she were barren, then Korin would have no use for her. Perhaps he would put her aside for another and she would be free!

She composed herself quickly and took up her embroidery hoop. "You say my husband has had children with other women? Can none of them be his heir? What about his first wife?"

"A sad tale, that. She kindled twice, but lost the first too early and died trying to birth the second."

"What about the child?"

"It died, as well, poor little mite. If he's got bastards, I haven't heard of them. Besides, only a trueborn heir will do, says Lord Niryn. That's what makes you such a precious jewel, my lady. You have the blood and Lord Niryn claims your family breeds girls. If you give the king a daughter, then who can dispute her claim to the throne? Not that pretender in Ero!" She made an ill luck sign. "Necromancy or pure lies, that's all that is! Mad as his mother, that one, so everyone says."

"Prince Tobin, you mean?" asked Nalia. Korin seldom spoke of his cousin except to call him "usurper" and mad.

"Your poor husband loved him like a brother. But during the Battle of Ero Prince Tobin ran away and come back with a gang of renegades at his back, claiming to be a *girl* and the queen!"

Nalia stared at her, then burst out laughing. "Don't tell me anyone believed that?"

"Why do you think we're way up here, rather than in the capital?" Tomara asked. "Traitors and fools, they are, but there are enough of them to back the boy's claim. It'll be war, I warrant, if they try to go against King Korin. Such nonsense! It's those Illiorans and a pack of mad priests and wizards that's behind it." Her faded eyes went hard and angry. "The old king had the right idea. Burn 'em and be done with it. Now look what we've come to? No, my lady, you must bear a daughter for your dear husband, and soon, for the good of the land."

As Nalia had hoped, news of her menses kept Korin away for the required days. She embroidered and played cards with Tomara and read her books, tales of knights perishing for the love of their ladies. Tomara brought her special teas, brewed from cane berry leaves, honey, and unicorn root, to make her womb more fertile.

The thought of the king's other wife and whatever other children he might have fathered preyed on her mind, much to her surprise. She was not jealous, just bored to death and hungry for any sort of gossip.

"You could find out for me, Tomara. He is my husband, after all. Don't I have a right to know? Perhaps it might help," she wheedled, sensing she had Tomara's attention. "I do so want to please him," she lied. "There must be some among his men who know his—tastes?"

Fortunately, Tomara was a bit of a gossip herself, and easily won over to the task. When she brought in the supper tray that night, she was smiling very smugly.

Nalia clasped her hands eagerly. "You learned something, didn't you?"

"Aye, perhaps," the old woman teased as they sat down to eat beside the hearth.

Nalia kissed her, the way she used to charm her nurse into telling secrets. "Come on now, who did you speak to?"

"Your husband's manservant. He told me that the king's fathered no living children at all! Not so much as a bastard. Bellies have swelled, but not a child has lived."

"Not one? How sad!" Nalia said, forgetting her own hopes for a moment. "No wonder Korin is so glum when he comes to me."

"Aye, bad luck," Tomara murmured, nibbling at a slice of bread with an arch look.

"There's something else, isn't there?"

"Well, I shouldn't tell you—"

"Tomara, I—I command you!"

"Well, it's only gossip, mind you. Soldiers are worse than old women when it comes to that, and superstitious."

"Out with it!" Nalia cried, resisting the urge to pinch her.

"Well, just between the two of us, my lady, I've heard a few among the ranks whisper that Korin's seed is cursed, on account of his father seizing the throne from his sister. But Princess Ariani was mad as a spring weasel, and she had no daughter. Stillborn, the girl babe was, or perhaps she killed the child. Who knows? It's no wonder that son of hers turned out a bad sort."

"Oh, you'll drive me mad with your rambling! I don't give a broken pin for Prince Tobin. Tell me about Korin!"

"It's on account of the prophecy. Surely you know of that?"

"The Prophecy of Afra, you mean? The old king and my husband are cursed by that?"

"That's what the Illiorans would have us believe," Tomara sniffed. "All the droughts and crop blight and that plague? All because a 'daughter of Thelátimos' doesn't sit on the throne. Didn't stop the rains from coming back this spring, though, did it?"

Nalia pondered this. "But King Erius is dead. Maybe that broke the curse?"

"Which doesn't say much for the Illiorans' claim to a queen. And all the more reason for that other prince to give way, I say. Korin's claim is the stronger, being the child of Agnalain's firstborn."

"But what about the curse on Korin's children?" Nalia asked impatiently.

Tomara leaned close and whispered, "It's said that he's fathered nothing but monsters, dead before they could draw breath."

Nalia shivered in spite of the day's lingering heat. "His other wife, she died in childbirth?"

Tomara sensed her misstep at once. "Oh pet! She wasn't of the royal line, was she? Not like you. The old king died and took the curse with him. The sun shines on the new king, and on you. You're the last, you see! With nothing but two princes left, you *are* the daughter of Thelátimos, and your children have the true claim. You'll be the mother of queens!"

Nalia nodded bravely, but fear turned the bread to ashes in her mouth.

* * *

Her bleeding passed on the sixth day, and the following night Korin resumed his cheerless visits, sometimes coming to her drunk and barely able to consummate the act.

Tomara brought her those herbal infusions again, too, but Nalia only pretended to drink them and poured them into the commode when the woman was out of the room.

Chapter 21

Tamír stayed in Ero long enough to celebrate Ki's name day. It had been a small celebration this year, just the Companions and a few close friends, with lots of wine and honey cake. Tamír joined in the drinking and jokes, but found herself watching Ki with different eyes as he teased the new squires about fidgeting with their braids. They were still children, really, but he was a man grown.

An age to be thinking of marriage.

Since the night of the victory feast, he'd gone back to his cot in the dressing room, as if nothing had happened between them. *Perhaps nothing did,* she thought sadly.

She had more wine than usual and woke the next morning with a heavy head. As the column set off for Atyion, she saw most of the others wincing and blinking in the hot sun.

Ki looked fresher than any of them. "Are you unwell?" he teased, and grinned at the dark look she gave him.

Tamír rode out with her Companions and wizards, dressed for show in a riding gown under her breastplate and sword belt.

Outside, the great column filled the road, banners and armor bright in the sunlight. Baggage carts and foot soldiers brought up the rear. It wasn't only soldiers in the column today. Illardi, Iya, and Nikides had spent weeks tracking down the remaining scribes and functionaries who'd served at Erius' court and testing their loyalty. Most gladly gave their allegiance to the new queen, some out of loyalty to who she was and what she represented, others in hopes of keeping their positions at court.

Nearly forty now rode with the baggage train: scribes, chamberlains, document keepers, footmen, and bailiffs. It was virtually a ready-made court.

The crowds that gathered along the road to see them off were smaller and more subdued than they had been a few days earlier, their mood almost sullen.

"Don't leave us, Majesty!" they called out. "Don't abandon Ero!"

Riding just behind Tamír with the other wizards, Arkoniel could tell the words stung. She was young and craved her people's love.

Once they were well on their way Arkoniel rode back to check on his younger charges, who were making the long journey in a cart.

It was a large, comfortable cart with a canvas awning, and the bed was filled with soft straw for the children to lie in. Ethni had been disappointed at having to stay with the younger ones, and insisted on taking the reins. Wythnir sat on the driver's bench beside her and waved as Arkoniel rode up to them. A crowd of foot soldiers had gathered around it, entranced at the little spells the children knew. They gave Arkoniel respectful nods and made way for him to ride beside the cart. The wizards had noticed more goodwill among the common soldiers since the battle.

The children rose and clung to the side of the cart at his approach.

"How are you faring so far?" he asked.

"I have to pee!" Danil declared.

"He's been twice already since we left," Rala said, rolling her eyes.

"You'll have to work out that for yourselves," Arkoniel replied. "And how are you?" he asked Wythnir.

The child just shrugged.

"Come now, what's the matter?" Arkoniel chided, already guessing the answer.

"Nothing," the child mumbled.

"Your long face says otherwise."

Wythnir ducked his head and mumbled. "Thought you'd gone away again. Like before."

"When I left you in the mountains, you mean?"

The boy nodded. "And when you went off to fight."

Ethni had told him how upset the boy had been, but there'd been no help for it then. He had to learn that Arkoniel's duty to Tamír would always come first.

All the same, he did the best he could to make it up to him. Arkoniel could only guess at the life the child had known before he'd come to Kaulin in return for some debt. The man had not been cruel as far as Arkoniel knew, but treated him little better than a useful hound before passing him off to Arkoniel.

Arkoniel shifted the bag hanging from his saddlebow and held out a hand, lifting the small boy over to sit in front of him on his horse.

"But you see, I'm taking you all with me this time, to that great city I told you about," he told him, settling an arm around Wythnir's waist. "We're all to live in a castle now."

"Lord Nyanis says there are lots of cats and kittens there, too," Rala said from the cart. "Will Queen Tamír let us play with them?"

Arkoniel chuckled. "The cats of Atyion rule themselves and play with whomever they like."

"Will you stay there with us, Master?" asked Wythnir.

"Of course. Unless the queen needs me to help her, as she did with the battle. But I came back again, didn't I?"

Wythnir nodded. "Yes. That time."

The sun was shining, and the huge double towers of the castle glowed white against the blue sky as Tamír came in sight of Atyion a few days later.

"They've got your colors up this time, at least," Ki noted.

Banners fluttered from the turrets, and from walls and rooftops in the town below, as if it was a festival week.

Lytia and a host of retainers rode out to meet them just outside the town walls. The grey-haired steward reined her palfrey in beside Tamír's horse. "Welcome home, Majesty! Your castle is in good order and a feast is prepared for tonight. I anticipated two hundred. Is that acceptable?"

"Yes, that's fine," Tamír replied, amazed as always by the woman's efficiency. "You've taken good care of my holding, as always, and you've done well supplying Ero. I hope it was not too much of a burden on my people here?"

"Atyion is rich in every way," Lytia assured her. "The people here have plenty and were honored to share with their less fortunate brethren in poor Ero. Is it true you're going to burn it?"

"It has to be done."

Lytia nodded, but Tamír saw the way her gaze swept her own fine town, as if she was trying to imagine such a calamity here. As steward, she ruled in the absence of the noble. According to Tharin, his family had served Tamír's family here as long as anyone could remember. His aunt took her duties seriously and loved the town and castle as if it were truly her own.

The townspeople streamed out to meet her on the road. Beyond the vineyards, on the rolling river mead between the town and the sea, a district of new wood-and-stone houses was being erected on the lands Tamír had designated for the Ero survivors.

"You've been busy, I see."

"We've settled over a thousand so far, Majesty. They've named the village Queen's Mercy, in your honor."

Tamír smiled at that, but as they approached the castle gates a grisly sight greeted her. The pitiful remains of Duke Solari's corpse still hung from the battlements overhead, reduced to a few blackened scraps and bones in faded yellow silk. "Why hasn't he been cut down yet?" Tamír demanded. Riding beside her, Lord Nyanis had gone pale at the sight of his onetime friend.

"He was a traitor and has been treated as one," Lytia replied. "It's customary to leave the body for the birds, as a warning to others."

Tamír nodded grimly, but the sight pained her. Traitor he might have been in the end, but she'd known him all her life. "What of Lady Savia and the children?"

"Gone back to their own estate. But the eldest son, Nevus, gathered the remains of his father's forces and has sworn in with Korin. I had it from Lady Savia herself that he means to avenge his father's death on you."

"What will you do to them?" Nyanis asked.

Tamír sighed. "If Lady Savia will swear fealty to me, then she can keep her lands."

"I wouldn't be too trusting," Tharin warned. "Her husband was a turncoat and a serpent. She has no reason to bear you any goodwill."

"I'll sort that out later, I suppose. If her son has the forces of the holding away with him, then she's not an immediate threat, is she?"

The greensward between the curtain walls was filled with livestock and fowl. The yards were filled with soldiers, and all the gardens were bright with summer flowers. A crowd of liveried servants stood waiting to greet Tamír as she dismounted and handed her reins to a groom. She spoke briefly with them, then strode inside.

She paused at the large household shrine in the receiving chamber and made offerings to the Four. As she cast her feathers on the brazier of Illior, something brushed against her leg. She looked down to find Ringtail regarding her with lazy green eyes. She scooped up the big orange cat and winced as he bumped his head against her chin. Kneading her arm with his big, seven-toed paws, he broke into a deep purr.

"Looks like he's glad to see you again, too," Ki said, chuckling.

She let Ringtail down and he trotted along at her heels as she continued on through the gallery to the great hall. More cats appeared from under tables and the tops of shelves, as if they'd been expecting her.

Afternoon sun streamed through the high windows, illuminating the rich tapestries and war trophies on the walls, and the myriad silver and gold vessels on the age-darkened oak sideboards. The long tables were set up facing the dais and high table, and were spread with shining white linen and colorful silk runners. Servants in blue livery were already bustling about with platters and mazers.

Home, she thought, trying the word out as she gazed around. It still didn't quite fit, not the way it did at Alestun, even after all her years at court.

Nobles and royal retainers were everywhere, already having taken up residence in what was now the royal palace. There was certainly room, hundreds of them in fact, in the great, two-towered edifice.

"This is how it was in your father's day," Lytia said as she accompanied her up to the room with the swan hangings. "You've made this castle come alive again. Will you have an official progress? A festival might be in order, as well. The people have had no chance to celebrate your reign, and those poor displaced souls up from Ero could certainly do with a bit of merriment."

"Perhaps." Tamír wandered over to the window as Baldus and Ki oversaw the servants with her meager baggage. Ringtail jumped up on the sill and she stroked him absently.

From there she could see more of the herds, now being tended in the close. "It looks more like you're preparing for a siege than a festival."

"I thought it best, with things as they are. Any word from Prince Korin?"

Tamír shook her head, wondering if her herald had made it safely to Cirna.

Tamír made a progress around the entire extensive holding the following day, and was pleased by the reports of her reeves and householders. The summer fields were ripening and the grapevines were heavy with fruit. According to her herd master—another relation of Tharin's—three hundred new colts and fillies had been born in the royal herds that spring, the most in years.

She left it to Nikides and Lytia to choose her lesser courtiers, and the pair proved invaluable in their knowledge of such details. A royal court needed its own small army of functionaries.

Tamír chose her principal ministers, with help from Tharin and the wizards. Jorvai and Kyman wanted nothing to do with court responsibilities, respectfully requesting to remain her commanders. Nyanis—charismatic, intelligent, and clever—would retain his command, but also serve as a chief emissary, helping to court those nobles who'd still not declared for her.

Duke Illardi had proven his worth at Ero, and she appointed him her Lord Chancellor. Tharin was pressed into accepting the title of duke at last, and made Lord Protector of Atyion, charged with the defense of the castle and the queen's person. Ki stubbornly refused any change in his status and told her so in no uncertain terms when they were alone.

Nikides also remained a Companion for now, but accepted an appointment as Royal Secretary, overseeing her correspondence and petitions. He, in turn, would organize the many scribes required.

At Tamír's suggestion, one of his first choices was young Bisir, whom she'd known in Lord Orun's household. She had not forgotten his kindness, or his company the winter he'd gotten snowed in with them at the keep.

"You do me too great an honor, Majesty!" he exclaimed when he presented himself at court at her summons. He was still pretty and soft-spoken, but the kindness he'd known from her, and from the woman who'd taken on his training here in Atyion had driven the haunted look from him at last.

"Those were dark days for both of us," she reminded him. "You were one of the few who showed me any kindness. But you also saw many of the most scheming lords among his friends. I'll rely on that knowledge. You are to alert me to anyone you recognize and tell me all you can of their dealings with my guardian and my uncle."

Bisir nodded gravely. "I never thought I would be grateful for my service there, Majesty. I am honored to be of use to you."

There were also the wizards to consider. Many of her nobles, who hadn't been with her at Ero, still had a strong distrust of wizards.

"It's important that we be seen as your allies, just the same as your generals," Iya advised. "Niryn left a bad taste in people's mouths. The Third Orëska must be seen to be loyal and above reproach."

"I will rely on you to make certain they are," Tamír replied.

Lytia had found comfortable rooms for them in the west tower, overlooking one of the private garden courts.

Tamír made a point of visiting the hall where the wizards practiced and found a warm welcome there, especially among the children. They delighted in showing off newly learned skills, and happily spun acorns and spoons in the air for her, and showed her how they could make fire without flint or wood.

Messengers arrived almost daily with word from towns

along the coast and the western hills. The harvests were good, and no plague had come, even during the dog days of summer. There were still too many empty villages, and too many orphans and widows on the roads, but a new sense of hope flowed out from Atyion.

Tamír shared in that hope for the land, but for herself there was less joy.

Her friendship with Ki was no secret to anyone. He was at her side constantly and had the room next to hers. The other Companions were housed along the same corridor, but none of them excited the sort of gossip that he did. Jealous courtiers whispered "grass knight" and "queen's favorite" thinking she would not hear of it. But she did, and so did Ki. He bore it stoically, but wouldn't talk about it, not even to her. Instead, he became more careful and spent less time alone with her in her room, finding excuses to include Lynx and the others, and leaving her when they did. They rode and sparred and practiced their archery together, as they always had, but the tenuous thread of attraction she'd thought she'd felt that last night together seemed to have broken. Alone in the huge bed with only Baldus and the cat for company, Tamír bore the nightmares and visitations from Brother in silence, torn between hurt and concern for her friend's honor and too proud to ask anyone else for help. She thought nothing of it; since childhood, she'd suffered such burdens alone.

Even so, the pain did not go away. Sometimes, unable to sleep, she shyly explored her body with her hands beneath the covers, testing its curves and folds with trembling fingertips. Her breasts were a bit rounder, but still small. Her hipbones and ribs were as sharp beneath her skin as they had ever been, though, and women's girdles had been taken in to keep them from slipping off her narrow hips. Tobin's hips, she thought darkly. Hardest of all to touch was the hidden cleft between her legs. Even after all these months, she felt the lack of what had been there before, still missed the comforting weight of cock and balls against her thigh. Behind the downy triangle of soft hair that remained, there was only a mysterious cleft she could hardly bear to touch. She made herself do it now, though, and gasped at the textures and sensations there. It was warm, and moist, not at all like it had been before, and left the smell of the ocean on her fingers. She turned on her stomach and buried her burning face in the coolness of her pillow, unable to bear the powerful mix of wonder and revulsion she felt.

What am I, really?

And close on the heels of that, *What does he really see when he looks at me? Is that why he stays away?*

Never had she missed Lhel more. Who else would understand? Lying in the dark, fighting back tears, she vowed to go back to the keep as soon as she could. It was almost a relief when Brother came whispering that night.

"What do you see when you look at me?" she demanded softly.

What I always see, Sister, he replied. *I see the one who has my life. When will you let me rest?*

"I want you to be free," she told him. "I want us both to be free. Can't you tell me anything more?"

But as always, he was no help at all.

By day she had no choice but to put such thoughts out of her mind, but there were daylight worries to take their place. As the weeks passed, she searched the audience chamber for her herald, but there was no sign of him.

Arkoniel noticed her distraction and drew her aside into the gallery one day after the morning's audience. Ki followed, as usual. In daylight he was her faithful shadow.

"You haven't been reading my thoughts have you?" she demanded suspiciously.

"Of course not. I merely took note of your obvious disappointment each time a herald arrives."

"Oh. Well, you might as well know, I wrote Korin a letter."

"Ah, I see. You still think Korin can be reasoned with?"

"Maybe, if I could get him away from Niryn."

"What do you think, Ki?" asked Arkoniel.

"Tamír knows what I think," Ki said, frowning. "I pegged him as a weak reed from the first."

"A weak reed?"

"It's what my old dad used to say of a man who was too easily swayed. Korin may not be a bad sort at heart, but he's got no grit when it matters. We saw it in that first fight we had, against those bandits, and again at Ero. And he always let Alben and the others lead him into mischief, too. Now it's Niryn."

"Hmm. Well, you also can't discount the fact that Korin really does believe he's the rightful king."

"What else can I do?" Tamír asked, frustrated.

"Eyoli has volunteered to go north for you. I believe he can get inside the court and be your eyes and ears there. His magic is not strong enough to attract the notice of the Harriers but does allow him to move about freely."

"Risking his life for me again?" Tamír noted. "I think he may be the bravest of all your wizards."

"He is devoted to you and all you stand for. Shall I tell him to go?"

"Yes. If nothing else, perhaps he can tell us if Lutha and Barieus are still alive."

When Arkoniel was gone, Ki sighed and shook his head. "If they are still with him, then it's by choice."

He left the rest unsaid, but she knew what he was thinking. If their friends had made that choice, then there were two more people they both dreaded having to face in battle.

She turned to go, but Ki caught her by the arm and stepped close, looking at her closely. "You're pale these days, and thinner, too, and—" His other hand came up to clasp her shoulder, as if he expected her to run away. "Well, you just look worn-out. You can't keep on like this."

"Like what?" she asked, wondering if her fears about him showed after all.

He smiled and she felt a shiver run up her spine. She could feel the warmth of his hands through the sleeves of her gown. She could feel the warmth of his breath on her cheek and smell the ripe pear he'd eaten during the assembly. Stunned, she wondered suddenly if his lips still tasted of the fruit?

"You haven't given yourself a moment to rest since Ero fell," he replied, oblivious to her turmoil. "You've got to rest, Tamír. There's no battle to fight right now and those damn courtiers have no right to run you into the ground like this. We should take off and go hunting or fishing—anything to get away from all that." He gestured in the direction of the hall. "Hell, I'm worried about you and so are the others."

He sounded so much like his old self that it brought tears to her eyes. "There now, you see?" he murmured, and pulled her into an embrace.

And once again, Tamír felt torn in two—half of her still Tobin, glad for the gesture of a friend, the other—Tamír—caught up in emotions she didn't fully understand, except that she still wanted to taste Ki's lips.

She pulled back a little, heedless of the tear that escaped down her cheek and looked up into his eyes. Their lips were just inches apart, so close . . .

Like my dreams, she thought. It would be so easy to just lean forward a little and kiss him.

Before she could, the sound of approaching footsteps made her start and pull back. A pair of young nobles passed by, making her a hasty bow as they caught sight of her behind the pillar.

She returned it with what dignity she could manage and when they were gone she saw that Ki was blushing furiously.

"I'm sorry. I shouldn't have— No, here. Look, I'm going to go fetch our horses and we're going for a ride. To hell with all this, at least until supper. Just us and the Companions, all right?"

She nodded and went to find the others, thinking glumly *Just like my dream, in every way.*

Chapter 22

Yawning through another dreary evening feast, Lutha was about to invite Caliel and some of the younger officers back to his room for a game of bakshi when there was a stir among the guards by the door. Porion rose from his place and went to see what was going on. He returned a few moments later with a herald, who'd just arrived.

The man was young, and notable both for his striking long blond braid and the bloody bandage wrapped around his left arm.

"I've never seen a wounded herald before," said Barieus. Heralds were sacred.

The young man came forward and bowed gracefully to Korin. "Your Majesty, please forgive my tardy delivery of this message. I should have been here a week ago, but I was delayed on the road."

"I see that you're hurt. Were you attacked?" asked Korin.

"Yes, Majesty. I met with some brigands on the road, but the message I carry remains safe." He pressed a hand to his breast and bowed again. "It is a most important letter, and the person who sends it requires that I give it to you in private. If it please Your Majesty, may we withdraw?"

Lutha glanced over at Niryn, but the man appeared to be taking little notice.

Korin raised a questioning eyebrow, however. "Who is this message from?"

"That, too, I may only impart to you alone, Majesty." Even a king could not order him to go against a vow he'd given to the one who'd entrusted him with the message.

Korin rose. "My lords, I'll bid you good night now. We'll speak more of strategy in the morning."

Alben yawned and ran a hand back through his long hair, which he'd taken to wearing loose except for the braids. "Tell Korin I'm in my room if he needs me. Mago, go find us that brace of pretty little dairymaids I met this morning and ask them if they'd like to see our chamber. Good night, boys." He gave the others a rakish wink; handsome Alben wasn't often refused.

"Would you boys like to join us for a last cup?" Niryn offered, knowing full well they wouldn't take him up on it.

"Thank you for the offer, my lord, but I've already made plans for the evening," Caliel replied coolly, then caught Lutha's eye. "You do still want that game of bakshi, don't you, Rattie? I promise I'll let you try and win your money back."

Rattie? thought Lutha. It was an affectionate nickname from his early days with the Companions; as a child Lutha had been small, quick in a fight, and had borne an unfortunate resemblance to said rodent. But no one had called him that in years. He shrugged and replied, "You'll do better to try and hang on to your own."

"Come on then. The stones are in my room."

Niryn waited until the other Companions were out of sight, then murmured, "Watch those two, Moriel."

He made his way alone up to Korin's door, where he swiftly sketched a pair of spells on the air, weaving in the proper intents.

Korin opened the door to his knock and waved him inside impatiently. "Come along, won't you? I want you to hear this."

The herald's mind had proven suitably malleable as well. He showed no hint of surprise or objection as Niryn stepped in and closed the door softly after him.

*   *   *

Caliel's chamber was much like Lutha's: narrow, damp, and sparsely furnished. Caliel had not taken a new squire, even when Barieus offered to help him find somebody. Lutha understood his friend's hesitation. Who would you trust here? As far as Lutha knew, Cal hadn't had a woman to his bed since they'd been here, either, though Lutha and Barieus, like Alben, had found plenty of willing girls among the servants of the keep.

Barieus started for the small wine table against the wall, looking for cups. Before he could pour for them, however, Caliel said, "Barieus, would you lend me your lord for a little while?"

"Sure, Cal." Barieus shot Lutha a curious look and went out.

"So, are we going to play?" Lutha asked.

Instead, Caliel held a finger to his lips and went to the narrow keyhole window.

"Rattie?" Lutha whispered. "You haven't called me that in—"

"I just wanted to get your attention. And I need a clever rat to climb out this window."

Lutha blinked. It was a sheer drop on this side of the fortress.

"Not all the way out," Caliel amended. "Come here. If I hold your feet, I think you can fit out the wide part."

Caliel pushed a wooden stool under the window for Lutha to stand on. He stepped up and examined the window. The slit had a round cutout at the bottom for an archer to shoot through, just large enough for someone small and flexible to squeeze out.

"But why?" he asked, peering out at the very long drop below.

Caliel gave him an impatient look. "I want to hear what that messenger has to say, of course!"

"What? How drunk are you?" Lutha hissed. "It's a herald! It's Korin! It's—"

Caliel clapped a hand over Lutha's mouth and pushed

the shutter closed with his other hand. "Do you want him to hear you?"

Lutha pushed Caliel's hand away but shut his mouth.

"I know it's Korin!" Cal whispered. "That's why I want to know what's going on. This message might be from Tobin. At least I hope it is!" He pushed the shutter back again and gave Lutha an expectant look.

"If you drop me, I swear to Bilairy I'll haunt you."

"Fair enough. Hurry now, before we miss it all."

Caliel snuffed the lamp. Lutha stepped onto the stool and squeezed out the loophole. It was a snug fit even for him, but once his shoulders were through the rest of him fit easily. With Caliel's arms wrapped tightly around his thighs, he was able to push himself out from the wall and twist himself toward Korin's window. *I must look like a caterpillar on a branch,* he thought sourly, straining every muscle.

Korin's bedroom window was only a few feet away. Twisting himself to the side and grasping the edge of the stonework that framed the loophole there, he got close enough to hear what was going on inside, though the angle was wrong to see anything but a sliver of tapestry-covered wall. The breeze was in his favor. He could hear the voices clearly.

"—word from your cousin, the Princess Royal Tamír, of Ero and Atyion."

"You are ill informed, Herald. There is no such person as this princess."

Lutha stifled a grunt of surprise. That was Niryn's voice, not Korin's.

"Forgive me, Majesty," the herald amended hastily, sounding frightened. "I am instructed to say that your cousin sends most loving regards. May I read the missive?"

"Go on." That was Korin.

Lutha heard the rustle of parchment, then the clear, carrying voice of the herald in his official capacity.

"*To Prince Korin, Beloved Cousin and Brother. I know*

you've had word of me, and what has happened. I know how hard it must be to believe, but it's true. I am a girl, but the same cousin you've always known. You only have to meet with me to have the proof. The high priest of Afra and most of Atyion witnessed the change and can vouch for me. I write to you now in my true form, as Tamír, daughter of Ariani and Rhius, the scion of Atyion. My seal bears witness.'"

Lutha caught his breath. That certainly sounded like Tobin's manner of speech, and he claimed powerful witnesses.

"'I'm sorry I had to lie to you and the others,'" the herald continued. *"'I've only known for a few years myself, but it was hard all the same, keeping the secret from my friends. I never meant to betray you when I joined the Companions. I didn't know then, I swear by the Flame. I never brought harm to you or your father, though he did great harm to my mother and her kin, whether you want to believe it or not. My mother should have been queen, and me after her. It breaks my heart to write this to you, Kor, but your father brought a curse on the land, one it is my burden to lift and heal.*

"'I mean you no harm, cousin. I never could. You were always kind to me. I have always loved you as a brother and I always will. Does it matter so much between us, who wears the crown? You are a rightful prince of Skala. I want you at my right hand, in my court and on the battlefield. Your children will be secure in their inheritance.

"'Please, parley with me. I want things to be right between us again.'"

The herald paused. "If you'll forgive me, Majesty, it is signed as follows: *'Your loving cousin and sister, Princess Tamír, who was Tobin.'"*

"I see." Something in Korin's voice caught at Lutha's heart. He sounded sad, not angry.

"Utter nonsense and subterfuge!" Niryn cut in sharply. "Majesty, you cannot possibly—"

Korin said something too softly for Lutha to catch.

"Majesty?"

"I said leave me! Both of you," Korin shouted with such vehemence that if Caliel hadn't had still a secure grip on Lutha, he'd probably have fallen. Caliel dragged him back through the window.

Lutha collapsed in a trembling heap on the floor, heart hammering in his chest. Caliel closed the shutter and set the hasp.

"What is it? What did you hear?" he demanded softly.

"It was from Tobin. At least that's what the herald claims, and they can't lie, can they? Only he says he really is a girl and—"

"You're babbling. Slow down. Start from the beginning."

So Lutha did, repeating as much of what he'd heard as he could remember.

"Niryn was in there?"

"I bet he put some spell on the herald and made him break his vow."

"Korin, too. And you're right; that does sound like Tobin. And he offers proofs? Still, it could be a trick. Or a trap."

"That's what Niryn said."

"I don't like to agree with that bastard, but it makes more sense than the alternative."

"Come on, Cal! Tobin would *never* betray us like that, or Ki either. Not of their own free will, anyway. I've been thinking and thinking on it. There are wizards at Tobin's court, too. I wonder if maybe one of them put some kind of spell on *them*, like Niryn is trying to do with Korin? There was that one old woman who came around. Tobin said she was attached to his family somehow."

"Mistress Iya? I think she was a friend of his father's."

"You couldn't call Tobin a traitor, could you, if someone was making him do all that?" Lutha was still stubbornly clinging to hope.

"I don't think that would change the minds of most of the nobles supporting Korin."

Caliel lit the lamp, then sat down on the bed. "Damn it, Lutha, we've got to get this settled once and for all, especially with this latest victory at Ero still fresh in everyone's minds. I don't know how much longer Korin can keep his supporters if he won't fight." He rubbed absently at the ring Tobin had made. "The only spies we have word from are those sent by Niryn. If only we could go see for ourselves—We're the damn Companions, for hell's sake! We're sworn to protect Korin. We should be the ones to bring him proof one way or the other. I don't trust Niryn to do that, not the way he hangs on Kor like a red leech."

"Neither do I, but what can we do?" asked Lutha.

"I think you know that as well as I do, but I want one more chance to reason with Korin. You say he sent Niryn out just now? Good. Then I think I'll go and see if I can have a quiet chat with him without an audience for once."

"Do you want me to come with you?"

Caliel smiled and clapped him on the shoulder. "Let me talk to him alone first."

Lutha nodded and turned to go, but Caliel caught him by the hand. "I've been glad of your company here, Lutha. I can still talk with you honestly."

"You always can," Lutha assured him. "Barieus, too. We don't like how things are, but I know it's been worse for you. You were always so close with him."

Caliel nodded slowly, looking so sad all of a sudden that Lutha nearly hugged him. If they'd both been a few years younger, he might have.

Lutha lingered a moment, watching as Caliel knocked softly at Korin's door. To his relief, Korin let him in.

Things just can't be as bad as they seem, he decided, heading back to his own room. Hadn't Korin thrown Niryn out, just now, and let Caliel in? That had to be a good sign. *If only someone would stick a knife in that red bastard, maybe things could get back to normal.*

Rounding the corner, Lutha suddenly found himself face-to-face with the Toad and Niryn himself. He'd have plowed right into them if Niryn hadn't caught him by the arm. The wizard's grip was strong, and his hand lingered a moment longer than necessary. Lutha felt a chill run through him, like the onset of a fever. His belly did a queasy roll and he had to swallow hard to keep his wine down.

"Have a care, my lord," Niryn murmured. He patted Lutha's arm, then tucked his hands back into his own voluminous silver-and-white sleeves. "Rushing around headlong like that, you'll do yourself harm."

"Forgive me, my lord," Lutha said hastily. "I—I didn't expect to meet you here."

Niryn gave him an odd look and Lutha's stomach tightened again. "As I said, you should have a care. Come along, Moriel."

Lutha watched until he was certain they were really gone, clutching his sword hilt, heart pounding loud in his ears. He felt cold despite the warmth of the summer night.

Barieus looked up from the boot he was polishing as Lutha came in. "What happened to you?"

"Nothing. Why?"

Barieus came over and pressed a hand to Lutha's brow. "You're white as milk and all covered in sweat. I knew you were drinking too much! Honestly, you're getting as bad as Korin."

"It's not that. I'm pale?"

"Awful. Come on, I'm putting you to bed."

Lutha suffered his friend's fussing and kept his new fears to himself. Niryn had done something to him, something that showed. Was he cursed? Would he die before dawn? He'd heard stories of some of the things wizards could do if they were very powerful.

Unlike some of the other Companions, he and Barieus had never been anything more than friends, but he was glad to sleep close beside him tonight.

*　　*　　*

Niryn hadn't needed to touch the young Companion to know what he'd been up to with Caliel. Moriel had been most informative, as usual. The boy had a true talent for listening through doors.

The young lords were getting quite bold lately, and Niryn enjoyed immensely watching them plot against him. The guilty look on that boy's face just now had been so amusingly obvious that Niryn hadn't been able to resist putting the lightest touch of a curse on him, just enough to give him bad dreams for a few nights.

He'd taken no direct action against Lord Caliel as yet. There had been no need. Korin's own growing fears and the self-serving attitudes of some of the other Companions were doing the wizard's work for him. Caliel's obvious stubbornness about their position here, his outspokenness in company, and his misplaced friendship with Prince Tobin had cost him Korin's trust with very little prompting on Niryn's part. The ground was now fertile for his revenge whenever he chose to take it.

Moriel moved about the chamber, folding away Niryn's overrobe into a chest and pouring a cup of sweet cider from a jug on the sideboard. Niryn drank it gratefully and Moriel refilled it.

"Thank you. That was dry work tonight." Niryn had never had much taste for wine; it weakened the mind, and he knew all too well how such weakness could be exploited. At table he made a show of lingering over his mazer, taking no more than a few sips.

Moriel knelt to remove his master's shoes. Orun had made certain this one was trained well in all the arts and war skills a squire would have needed. Tobin's refusal to take Moriel in place of Ki had left the boy suitably bitter and eager for revenge. Orun had trained Moriel in other ways, as well, but Niryn did not take boys to his bed, not even willing ones like Moriel.

"Were you successful, my lord?" he asked as he placed the shoes neatly by the clothes chest.

"Of course. You know how persuasive I can be."

Moriel smiled. "And the herald?"

"He was no challenge at all."

"Was the letter from Prince Tobin?"

"Yes, quite a cunning piece of work. He pleaded with Korin to forgive him for his treachery and thought to convince the king to give over his crown without a fight."

"It would be just like him," Moriel sneered. "What sort of reply did Korin give, if I may ask, my lord?"

"He said he'd give his answer tomorrow. Be a good lad and make certain that herald never leaves the isthmus, won't you? Take a few of my guard with you and bring me back the king's letter. I'll be most interested to see what he has to say."

"Of course, my lord. But won't Prince Tobin wonder if his messenger doesn't return?"

Niryn smiled. "Yes, I'm certain his cousin's silence will be quite unsettling for him."

Chapter 23

Korin answered Caliel's knock with a curt, "Who is it?"
    "It's me, Kor. Let me in."

There was a pause, and for a moment Caliel thought Korin would refuse.

"It's not locked."

Caliel slipped inside and closed the door.

The royal chamber was better appointed than the other rooms of the fortress, at least by Cirna standards. The large, carved bedstead was fitted with heavy, dust-laden velvet hangings. A few faded tapestries hung on the walls.

Korin sat at the writing table in his shirtsleeves, looking worn and unhappy. His face was flushed with wine and a full mazer stood at his elbow. He appeared to be in the midst of writing a reply to Tobin's letter, which lay before him. Caliel went to Korin and picked up the cup, glancing down as he did so at the sheet of parchment in front of him. Korin had gotten no further than, "To the pretender, Prince Tobin—"

He took a sip, watching for Korin's reaction. He was glad to see no more than the usual level of irritation at the familiar liberty. He drew up another chair and sat down. "How are you?"

"Is that all you came to ask me?"

Caliel sat back and stretched out his long legs, pretending an ease he didn't feel. "That herald got me curious. I thought I'd come see what all the fuss was about."

Korin shrugged and tossed him Tobin's letter. Caliel read the contents quickly and felt his heart skip a beat. Lutha had gotten most of it right, but it was even more shocking to see the words written out in Tobin's own unmistakable scrawl.

Korin had reclaimed his mazer and was currently staring morosely into its depths. "Do you believe him?"

"I don't know. Some of it—" *I'm sorry I had to lie . . . I never meant any harm . . . be my brother still . . . I want things to be right and proper between us . . .* "I do think you should meet with him, face-to-face."

"No! Madman or necromancer's monster, he's a traitor, and I can't be seen justifying his claim in any way."

"Is that what Niryn counseled?"

"And he's right!" Korin's bloodshot eyes were wide now, and burning with a sudden, unreasoning fury. "Tobin haunts my dreams, Cal. I see him, all pale and leering, calling me usurper and a murderer's son." He rubbed at his eyes and shuddered.

"All the more reason to find out for yourself what his intentions really are."

"I said no!" Korin snatched the letter back and slammed it down on the desk. He drained the cup and slammed that down, too.

"Damn it, Kor, I can't believe you're just going to take the word of others on this."

"So you're saying I should honor this—this *request*?"

"Korin, look at yourself! This is Niryn's doing. He's on you like a leech! He made you run from Ero. He brought you that ill-made girl you've got hidden away up in the tower. Is that how you treat a wife, Kor? A consort? Is this how the king of Skala lives? I say we gather your army tomorrow and ride for Ero. Parley with Tobin or fight him. Either way, you can see for yourself what the truth is!"

"I know the truth!"

"From who? Niryn's hounds?" Desperate, Caliel leaned forward and captured Korin's hand in his. "Listen to me, please. I've always been true to you, haven't I?"

It hurt, the hesitation he saw before Korin nodded. Caliel pressed on. "Whatever Niryn has told you, you have

my loyalty and my love, now and always! Let me go as
your emissary. I know the city. I can slip in and be back in
no time. I might even be able to talk to him. Give the
word, Kor. I'll go tonight!"

Korin wrenched his hand free. "No! I can't spare you."

"Spare me for what? Watching you drink yourself to
death?"

"Take care, Caliel," Korin growled.

"Lutha, then—"

"No! None of the Companions." Something very close
to fear flitted in Korin's red-rimmed eyes. "Damn it, Caliel,
why are you always fighting me? You used to be my
friend!"

"And you used to know who your friends are!" Caliel
stood and backed away, fists clenched helplessly at his
sides. "Bilairy's balls, Korin, I can't just stand by and watch
you piss away—"

"Get out!" Korin yelled, staggering up to his feet.

"Not until I've made you see sense!"

"I said get out!" Korin grabbed up the mazer and flung
it at Caliel. It struck him in the face and cut across his
cheekbone. The dregs stung the open wound.

The two young men stood staring at each other in
shocked silence and Caliel saw that Korin had his hand on
his sword hilt.

He slowly wiped his cheek with the back of one hand.
It came away bloody. He held it out for Korin to see. "Is
this what we've come to? You couldn't even take an honest
swing at me?"

For a moment Caliel was certain Korin would break
into that shamefaced grin that had always won him over,
the one that had always been enough to make Caliel forgive him anything. It was all it had ever taken and he
ached to forgive him now.

Instead, Korin turned his back on him. "Things have
changed. I am your king, and you *will* obey me. Good
night."

The curt dismissal stung far worse than the wound. "We've had some hard days," he said quietly. "The world is out of joint right now. But remember this: I *am* your friend, and I have nothing in my heart for you but the same love I have always felt. If you can't see that, then I pity you. I won't stop being your friend, no matter how big an ass you make of yourself!" He had to stop and force down the lump of bitterness that was rising to choke him. "Sleep on your belly tonight, Kor. You're drunker than you think."

He slammed out and stalked back to his room. Alone, he threw his wine-stained coat aside and paced the bare floor.

I am your friend, damn you! What can I do for you? How can I help you?

Too agitated to sleep and longing for company, he thought of going to Lutha's chamber. What did it say, he wondered darkly, when the youngest Companions were Caliel's sole confidants? The last honest men.

"No, not the last ones," he muttered.

Porion's chamber was in the lower level of the keep, close to the guardroom. As Caliel made his way down through the torchlit corridors, the golden hawk ring on his forefinger caught his eye again, and he regarded it sadly, recalling Tobin's shy smile the day he'd given it to him. It had been a gift, in return for all the time Caliel and their friend Arengil had spent teaching him falconry. Tobin was good with the birds, patient and gentle. He was like that about everything. Or had been, anyway. Caliel still couldn't bring himself to take the ring off.

Porion answered the door in his shirtsleeves and raised an eyebrow at Caliel's bloody cheek as he motioned him to the plain room's only chair.

"What have you done to your face?" he asked, sitting down on the narrow bed.

Caliel dabbed the cut with his sleeve. "It's nothing. I need to talk with you."

"About King Korin."

"Yes."

Porion sighed. "I figured you'd come to me, sooner or later. Speak your mind, boy."

Caliel smiled in spite of himself. The Companions would always be "boy" and "lad" to their old swordmaster. "I was just with him. The letter he got was from Tobin. He let me read it."

"And what did Tobin have to say?"

"He claims outright to have changed into a girl. He didn't explain, just said he had witnesses, including some Afran priests and most of Atyion."

"What do you believe?"

"I don't know." Caliel fidgeted with the ring. "Fantastic as it sounds, it makes more sense than Tobin turning traitor, don't you think?"

Porion ran a hand over his short grey beard and sighed. "You're young, and you have a good heart. And thanks to Erius, you boys led a sheltered life for too long. I've lived through two queens and a king and seen what people are capable of when great power is involved. I've been thinking about Tobin, too. I always thought it was queer, him being kept away from court most of his life, off in secret."

"His father was an honorable man, though, and served Erius all his life."

Porion nodded. "I knew Rhius from a boy and I wouldn't have thought him capable of intrigue like this. Still, he did keep more to himself after his marriage, and even more after that child was born. For all we know, he and that wizard of his were planning this all along, to avenge Erius' taking Ariani's place on the throne."

Caliel shifted uneasily in his chair. "I didn't come to speak of Tobin. Do you think Korin's acting like himself?"

Porion picked up his scabbard and found a flask of mink oil in a box under the bed. The musky smell rose in the air between them as he worked it into the scarred leather. "You've been Korin's friend longer than anyone else, but he's not only your friend, nor was he ever. He's the king. I didn't like everything his father did, and I sure as hell didn't care much for his grandmother, but the crown is the crown, and duty is duty. Korin's young, and green, it's true, but you know the worth in him."

"You know him as well as I do, Porion. We've both seen his weaknesses, too—the drinking, and—" Caliel clenched his fists against his knees, hating what he had to say next. "He's no good in battle. It wasn't just that first time, against those bandits. He nearly got us all killed at Ero, then he let that damn wizard talk him into running!"

Porion kept at his work. "It takes time, with some."

"Tobin—"

Porion looked up sharply, and Caliel was taken aback by the sudden anger in his old mentor's eyes. "That's enough, Caliel. I won't hear it, you comparing the two of them. Korin is king, and that's that. I served his father and now I serve him. If you don't think you can do that, then it's best if I know it now."

"That's not what I'm saying! I love Korin. I'd lay down my life for him. But I can't stand by any longer while that serpent ruins what's left of him! Bilairy's balls, Porion, you're not going to tell me you think this great friendship between them is natural? How can you sit there in the hall night after night, seeing that cur in Tobin's place—"

"Tobin again, is it?" Porion regarded him levelly. "That name is on your lips a great deal, my lord."

Caliel went cold. Porion had been his swordmaster since he was a boy, a friend and a good teacher. He was looking at him now with the same distrust that Korin had earlier, taking his measure.

"Something isn't right with that, Porion. That's all I'm trying to say."

"Times change, lad. People change. But the crown's the crown, and duty is duty. You're old enough to understand that."

"You're saying I should just keep my mouth shut and let Lord Niryn have his way?"

"Who the king chooses for his councilors is his concern. The best you can do is stand by him. Can you look me in the eye and swear your loyalty to him?"

Caliel met the old man's gaze unflinchingly. "I swear by the Flame and all the Four, I serve Korin as my friend and my king."

Porion wiped more oil on the scabbard. "I believe you, but there are those close to the king who think otherwise."

"Niryn, you mean? I know. Moriel's under my feet all the time, spying for him. He can lurk all he likes. I've done nothing I'm ashamed of."

Porion shrugged. "All the same, watch your step, lad. That's all I'm saying."

The exchange, with its hint of a threat, upset Caliel even more than his argument with Korin, and not only because the man had questioned his loyalty. His bedchamber had all the allure of a tomb. Instead, he went out and walked the battlements, warring silently with himself.

Porion's admonishments had cut deep; in his heart Caliel *did* feel disloyal. But his fear for Korin was real, too. Now it seemed that Niryn had even won over Porion. He and Lutha were truly the only ones left who could see that Korin was growing weaker under Niryn's influence.

He wandered down to the courtyard well for a drink, still trying to figure out what to do. Somehow, he didn't think murdering Niryn in his sleep was his best plan, tempting as it was.

He was still fretting when he heard a door open. He glanced in that direction, then hastily crouched down behind the low well. It was Moriel, and he had one of the Harrier captains with him, a tall man named Seneus. The pair stopped in the shelter of a farrier's shed. The Toad looked around carefully, then took a purse from his belt and gave it to the Harrier.

"Station your men on all the roads and have someone follow when he leaves."

"I know my business!" Seneus snorted. "I've hunted wizards, you know. This one shouldn't give any trouble." He weighed the purse, then opened it. "This better all be gold. I'm courting Astellus' curse."

"It is, and more than enough for any offerings to lift it," Moriel replied. "But what does a Sakor man like you care for the watery Traveler, eh? My master will give you more, when you bring back the king's letter. Go on now, and do your duty."

Caliel caught his breath as the import of the conversation came clear. The only Astellian in the keep tonight was Tobin's herald.

He waited until both men were safely gone, then slipped back up to his room. He quickly put on his hauberk, then a plain tunic and cloak over it, and buckled on his sword. He didn't allow himself to pause as he passed Korin's door, or the corridor leading to Lutha's. He and Barieus must remain blameless.

Instead, he stole across the shadowy yard to the kitchen entrance and the rooms set aside for heralds there. There were several, but only one with a pair of boots outside the door.

He scratched softly, keeping an eye out for watchmen. The herald answered, yawning, his long yellow hair loose around his shoulders. "Is it dawn already?" He broke off in surprise as Caliel pushed him back into the room and closed the door. "Lord Caliel, what are you doing here?"

"Did King Korin give you a message to carry back to Prince Tobin?"

"You know I can't tell you that, my lord."

"I come as a friend. There's a plot on your life, to keep that message from being delivered. I mean to ride for Atyion right now. I'll carry it, and you can leave by another way. I swear by your Traveler and all the Four, this is the truth."

"I cannot, my lord, though it means my life."

Caliel ran a hand over his face in frustration. "The message will be lost. You're already wounded. You'll be no match for the men being sent after you."

The man smiled and held up his bandaged arm. "As you can see, heralds are not so easily caught. There were twenty brigands, and I came away with my life and my message. There are other roads I can take, thanks to your warning."

"You'll be watched from the moment you leave the gate. There'll probably be a wizard in the pack."

"So you say, my lord, and again, I'm grateful, but my duty is sacred. I cannot do as you ask."

Caliel shook his head, caught between the desire to knock the man out for his own good, and admiration for his courage. "You'll be dead by sunset tomorrow."

"That is for Astellus to decide, my lord."

"Well, I hope your god loves you. Will you keep this conversation to yourself?"

The herald bowed. "You were never here, my lord."

Leaving the man to his fate, Caliel went back to the yard and left by a small postern gate on the seaward side. Moriel's henchmen wouldn't have had time to set their ambush yet and would be looking for a herald with a blond braid when they did. If he didn't hesitate, he might have a chance.

With no immediate threat of attack from without, the guards were lax. He slipped out unchallenged and followed a rough footpath along the cliffs, then stole a horse from a picket line. He smiled darkly to himself as he rode off, thinking with satisfaction of the bad report he could make of the Harrier officers when he got back.

The high road shone like a pale ribbon before him in the starlight. The farther he got from that cursed fortress, the lighter his heart felt. By dawn he was miles away, watching the sun come up over the Inner Sea. In a few days he'd see for himself if Tobin was friend or foe. The

cut on his cheek was already scabbed over, the hurt Korin
had done him already forgiven. With Korin's faith or without it, Caliel would serve his king the best way he could.

He looked down at the ring again. *If you are still our
friend, then Korin needs you. If not, I'll deal with you myself, for his sake and in his name.*

Chapter 24

Lutha spent the night lost in terrifying dreams he could not escape and woke with the sun in his eyes and someone pounding furiously at his door.

"Lutha, are you there? Open in the name of the king!"

Lutha lurched up to find Barieus bent over the washstand, looking back wide-eyed at him, water dripping from his cupped hands. "That sounds like Alben."

Lutha went to the door, his sweaty shirt clinging uncomfortably to his back between his shoulder blades, and opened the door a crack to peer out.

Alben greeted him with a look of relief. "You are here! When you didn't appear at the morning meal—"

"I overslept. What's all the shouting about?" He opened the door wider and found himself facing half a dozen grey-back Guards. He was also aware of Barieus at his back. "What's going on, Alben?"

"Caliel deserted last night."

Lutha stared at him in disbelief until cold realization hit. "And you assumed we ran off with him."

Alben had the good grace to look embarrassed. "Master Porion sent me. Korin's in a state. He's already had Cal declared a traitor and set a price on his head."

"That's ridiculous! There must be some other explanation."

"He's gone, Lutha. Did you know he was planning this?"

"Are you mad? Of course he didn't!" Barieus cried.

"Perhaps Lord Lutha should answer for himself?" Niryn stepped into view behind his men. "Lord Lutha, you have been seen by witnesses, meeting in secret with Lord Caliel and plotting against the king. I'm only sorry I didn't take action sooner, before Lord Caliel escaped."

"Plotting?" Lutha sputtered. "We never— Is that what Korin thinks? Let me talk to him!" He turned, looking frantically for his clothes. Barieus tried to fetch him his trousers, but the grey-backs surged in and seized both of them.

"Alben, you can't believe this?" Lutha cried as they were dragged away. "Let me talk to Korin. Alben, please! This is Niryn's doing. *Alben!*"

They were dragged, half-dressed and struggling, downstairs, in front of all the warriors and nobles gathered there, and out to a damp, dark little cell beside the barracks.

The guards shoved them inside and slammed the heavy door on them, plunging them into darkness. There was a heavy thud as the thick bar was dropped into place.

"Lutha, what's going on?" Barieus whispered.

"I don't know. Maybe Korin's really gone mad at last." Lutha found a damp stone wall with his hand and sat down with his back to it, drawing his bare legs up under his shirt. "You saw who came for us. Damn that wizard to the crows!"

There were chinks in the stonework where the roof beams met the wall. As his eyes adjusted he could make out Barieus crouched beside him, and the narrow confines of their cell. It was barely two arm spans wide.

They sat in silence for a while, trying to comprehend this sudden reversal of fortune.

"You don't think Cal would really turn traitor?" Barieus asked at last.

"No."

"Then why did he leave like that, without saying anything to you?"

"We've only got Niryn's word that he did. More likely

Niryn had him murdered. Damn him! I should have warned Cal."

"Warn him about what?"

Lutha told him how they'd spied on Korin, and how he'd run into the man afterward. "Niryn probably knew all along. I should have guessed by the way he looked at me. Damn, I should have gone back to Caliel!"

They sat in silence again, glumly watching a thin ray of sunlight track down the wall.

At last they heard the bar being lifted, and daylight flooded the cell, making them blink. A guard tossed in their clothes. "Get dressed. King Korin has summoned you."

They dressed hastily and were escorted to the hall. Korin sat on his throne, flanked by the two remaining Companions and Niryn's wizards. Master Porion stood at his right hand today, and he held a long whip in his hand, the same sort that Tobin had been made to use on Ki.

Lutha drew himself up to attention, trying not to let his anger and fear show. He might be barefoot, with straw in his hair, but he was still a Royal Companion and a nobleman's son.

"A complete search has been made for Caliel. He's nowhere to be found," Korin said. "What do you know of this?"

"Nothing, Majesty."

"Don't lie to me, Lutha. You'll only make things worse for yourself."

"Oh, so I'm a liar now, as well as a traitor?" Lutha snapped. "Is that all you think of me, *Majesty*?"

"Lutha!" Barieus murmured in alarm.

"Companion, you will address your liege with the proper respect!" Porion barked.

Quivering with outrage, Lutha shut his mouth and fixed his eyes on the floor.

"You will mind your tongue or lose it, my lord," Niryn said. "Speak the truth, or I will compel you."

"I always speak the truth!" Lutha retorted, not bothering to hide his disdain for the man.

"I've sent my best trackers after him," Niryn told him. "Lord Caliel will be found and brought back very soon. You only do yourselves harm by lying for him. He's gone over to Prince Tobin."

Lutha ignored him. "On my honor as your Companion, Korin, Cal said nothing about leaving or going back to Ero, and we never planned to desert. I swear by the Flame."

"As do I, Majesty," said Barieus.

"Yet you admit to sympathizing with the false queen?" Niryn said.

"Sympathizing? I don't know what you mean," Lutha replied. Korin was still impassive on his throne, and the distrust in his eyes scared Lutha. "We only thought it was odd you wouldn't let us go find out the truth about Tobin. But Cal never said anything about leaving! He's as loyal to you as I am."

"That may not count for much, Majesty," Niryn sneered. "If you will allow me, I can soon give you the truth."

Lutha's heart sank as Korin nodded. Niryn stepped down from the dais and motioned to the men flanking Lutha. They grabbed his arms, holding him fast.

Niryn stood before him, and made no effort to hide his nasty, gloating smile. "This may hurt a bit, my lord, but it is your king's will."

He clasped Lutha under the chin with one cold hand and laid the other on top of his head, palm to Lutha's brow. His touch made Lutha shudder, like having a snake crawl across your bare foot in the dark. He fixed his gaze on the wizard's chest. The white robe was spotless, as always; Niryn smelled of candles and smoke and something sweet.

Lutha had nothing to hide. He concentrated on his loyalty to Korin until a bolt of searing pain obliterated all conscious thought. It felt like his head was being crushed and plunged into fire, all at once. He didn't know if he was still on his feet or not, but felt like he was falling endlessly into a black pit. Despair swept aside pride; he wanted to cry, scream, beg Korin or even the wizard for this torture to end. But he was blinded and lost, his tongue numb in his mouth.

It went on and on, and just when he thought he would die from the pain, he found himself on his hands and knees in the stale rushes at Niryn's feet, gasping for breath. His head throbbed horribly and his mouth tasted like bile.

Niryn was already gripping Barieus' head in the same manner. Lutha watched helplessly as his friend stiffened and went white.

"Korin, please! Make him stop," Lutha begged hoarsely.

Barieus let out a strangled whine. His eyes were open, but unseeing, and his fists were clenched so hard his knuckles showed white through his sun-browned skin. Niryn looked serene, as if he were healing the boy rather than tearing into his soul.

Lutha struggled unsteadily to his feet. "Let go of him! He doesn't know anything." He grabbed at the wizard's arm, trying to stop him.

"Guards, restrain him," Korin ordered.

Lutha was too weak to fight but he did anyway, struggling fruitlessly between the two guardsmen.

"Lord Lutha, don't! There's nothing you can do," one of them warned.

Niryn released Barieus and the boy collapsed unconscious to the floor. The guards let go of Lutha and he fell to his knees beside him. Barieus' eyes were tightly shut, but his face still bore a look of utter horror.

"They speak the truth regarding Lord Caliel, Your Majesty," said Niryn. "They know nothing of his disappearance."

Was that relief in Korin's eyes? Lutha was weak with it himself, but it proved short-lived.

Niryn gave him a withering glance. "However, I do

find in both of them a strong loyalty to Prince Tobin. I fear their love for him outweighs their loyalty to you, Majesty."

"No, that's not true!" Lutha cried, but even as he said it, he feared it might be true. "Please Korin, you must understand. He was our friend! He was your friend! We only wanted you to talk with him, as he asked—"

Korin's eyes went hard again. "How do you know of that?"

"I—That is, Cal and I—" The words died on his lips.

"He admits to his spying, Majesty," Niryn said, shaking his head. "And now Caliel has gone to Tobin, no doubt to give him all the particulars of your strength here."

"No, Caliel wouldn't," Lutha said weakly, cringing under the hostile looks from Korin and the other Companions. He knew then that he was lost. He would never be allowed to stand with them again.

Barieus stirred and opened his eyes, then shivered as he saw Niryn standing over them.

Korin stood and advanced on them. "Lutha, son of Asandeus, and Barieus, son of Malel, you are cast out of the Companions and condemned as traitors."

"Korin, please!"

Korin drew his dagger, his face harsh as winter. The guards held Lutha and Barieus tightly as Korin stepped down from the dais. He cut off their braids and cast them at their feet, then spat in both their faces.

"You are nothing to me, and nothing to Skala. Guards, take them back to their cell until I decide their sentence."

"No, Niryn's lying!" Lutha howled, struggling as the guards dragged him and Barieus away. "Korin, please, you have to listen to me. Niryn's evil. He's lying to you. Don't believe him!"

He got no further before his head exploded with pain again and the world went black.

ᚻis head still hurt terribly when he came to, and for a moment he thought he'd been struck blind. He could feel that he was lying with his head in someone's lap and heard the sound of Barieus' soft weeping, but he couldn't see a thing. As his mind cleared he recognized the smell of moldy hay and knew they were back in the cell. Looking up, he found the chinks in the wall, but the light was much fainter now.

"How long was I asleep?" he asked, sitting up. He felt gingerly at the back of his head and found a sizable lump, but no blood.

Barieus wiped hastily at his face, probably hoping Lutha hadn't heard him crying. "A few hours. It's past midday. I heard the drum beat for the guard change."

"Well, looks like we're for it now, eh? Cal was right, all along. Niryn has just been biding his time." Lutha clenched his fists in helpless anger.

"Why—" Barieus paused, shifting uncomfortably. "Why do you think Caliel left us behind?"

"He wouldn't desert us, not if he meant to go over to Tobin's side. I still think he's dead." He'd rather that was the truth than think that Caliel had betrayed them.

Nalia lingered on her balcony, waiting nervously to see what was going to happen to the poor boys who'd been dragged out to the cells.

Tomara had brought word of the uproar with the morning tea. Shortly after she arrived with the tray, they heard the clatter of hooves and watched as parties of armed men rode off north and south at a gallop.

"They're after Lord Caliel," said Tomara, shaking her head. "We'll see his head on a spike before the week's out."

"How horrible!" Caliel had been particularly kind to her. He was handsome, too, with his golden hair and dark eyes. Korin had always spoken of Lord Caliel as his dearest friend. How could he give such an order?

Nalia had little appetite for her bread and eggs that morning. For the past several days she'd had spells of dizziness and moments of hot nausea that nearly sent her to the basin. She'd said nothing to Tomara or Korin. She'd learned enough from her woman's prattling to realize what such distemper might signify. Her next moon flow was due in a few days and she was counting the days with a heavy heart. If she were with child, then Korin would never let her go.

Late-afternoon sunlight streamed down through the forest canopy, painting shifting patterns across the moist earth of the game trail Mahti had been following.

Lhel and the Mother had been drawing him north and west instead of south this past week, toward the great bridge. At night, hidden away from prying eyes in forests or deep meadows, he played Sojourner softly and let the songs bring visions of landmarks and vistas to guide him. By day he let his feet take him where his heart guided, and he found them.

Mother Shek'met's voice was stronger now, so strong that he stopped beneath the spreading arms of a grand-mother oak and closed his eyes, swaying slightly as the witch marks tickled and burned under his skin. The sounds of the breeze and birdsong faded around him, obscured by the slow, deep beat of his heart. He brought the oo'lu to his lips and let the song take its own form. He did not hear it, but saw the pictures it made.

He saw a great sea, the one that lay on the other side of the great bridge. He'd heard tales of it and knew it by the lighter blue of its waters. Gulls flew in great flocks over it, and in the distance he saw a huge stone house with high walls.

The song told him of deep sorrow in that house, of spirits broken, and a cold heart that could not be warmed. His path lay in that direction, and he must hurry.

Quickly! the Mother whispered in the silences under the oo'lu's song.

Mahti lowered the instrument and opened his eyes to find the sun nearly gone from the sky. Shouldering the oo'lu and his food bag, he hurried on. The swift-footed deer that made this path had marked the earth with their cloven hooves. The double-pointed marks guided his bare feet long after the stars came out.

Lutha and Barieus marked the passing of the day by the thin rays of light that tracked across the far wall. Darkness fell, but no one brought them food or water. They could hear guards outside shifting restlessly and muttering among themselves.

Moving slowly to spare his aching head, Lutha crept to the door, hoping for some word of Caliel, but the men outside talked only of gaming and women.

He explored the confines of the cell, even climbing up on his squire's shoulder to reach the beams and thatch overhead. There was a bucket to piss in, and another for water, but no way out, not even for a clever rat like him.

Past hope, they fell asleep with their backs to the wall and woke the next morning to the grating of the bar. They blinked in the midmorning glare as another man was dragged in and slung down in the straw. He landed face-down, hands bound behind his back, but they knew Caliel by his blood-matted hair. From the looks of him, he'd been beaten and dragged, and probably put up a good fight besides. Two ragged tufts of hair at his temples marked where his braids had been.

The door slammed and for a moment Lutha couldn't see a thing, still dazzled by the sudden light, but he crawled to Caliel and ran his hands over him, looking for wounds. There was a sizable lump on the side of his head and bloody abrasions on his arms and legs. He didn't move, but moaned as Lutha felt his chest and sides. His breathing was labored.

"They cracked a rib or two, the bastards," Lutha muttered. He freed Caliel's hands and chafed the cold flesh to get the blood moving, then settled down beside him, with nothing left to do but await their fate. The light had shifted to midafternoon on the wall when Caliel finally stirred.

"Cal? We're here with you. What happened?" Lutha asked.

"They caught me," he whispered hoarsely. "Grey-backs—and one of those cursed wizards." He struggled up, blinking in the dim light. The right side of his face was dark with dried blood and his lip was split and swollen. "They wouldn't fight me properly, but came at me with cudgels. I think the wizard cast a spell on me in the end. I don't recall anything after that." He shifted painfully, favoring his side. "What are you two doing here?"

Lutha quickly told him what had happened.

Caliel groaned again. "But that's why I left the way I did, so you wouldn't be tied into it and get into trouble!"

"The Toad's been carrying tales to his master. We're accused of conspiring with you against Korin."

Caliel sighed. "Tanil and Zusthra die, but a serpent like Moriel wiggles through and survives. Sakor's fire, where's the justice in that?"

"It's Korin's justice we're facing now, and I don't like our odds," Lutha replied sadly. "Niryn's cut us off from him, neat as a tailor."

"I should have expected this. Damn, if only I'd been able to get away and talked sense to Tobin!"

"I'm sorry you got caught, but I'm glad to know that you didn't just run off," Barieus said softly. "At least I can think of that before they hang us."

"Do you think they will, Cal?" asked Lutha.

Caliel shrugged. "I imagine they'll hang me but you two didn't do anything! It's not right."

"Nothing's been right since we left Ero," Lutha said glumly.

Niryn stood by Korin in the council chamber. He remained silent as the handful of lords debated the traitors' fates, but he was not idle.

The corridors of the young king's mind were familiar territory, but he still found surprising twists and turns there, walls of resistance that even his insinuations could not breach. Lord Caliel had been the catalyst for far too many of these, and that little rat-faced one was no better. Deep in his heart, Korin still loved them.

"Your Majesty, they have betrayed you," Duke Wethring urged. "You cannot be seen as weak! They must be punished for all to see. All of them."

Korin still clutched three slender braids in his hand: one blonde, one ruddy, and one dark.

Such loyalty, even after his friends have turned their backs on him, thought the wizard. *A pity it is so misplaced.* Niryn focused again and concentrated on the images it brought him of a younger Prince Korin, lost in the shadow of his family. Sisters who would be queen. Brothers with stronger arms, swifter feet. A father who'd favored this one or that, or so it had seemed to a little boy who was never quite certain of approval until plague carried away his competition. And then the guilt. Even with the others out of the way, he still wasn't good enough. Niryn had long since found memories of overheard conversations— Swordmaster Porion instructing the other Companions to let Korin win. A deep wound, that, rubbed with salt. Caliel had known.

Niryn gently tended that deep-buried hurt. Korin didn't suspect a thing, only felt his heart harden as he tossed the braids aside and gritted out, "Yes, you're right, of course."

Niryn was pleased.

It was evening when the door swung open again, and Niryn himself stood there, gloating. "You're to be brought before Korin for judgment. Come now, or would you prefer to be dragged, as you deserve?"

"Be brave," murmured Caliel as he rose unsteadily to his feet. Lutha and Barieus were already up. No matter what anyone said, they were Royal Companions; they cowered for no man, not even the king.

They stepped from the cell to find a tribunal waiting for them in the courtyard. The garrison was formed up in a hollow square around the yard, and Korin stood on the far side, flanked by Porion and his chief generals.

Their guards marched them to the center of the square. Niryn went to stand at Korin's right hand, among the generals and nobles.

Lutha glanced around, searching faces. Many simply glared back at him, but a few could not meet his eye.

Korin was dressed in full armor and held the Sword of Ghërilain unsheathed before him.

Porion spoke the charges. "Lord Caliel, you stand accused of desertion and treason. You were expressly forbidden to go to the usurper prince, yet you stole away like a thief in the night to join his camp. What do you have to say for yourself?"

"What can I say, Korin, if you're too blind to see the truth for yourself?" Caliel replied, lifting his chin proudly. "If you think I deserted you, then you never knew my heart as I thought you did. There's nothing I can say now to change that."

"Then you admit you were making for Prince Tobin's army?" Niryn demanded.

"Yes," Caliel replied, still speaking to Korin, and Korin alone. "And you know why."

Lutha saw Korin's hand tighten around the hilt of his sword. His eyes went flat and dead as he proclaimed, "Disloyalty against one's lord is the greatest crime for a warrior at any time, but in these dire days, when I expect those closest to me to set an example, it is all the more unforgivable. Caliel and Lutha, you have both questioned my will since we left Ero. I have shown forbearance, hoping you would mend your ways and be the loyal Companions I have known. Instead, you have fomented unrest and doubt among others—"

"What others?" Lutha demanded. "We were worried for you, because—"

A crushing force closed around his heart and throat, choking off his protest. No one else seemed to notice, but once again he found Niryn watching him with amusement. This was magic! Why couldn't anyone see what he was doing? He swallowed hard, wanting to denounce the man, but the more he tried to force the words out, the harder the pain closed around his throat. He fell to his knees and clutched his chest.

Korin mistook his distress. "Stand up! Shame your manhood no more than you already have."

It was hopeless. Niryn knew what Lutha wanted to say and was stopping the words in his throat. Staggering to his feet again, he croaked, "Barieus knew nothing of this. He's guilty of nothing."

Beside him, Barieus threw back his shoulders and said loudly, "I am Lord Lutha's squire and follow him in all things. If he is guilty, then so am I. I am ready to share any punishment."

"And so you shall," said Korin. "For the crime of disloyalty, you shall first be flogged before this company. Twenty lashes of the cat for Lutha and his squire, and fifty for Caliel, for his greater crime. At dawn tomorrow you shall be hanged, as befits your false friendship and treachery."

Lutha kept his head high, but he felt like a horse had kicked him in the belly. Despite his harsh words in the cell, he hadn't really believed Korin would go so far. Even Alben looked shocked, and Urmanis had gone pale.

"All of them hanged?" asked Master Porion, his tone carefully guarded. "Lutha and Barieus, as well?"

"Silence! The king has spoken," Niryn snapped, fixing the old swordsman with a sharp look. "Would you challenge His Majesty's wisdom, as well?"

Porion flushed angrily, but bowed to Korin and said nothing more.

"If Master Porion won't speak, then I will!" Caliel cried angrily. "Before these witnesses, I say that you are unjust. Hang me if you must, but in your heart, you know I was acting on your behalf. You say you are punishing treachery, but I say you are rewarding it." He cast a scornful look at the wizard. "If you hang these two boys, who have done nothing but serve you loyally, then let this company witness your justice and see it for the evil it is! You have forgotten who your true friends are," he finished angrily, "but even if you kill me, I will not stop being yours."

For just a moment Lutha thought Korin might relent. A hint of pain crossed his face, but only for an instant.

"Let the lesser infractions be punished first," he ordered. "Companions, see to your duty."

Alben and Urmanis avoided his eyes as they stepped forward and roughly stripped off Lutha's shirt. Garol and Mago took charge of Barieus and did the same.

A feeling of unreality settled over him as they were led back toward the stone building that housed the cells. There, large iron rings were set high on the wall. Soldiers were already busy, fixing short lengths of rope through them.

Lutha held his head up and looked straight ahead, refusing to give any show of fear. From the corner of his eye, the massed ranks of silent warriors were nothing more than a dark, ominous blur.

He'd witnessed floggings enough to know that twenty lashes was a serious sentence, but the threat of it paled beside the proof that all their years of loyalty and friendship meant nothing to Korin. Not if they could be wiped away so brutally, on nothing more than the word of a wizard.

The other Companions strung them up, binding their hands to the rings with their faces pressed to the rough wall. The rings were so high that Lutha's feet scarcely touched the ground. It felt like his arms were being pulled from their sockets.

He turned his head, looking at Barieus. He had his lips pressed grimly together, but his eyes were wide with fear.

"Courage," Lutha whispered. "Don't let them hear you cry out. Don't give them the satisfaction."

He heard movement behind him, and what sounded like a collective intake of breath. A burly, shirtless man with a cloth mask obscuring his face stepped close and showed them the knotted cat they would be punished with. A dozen or more long lengths of cord were fixed to a long wooden handle.

Lutha nodded and looked away. Gripping the iron ring, he braced for the first blow.

It was worse than he could have imagined. Nothing he'd experienced on the practice field or in combat compared to that first brutal stripe. It stole the breath from his lungs and burned like fire. He felt a trickle of blood under his shoulder blade, tracking down his side like a falling tear.

Barieus took the next stroke and Lutha heard his strangled grunt of pain.

The man wielding the cat was well versed in the art. He carefully distributed the stripes, marking them evenly down both sides of their backs and crosshatching the welts, so that every new strike hit already torn skin to cause more pain.

Lutha managed the first few well enough, but by the time the first ten had been meted out he had to bite his lip to keep from crying out. Barieus cried out at each stroke now, but to the boy's credit, he was not weeping or begging. Blood blossomed bright and metallic across Lutha's tongue as he bit his lip and forced himself to silently count down the last few strokes.

When it was over at last, someone cut the rope securing his hands to the ring, leaving his wrists bound together. Lutha's legs betrayed him and he ended up in a trembling heap in the dirt. Barieus collapsed, too, but was up almost at once. He bent down, holding his bound hands out to

Lutha. His face was streaked with tears and blood was running down his sides, but his voice was steady as he said,
loud enough for all to hear, "Let me help you up, my lord."

It gave Lutha the strength he needed. They turned and
stood shoulder to shoulder, facing Korin, and Lutha realized that any love he'd felt for him was dead.

Guardsmen pulled them aside roughly and made them
stand and watch from close range as Caliel was stretched
against the wall. Everyone heard his sharp hiss of pain as
his arms were pulled over his head, straining his broken
ribs.

How will he stand it? Twenty strokes had left Lutha
limp and weak, his back a throbbing mess. Fifty strokes
could strip the flesh from a man's bones, perhaps even kill
him, and Caliel was already badly hurt.

Caliel was taller, with longer arms. He gripped the iron
ring easily and braced his feet, head bowed. And it began
again.

Caliel shuddered under the first few stripes. After ten
strokes he was bleeding. After twenty, he was shaking vis-
ibly. Each stroke of the cat opened bloody lines across his
skin, and after several complete passes over his back the
skin was raw and streaming blood.

Perhaps Niryn had secretly instructed the man with the
whip not to ruin Cal for the hanging, for he did not open
him to the bone, but after the thirty-ninth lash Caliel
fainted. Men came forward with buckets of seawater. The
cold and the sting of the salt brought Caliel around. He
writhed against the wall, biting back a cry, and the punishment proceeded to its conclusion. Caliel bore the rest in
the same stubborn silence. When they cut him down he
fell insensible to the ground, bleeding into the dirt.

"The king's justice has been served," Porion announced heavily. "Take them back to their cell. Tomorrow,
they shall be hanged. Let the king's justice be done."

Every warrior around the yard struck their sword hilt

or bow to his chest. The sharp clatter of obedience went through Lutha's belly like a knife thrust.

He and Barieus managed to make it back to the cell on their feet, but Caliel was roughly dragged by the arms and dropped facedown in the straw. Lutha fell to his knees beside him, fighting back tears of pain and betrayal.

"Sakor's Flame, he'll bleed to death!" he gasped, looking down helplessly at the bloody mess the cat had made of Caliel's back. "Tell the king he needs a healer, please!"

"Not much point," one of their gaolers muttered.

"Shut up, you!" the other one snapped. "I'll ask, Lord Lutha, though I don't know what he'll allow. Maker's Mercy be with you all, whatever happens."

Lutha looked up in surprise at this kindness. The man wore the red hawk insignia, but his eyes were filled with a mix of pity and disgust. He sent the other man away to ask for a healer but lingered a moment.

"It's not my place to say anything, my lord," he whispered, "but all three of you did yourselves proud out there. And—" He paused and stole a nervous glance at the door. "And there's them that don't hold with the king's idea of justice. Maker's Mercy be with you all." He stood and hurried out. Lutha heard the heavy bar fall into place.

No healer came. Working painfully with their bound hands, Lutha and Barieus managed to tear strips from the legs of their breeches and laid them across the worst wounds on Caliel's back to staunch the bleeding. Lutha's own back burned every time he moved, but he didn't stop until they'd done what little they could for Caliel.

It was too painful to sit with their backs to the wall, so they stretched out on either side of Caliel, trying to sleep.

Lutha was just slipping into a fitful doze when he felt a foot nudge his own.

"You were brave," Caliel rasped.

"Not half as brave as you," Lutha replied. "By the Four, Cal, you spoke your mind and you never cried out, not once!"

"Really? I—I don't recall much of it." He mustered a rusty chuckle. "Well, at least I don't have to worry about the scars, eh?"

"I guess not." Lutha rested his head on his arm. "Are you frightened?"

"No, and you shouldn't be, either. We'll walk up to Bilairy's gate together, with our heads up. I'm just sorry I got you both into this. Can you forgive me?"

"Nothing to forgive," Barieus whispered. "All any of us tried to do was our duty. Fuck Korin if he'd rather listen to Old Fox Beard."

It hurt to laugh, but it felt good, too. "Yeah, fuck him!" Lutha gasped. Raising his voice, he yelled hoarsely, "You hear that, Korin? Fuck you, for not knowing how to treat those who loved you! You can just go to—"

"That's enough," Caliel croaked. "Both of you, that's no way to be remembered. It's not—I don't think this is all Korin's fault."

"How can you still say that?" Barieus hissed bitterly. "He's going to hang us tomorrow. Are you saying you still care about him?"

"I wasn't lying out there," Caliel replied softly. "I should have killed Niryn when I had the chance. I'd rather have hanged for that than die like this. At least that would have done some good. This will be a damn useless death."

Nalia had watched in horrified fascination as Lord Lutha and his squire were strung up, but after the first few lashes she'd run from the sight and vomited into the basin. Tomara held her until she was finished, then helped her to bed.

"Close the doors!" Nalia begged, pulling the pillows around her ears. She could still hear the sounds of the whip and the cries that drifted up.

Tomara closed the balcony door and all the shutters, then returned to sponge Nalia's temples with rosewater.

"Poor dear, you shouldn't see such things. You're too tender for such sights."

"Those were the king's Companions!" Nalia gasped. "Why would he do such a thing?"

"There, there. You mustn't spare any tears for traitors, my dove," Tomara soothed. "If that's the worst that happens to them, then King Korin is a more merciful ruler than his grandmother or father ever were. Queen Agnalain would have had them drawn and quartered."

"Then it's true?" Korin's friends had turned against him. She could still almost feel sorry for him, knowing how deeply such betrayal cut, but it frightened her to see what he was capable of. "Tomara, go down among the guards and see what you can learn."

All too pleased to be sent gossiping again, Tomara hurried off.

Nalia lay back among the pillows, anxious for news. When Tomara did not immediately return, curiosity won out and she went to the window overlooking the courtyard again, and cracked the shutters open.

Lord Caliel hung there now. His back was already bloody and the man wielding the whip was still beating him. At once repelled and fascinated, Nalia began to count the strokes. She reached thirty-one before the flogging was done.

As she watched, Nalia had a revelation. If this was how Korin served his dearest friend, what might he do to her if he ever discovered how, deep in her heart, she now loathed him?

Mahti had walked all night and all day without stopping. He chewed dried snakeroot berries and sang softly under his breath, a tuneless chant that kept fatigue and hunger at bay. By the time he stopped he could see the huge water of his vision shining in the distance, the Sunrise Sea. He stopped, gazing at it in wonder. In the days before the coming of the pale-skinned lowlanders, before his people had been driven back to become mountain dwellers, the Retha'noi had traveled between the two seas and worshipped the Mother. There were sacred places on this lost coast. He wondered if anyone was left to tend them.

He ate a little of the food he'd taken from a house he'd passed, slept for a while in the shelter of an abandoned shed, then walked on, drawn by the shimmer of the sea.

There were no forests here to protect him, only open fields and the scattered houses of lowlanders. In the darkness he saw clusters of light in the distance that marked a town and kept well away from that place.

The Mother's voice pulled him on until he reached a lowlander's road. It shone pale in the moonlight and he paused at the edge of it as if it were a swift river that would carry him away if he stepped too carelessly into it. His witch marks tingled and itched again and his eyes closed, but his feet moved. He let them, trusting in Mother Shek'met, whose pale, comforting face looked down on him from the clear night sky. Her light was like cool springwater, soothing his aching legs and parched lips.

He walked on the road for a long time, the dusty packed earth strange under his feet. No deer had walked here, only horses, and their marks gave him nothing. He walked until something hard pressed into the arch of his foot, making him stumble.

He stooped down, surprised by the glint of gold in the hoofprint he'd just stepped in. It was a ring. He'd seen such ornaments on the hands of lowlanders before. This one was damaged, bent in on itself and flattened.

Perhaps a horse stepped on it, he thought. As he turned the bit of metal over in his hand, he saw that part of it was made to look like a bird.

Lhel appeared ahead of him in the road, waving for him to follow. *Hurry,* she whispered on the night breeze. *Hurry, or you will be too late.*

In the distance the road divided like a river around a rock. One way went along the cliffs to the east. The other way was narrower, and headed toward the dark shape of a forest. Lhel gestured in that direction and he was glad. It would be good to be among trees again.

Chapter 25

Caliel and Barieus fell silent as the night dragged on. Lutha didn't know if they were asleep or not and didn't have the heart to disturb them.

Pain was a good distraction, or perhaps he really was brave, for he couldn't muster much fear. Perhaps that would come later, when he was climbing the gibbet? He tried to picture his own head on a pike, beside those already rotting on the battlements, but felt nothing but a numb disinterest. When he imagined the others dead, though, especially Barieus, it broke his heart.

He had no idea how close dawn was when he heard a laugh and the murmur of voices, then a soft thud against the door. He lay very still, like a rabbit frozen in front of a fox.

A moment later he heard the grating of the door bar. Fear found him then, as the door swung open with a small creak of hinges.

It was still dark outside and the guards had no torches. Lutha could make out nothing more than the indistinct outline of a smallish figure standing there.

"Who is it?" Lutha demanded, throat so dry he could scarcely get the words out.

"A friend." Lutha didn't recognize the whispered voice, but it sounded like a young man. "Get up, all of you. Hurry!"

Lutha struggled painfully to his knees. There was a faint rattle, then the sudden brightness of a small, shuttered lantern. A fair-haired young man stood holding it, and a bundle of clothing.

"Hurry, put this on," he urged, shaking out his bundle and handing them each a shirt and plain cloak. He looked down at Caliel and gasped. Caliel hadn't stirred. His back was black with dried blood and raw wounds.

"Who are you? Why are you doing this?" Lutha whispered, gingerly pulling on the shirt.

"A friend of the queen's," the young man replied impatiently. "She'd be very unhappy if you died. Please, hurry before someone comes."

"Caliel, wake up," Lutha urged softly, shaking him by the foot.

Caliel groaned. Barely conscious, he was too weak and disoriented to stand by himself. With the stranger's help, Lutha and Barieus got him on his feet. His skin was hot and dry, and he let out another ragged groan when the stranger draped the cloak around him. "What—What's happening?"

"I'm getting you out of here before Korin hangs three more good men," the stranger told him. He shuttered the lantern again and opened the door a crack to peer out. "Clear. Go now. The guard is about to change."

"No, can't!" Caliel muttered, confused. "Won't desert—"

Lutha tightened his grip around him. "Please, Cal, don't fight us. We're helping you."

Between the three of them they managed to get him out the door. The yard lay in shadow, the torch by the door extinguished, but Lutha could make out two prone forms on the ground. He wondered how this slight young man had overpowered them, and if one of them was the man who'd spoken kindly to him before. He hoped not.

Keeping to the shadows and avoiding the guards stationed at the main gate, they made it to a small postern gate on the west side of the wall. Another guard lay dead or unconscious there.

"There was no way to get horses for you, so you'll have to get him away on foot as well as you can. Take the path along the cliffs and stay clear of the encampments. If you hear anyone coming after you, you can hide—or jump."

Lutha was less shocked by the advice than he might have been a few days ago. "At least tell me your name."

The fellow hesitated, and then whispered, "I'm Eyoli. Please tell Tamír that I'm still here, and will get word out as soon as I can. Go on now, hurry! Steal horses if you can find them, but get from here before the sun comes up."

With that, Eyoli all but shoved them through the postern and closed the door after them before Lutha thought to thank him.

The outer walls reached almost to the cliffs. A narrow strip of grassy, uneven land lay below, and in the starlight a well-worn goat path showed in a pale line, winding away between the rocks and hummocks. Not far away lay the outer watch fires of the southern encampment. Lutha squinted around in the darkness, praying they didn't meet anyone on this trail so late at night. They were in no shape to run or fight.

They had to all but carry Caliel—not an easy task. He wasn't heavy, but he was taller than either of them and half-dead on his feet. Lutha could feel the warmth of blood soaking through the cloak under his arm and running down his own back as the effort pulled the lash cuts open again. By sheer determination, they managed it; but Lutha scarcely dared breathe, expecting an outcry from above or the angry hiss of arrows.

But luck was with them, it seemed. They got away from the keep and met no one on the trail. Carefully skirting the outlying tents, they followed it for a mile or so, resting often as their strength threatened to give out and Caliel drifted in and out of consciousness. When they were past the last of the pickets, they cut across to the road leading into the small forest in the distance.

Lutha was in terrible pain and had had no water in nearly a day. He felt increasingly light-headed as they went along, and Barieus was in no better condition.

"What are we going to do?" Barieus whispered, voice filled with pain and fear. The trees still seemed very far away and the first hint of dawn was visible on the eastern horizon.

"To Tobin," Caliel rasped, lurching deliriously along between them. "We must—we have to find out—"

"Yes." This would mark them as traitors for sure, but their lives weren't worth a lead sester if Korin caught them. *Ah well, he can only hang us once.*

Still, he found himself looking across Caliel's shoulder at Barieus. They'd known each other since birth. If anything more happened to Barieus because of him—

Barieus caught him looking and rasped out, "Don't say it. I go where you go."

Lutha grinned to hide his own relief. Atyion was a very long way off. He wasn't certain they could even make it to the forest ahead.

There were no steadings or villages on this stretch of the isthmus, nowhere to steal a horse. As dawn slowly lit the sky, they struggled on, and finally managed to get Caliel into the cover of the trees as the first bright edge of the sun appeared over the sea. A narrow dirt road wound away into the dark wood. Brambles and cane berry bushes lined the road, too thick to get through. For now at least they had to keep to the road.

The birds woke around them and sang to welcome the new day, their calls mingling with the sigh of a freshening breeze through the leaves overhead.

They didn't hear the sound of horses until the riders were quite close.

"They're right behind us!" Barieus moaned, staggering and nearly dropping Cal as he looked back over his shoulder.

Despair overwhelmed Lutha. They couldn't escape, except by hiding, and if the riders were from the keep, they were probably being guided by the same wizardry that had found Cal so quickly.

"Leave me. Run for it," Caliel mumbled, struggling weakly in their grasp.

"We won't leave you." Lutha looked in vain for some sort of cover.

"Don't be stupid!" Caliel groaned, sinking to the ground.

They could hear the jingle of harness clearly now, and the staccato beat of hooves. "Bilairy's balls, there's at least a score," Barieus said.

"Help me get him off the road," Lutha ordered, trying to drag Caliel's limp body into the brambles.

"Too late!" Barieus moaned.

The sound of the horses was louder, drowning out the early birdsong. They could see the glint of metal through the trees.

Suddenly they were startled by the strangest sound they'd ever heard. It was close by and seemed to come from all sides at once. To Lutha it sounded like the combination of a bullfrog's croak and a heron's call, but blended and drawn out in a weird pulsing drone.

He and Barieus closed in to protect Caliel from this new threat. The sound grew louder, rising and falling, and making the hair on the backs of their necks stand up.

The horsemen rounded the bend and came on hard in a pack. There was a wizard in the front rank, his white robe unmistakable. Lutha and Barieus tried to drag Caliel into a bramble brake, but it was so thick they couldn't get through. Huddled there, thorns piercing painfully through the backs of their cloaks, Lutha crouched over Caliel.

The riders thundered past, some of them so close Lutha could have reached out and touched their boots. Not one of them spared a glance for the ragged fugitives watching incredulously as they all but rode them down.

The weird drone went on until the last rider had disappeared around another bend and the last jingle of harness had faded in the distance, then stopped as abruptly as it had begun. In its wake Lutha could hear the cries of the gulls and the hammering of a lone woodpecker.

Caliel was awake again, and shuddering with exhaustion. His wounds had opened; dark patches of blood and sweat stuck the coarse material to his back.

"What in the name of all the Four just happened?" whispered Barieus.

"Your guess is as good as mine," Lutha muttered.

A moment later they all heard the unmistakable sound of footsteps in the forest beyond the bramble brake. Whoever it was made no attempt at stealth. Along with the loud, careless snapping of twigs underfoot, the traveler was whistling.

A moment later a dark little man appeared out of the brambles in the road behind them. He had a small sack strung over one shoulder and was dressed in the long, belted tunic and ragged leggings of a peasant farmer. He didn't appear to be armed, apart from a long sheath knife at his belt and the odd-looking staff he carried over his other shoulder. It was about a yard and a half long, and covered with all sorts of designs. It seemed overly ornate for a weapon and too thick for a quarterstaff.

As he came closer, Lutha realized this was no Skalan. The man's wild, black hair hung in a mass of coarse curls past his shoulders. That, together with his dark, nearly black eyes marked him as a Zengati. Lutha watched him warily, trying to tell if he was facing friend or foe.

The fellow must have guessed what was on Lutha's mind. He stopped a few yards away, balanced his staff in the crook of one arm, and held both hands out to show that they were empty.

Then he smiled and said, in a thickly accented voice, "Friends, you need help."

Now Lutha could see that what he'd taken for a staff was a wooden horn of some sort. The man wore a necklace made of decorated animal teeth on a leather thong, and bracelets of the same design.

"What do you want with us?" he demanded.

The man gave him a puzzled look. "Friend." He pointed in the direction Niryn's men had gone. "I help, yes? They gone."

"That noise, you mean? You did that?" asked Barieus.

The man raised his horn for the others to see, then puffed his cheeks out and set his lips to the top of it. There was a sort of broad mouthpiece made of a ring of wax. A throbbing blat issued from the other end. He made a few more of those odd noises, like a piper warming up his instrument, then the sound changed and settled into the deep drone they'd heard before. Lutha found his gaze drawn to the man's feet as he listened. They were very dirty and callused, as if he'd never worn boots. His hands were grubby, too, but less so, and the nails were carefully trimmed. There were bits of dead leaves and twigs caught in his hair.

The music was as odd as the man, and there was no question that this is what they'd heard before.

"It's magic, isn't it?" Barieus exclaimed. "You're a wizard!"

The man stopped playing and nodded. "They don't hear, those riders. Don't see."

Lutha laughed outright. "That's some good magic. Thank you!"

He started forward to clasp hands with their savior, but Caliel caught his arm. "No, Lutha! Don't you see?" he gasped. "He's a witch!"

Lutha froze. He'd have been less shocked to encounter a centaur mage, come down from the Nimra Mountains. They were more commonly met than hill witches, and a good deal more welcome. "Is that true?"

"Witch, yes. I Mahti." He touched his chest, as if Lutha might not understand. "Maaaah-teee? Retha'noi. What you call *'heeel fok'.*"

"Hill folk," Caliel grated out. "Don't trust him—Probably scouting for a raid."

Mahti snorted and sat down cross-legged on the dusty road. "No raid." He walked two fingers across the ground. "Walk long days."

"You're on a journey?" asked Lutha, intrigued in spite of Caliel's reaction.

"Long walking, this 'joor-nay'?"

"Yes. Many days."

Mahti nodded happily. "Joor-nay."

"Why?" Caliel demanded.

"Watch for you."

The three Skalans exchanged skeptical glances.

Mahti dug into a greasy pouch at his belt, popped something dark and wizened into his mouth, and began to chew loudly. He offered the pouch to the rest of them and smirked when it was quickly declined. "See you in my dream song—" He paused and held up two dirty fingers. "These nights."

"Two nights ago?"

He held up three fingers and pointed at each of them. "See you, and you, and you. And I find this."

He dug into another small pouch and held out a bent gold ring. Caliel stared at it. "That—that's mine. I lost it when they caught me."

Mahti leaned over and placed it in the dirt in front of Caliel. "I find. I run hard to get here." Mahti held up one bare foot, showing them a few dirt-caked cuts in the thickly callused sole. "You run, too, from friend who has—" He paused again, searching for the right word, then looked sadly at Caliel. "Your friend, he who turns his face away."

Caliel's eyes went wide.

Mahti shook his head, then touched a hand to his chest above his heart again. "You have pain from that friend."

"Shut your mouth, witch."

"Cal, don't be rude," Lutha murmured. "He's only speaking the truth."

"I don't need to hear it from the likes of him," Caliel shot back. "It's just some trick, anyway. Why don't you ask him what he wants?"

"I tell you," Mahti replied. "You my guides."

"Guides? To what?" asked Lutha.

Mahti shrugged, then cocked his head at Caliel and frowned. "First I heal. Friend who turn face away hurt you."

Caliel leaned back, too weak to do more. But Mahti didn't try to approach him. He didn't move at all, except to raise his horn to his lips. The open end rested on the ground in front of him, pointing at Caliel. Puffing out his cheeks again, he warmed the horn.

"Stop him!" Caliel tried to struggle away, eyes fixed on the horn as if he expected it to spew fire.

Mahti ignored his protests. Fitting the horn more comfortably against his mouth, he began the spell drone. To Lutha's horror, black lines appeared on the man's skin as he played, crawling like centipedes across his skin to form intricate, barbaric patterns of lines and circles.

"You heard him. He doesn't want your magic!" Barieus cried, jumping between the witch and Caliel. Lutha did the same, ready to fend off who knew what sort of attack.

Mahti glanced up at them, amusement clear in his eyes, and the horn made a rude, laughing sound. Then the tone changed to a completely different sort of sound.

It began with a drone, but immediately fell to a deeper, softer sound. The symbols completely covered his face, hands, and arms now, and the exposed skin of his chest, too. It reminded Lutha of the markings he'd seen on Khatme people, but these markings were different, more angular and crude. The designs etched into the animal teeth and fangs that decorated his neck and wrists were the same. Barbaric; there was no other word for it. The sight of that reminded him of all the gruesome tales he'd heard of the hill folk and their magic.

Yet in spite of his instinctive alarm, the sounds coming from the horn were strangely soothing. Lutha slowly succumbed to its mesmerizing effect and felt his eyelids grow heavy. On some level he realized that he was bespelled but was helpless to resist. Barieus was blinking and wavering where he stood. Caliel was still panting, but his eyes had fluttered shut.

The buzzing went on for a few minutes, and to Lutha's surprise, he found himself sitting on the ground beside Caliel, urging him to lie down and rest his head on his thigh. Caliel stretched out on his side, grimacing as the lacerations on his back pulled and caught on his bloodstained cloak.

The horn sound had shifted again without Lutha even noticing. Now it was lighter and higher, quick little bursts of sound followed by long trills. Caliel sighed and went limp against him. Lutha couldn't tell if he'd fallen asleep or fainted, but his breathing was easier than it had been. He looked over at Barieus; the squire was fast asleep where he sat, a peaceful smile on his lips.

Lutha fought off sleep and kept guard over the others, watching the witch with a mix of suspicion and wonder. He might look dirty and ordinary, but clearly he was a man of power. He'd gained control over the three of them with nothing more than this strange music, if you could call it that.

Stranger still was the way it seemed to draw the pain from Lutha's back. His skin itched and burned, but the worst of the pain from the lash cuts grew muted, almost bearable.

The sound died away at last and Mahti came over and rested a hand on Caliel's brow for a moment, then nodded. "Good. He sleep. I come back."

The witch left his bundle on the ground but took the horn with him as he wandered off into the trees across the road. The brambles there looked as thick as the ones that had stymied Lutha, but the witch passed through easily and disappeared into the trees beyond.

Now that the spell was broken, Lutha was chagrined at how easily they'd been snared. Not wanting to wake Caliel, he threw a pebble at Barieus to wake him.

The boy started and yawned. "I was dreaming. I thought—" He looked blearily around and spied the witch's bag. "Oh. Oh!" He leaped to his feet. "Where is he? What did he do to Cal?"

"Quiet. Let him sleep," Lutha whispered.

Barieus started to object, then a look of utter amazement spread across his face. "My back!"

"I know. Mine, too." He gently shifted his leg out from under Caliel's head and tucked his own cloak under his friend's head in its place. Standing, he lifted Barieus' cloak and shirt to examine his back. It didn't look much better, but there was no fresh blood. "I don't know what he did, but Caliel is resting easier for it. Mahti said he was going to heal him. Maybe he did?"

"He could be some kind of drysian."

"I don't know. The stories I heard never said anything about witches doing healing. What he did, magicking the ones chasing us; that's more like what I'd expect."

"What do you think he meant about us guiding him somewhere?" asked Barieus, looking around nervously for the man.

"I don't know." It could be that Cal was right about him and it was some kind of trick, but if so, why would he help them?

"You think he saw us in a dream, like he said?"

Lutha shrugged. If the man was a witch, then anything was possible, he supposed. "Maybe he's a madman and wandered off from his own kind. He acts a bit crazy."

A snort of laughter made them both jump and turn.

Mahti emerged from the brambles with a handful of small plants and squatted beside Caliel. Cal didn't wake as

Mahti rolled him gently onto his stomach and lifted the filthy cloak away from his back. The lacerations had scabbed and broken open again many times in the night, and were already red and swollen.

Mahti opened his bag and pulled out a wrinkled homespun shirt. He tossed it to Lutha, along with his knife. "Make to put on," he ordered, clearly intending for him to make bandages.

While Lutha cut up the shirt, Mahti took something else from his bag and began chewing it as he rubbed the young plants briskly between his palms. After a moment he spat a dark juice into the crushed leaves and kneaded it all together with some water from a flask, then began patting the crude poultice onto Caliel's wounds.

"Are you a drysian?" Barieus asked.

Mahti shook his head. "Witch."

"Well, at least he makes no bones about it," muttered Lutha.

Mahti picked up on the tone of the words and raised an eyebrow at him as he finished bandaging Caliel's back and ribs. "My people? We scare our babies with stories of *you*." He looked down at Cal and wrinkled his nose in disgust. "No Retha'noi do this." He finished with Caliel's back, then touched the swollen bruises over the damaged ribs. "I mend bone now. Take out sick water."

"What's that mean?" Barieus asked.

"I think he means pus," said Lutha. "And you heal with that, don't you?" Lutha pointed at the horn lying next to them on the ground.

"Yes. Oo'lu."

"And that's what you used to hide us earlier?"

"Yes. Witch men Retha'noi all play oo'lu for their magic."

"I've heard stories of your kind using them in battle."

Mahti just turned back to tending Caliel. Lutha exchanged a worried look with Barieus. The squire had noticed the lack of answer, too.

"We appreciate what you've done for our friend. What payment do you require?" asked Lutha.

"Payment?" Mahti looked amused.

"You helped us, so we give you something in return?"

"I tell you. You guide me when your friend can joornay."

"Oh, so we're back to that?" Lutha sighed. "Where do you want to go?"

"Where you go."

"No! I'm asking where it is you want us to guide *you*. Not that it matters. We are already going somewhere. I don't have time to wander off with you."

It was impossible to know how much of this the hill man understood, but he nodded happily. "You guide."

Barieus chuckled.

"Fine, we guide," Lutha muttered. "Just don't complain to me if we don't end up where you intended!"

Chapter 26

Thanks to her wizards and spies, Tamír now knew the hearts of six nobles who had estates within a few days' ride of Atyion. Four were against her, all well within striking distance if they chose to make trouble.

This was cause for concern. Tamír's army still numbered less than ten thousand warriors, and many were untrained farmers and merchants' sons and daughters. Disenchanted nobles who'd fled Korin's northern court brought reports of twice that number. If Korin moved in force, Tamír would have to rely on the strong walls and carefully stocked supplies of her new capital.

Something had to be done.

She met with her generals and wizards around the great round table in the map chamber. This room had been used since the time of the castle's founding to plan battles. Racks of maps and sea charts filled the walls. In quiet moments Tamír had searched through the excellent collection, finding many that bore notations in her father's hand.

At the moment Lytia was reading out castle inventories of armaments, and the number of various kinds of craftsmen. Tamír tried hard to concentrate on the lists of farriers and armor makers, but her mind wandered. It was hot and still today, and the steady drone of the cicadas made her eyelids heavy. She was sweating in her summer gown. It was close to her moon time again, too, and the heat seemed to bother her more. Or maybe it was these wretched long skirts!

She drifted over to a large open window, trying to cool

herself with a delicate sandalwood-and-ivory fan. She'd
found a box of them in one of the wardrobes in her dressing room and decided to put them to use. She'd felt a bit
odd at first, as she did with most feminine accoutrements,
but the scented breeze it created more than made up for
any embarrassment. No one seemed to think it odd.

With no battles to fight, she wore dresses most of the
time. Lytia had set the castle seamstresses to making over
her mother's gowns into the newer fashion. This one, light
blue linen trimmed with silver stitching, had been one of
Princess Ariani's favorite summer riding habits. Looking at
herself in the mirror, Tamír thought of that night during her
first visit here, when she'd snuck in and put on her
mother's cloak, trying to imagine what she'd look like as a
girl.

The sound of childish laughter from the garden below
caught her attention. Some of Arkoniel's youngest wizards
were splashing in a fountain with some of the castle children. A few others were sitting on the grass, playing with
some kittens. She envied them. Only last summer she and
her friends would have been off swimming naked in the
sea on a day like this, or lying in a shady corner somewhere with their shirts off.

Illardi broke in on her reverie. "Majesty? What do you
think?"

She sighed and walked back to the table. "I was woolgathering. About what?"

Nyanis had another map spread out. On it Tamír's
known allies were marked with blue ink, those loyal to
Korin in red, and those whose intentions remained un-
known in green. The red and green marks outnumbered
the blue and were heavily concentrated to the north,
where some of the largest holdings lay. The blue marks to
the south were mostly towns and the holdings of lesser
lords and knights.

"You've shown great forbearance, Majesty," Illardi

said. "It's time to show that the true queen has power and a limit to her patience."

"I'd start here, with Lord Erian," Nyanis advised, pointing to a location two days' ride north. "He has a strong keep, but less than two hundred warriors, and his holding was hard hit by the famine. He shouldn't be able to hold out long in a siege. Send a company up there and make an example of him. The same tactic can be used against Duke Zygas and Lady Alna. Word will soon spread."

"So it's come to this finally, has it? Skalans fighting Skalans. Still, if I am to be accepted as a warrior queen, then I must be seen acting like one."

"No, Majesty. Because you are queen, you must let your captains and generals take care of small fish like these," Illardi explained.

"What? Stay here while you go fight?"

"He's right, I'm afraid," said Nikides. "These small holdings are below your notice. I'll draft an ultimatum to be read out at the gates. That will give them a chance to change their minds if they think better of it."

"What did I train for, then?"

"To lead battles, not skirmishes," said Tharin. "Your father and I carried out these little fights in the king's name. He didn't have to be there. We were his arm and his will." He smiled at her obvious disappointment. "You've already proven yourself, Tamír, from your very first fight. Word of your victories against the Plenimarans is spreading. Besides, as you say, this is Skalan against Skalan. Better you keep your hands clean. Let your warriors go make an example of these upstarts. Perhaps that will be enough for others, especially those who remain undeclared."

Tamír suddenly realized that she'd been using the fan rather emphatically. Bilairy's balls, no wonder they were telling her to stay home, standing here in a dress like some fluttery courtier! "We'll talk about this more after lunch," she muttered. She was hungry, but if she didn't get out of this dress and bathe, she was going to go mad.

The others bowed and took their leave, except Ki and Tharin.

"Could I have a word, Majesty?" Tharin murmured before she could escape, giving her a look that said it was important. "Alone?"

She sighed. "Oh, all right. But let's talk in the garden. It will be cooler there. Ki, have Baldus order a cold tub in my room, would you? I'll eat with you shortly."

Ki shook his head. "That's your third bath this week. People will take you for Aurënfaie if you keep this up."

The sun had moved behind the west tower and there was a breath of a breeze. Patterned beds of flowers scented the air, and the tinkling of fountains mingled with the droning of bees busy among the blossoms.

Tharin seemed glad of the shade, too. He dressed like a proper courtier here, his tunic and short cape somber in tone but of a fine cut and trimmed with embroidery. A duke at last, he wore the gold chain and signet of his rank, and tied his hair back with a black silk ribbon instead of a greasy leather cord, but he cared no more for titles and fine things than he ever had. And he remained at her side, unmovable as a barnacle on a rock and her most trusted source of counsel.

She could tell he had something on his mind now as they strolled along under a line of flowering trees. There were courtiers and servants all around, though, and he waited until they'd reached the relative seclusion of a thickly overgrown grape arbor to speak.

Dappled shade played over his face as he sat down on the wooden bench. "You may not like what I have to say."

"You know I'll listen, though." She sat down and pulled her skirt up over her knees to cool her legs. Ringtail emerged from a clump of flowering roses and jumped into her lap. She scratched his ears, then winced as he kneaded sharp claws into her thigh. "Go on, then. What is it?"

"It's about Ki. The way things are now? It's not good for him."

That caught her off guard. She'd expected talk of war. "Has he said something to you?"

"No, and he wouldn't thank me for interfering if he knew. But I've been at court longer than either of you, and I don't like how the talk is running. He's already labeled as your favorite, and more. That breeds jealousy, and that can lead to trouble for both of you." He paused, plucking a few ripe grapes and passing some to her. "I'm guessing your feelings for him haven't changed?"

She ducked her head, blushing, and said nothing. They had; they were stronger than ever.

"I know you try to hide it, but the mere fact that you keep him so close is enough for the gossips— That and the fact that he's not highborn."

"You know I don't care about that!"

"No, but you're at court now, and things are as they are; too many people with too much time to wonder." He ate a grape, chewing slowly. "But there's more to it than that. You've got him acting like a lady-in-waiting. That's no position for a warrior."

"I do not!" But Tharin's words stung in a way that told her he was right. "He's my squire. If I was still a boy, they wouldn't be talking like that, would they?"

"People were talking before. But that's neither here nor there. You are a young queen, and he's a squire from a family no one knows of except as rough characters. When you were just a prince and still a child, it didn't matter as much. Things have changed, and they're never going back to what they were."

"What would you have me do? I don't want Ki suffering on my account, but I can't just send him away." When Tharin said nothing, she bridled angrily. "No, I won't do that, not for anyone!"

"I'm not saying discharge him, but have a care for his feelings, too. Ki's a fine warrior and a smart young man. If he'd risen under some other lord—Jorvai say, like his sister—then he'd be praised for his ability. As it stands now, no matter what he does, some will see it as your favor rather than him rising on his own merits."

"And Ki's said nothing about all this to you?"

"No. As long as you want him at your side, he'll be there, no matter what's made of it. But is this what you want for him?"

"Of course it isn't! I wish— Oh, Tharin, why does it have to be so damn difficult? Ki's changed, too, and I've changed and—"

Tharin regarded her knowingly. "You want him for your consort, don't you?"

Tamír reddened miserably. "Illardi and Nik both say I must have one soon, and that I have to think about proving that I can provide an heir." Her stomach tightened in fear at the thought of what *that* meant. "It's bad enough, thinking of—that, but I can't imagine being with anyone but him! I love him, Tharin! I always have. But he doesn't love me. Not that way."

"Has he said so?"

"He doesn't have to. He still treats me like a boy most of the time."

"Sometimes when we're so close to someone all the time, we can't really see them anymore. Perhaps what you both need is a bit of distance."

"Then you are saying I should send him away?"

"No, I'm thinking of what Nyanis was saying. Ki needs to prove himself. He's trained to fight and lead, just as you are. Have him take a force of his own against some of those lords."

"But won't people still say that he got his commission because of me?"

"When a princess becomes a queen, her Companions almost always become her commanders and councilors, like your father and Erius. Once Ki leads and wins on his own, that will be to his credit."

Tamír nibbled a grape as she considered this. It snapped between her teeth, flooding her mouth with sweet juice. "He won't like it."

"Doesn't matter if he does or not. He's your liegeman, and honor-bound to obey your orders. Your father would be telling you the same if he were here now."

Tamír popped another grape into her mouth. The more she thought about it, the more it made sense. "If I make him a commander, then he can't be just my squire anymore. He's been fighting me on that, but he'll have to accept a title. He's more stubborn than you on that account. Oh, but wait. Does this mean I have to take another squire in his place?"

"No. You don't need one around here, and when you do go into battle he'll ride with you, as I did with your father."

Tamír grinned. "That's all right, then! Let's go tell him."

Ki was in her chamber, helping Baldus oversee the filling of the silver-lined tub. Tamír sighed inwardly at the sight. Tharin was right; she had reduced him to duties far below his worth.

"That's enough," she told the girls with the buckets though the tub was scarcely a quarter full. "You can leave us. You too, Baldus. Go play with your friends. I don't need you until after supper."

The boy bowed and dashed off. Ki moved to follow, assuming she was going to bathe.

"No, wait. We have something to talk to you about."

"Oh?" Ki cast a curious look at Tharin.

"Well, I think—And Tharin agrees . . ." It was much harder than she'd expected, with him giving her that suspicious look. "I've decided to give you a commission."

Ki folded his arms and arched an eyebrow. "What sort of commission, exactly?"

"You'll go after these local lords for me. You could

take a company from the garrison and support Jorvai for starters, and then—"

Ki bridled at once. "You're sending me away?"

"No, of course not! You shouldn't be gone more than a few weeks, barring sieges. Listen, Ki, I trust you. And since I can't go out on these raids, I need someone I trust to do it for me. Besides, I need a few commanders who aren't old enough to be my grandfather."

Ki said nothing, but she saw interest warring with that stubborn gleam in his eye.

"You can take Lynx with you, and the men from Alestun. They know you and they'll set an example for the others."

"I see." He shot another look at Tharin and shrugged. "Thank you. I'm honored." Then, just as she'd expected, his eyes narrowed again. "Will you be replacing me with another squire?"

"Never, Ki. When I go to battle, you'll be at my side, I promise. Tharin will stay with me while you're gone. Hell, he's worse than a burr on a wool sock."

Tharin chuckled. "I am that. Don't worry, Ki. You know I'll look after her for you. It's time you showed your mettle."

Tamír punched Ki lightly on the shoulder. "You'll have all the fun, while I have to stay here—in a dress!"

Chapter 27

For Ki, the next three days passed too quickly, and he found himself torn between the excitement of his first command and guilt over leaving Tamír. He spent the days seeing to the equipage of his company and laying plans with Jorvai for the first confrontation, in which he would assist. In the evenings, though, he kept close to Tamír, and looked for some regret in her eyes, but she seemed glad for him and anxious to have him prove himself.

The night before he was to leave, he lingered behind in her chamber after the others had withdrawn. As they sat by the open window, sipping the night's last wine and listening to the sounds of the crickets, he found himself caught by the sight of her. She was gazing pensively out at the stars, one slender finger slowly tracing the raised pattern on her silver mazer. She wore a gown of dark red embroidered with golden vines tonight and the color suited her. The candlelight softened her features and caught the sheen of her hair as it lay loose over her shoulders and breast.

In that moment Ki lost sight of Tobin, as he never had before. Her lips looked as soft as any he'd ever kissed, her cheeks smooth as a maiden's, not a beardless boy's. In this light she looked almost fragile. It was as if he were seeing her for the very first time.

Then she turned and raised an eyebrow at him in a way he'd seen a thousand times before, and there was Tobin again, gazing at him with the same eyes as ever.

"What's wrong, didn't your dinner agree with you?"

He gave her a sheepish smile. "I was just thinking—"

He paused, heart racing. "I wish you were coming with me tomorrow."

"Me, too." Her wry smile was Tobin's, too. "Promise me you'll—" Now she paused and looked embarrassed. "Well, don't have so much fun you get yourself killed."

"I'll do my best not to. Jorvai thinks most of them will give up without a fight anyway, once they see that you are willing to move against them. I may not have my sword out of its scabbard at all."

"I don't know which to wish you: safety or an honorable fight. In case you do fight? Well, I made you this." She reached into her sleeve and took out a golden disk an inch or so across and gave it to him. On it in a raised design was a stylized owl with wings outstretched, holding a crescent moon in its talons. "The idea came to me a few days ago. I made it in wax and had it cast in the village."

"It's beautiful! It's good to see you making things again." Ki untied the leather cord around his neck and slid the charm on to dangle beside the carved horse. "Now I have both gods on my side."

"That was the idea."

Rising, she held out her hand. He stood and clasped with her. "Sakor's fire, Ki, and Illior's light to guide you."

Her hand was warm in his, the palm roughened from the hilt of a sword, the fingers strong and callused from the bowstring. He pulled her into his arms and hugged her tight, wishing he knew his own heart. She hugged him back, and when they stepped apart again he thought he caught a glimpse of his own confusion in her eyes. Before he could be sure, though, she turned away and reached for her cup again. "It's late. You should get some rest while you can."

"I guess so." She still wasn't looking at him. Had he hurt her somehow? "I—I could stay a bit longer."

She smiled back at him and shook her head. "Don't be silly. Go on and get your rest. I'll be there to see you off. Good night, Ki."

He could think of nothing more to say, or even what he wanted to say. "Thank you for my commission," he said at last. "I'll make you proud."

"I know you will."

"Well—good night."

His own door was only a dozen paces from Tamír's, but it seemed a mile by the time he gained his room. He was startled to find Tharin there, standing at the rack that held Ki's armor.

"There you are. Since you don't have a squire of your own, I thought I'd make a last inspection of your arms." Tharin paused, looking at him oddly. "What's the matter with you?"

"Nothing!" Ki exclaimed quickly.

Too quickly from the way Tharin's eyes narrowed. "You were just with Tamír?"

"Yes. I wanted to—to thank her, and she's worried about me and—" He faltered to a halt.

Tharin regarded him in silence for moment, then just shook his head.

*T*amír spent a sleepless night. Every time she closed her eyes she saw the anguished look she'd caught on Ki's face, and the way it had felt when he embraced her. *He still doesn't know what to make of me, and neither do I!*

Before dawn she bathed at the washstand and put on a dark gown and a ceremonial breastplate. There was one last thing she meant to do. Tharin and the Companions were waiting outside and fell into step behind her. For the first time, Tamír was achingly aware of Ki's absence at her side, and Lynx, too, who was going off as one of Ki's captains.

"You're really going to do it this time, aren't you?" Nikides asked.

"He can't very well refuse this time," she murmured with a wry smile.

*   *   *

The mounted companies had already formed up when they reached the courtyard, and hundreds of courtiers lined the walls and stairways to see them off.

Jorvai and Ki were there to greet her in full armor. Tamír wished them both luck and said a few words to the captains. Then, trying not to grin, she turned back to Ki. "There's one more thing. Kneel and present your sword."

Ki's eyes widened at that, but he had no choice but to obey.

Tamír drew her own and touched him on the cheek and shoulders. "Before these witnesses, for your years of honest and loyal friendship, and for saving my life more than once, I dub you Lord Kirothieus of Oakmount and Queen's Mercy, and grant you the steading of your birth, as well as the rents, holdings, and main right of the village of Queen's Mercy. In addition, you are granted a founding gift of five thousand gold sesters. May you use it wisely, to the honor of your house and Skala. Rise, Lord Kirothieus, and accept your arms."

Several young women came forward. One held his banner on a standard pole. Two others displayed a tabard. Both showed his new device, laid out by Nikides. The shield was diagonally divided from left to right with the white bar representing legitimate birth. Centered on the bar was a lion skin draped over a stick, to commemorate the first time Ki had risked his life to defend her. She saw him smile at that. The left field was green, with a white tree, for Oakmount. The right was black, with a white tower, for Queen's Mercy. A silver flame cupped by a crescent moon, honoring the two gods, surmounted the design.

"You have been busy, haven't you?" Ki muttered, trying to sound put out, but his shining eyes and reddened cheeks said otherwise. He pulled on the tabard and held his sword up before his face. "The house of Oakmount and Queen's Mercy will ever be your most loyal servants, Majesty."

Tamír took his hand and turned him to face the assembly. "My people, welcome Lord Kirothieus, my friend and my right hand. Honor him as you honor me."

A cheer went up and Ki blushed harder. Tamír clapped him on the shoulder and mouthed, "Be careful."

Ki mounted his horse and fastened his helmet. Jorvai drew his sword and shouted, "For the honor of Skala and the queen!" and his riders took up the cry.

Ki did the same, shouting "For Tamír and Skala!" and a thousand throats behind him took it up.

"I hope you appreciate how jealous I am," Tamír said, when the shouting died down.

"It's your own doing." Jorvai laughed, clapping on his battle-scarred helmet. "Don't worry. Ki and I will keep each other alive if we can and carry the other's ashes if we can't."

"Good. Go show them this 'mad boy in a dress' is not to be trifled with."

They rode first to the large holding of Duke Zygas, a hard-bitten old lord. He had a large stone keep with strong out-lying walls but his wealth lay in his grainfields, which were ripe. He had a few turma of fighters stationed on the road at the outskirts of the holding, but Jorvai and Ki had marched through the night and took them by surprise just after sunrise. Ki led a forward party and quickly dispatched any resistance. Leaving the captains to bring up the foot, Jorvai and the riders rushed on at a gallop to the gates of the keep and sent out a herald under the white banner.

The walls above the earthen moat bristled with archers and gleamed with the reflected light off helms and weapons, but no shaft could be loosed on either side until the herald had spoken and withdrawn.

Zygas' white-and-black banner with its three horses rose above the barbican. A man leaned over and called down angrily, "Who abuses my rights and hospitality in this manner? I recognize only one banner there. Jorvai of

Colath, we have never had bad blood between us. Why are you at my gates as if I were a Plenimaran?"

"The herald speaks for me," Jorvai called back.

"Your grace, I bear a letter from Tamír Ariani Ghërilain, Queen of Skala," the herald announced.

"I know no such queen, but I will honor the white banner. Speak your letter."

"The banners of Lord Jorvai of Colath and Lord Kirothieus of Oakmount and Queen's Mercy fly at your gates, the liegemen of Tamír Ariani Ghërilain, Queen of Skala by right of blood and birth.

"Be it known, Zygas, son of Morten, Duke of Ellsford and Fire River, that by your obdurate and ignoble disloyalty, you have incurred the displeasure of the Crown. If you do not this day desist from such action and ride at once under safe passage to Atyion to swear fealty to the rightful queen, forswearing all other loyalties, then you shall be declared a traitor and stripped forthwith of all titles, lands, rents, and chattels. If you hold your gates against these, the queen's chosen lords, your fields will be burned, your livestock taken, your gates broken, and your house razed. You and your heirs will be taken prisoner and carried forthwith to Atyion to face the queen's justice.

"Queen Tamír, in her wisdom, abjures you to seize the hand of mercy extended today and turn your back on all other erroneous alliances. Delivered this day by my hand."

A lengthy pause followed. Ki craned his neck, trying to make out his opponent's face, but Zygas had stepped away from the battlements.

"What do you think?" he said quietly to Jorvai as they sat their horses, waiting.

"Erius guested here often, and Zygas fought for him across the sea. I don't know that he knows any more about Korin than he does Tamír, though."

They sat there as the sun rose higher and the air grew warm. Sweating in his armor and tabard, Ki listened to the barking of dogs and bleating of sheep from beyond the keep walls. The drawbridge across the moat was pulled up to shield the doors. It was fashioned of thick timbers, and studded with brass bosses the size of bucklers. It would probably take catapults and fire to breach the place, if it came to that.

The shadows cast by his horse's legs had clocked nearly an hour's passage before they heard the sound of riders coming around the keep from the left at a gallop. Zygas had a back door somewhere, and had used it to ride out.

He was mounted on a tall bay warhorse, but wore no armor. Instead, he was accompanied by his own herald under a sacred banner. He galloped up to them, head high, and reined in. He nodded to Jorvai, then gave Ki a cold, appraising look. "I don't know you."

"Allow me to present Lord Kirothieus. He's the queen's man, same as I am," Jorvai told him. "Well, what do you say? You haven't gone north, so perhaps you're having a few doubts?"

"You believe this nonsense about a boy turning into a girl, do you?"

"I saw it with my own eyes, and you've never known me for a liar, have you? It happened on the very steps of Atyion castle. Lord Kirothieus has been friend and squire to her since they were both younglings."

"On my honor, Your Grace, it is true," Ki said.

Zygas snorted at that. "On the honor of a stripling lord raised by the so-called girl queen, eh?"

"You have only to come to Atyion and see for yourself. Would you call the priest of Afra a liar to his face, as well?" Ki replied evenly. He glanced up at the battlements again. "I don't see Korin's banner flying there, only your own. Are you waiting to see them clash, then back the winner?"

"You watch your tongue, you young upstart!"

"He's right, Zygas," Jorvai chided. "I never put you down as anything but a solid man, but it seems you're growing indecisive in your old age."

The duke glared at them both for a moment, then shook his head. "I've waited months for Korin to march and defend his throne, but he sends me nothing but excuses. Instead here you two are. You were always an honest fellow, Jorvai. Can I trust this offer of hers?"

"You can trust her to accept your fealty if you ride today, just as you can trust us to set fire to every field and byre and cottage the moment you say otherwise."

"Aye, and you've brought a force to do it, too, haven't you?" Zygas sighed. "And if I say that I will go, to see for myself?"

"Not good enough. If you take the right path and offer fealty, I'm to tell you to ride at once under the protection of my own men, and that you must take your wife and children with you. You have a son on his own lands now, as I recall, and a few younger ones still under the roof?"

"She requires hostages, does she?"

"That's for her to say when you get there. You shouldn't have waited so long. It's only her kind heart that's kept your lands untouched today, but her patience has reached its end. Decide now, and let's get on with it."

Zygas looked around at the fields and steadings that lay beyond the line of armed riders. In the distance the foot soldiers were coming on fast, raising the dust from the road as they jogged along with weapons ready. "So she really is the princess' daughter, hidden all this time?"

"That she is. You'll see Ariani in her. It's clear as day. The lords of the southlands are flocking to her. Nyanis is with her, and Kyman. You don't think them fools, do you?"

Zygas rubbed a hand over his grizzled beard and sighed. "No, nor you either. If I do go, will she take my lands?"

"That's for her to say when she's seen you," Jorvai replied. "But it's sure as the Maker's rain in spring that she will if you don't."

Ki could see the man warring with himself. At last Zygas said, "I'm to take my little girls, as well? How will I protect them on the road, with no escort of my own? I won't have them abused."

"Tamír would kill anyone who touched them, and so would I," Ki told him. "I have women among my warriors. I'll send some of them as your escort. They won't let anyone touch your girls."

Zygas took one more look around at the armed fighters massed at his gate. "Very well, but my curse will be on all of you and your queen if this is a trick."

"Tamír wants nothing from you but your loyalty," Ki assured him.

Zygas gave them a resigned bow. "If this queen of yours is as merciful as you paint her, then perhaps she's worth backing, rightful or not."

He rode off the way he'd come and Ki let out a pent-up breath. "That wasn't so hard."

Jorvai chuckled darkly and pointed back at their forces. "That's a persuasive argument. So, you've seen how it's done. I hope you find Lady Alna as amenable."

Unfortunately, she was not. Ki and his company marched three days through sweltering heat, only to find the village deserted, the fields harvested, and the noblewoman ready and waiting.

She was a widow of middling years, with long yellow hair and a proud, hard face. She rode out, as Zygas had, but listened with thinly veiled impatience as the herald read out his missive.

"Lies or necromancy? Which is it, my lord?" she sneered, clearly less than impressed by Ki. "I have a thousand men-at-arms behind my walls and my grain is safe there, too. King Korin has sent assurances that my lands will be expanded and my title protected under his banner. What do I have from your queen, but threats?"

"You were summoned more than once and given every chance to align yourself with the true queen," Ki replied, keeping his temper in check.

She sniffed at that. "True queen! Ariani had no daughters."

"She did and you have heard the tale of her changing, I'm sure."

"Then it's necromancy. Are we to bow down to an overlord backed by dark magic like the Plenimarans do?"

"It wasn't dark magic . . ." Ki began, but she cut him off angrily.

"Half my kin were wizards, free wizards of Skala, boy, and powerful ones. They could not do such magic as you describe."

Ki wasn't about to tell her that a hill witch had done the deed. "You have your choice," he told her. "Go to Atyion with your children now, under safe conduct, or I will not hesitate to carry out my orders."

"Won't you?" Alna took a long look at him. "No, I don't suppose you will. So be it. I was loyal to King Erius and I will not forsake his son." With that she wheeled her horse and rode back to her own gates. Under the rules of parley he had no choice but to watch as they closed heavily after her.

Ki turned to find Lynx and Grannia watching him expectantly. "Grannia, you burn the village. Lynx, bring up the sappers and fire carriers. Show no mercy to anyone carrying a weapon. Those are your orders."

Chapter 28

Tamír's heart leaped at the sight of every herald.

At last the first came in, bearing greetings and apologies from Duke Zygas, now on his way to swear allegiance. He'd been the one most likely to hold out and she took it as a good omen. He and his family arrived a few days later by cart. Tamír received him sternly, but he was so fearful for his children and so earnest in his oath that she gladly upheld his title.

A few days later Jorvai's second herald brought word of another bloodless victory. Lord Erian had come out to surrender the moment Jorvai's force appeared over the horizon, apparently not knowing if it was to Korin or Tamír he was surrendering. Jorvai's letter was disdainful. "'Keep this one well under your thumb. It's the cowardly dog that most often bites.'"

But still no word from Ki. The nights were long, knowing the room next door was empty, and Brother had returned to trouble her dreams again.

At last, on the last day of Shemin, a herald arrived with word that Ki had been victorious and was close behind.

He arrived just after nightfall with his cavalry and came straight to the great hall, flanked by Grannia and Lynx. All three looked tired and grim, and their tabards still carried the dark stains of battle.

"Welcome back," she said, trying to maintain her dignity before the court when all she really wanted was to jump off the dais and hug Ki. "What do you have to report?"

"Majesty, Lord Ynis surrendered and is on his way to you. Lady Alna refused." Ki nodded to Lynx.

Lynx took a leather sack from under his cloak and opened it. Ki reached in and pulled out a woman's head by its bloodstained blond hair.

Tamír did not flinch at the sight of those slack lips and dull, milky eyes, but the sight saddened her. "Mount it on the battlements above the gate, near Solari's remains, with a sign giving her name and crime. Did you kill her, Ki?"

"No, Majesty, she died by her own hand on the fourth day of the siege. She killed her two daughters and her son as well, or had them killed. We found them lying together in her chamber."

Tamír had no doubt that Ki would have done it himself if it had been necessary, but she was secretly relieved that he hadn't had to. In any case, Alna had spared her the trouble of an execution.

"Let the heralds carry the news to every town and holding," she ordered. "Have the town criers spread the word. I have been merciful to those who gave me their loyalty. The traitor was not spared. Lord Kirothieus, you have my thanks, and the gratitude of the land. I hereby grant you all the lands of Lady Alna, in honor of your first victory under your own banner."

She smiled to herself as Ki bowed again. There could be no murmuring about that. Such were the spoils of war.

Instead, it was Ki who complained, as soon as they sat together at the feast that night.

"You didn't have to do that," he grumbled. "You've already saddled me with enough land and rents, as well as a title."

"And now you have men-at-arms and riders of your own to draw on, the next time I need you," Tamír replied happily. "No more taunts of 'grass knight' for you, my lord."

Ki folded his arms, acknowledging defeat. "Just so

long as you let me fight again, I suppose I can bear up under the strain."

"Tell us about your first command!" Una urged. "And you, too, Lynx. How do you like being Ki's captain?"

"It's Ki's story to tell," Lynx demurred modestly, but Tamír caught sight of his squire standing by the kitchen doorway, talking excitedly to Lorin and Hylia.

"I'll make him tell his part, don't worry." Ki laughed. "He and Captain Grannia did me proud."

"Maybe, but you were in the forefront, every step," Lynx pointed out.

Tamír studied Ki's face as he went through the details. The keep had been a strong one, and prepared for a siege. Ki outlined the fight, using bits of bread and dishes to illustrate. He was modest in the telling, giving away much of the credit. He grew grim, though, when he finally came to the moment they'd found Alna and her kin.

"It was just as well," Grannia put in from her place at the lower table. "More honor in that than being hanged for a traitor."

"I wouldn't have harmed her children," Tamír said sadly.

As Ki and the Companions accompanied her back to her room that night, she thought the looks he got from the various courtiers they met along the way were more respectful than they had been before. All the same, she was mindful of prying eyes as she invited him into her chamber.

They looked at each other for a moment. The weeks apart only seemed to have strengthened the awkwardness between them. Tamír sighed and gave him a hug, and he returned it, but it was brief and they quickly moved to the gaming table by the window.

"So, you're a blooded commander now," she said, toying with a carved pawn. "How does it feel?"

Ki smiled as he ran a finger over the lines on the

board. "I didn't like fighting without you there, but otherwise?" He grinned at her, eyes warm again. "Thank you."

"I'm sorry about Alna."

Ki nodded sadly. "It wasn't a very pretty sight. The children's throats were cut. I wonder if the keep will be haunted now?"

"Probably, with those kinds of deaths."

"Well, I don't mean to live there. You're not going to force me, are you?"

"No, I want you here," she said, then cursed herself for blushing. "But now that you're back, with no fighting to do, won't you be bored?"

Ki took out his bag of bakshi stones. Rattling them in challenge, he said, "There are other kinds of fighting we can do here. And now I have gold of my own to wager."

They played half a dozen games, not really caring who won or lost, and when they were done he rose to go. Fidgeting nervously with the stone bag, he said, "I meant what I said, about it not feeling right to be fighting without you." He leaned down and gave her a hasty kiss on the cheek. Before she recovered, he was gone.

She sat for some time, fingers pressed to her cheek where his lips had touched, wondering what to think of it and trying not to give in to false hope.

Chapter 29

Niryn had spied Nalia peeking down from her balcony the night of the floggings and was pleased with how the spectacle had cowed her. She'd been very quiet since. Even Korin had remarked on it.

She'd still had some spirit when Korin first arrived. Her hatred and anger had been palpable, as well as her despair. Concerned, Niryn had gone so far as to bespell the balcony and windows to prevent her from leaping to her death.

Time and Korin's attentions had calmed her, and the sight of her husband's hard justice seemed to have dampened the last of her resistance. She was meek at table and during her evening strolls on the walls. Niryn was careful to make sure she passed the heads of the traitors displayed there. The only one missing was that of whoever had let Caliel and the others escape.

Korin, however, grew increasingly difficult to manage. Drink was taking its toll, and Alben and Urmanis were helpless to stop him. At his worst Korin was by turns restless and morose. The treachery of his Companions had hurt him deeply; Niryn had carefully nurtured that pain to his own ends. Several new gibbets had to be built outside the fortress walls. The bodies bloating there served as a good reminder for the rest.

What Niryn could not control, however, was the demand among Korin's allies for battle, which only grew stronger when spies brought word that Tobin had sent his army against some of the nobles who refused to recognize his claim, and that his generals were having one success after another.

Korin's warlords were equally successful once the lead was slipped against a few minor nobles who opposed him. Some fought for the king's honor, but more were in it for the spoils. There was some grumbling over their shares of the lands and gold captured, but Korin had an army to pay and men to feed. Northern taxes flowed into Cirna, but without a royal treasury to draw from, Korin took the full royal share of all spoils.

Reading through the day's reports one evening in his chambers, Niryn saw a few familiar names. Lord Jorvai was with Tobin at Atyion, and the forces he'd left behind at his estate were no match for Duke Wethring and his army. The keep and town had been put to the torch and the fields burned.

Nevus currently had a smaller holding under siege. It was a miserable little keep in the hills called Rilmar, but Niryn smiled as he read the name of the old knight who held it: Marshal of the Roads, Sir Larenth.

"Dear me," he smirked, showing the report to Moriel. "I do believe that's young Ki's family, isn't it?"

Moriel's gloating smile was poisonous. "Yes, my lord. King Erius granted him those very lands as a favor to Prince Tobin."

"Well then, it's only right that the king's son should take them back."

Earlier, Korin had given in to a momentary regret over that. "Father sent the Companions there to get us blooded against some bandits. Sir Larenth was a fine old fighter in his day and a good host in his way."

"He was offered terms, Majesty, and he refused in the most colorful terms," Master Porion assured him.

"You cannot afford to show them mercy, any more than you could those rebel Companions. False friends make the bitterest enemies," Niryn reminded him.

All the same, Niryn caught a flicker of guilt in Korin's eyes and pursued it, winding his way into the young man's memory. There was shame there, some failure involving Rilmar. Niryn crooked hidden fingers into a spell, fanning the pain of the buried memory.

"You're right, of course," Korin whispered, rubbing his eyes. "There can be no mercy for rebels, no matter what." He summoned a herald. "Go to Lord Nevus. Tell him it is my will that he spare the girls who aren't trained to arms and the little children. Hang the rest."

Look there," Korin said as they strolled the walls later that evening, pointing up at the constellation just above the eastern horizon. "There's the Hunter. Summer's nearly gone and still I lurk here, tied down by the tide in a womb! By the Flame, it's as if I have no use but to get babies on a woman."

"It's not for lack of trying, now is it?" Alben chuckled. "You're up there often enough. I hope for your sake she's not barren—"

"My lord!" Niryn made a sign against ill fortune. "It's said the women of her family kindle slowly, but that they bear healthy babes, and they tend to girls."

Korin sighed. "I *must* face Tobin on the battlefield before the snow comes and defeat him once and for all!"

A little longer, my king, thought Niryn. According to old Tomara, Nalia was having trouble keeping her breakfast down.

Chapter 30

News of Tamír's actions against the recalcitrant nobles spread quickly and heralds bearing conciliatory letters soon began to arrive from nobles up and down the coast. The powerful lords of the north and some of the west remained staunch in their support of Korin, however. Jorvai had been one of the few from that region to support her. According to Tamír's spies and Arkoniel's wizards, Korin was still stubbornly sitting at Cirna.

Tamír wasn't certain what to make of that. In his place, with superior forces, she'd have marched long since, yet there was still no sign of movement. Ki was of the opinion that Korin was scared to fight, but Tamír was certain there must be something else.

Whatever the case, they now found themselves in a period of relative peace and Imonus seized the opportunity once again to urge Tamír to go to Afra.

"It's time, Majesty. If nothing else, you must be seen honoring the Lightbearer as your ancestors always have."

"He's right, you know," said Illardi. "Every new queen has gone there and brought back a prophecy for the people."

Tamír needed no convincing. She'd had her fill of court life, and if she couldn't fight a battle, then the prospect of a journey had its appeal.

On Imonus' advice, Tamír set the date for their departure for the first week of Lenthin. That would bring them to Afra during the moon's first waxing—a most fortuitous time, according to the priests.

There was no question of taking a large force. The

shrine lay high in the mountains west of Ylani, and was reached by a single, switchback road, which, according to Imonus and Iya, was barely wide enough in places for a single rider to pass.

"The place is sacred ground. Not even Niryn would dare defile it by attacking you there," Imonus assured her. "And no one would follow Korin if he committed such a sacrilege."

"I hope you're right," said Tharin. "All the same, she must take a sufficient guard to protect her on the road."

"My personal guard should be enough, especially with Iya and Arkoniel with us," said Tamír. "With any luck, I'll be back before Korin's spies can carry the news that I was gone."

"Saruel has asked to accompany us," said Iya. "The Aurënfaie hold the Oracle in high regard, and she would like to visit the place."

"I'm glad to have her," Tamír replied. "She's one of your more powerful wizards, isn't she? I'll feel that much safer, with her along."

The night before their departure Tamír was too restless to sleep. She sat up late, gaming with Ki and Una, then sat by the window as they played the final game, watching the last waning half-moon rise and tugging absently at a braid. Una won at last and took her leave, eager to be off tomorrow.

"What's the matter? I thought you'd be anxious to go," said Ki as he scooped their bakshi stones back into their respective bags and put away the wooden board.

"I am."

"Well, for someone who's cool as springwater before a battle, you seem awfully fretful over a little ride. Are you afraid of the Illiorans? I know I am."

She turned to find him grinning at her. "Stop teasing. You're not the one god-touched. It was eerie, that vision I

had, and that was just a little one! This is the greatest
Oracle in the land."

"And who could be safer there, than you?" Ki coun-
tered. "Come on, there's something else, isn't there?"

"What if I don't like what she tells me? What if I'm des-
tined to fail, or go mad like the rest of the family or—I
don't know."

"And?"

"And Brother. He's still after me about his death. I
want to know the truth, but I'm afraid to, too. I can't explain it, Ki. It's just a gut feeling."

"Which are you more afraid of? That he won't go away
once you've satisfied him or that he will?"

"I want him gone. I just don't know if I can give him
what he wants to do it."

They set off early the next day, riding at a trot through the
sleeping town. Tamír felt a stir of excitement as the southern high road stretched away before them. It wasn't just
the anticipation of at last meeting with the Oracle who'd
defined her life. To ride at full gallop with armed riders at
her back was one of the finest feelings she knew.

Lain, youngest of the Afran priests who'd come north
with Imonus, rode in the forefront with her as their guide,
though Iya and Arkoniel knew the way as well. He was a
quiet sort, and Tamír hadn't paid him much mind, but he
was positively glowing today.

"It's a great honor, Majesty, to conduct a new queen to
Afra. I pray you receive a clear answer there, and comfort."

"So do I," she replied.

Arkoniel had brought Wythnir with him this time, and
the boy rode proudly on a pony of his own, dressed in a
fine new tunic and boots. It made him look older. The wizards spent much time riding together and though the boy
said little, as always, Tamír could see that he was taking in
every word his master said. He bore the long hours of rid-

ing without complaint, apparently content to be near Arkoniel rather than left behind again.

They slept at Ero on the second night, and the following day Illardi's steward proudly showed her the new town springing up along the northern edge of the harbor. Many people were still in tents and makeshift shelters, but men were at work everywhere, hauling stone and hammering away at new house frames, and the air was sweet with the scents of lime and raw lumber. She paused frequently to watch the craftsmen.

Arkoniel smiled as she lingered to watch a woodcarver at work on a fancy lintel. "Do you ever wish you'd been born into a craftsman's family instead?"

"Sometimes. I lost all my carving tools and haven't had time to find any new ones."

Arkoniel reached into his purse and handed her a small lump of fresh beeswax. "Will this do, for now? You never used to be without it."

Tamír grinned; Arkoniel had been among the first to recognize and support her gift.

But not the first.

The sweet aroma brought back a few precious moments of peace with her mother—a rare smile as her mother had warmed a bit of wax between her hands. *It smells of flowers and sunshine, doesn't it? The bees store up all of summer for us in their waxen houses.*

The sting of tears behind her eyelids surprised her. Tamír had so few good memories of her. She looked down at the serene carved countenance on her ring, wondering what Ariani would think, to see her in her true form? Would she love her at last, as much as she'd loved Brother? Would she have loved them both and not gone mad if Brother had lived?

Tamír shook off the bittersweet thought and strode on, hoping Arkoniel and the others hadn't noticed her weakness.

*   *   *

They soon left the sea road behind, striking south and west toward the mountains for the next few days. This was the same road she'd taken the first time she'd come to Ero. She and Ki shared a silent look of longing as they passed the crossroads that would have taken them to the Alestun keep. Who knew when they would have the time to go there again? Her old nurse, Nari, wrote often, and Tamír always answered, but she couldn't promise a visit.

Beyond the Alestun road, Lain led them along back roads that avoided the larger towns, moving ever inland. The first few nights they slept in small roadside inns, where people greeted her with respect and wide-eyed amazement, especially when their new queen was content to dine with them in the common room. She and the Companions joined in songs around the hearth at night, and Iya and Arkoniel entertained with simple, colorful spells and cast mendings for those who dared ask.

In return, the villagers spoke to Tamír of crops and bandits. Rogues of all sorts had grown bolder since Ero fell. Tamír sent a rider back with word for Illardi to have some of their idle warriors sent out to deal with brigands.

The great range that formed the spine of the Skalan peninsula loomed closer each day, the jagged peaks still snow-capped.

On the afternoon of the seventh day Lain guided them onto a well-traveled road that led into the mountains. Evergreen forest gradually gave way to thinner groves of quakeleaf and oak.

The way grew steep and began to twist, forcing them to rein their horses back to a walk. The air grew steadily cooler around them and carried the scents of plants Tamír did not recognize. Stunted, wind-twisted trees clung to the rocky slopes, and hardy mosses and small plants lined the road. It was still summer in Atyion but the air here already carried the first hint of autumn, and the quakeleafs were showing golden edges to their round leaves. Far above them the snow-capped peaks shone so brightly against the clear blue sky it hurt to look at them for long.

"It reminds me of my home. Many of these plants are the same," Saruel remarked, riding beside Tamír.

"You're from the mountains?"

"Yes. As a child I saw level ground only when we traveled to Sarikali for the clan gatherings." She inhaled deeply, and the black tracery around her eyes pulled and bunched as she smiled. "I've missed these smells, and the coolness. I enjoyed my time in your capital, but it was very different than what I'm used to."

Tharin chuckled. "Stinking Ero. It came by the name honestly, for certain."

"I understand. I grew up in the mountains, too," Tamír said.

"This feels like one of our hunting trips, doesn't it, Tharin?" Just then something caught Ki's eye and he leaned far over in the saddle to pluck a blossom from a clump of bell-shaped pink flowers growing from the cliff face. He kept a precarious grip on his horse's sides with his knees, and came back up with a grin to present the flower to Tamír. "Look. Heart's Ease, for better memories."

Tamír sniffed at it, savoring the familiar heady scent, and tucked it behind her ear. Ki had never done such a thing before. The thought sent a giddy flutter through her chest and she nudged her horse into a trot so the others wouldn't catch her blushing.

They camped beside a stream in a high, windswept valley that night. The stars showed large in the velvet sky, just as they had at Alestun, so bright they turned the snow on the peaks to silver.

Saruel and Lain gathered handfuls of small blue berries and brewed a sweet, resinous tea from them.

"Most of you haven't traveled such high passes. The air grows thinner as we climb," the priest explained. "Some feel ill with it, but this tea will help."

Tamír had felt no ill effects so far, but Nikides, Una, and the new squires admitted to feeling a little dizzy toward the end of the day.

The owls here were numerous and larger than the ones in the lowlands, with tufts like a cat's ears on their round heads and bands of brilliant white on the ends of their tail feathers. Ki found a few fallen feathers in the gorse by their campsite, and gave them to Tamír. She cast a few into the campfire with a murmured prayer for luck.

They slept on the ground, wrapped in their cloaks and blankets, and woke to find the valley in a thick, chilly mist that coated their hair and their horses' coats with jeweled droplets. Sounds carried oddly. Tamír could hardly hear the conversation of those standing across the campsite, but the knocking of a woodpecker sounded as close as over her shoulder.

After a cold breakfast and more of Saruel's tea, they continued on, walking their mounts until the mist cleared.

The peaks closed in around them and the way narrowed. To their right sheer rock face bore down on them, even overhanging the narrow trail in places so they often had to duck and lean precariously as they rode in single file behind the wizards and priest. On their left a sheer precipice fell away into the lingering mist below. Tamír cast a stone over the edge, but never heard it strike.

The afternoon was waning when Tamír noticed the first crescent shapes and bits of writing scratched into the bare rock face, left by other wayfarers and pilgrims.

"We're getting close," Iya told her as they rested their horses and let them graze on the sparse grass that lined the trail. "A few more hours will bring us to the painted gate you saw in your vision. Afra lies just beyond."

Arkoniel scrutinized the inscriptions as they rode on. Presently he reined and pointed to one in particular. "Look, Iya, here's the prayer I left the first time you brought me up here."

"I remember," Iya said with a smile. "I must have a few marks around here somewhere, too."

"Why do you do this?" asked Saruel.

"Custom, I suppose. For luck, too," Iya replied.

"Isn't that what people always say about such things?" said Lynx, still a staunch Sakoran despite all he'd seen.

"You'd do well not to mock the devotions of the Illior, young lord," Lain said, overhearing. "These prayers last far longer than any charm burned up in a fire. They shouldn't be taken lightly, or made thoughtlessly." He turned in the saddle. "You should write something, Queen Tamír. All your forebears have done so, somewhere along this route."

The thought was a comforting one, and gave her a sense, once again, of being connected to the line of women who'd come before her.

Everyone dismounted and hunted for sharp stones to scratch their names and messages.

Saruel joined them, but instead passed her hand across the stone. A small silver crescent and words in fine script appeared. "It's a good thing, to honor the Lightbearer on the way to his sacred place," she murmured, watching approvingly as Lynx's young squire made his mark.

"You've 'faie blood in you, Tyrien í Rothus," Saruel said. "I see it in the color of your eyes."

"So my grandmother told me, but it's a long way back, so I can't have much," the boy replied, those grey eyes alight with pleasure that she'd noticed. "I'm no wizard, anyway."

"The amount makes no difference, but the lineage, and even that's no sure thing," Iya told him, overhearing. "A good thing, too. If every Skalan with a drop of 'faie blood in their veins was wizard-born, there'd be little for warriors to do."

"Were your parents mages?" Saruel asked Wythnir, who was making his mark a little way on.

"I don't know," the boy replied softly. "I was just little when they sold me off."

That was more than Tamír had ever heard him say at one go, and the most he'd ever confided. Tamír smiled at the way Arkoniel's hand rested on the boy's shoulder, and the worshipful look it earned him. Tamír found herself wishing she'd given him more of a chance as a child. He'd been just as kind with her, then and now. He was her friend.

Ask Arkoniel! Brother's challenge still sent an uneasy chill through her.

Tamír pushed the thought aside for later and stared at the bit of flat wall she'd chosen, at a loss as to what she should write. Finally she scratched in simply, "Queen Tamír II, daughter of Ariani, for Skala, by the will of Illior." She added a small crescent moon under it, then passed the stone she'd used as a stylus to Ki.

He leaned in beside her and scratched his name and a crescent moon under hers, then drew a circle around both their names.

"Why'd you do that?" she asked.

It was Ki's turn to blush as he said softly, "To ask the Lightbearer to keep us together. That was my prayer."

With that he hurried away and busied himself checking his girth strap. Tamír sighed inwardly. First the flower, and now this, but he still kept his distance. Once she'd thought she'd known his heart to the core. Now she had no idea what was held there, and feared to hope.

The sun was sinking behind the mountains when Tamír rounded a bend and was struck with a dizzying sense of familiarity.

The vista before her was the exact scene from her vision in Ero. The narrow track twisted out of sight, then back into view in the distance. There stood the incongruous gate straddling the road, painted with bright colors that glowed in the fading light. She knew it was real, but it still seemed like something from a dream. As they rode closer, she made out stylized dragons painted in brilliant shades of red, blue, and gold twined around the narrow opening, as if they were alive and guarding this sacred way with fangs and fire.

"Illior's Keyhole."

"Beautiful, isn't it?" said Arkoniel. "Do you recognize the style?"

"I saw work like that in the Old Palace. It's centuries old. How long has this been here?"

"At least that long, and it's only the most recent one," said Iya. "Others have fallen to ruin and been replaced. Legend says a gate already stood here when the first Skalan priests followed a vision to the sacred place. No one knows who built the first gate, or why."

"We are taught that a dragon built the first gate, from the stones of the mountain, to guard Illior's sacred cavern," Lain told them.

"My people tell the same tale of our sacred places," said Saruel. "Of course, dragons still do things like that in Aurënen."

"Dragon bones are sometimes found in the higher valleys. Now and then we even get little fingerlings at the shrine." Lain turned back to address the others. "I should warn you, if any of you see what appears to be a little lizard with wings, pay it proper respect and don't touch it. Even fingerling dragons have a nasty bite."

"Dragons?" Wythnir's eyes lit up with a child's excitement.

"Tiny ones and very rarely seen," Lain replied.

They had to dismount at the gate and lead their horses along a narrow, rocky trail. Afra lay up a narrow pass less than a mile or so beyond. Presently the cleft opened into a deep, barren place. It was already shrouded in shadow, but several red-robed priests and a handful of young boys and girls carrying torches were waiting for them. Behind them, the trail twisted away into the shadows.

Ki sniffed the air, which carried the smell of cooking.

"I hope they saved us some dinner. My belly thinks my throat's been slit."

"Welcome Queen Tamír the Second!" the lead priest cried, bowing low with his torch. "I am Ralinus, high priest of Afra in Imonus' absence. In the name of the Oracle, I welcome you. She has watched long for your coming. Praise to you, the Lightbearer's chosen one!"

"Did Imonus send you word?" asked Tamír.

"He did not have to, Majesty. We knew." He bowed to Iya next. "The Oracle bids me welcome you, too, Mistress Iya. You have been faithful and accomplished the difficult task set for you, all those years ago."

The priest caught sight of Saruel and held out his tattooed palms in welcome. "And welcome to you, daughter of Aura. May you be of the same heart with us, here in the Lightbearer's place."

"In the darkness, and in the Light," Saruel replied with a respectful nod.

"Quarters have been prepared for you, and a meal. This is most fortuitous, Majesty. A delegation of Aurënfaie arrived three days ago, and await your coming at the guest-house across the square from your own."

"Aurënfaie?" Tamír glanced suspiciously at Iya and Saruel. "Is this your doing?"

"No, I've had no contact with anyone there," Saruel assured her.

"Nor have I," said Iya, though she looked very pleased with this news. "I did think some might show up, one place or another."

The torchbearers took charge of their horses and led them around the final bend in the trail.

Pinched in a deeper cleft between two towering peaks, Afra at first glance was nothing more than a strange configuration of deep-set windows and doorways carved into the cliffs on either side of a small paved square. This was ringed with tall torches set into sockets in the stone. Carved fretwork and pillars of some ancient design framed the doors and windows, similar to the decorative work on the Keyhole, Tamír noted absently.

What captured her attention at the moment, however, was the dark red stone stele standing at the center of the square between two brightly burning braziers. There was a bubbling spring at its base, just as the wizards had described, welling up in a stone basin and flowing away through a paved channel into the shadows to her left. In the waning daylight, the leaping flames cast dancing shadows across the inscriptions that covered it.

She touched the smooth stone reverently. The Oracle's words to King Thelátimos were carved there in Skalan and three other languages. She recognized one of them as Aurënfaie.

"'So long as a daughter of Thelátimos' line defends and rules, Skala shall never be subjugated,'" Ralinus said, and all the priests and acolytes bowed deeply to her. "Drink from the Lightbearer's spring, Majesty, and refresh yourself after your long journey."

Tamír again felt that deep sense of connection and welcome. Suddenly the air around her stirred, and from the corner of her eye she caught the faint, misty shapes of spirits. She couldn't tell who they were, but their presence was comforting, nothing like Brother's cold anger. Whoever they were, they were glad she'd come.

There was no cup. She knelt and rinsed her hands, then scooped up a handful of icy water. It was sweet, and so cold it made her fingers and teeth ache.

"Can the others have some?" she asked.

The priests all laughed at that. "Of course," Ralinus told her. "The Lightbearer's hospitality knows no rank or limit."

Tamír stood back as her friends and guard all took a ritual sip.

"It's good!" Hylia exclaimed, kneeling to drink with Lorin and Tyrien.

Iya was the last to drink. She moved a bit stiffly after

the long ride, and Arkoniel gave her his arm to help her back to her feet. The old woman pressed her hand to the stele, then to her heart.

"The first Ghërilain was called the Oracle's Queen," she said, and Tamír was amazed to see tears in her eyes. "You are the second queen foretold here."

"And yet you took the name of a different queen, and one of the lesser ones, at that," Ralinus noted. "I've wondered about that, Majesty."

"The first Tamír appeared to me in Ero, and offered me the great Sword. Her brother murdered her, just as so many of my female kin were murdered by my uncle, and her name was all but forgotten in my uncle's time. I took it to honor her memory." She paused, staring down at the silvery ripples of the spring. "And to remind myself and others that such ruthlessness must never be repeated in the name of Skala."

"A worthy sentiment, Queen Tamír," a richly accented man's voice said from the shadows across the square.

She looked up to see four men and a woman approaching. Tamír knew them for Aurënfaie at once by the sen'gai they wore, and the fine jewelry at their throats, ears, and wrists. They all had long, dark hair and light eyes. Three of the men were dressed in soft-looking tunics of woven white wool, over deerskin trousers and low boots. The woman wore similar clothing, but her tunic reached below her knees and was slit up both sides to her belt. The fifth, an older man, wore a long black robe. His fringed, red-and-black sen'gai, facial markings, and the heavy silver earrings dangling against his neck marked him as a Khatme. The woman and one of the younger men wore the bright red and yellow Tamír recognized as the colors of Gedre. The others wore dark green of some other clan.

As they came into the brighter light by the stele, Ki let out a happy whoop and ran to embrace the younger Gedre.

"Arengil!" he exclaimed, lifting their lost friend off his feet in his excitement. "You found your way back to us!"

"I promised I would, didn't I?" Arengil laughed, regaining his feet and clasping Ki by the shoulders. Ki was half a head taller than he was now, though they'd been the same height when Arengil had been sent home. "You're bigger, and you've sprouted a beard." He shook his head, then caught sight of Una among the Companions. "By the Light, is that who I think it is?"

She grinned. "Hello again. Sorry I got you into so much trouble that day. I hope your father wasn't too angry."

His aunt arched an eyebrow at that. "He was, but Arengil survived, as you see."

Tamír took a hesitant step forward, wondering what his reaction would be to the changes in her appearance. Arengil's smile only widened as he closed the distance between them and hugged her.

"By the Light! I didn't doubt the seer, but I didn't know what to expect, either." He held her at arm's length and nodded. "You look very good as a girl."

The Khatme man looked scandalized by such familiarity, but the others only laughed.

"My nephew had a great deal to do with our coming, and would not be left behind," the other Gedre told her. Her Skalan was perfect, with only the slightest accent. "Greetings, Tamír, daughter of Ariani. I am Sylmai ä Arlana Mayniri, sister of the Khirnari of Gedre."

"I'm honored, lady," Tamír replied, not sure what to make of all this, or how to address them. The Aurënfaie used no formal titles, apart from the clan chief, or khirnari.

"Greetings to you, as well, my friends," Sylmai said to Iya and Arkoniel. "It has been some time since we saw you in our land."

"You know each other?" asked Tamír.

Iya clasped hands with Sylmai and kissed her on the cheek. "As she says, it has been years, and only a single visit. I'm honored that you remember us. Arkoniel was only a boy."

Sylmai laughed. "Yes, you're much taller now. And this?" She touched her chin as if stroking a beard and grimaced playfully. "Even so, I'd know you by your eyes. The blood of our people shows there. And you have more of our cousins, too, I see," she added, smiling at Tyrien and Wythnir.

Tamír extended her hand to the dour Khatme. "And you, sir? Welcome to my land."

"I am honored, Tamír of Skala. I am Khair í Malin Sekiron Mygil, husband of our khirnari." His voice was deep and his accent much thicker. "One of my clan stands with you, I see."

Saruel bowed. "I am honored to meet you, Khair í Malin. It has been many years since I've been home."

The two men wearing dark green sen'gai came forward last. The older one looked no older than thirty, and the younger one was hardly more than a boy, but that was no measure with the 'faie. They might be two hundred years old, for all she knew. They were also two of the handsomest men she'd ever seen, and her heart tripped a beat as the taller of the two smiled and bowed to her in Skalan fashion.

"I am Solun í Meringil Seregil Methari, second son of the Khirnari of Bôkthersa. This is my cousin, Corruth í Glamien."

Corruth took her hand and bowed, giving her a shy smile. "I am honored to meet a queen of Skala. My clan stood with your ancestor against Plenimar in the Great War."

"I am honored to meet you," Tamír replied, feeling a bit shy herself. The beauty of these men, even their voices, seemed to weave a spell, making her heart race. "I—that is, I understand you are not here by chance?"

"Our seers claimed there was a queen in Skala again, one who bears the mark of Illior," Solun replied.

"I see for myself that you are indeed a woman," said Khair of Khatme. "Do you still bear the mark?"

"Your birthmark," Arengil explained. "It's one of the signs we're to know you by. That, and that moon-shaped scar on your chin."

Tamír pushed back her left sleeve, showing them the pink birthmark on her forearm.

"Ah, yes! Is it as you remember, Arengil?" the Khatme asked.

"Yes. But I'd have known her without it by those blue eyes."

"But you've only just arrived, and you have business of your own here," Solun interjected. "You should eat and rest before we talk."

"Please, won't you join us?" Tamír said a bit too hastily, and saw the annoyed look Ki gave her.

Solun's answering smile made her heart beat that much faster. "We would be delighted."

Chapter 31

Ralinus ushered Tamír across the square to another of the guesthouses. Beyond a thick, age-blackened oak door lay a spacious chamber carved into the cliff. Other doors led deeper into the cliff to the guest rooms. Young acolytes showed them to their rooms along one of the corridors.

These were very small, hardly more than cells, and simply furnished: just a bed, washstand, and a few stools. But the walls were whitewashed and painted with bright colors, like the Keyhole. Tamír's chamber had one tiny window covered with a screen of fretted stone. Ki took the room next to hers, and the rest of her people were distributed along the same corridor. There appeared to be a veritable warren of little rooms stretching back into the rock.

Tamír washed quickly and let Una help her change her travel-stained tunic for one of her gowns. Ki came in as they finished.

"That's something, those 'faie turning up like that," said Una, folding Tamír's tunic away on top of a chest.

"After all the stories I've heard of them, it doesn't really surprise me," Tamír replied, tugging a comb through her hair. "What do you think of them so far, Ki?"

He leaned on the doorframe, picking at a hangnail. "Good-looking folk, I guess."

Una laughed. "Beautiful is more like it! And I liked the way that young Bôkthersan blushed when you greeted him, Tamír."

Tamír grinned. "I haven't met an ugly Aurënfaie yet.

Do you think there are any?" she asked, still struggling with the comb.

Ki strode over and took it, then worked the tangle free, muttering, "Maybe they don't send the ugly ones abroad."

Una gave him an odd look, and Tamír realized that no one had ever seen Ki do this for her. Suddenly self-conscious, she retrieved the comb and said lightly, "Maybe the ones they think are ugly are still good-looking to us."

Ki made a noncommittal noise and strode to the door. "Come on, Your Majesty, I'm starving."

As Tamír rose to follow, Una caught her by the arm and whispered, "He's jealous! You should flirt with the handsome 'faie."

Tamír gave her an incredulous look and shook her head. She'd never played those court games and wasn't about to start now. She and Una followed Ki out to the hostel's large front chamber, where the rest of the company were already mingling with the Aurënfaie and temple folk. She doubted Una was even right about Ki's odd behavior; such a thing had never happened between them before. He wasn't even interested in her, not that way!

All the same, she felt self-conscious again as Solun bowed to her from across the room. She glanced at Ki, and though he was neither smiling nor frowning, his gaze did seem to keep wandering back in the direction of the handsome 'faie.

"Please, Majesty," Ralinus said, indicating a seat for her at the center of one of the tables. He sat with her, together with her wizards, Tharin and Ki, and the Aurënfaie. Young boys in white robes brought basins for them to dip their fingers in, while others poured wine. More introductions were made among Tamír's people as they took their places at the tables. Tamír was not displeased to be seated across from the handsome Bôkthersans.

She poured a libation to Illior and the Four, and the meal began. They exchanged pleasantries as they ate.

Tamír questioned the 'faie about their homeland and watched them as they talked with the others. Una and Hylia were both making eyes at Solun, and Lynx was looking a little flustered as he tried to make small talk with Corruth, seated beside him.

They truly were beautiful people, but Tamír would not let that blind her. They would not have come so far if they didn't want something in return. Beside her, Ki was giving Arengil an abbreviated description of the fighting they'd seen so far.

"If the king hadn't caught us that day, I'd have been with you," Arengil grumbled. "We train for war in Gedre, but all we get to fight are Zengati pirates."

"My nephew was quite taken with Tirfaie life," Sylmai said, giving him a fond look. "Perhaps he needs to see a real battle so that he will not be so hasty to seek them out."

The tables were cleared, and warm tarts and cheese were set before them, with a sweet wine.

"Ralinus said you came to meet me," Tamír said to Sylmai, who appeared to be the highest in rank among them. "Was it only curiosity that brought you all this way?"

The woman smiled knowingly, nibbling a bit of cheese, but it was Khair who answered. "It was foretold that you would set right what the usurper wrought against the faithful. This gives us hope that Skala might yet give up the blasphemies—"

"Our clan and Bôkthersa have some of the closest ties to Skala, so the khirnaris decided to send representatives to meet with you and learn the whole truth," Sylmai said, cutting him off rather abruptly.

"I took no offense," Tamír assured them. "My uncle's actions against followers of Illior were unforgivable. Do you wish to reestablish ties with my country?"

"Perhaps," the Khatme replied. "Our first task was to ascertain the validity of your claim and discover whether you mean to properly honor the Lightbearer, as your ancestors always have."

"I witnessed the acts of my uncle firsthand. I would never continue such policies. All the Four are honored in Skala, and Illior is our special patron."

"Please forgive Khair's bluntness," Solun said, narrowing his eyes at the man. It seemed the others found their companion as abrasive as Tamír did.

To her surprise, the Khatme touched his brow. "I meant no disrespect. Your presence here speaks well of your intentions."

"My clan would welcome reestablishing ties with Skala," Solun said. "There are still those living among us who remember your Great War, the children of the wizards who joined the great queen Ghërilain against the necromancers of Plenimar. We have paintings of her at Bôkthersa. Arengil is right. You have her eyes, Tamír ä Ariani."

"Thank you for saying so." She felt herself blush again, mortified at the effect the man had on her. "Are you offering to ally with me against my cousin, Prince Korin?"

"Yours is the true claim to the throne," said Khair.

"Will it really come to fighting?" asked Arengil. "Korin was not his father. We were good friends."

"He's changed since you left, and not for the better," Ki told him. "He's taken up with Lord Niryn. You remember Old Fox Beard, don't you?"

"This Niryn is the wizard who gathered the Harriers, is he not?" asked Khair.

"Yes," Tamír told him. "By all reports, he's attached himself to Korin. I've tried to contact my cousin, but he refuses to parley. He claims I'm either mad or a liar."

"Clearly you are neither," said Solun. "We will tell the Iia'sidra so."

Just then something flittered from the shadows overhead, just beyond the glow of the broad stone hearth.

"Master, look!" Wythnir exclaimed.

Una flinched back. "Bats?"

"I think not." Ralinus held up his hand, as if calling a falcon. A tiny winged creature fluttered down and settled on his outstretched finger, clinging with delicate clawed feet and a long slender tail. "Look, Majesty. One of the Lightbearer's dragons comes to greet you, after all."

Tamír leaned closer, remembering the warning not to touch. The dragon was beautiful, a perfect miniature of the huge beasts she'd seen in manuscripts and pictured on tapestries and temple walls around Ero. Its wings were similar in form to a bat's, but nearly translucent and faintly iridescent, like the inside of a mussel shell.

"I didn't think there were any dragons left in Skala," said Arengil.

"They are rare, but these little ones have been more common around Afra in recent years. The Lightbearer must have sent them to greet their new queen." Ralinus held the little creature out to Tamír. "Would you like to hold it? I'm sure it will come to you if you're very calm."

Tamír held up a finger. The dragon crouched lower on the priest's finger for a moment, baring tiny fangs and drawing its snaky neck back as if to strike. Its eyes were tiny golden beads, and spiky whiskers bristled out from its muzzle and head, fine as jeweler's work. She noted every detail, already thinking how she could re-create it with wax and silver.

She'd worked with hawks enough to know that she must make no sudden moves and show no fear. Instead, she slowly brought her finger against the priest's. The dragon flicked its wings nervously, then slowly climbed across to perch there, wrapping its tail around her fingertip. Its claws were sharp as thistle spikes. She'd expected its body to be smooth and cold, like a lizard's, but instead felt an astonishing heat where its belly rested against her skin.

She slowly moved her hand so that Wythnir could get a better look. She'd never seen him look so happy.

"Can it breathe fire?" he asked.

"No, not until it's much larger, assuming it survives. Most of the little ones don't, even in Aurënen," said Solun.

"These little fingerlings are hardly more than lizards," Corruth added. "They change as they grow, and get quite dangerous in the process. One of our cousins was killed by an *efir* last year."

"What's an effer?" asked Ki, equally entranced by the little creature.

"A young dragon about the size of a pony. Their minds are still unformed, but they're very fierce."

"This one doesn't look all that dangerous," Ki chuckled, leaning in for a closer look. Perhaps he moved too quickly, for the fingerling suddenly lashed out and nipped him on the cheek just under his left eye.

Ki jerked back with a yelp, clapping a hand to his cheek. "Damnation, that stings like snakebite!"

Tamír sat very still but the dragon tensed, bit her, too, and fluttered away into the shadows where it had come from. "Ow!" she cried, shaking her finger. "You're right, it does hurt."

"Hold still, both of you," laughed Corruth. The young Bôkthersan took a clay vial from his purse and quickly dabbed a bit of dark liquid on both bites.

The pain lessened at once, but when he wiped away the excess, Tamír saw that it had stained the tiny imprints left by the teeth. She had four dark blue spots on the side of her finger, just below the first knuckle. Ki had a matching mark on his cheek, and it was swelling.

"We match," she noted wryly.

Arengil chided Corruth in their language and the other boy blushed. "Forgive me, I didn't think," he said, abashed. "It's what we always do."

"Corruth meant well, but I'm afraid the marks are permanent now," Solun explained. "Lissik is meant to stain the bites and make them permanent." He showed her a much larger mark between his thumb and forefinger. "They're considered very lucky, signs of the Lightbearer's favor. But perhaps you'd rather not have had them?"

"No, I don't mind," Tamír assured him.

"That's quite the beauty mark for you, Ki." Nikides laughed.

Ki polished the blade of his knife on his leg and held it up as a mirror to see the mark. "It's not so bad. Makes for a good story if anyone asks about it."

"Dragons are rare here, and so are the bites," said Ralinus, inspecting the mark on Ki's cheek more closely. "Would you teach me the recipe for that unguent, Solun í Meringil?"

"The plants we use don't grow here, but perhaps I could send you some of our mixtures."

Khair took Tamír's hand gently between his own and looked closely at the mark. "It is the belief of our people that after it is grown to the size of intelligence, a dragon remembers the names of anyone it bites and has a bond with them."

"How long does that take?" asked Ki.

"Several centuries."

"Doesn't do us much good, then."

"Perhaps not, but you both will have a place in the dragon's legends."

"Should you ever come to Aurënen, a mark like that will gain you respect. There aren't many Tírfaie who have them," offered Corruth, still regretting his hasty act.

"Then it's worth the bite. Your medicine's already taken the worst of the sting out of it. Thanks." Ki grinned and shook hands with him. "So the little ones can't talk, either?"

"No, that comes only with great age."

"Only the Aurënfaie have dragons that large living in their land," said the priest. "No one knows why. They were in Skala long ago."

"Perhaps because we are the most faithful," Khair replied, reverting to his earlier bluntness. "You worship the

Four, while we acknowledge only Aura, whom you call Illior."

Ralinus said nothing, but Tamír caught a flash of dislike in his eyes.

"That's an old argument, and one better left for another time," Iya interjected quickly. "But surely even the Khatme cannot question the Lightbearer's love for Skala now, as evidenced by Tamír herself."

"She's already been granted a true vision, a warning before the second Plenimaran assault," Saruel told him. "With respect, Khair í Malin, you've not lived among the Tír as I have. They are devout and Aura has blessed them."

"Forgive me, Tamír ä Ariani," Khair said. "Once again I gave offense without meaning to."

"I grew up among soldiers. They're a plainspoken lot, too. I'd much rather you speak your mind openly to me than worry about etiquette and court manners. And you can expect the same from me."

Solun chuckled—a warm, friendly sound—and Tamír found herself blushing again for no good reason.

Solun exchanged an amused look with his Gedre companions, then took a heavy golden bracelet set with a polished red stone from his wrist and rose to present it to her. "Bôkthersa would be the friend of Skala, Tamír ä Ariani."

Tamír accepted the bracelet, and saw from the corner of her eye that Iya was motioning for her to put it on. She slipped it on her left wrist, trying to recall all his different names and failing. The gold was warm from his skin, a fact that did not help her composure. Still she managed not to stammer as she thanked him. "I am honored to accept, and hope you will always consider me to be your good friend."

Sylmai presented her with a golden neck chain of tiny leaves set with some sparkling white stone. "May the ships of Gedre and Skala share ports once again."

The Khatme was the last to come forward and his offering was different. He gave her a small leather pouch, and inside she found a pendant made of some dark, waxy green stone and set in a frame of plain silver. The stone was covered with tiny symbols or letters, surrounding the cloud eye of Illior.

"A talisman of Sarikali stone," he explained. "That is our most sacred place, and these talismans bring true dreams and visions to those who honor Aura. May it serve you well, Tamír ä Ariani."

Tamír guessed from the surprised expressions among the others that this was an uncommon gift for an outsider. "Thank you, Khair í Marnil. I will treasure it and the memory of your honesty. May all my allies be so forthright."

"A noble hope, if a slim one," he said with a smile. With that he rose and bade her good night. The others lingered behind.

Solun took her hand in his and examined the blue dragon bite mark again. His touch sent a pleasant tingle up her arm. "By this mark we will know you from now on, Aura's Chosen One. I believe my father will be well disposed to your support. Send word to us if you are in need."

"Gedre, as well," said Sylmai. "We've missed trading with your land." She turned to Iya and Arkoniel, who'd stayed close by, and spoke quietly with them.

"I'll come and fight for you, too," said Arengil, looking hopeful.

"And me!" Corruth said.

"You'll always be welcome, war or not. If your khirnaris are willing, you'll both have an honored place among my Companions," Tamír replied.

A young acolyte came in from outside and whispered something in the head priest's ear.

Ralinus nodded and turned to Tamír. "The moon is well up over the peaks now. This would be the best time for you to go to the Oracle, Majesty."

Tamír fought down the nervous flutter his words sent through her chest and slipped the Khatme talisman into her purse. "All right, then. I'm ready."

Chapter 32

The sky was a thin strip of brilliant stars between the towering cliffs, and the white-sliver moon hung overhead. Gazing up at it, Tamír felt a thrill of anticipation.

"Isn't there some sort of ceremony?" Nikides asked as the other Companions and wizards gathered by the spring. Wythnir was clinging to Arkoniel's hand again, as if he feared he'd be left behind.

Ralinus smiled. "No, my lord. There is no need, as you will see if you choose to descend."

A linkboy hoisted his lantern pole and led the way from the square up to a well-worn path that continued into the deeper darkness of the narrow cleft beyond.

The way grew steeper almost at once, and the path soon dwindled to a faint track winding up between boulders. Ahead of them, the lantern bobbed and swayed, making shadows dance in crazy patterns.

The way was surprisingly even underfoot, and slick in places, worn by the feet of thousands of pilgrims over the centuries.

The cliffs closed in around them, and the way ended in a small cul-de-sac where the shrine lay. A low stone well stood beside a small open-fronted shack, just as Arkoniel had described.

"Come, Majesty, and I will guide you," Ralinus said softly. "You have nothing to fear."

"I'm not afraid." Going to the well, she peered into the black depths below, then nodded to the rope bearers. "I'm ready."

The men passed the looped end of the rope over her

head and down to settle behind her knees. It was a bit awkward in a skirt. She wished she'd kept to trousers. The priests secured the rope behind her thighs and showed her how to sit on the edge of the hole, gripping the slack against her chest.

Ki watched with poorly concealed alarm as she dangled her legs into the hole. "Hang on tight!"

She gave him a wink, gripped the rope with both hands, and pushed off into the darkness. The last thing she saw was Wythnir's solemn little face.

She couldn't help a gasp as the rope took her weight. She grasped it tightly, twirling slowly as the priests lowered her.

Utter darkness closed over her like water. She could see nothing at all, now, except a dwindling circle of stars overhead. Iya had said the cavern was very large, and Tamír began to understand what she'd meant.

It was uncommonly silent; no sounds of a breeze or water moving, not even the twitter of bats—or dragons, for that matter. There was no sign of walls or floor, just the dizzying sensation of an endless void. It was like being suspended in the night sky.

The air grew colder the lower she went. She stole another glance upward, using the shrinking circle of stars above the wellhead as a visual anchor. After what felt like quite a long time, her feet touched solid ground. She got her balance with some difficulty and stepped free of the rope. Looking up, she couldn't find the wellhead anymore. She was in complete darkness.

She turned slowly, still unsure of her balance, and was glad to see a faint glimmer of light off to her left. The longer she looked at it, the brighter it became, until she could see just enough of the cavern floor to be certain of her way. Gathering her courage, she made her way toward it.

The light was coming from a crystal orb set on a tripod. At first that was all Tamír could see, but when she drew nearer she saw a dark-haired young woman sitting beside it on a low stool. Her skin was deathly pale in the cold light, and her hair fell over her shoulders and pooled on the floor on either side of her. Despite the chill, she wore nothing but a plain linen shift that left her arms and feet bare. She sat with her palms on her knees, her gaze fixed on the ground before her. All the oracles were mad, or so Tamír had been taught, but the woman only seemed pensive—at least until she slowly raised her eyes.

Tamír froze where she was. She'd never seen eyes so empty. It was like looking at a living corpse. The shadows closed in closer, even though the glow of the orb remained steady.

Her voice was equally devoid of emotion as she whispered, "Welcome, second Tamír. Your ancestors told me of your coming."

A silvery nimbus brightened around the woman's head and shoulders and her eyes found Tamír's again. They were no longer empty, but filled with light and a frightening intensity.

"Hail, Queen Tamír!" Her voice was deep and resonant now. It filled the darkness. "Black makes white. Foul makes pure. Evil creates greatness. You are a seed watered with blood, Tamír of Skala. Remember your promise to my chosen ones. Have you cared for the spirit of your brother?"

It was too much to take in at once. Tamír's legs felt like they'd turned to water. She sank to her knees before the fearful presence of the Lightbearer. "I—I have tried."

"He stands behind you now, weeping tears of blood. Blood surrounds you. Blood and death. Where is your mother, Tamír, Queen of Ghosts and Shades?"

"In the tower where she died," she whispered. "I want to help her, and my brother. In a vision, he told me to come here. Please, tell me what to do!"

Silence fell around them, so complete it made her ears ring. She couldn't be certain if the Oracle was breathing or not. She waited, knees aching on the cold stone. Surely she hadn't come all this way just for this?

"Blood," the Oracle whispered again, sounding sad. "Before you and behind you, a river of blood bears you to the west."

Tamír suddenly felt a tickling sensation on her chest, where the old scar lay hidden. Pulling open the neck of her gown, she gasped at the sight that greeted her there.

The wound she'd inflicted on herself that day in Atyion, cutting out the shard of bone and Lhel's careful stitching, had healed itself during the transformation, leaving only a thin pale line where it had been. But it had come open again now, so deep she could see bone, and blood was flowing down between her breasts. It welled over her hands and ran down the front of her gown, spattering on the floor at her knees. Oddly enough, there was no pain, and she felt strangely detached as the blood spread into a round pool before her.

When it was the size of a shield, the dark surface rippled and shapes began to form there. The loss of blood must have overtaken her then, for she grew faint, and the images in the blood swam in a dizzying blur of color.

"I—I'm going to . . ." She was about to faint.

The touch of a cold hand in hers brought her back. Opening her eyes, she found herself standing with Brother on a windswept cliff above the sea. It was the place she'd visited so often in her dreams, but it had always been Ki with her, and the sky was blue. This sky promised rain, and the sea was the color of lead.

Then she heard the clash of arms, just as she had at the temple in Atyion. In the distance she saw two armies fighting, but she had no way to reach them. A rocky gully lay between her and the field of battle. Far beyond them, she could just make out what looked like the towers of a great city.

Korin's banner rose from the shadows at her feet, floating in the air as if held by invisible hands.

You must fight for what is rightfully yours, Tamír, Queen of Skala a low voice whispered in her ear. *By blood and trial, you must hold your throne. From the Usurper's hand you will wrest the Sword.*

More blood! she thought despairingly. *Why must it be so? There must be another way, a peaceful way! I will not spill a kinsman's blood!*

You were born of spilled blood.

"What are you talking about?" she cried aloud. The wind caught the banner and blew it in her face, blinding her. It was nothing but a length of silk and embroidery, but it wrapped itself around her throat like a living thing, cutting off her breath.

"Brother, help me!" she wheezed, clawing at it but finding no purchase in the elusive, wind-torn fabric.

A chilling laugh answered her. *Avenge me, Sister. Avenge me, before you ask any more favors of the one wronged!*

"Illior! Lightbearer, I call on you!" she cried, struggling desperately. "How can I help him? I beg you, give me a sign!"

The silken banner evaporated around her like mist at dawn, leaving her in darkness again.

No, not darkness, for in the distance she saw a cool white glow, and realized she was back in the Oracle's cavern. Somehow, caught in the vision, she'd wandered away from the light. Her hands felt sticky. She raised them, squinting in the uncertain light and saw that they were bloody to the elbow.

"No!" she whispered, wiping them hastily on her skirts.

Slowly, on unsteady legs, she made her way back toward the Oracle's seat, but as she drew closer, she saw someone else in her place, a robed figure with a long, familiar grey braid, kneeling with bowed head before a much younger Oracle. Tamír recognized Iya even before the wizard raised her head. When had she come down, and why? The priest had said only one person was allowed down into the chamber at a time.

Iya held something in her arms. Coming closer, Tamír

saw that it was an infant. The child was limp and silent, and its dark eyes were vacant.

"Brother?" Tamír whispered.

"Two children, one queen," the child Oracle whispered in a voice too ancient and deep for her small frame. "In this generation comes the child who is the foundation of what is to come. She is your legacy. Two children, one queen marked with the blood of passage."

The girl turned to Tamír, her eyes full of searing white light that seemed to bore into Tamír's very soul. "Ask Arkoniel. Only Arkoniel can tell you."

Terrified without knowing why, she fell to her knees and whispered, "Ask him what? About my mother? Brother?"

Cold hands closed around her neck from behind, choking her as the banner had. "Ask Arkoniel," Brother whispered in her ear. "Ask him what happened."

Tamír's hands flew to her throat; she didn't really expect to touch Brother or stop him, any more than she'd ever been able to. But this time her hands found cold flesh and hard, corded wrists. She grabbed at them as a terrible stench rolled over her, making her gag.

"Give me peace!" a thick, gasping voice moaned close to her face. It was not Brother's ghost behind her anymore, but his corpse. "Give me rest, Sister."

He released her and she fell forward on her hands, then twisted around to face the horror behind her.

Instead, she found herself looking at the Oracle again, the woman she'd been speaking with. She sat just as Tamír had left her, hands open on her knees, eyes wide and empty again.

Tamír raised her own hands, and found them dry and clean. Her bodice was still laced. There was no sign of blood anywhere.

"You've told me nothing," she gasped.

The Oracle gazed stupidly past her, as if Tamír wasn't even there.

A rage she'd never experienced before came over her.

She grabbed the Oracle by the shoulders and shook her, trying to find the god's intelligence again in those blank eyes. It was like shaking a doll.

It was a doll, large as a woman, but made of cotton-stuffed muslin, with a crudely painted face and uneven limbs. It weighed nothing and flopped limply in her hands.

Tamír dropped it in surprise, then stared down in renewed horror. It was just like her old doll, the one her mother had sewn Brother's bones into. It even had a twisted cord of black hair tied tightly around its limp neck. There was no sign of the Oracle. Tamír was alone in the dark chamber and the light of the orb was slowly failing.

"What are you trying to show me?" she cried out, clenching her fists in desperation. "I don't understand! What has any of this got to do with Skala?"

"You are Skala," the voice of the god whispered. "That is the one truth of your life, twin of the dead. You are Skala, and Skala is you, just as you are your brother, and he is you."

The light was nearly gone when she felt something tighten around her chest. She looked down in a panic, wondering if the terrible doll had come to life, or if it was Brother's grisly corpse again. Instead, she saw that it was the priest's rope, somehow looped around her body again. Someone had taken up the slack and she just had time to grab on for purchase when she was lifted bodily off the ground to spin up through the solid darkness. She looked up frantically, found the circle of stars overhead, and kept her eyes fixed on it as it grew larger and closer. She could see the dark outline of heads there now, and hands were reaching down to help her up over the lip of the hole. It was Ki, and his arms were strong and sure around her as her knees gave out.

"Are you hurt?" he asked anxiously, helping her to a seat on the edge of the stone enclosure. "We waited and waited, but you gave no sign."

"Brother," she gasped, clutching at the neck of her gown.

"What? Where?" Ki cried, alarmed, still holding her.

Tamír leaned gratefully into that embrace. "No— It was only—only a vision." But she couldn't stop shaking.

"The god spoke to you," said Ralinus.

Tamír let out a harsh laugh. "If you could call it that. Riddles and nightmares."

Suddenly she heard a scratching sound behind her. Turning, she was horrified to see Brother gazing up at her from the cavern entrance, his face a mask of hate. His pale skin slowly shriveled on his skull, and hands like claws emerged and scrabbled at the ground as he began to pull himself from the hole.

You are he, and he is you, the Oracle whispered from below.

The words followed Tamír into darkness as she fainted.

Chapter 33

Tamír was as cold as a corpse when they lifted her from the Oracle's chamber. Ki pulled her away from the others and sat down, cradling her head against his chest.

"Master, did the Oracle hurt her?" Wythnir whispered.

"Hush! It's only a faint." Iya took charge, pushing Arkoniel and the priests aside as she knelt and rested a hand on the girl's clammy brow.

"It's a good sign," Ralinus told the others, trying to calm them. "She must have had an important vision, to be so overcome."

Tamír's eyes fluttered open and she looked up at Iya. A chill went through the wizard; those eyes looked as black as the demon's in the moonlight, and just as accusing. Tamír pushed Iya's hand away and struggled from Ki's arms to sit up.

"What—what happened?" she asked in a quavering whisper. Then she looked back at the well and began to tremble uncontrollably. "Brother! I saw—"

"Companions, carry your queen back to her lodging," Iya ordered.

"I don't need anyone to carry me!" Tamír gave Iya another dark look as she staggered unsteadily to her feet. "I have to go back down there. Something went wrong. I didn't understand what the Lightbearer showed me."

"Be patient, Majesty," the priest replied. "Though the vision may not be clear at first, I assure you, whatever you were shown is true. You must meditate on it, and in time you will see the meaning."

"In *time*? Damn it, Iya, did you know this would

happen? Why didn't you warn me?" She turned an accusing look on Arkoniel. "Or you?"

"All experience the Oracle in their own fashions. We couldn't risk coloring your expectations."

"Let your friends help you back," Iya told her sternly. "We don't need you falling and cracking your skull in the dark."

Tamír opened her mouth to protest, but Ki stepped in and put an arm firmly around her waist. "Calm down and stop being so damn stubborn!"

Tamír took a deep, shuddering breath, then grudgingly let him help her back to the guesthouse.

He's the only one who can sway her like that, Iya thought. *The only one she trusts so deeply.* The look she'd given Iya told a different story.

At the guesthouse, however, not even Ki could convince her to go to bed. "Ralinus, I must speak with you now, while the vision is still fresh in my mind."

"Very well, Majesty. The temple is just next door—"

"Iya, you and Arkoniel wait for me," she ordered. "I'll speak with you later."

The sharpness in her voice surprised Iya, just as that dark look had. She pressed her hand to her heart and bowed. "As you wish, Majesty."

"Ki, come with me." Tamír strode away, with Ralinus and Ki hurrying along behind her.

Arkoniel watched her go, then turned to Iya with a worried look. "She knows, doesn't she?"

"If it's Illior's will." Iya walked slowly into the guesthouse, ignoring the confused looks of the young priests and Companions, who'd witnessed the exchange.

I kept my word, Lightbearer. I will keep it still.

The temple of Illior was a tiny, low-ceilinged chamber carved into the cliff face. Inside, it was dank and ill lit by a single brazier burning before a large, painted carving of the Eye of Illior. The walls, or what Ki could see of them, were stained with smoke.

"Are you certain you want me here for this?" he whispered, watching as Ralinus put on a smooth silver mask.

Tamír nodded slowly, eyes fixed on the priest.

"But wouldn't it be better to have the wizards, too? I mean, they know about this sort of thing."

Her eyes went hard again at the mention of them. "No. Not now."

Ralinus knelt before the brazier and gestured for Tamír to join him there. "What did you see, daughter of Thelátimos?"

Ki stood awkwardly by as Tamír haltingly related what the Oracle had shown her.

"She said that I must take the Sword from the usurper's hand," Tamír said, her eyes filled with sorrow. "That means war with Korin, doesn't it? She was showing me that there's no peaceful way to settle this."

"I fear that is so," the priest replied.

"It's what we've been telling her all along," Ki said. "You've had it from a god now."

"It seems I have no choice," Tamír murmured.

"That was not all the Oracle showed you," said the priest. "Something else upset you."

She shivered again, as she had at the cavern. Ki moved closer and took her hand. She held his so tightly it hurt. "My brother—I saw him down there, but not—Not the way I usually do. He's always looked like me, or at least how I looked as a boy. He's a young man now, as I should have been." She let out a humorless little laugh. "He even has the beginnings of a beard. But this time—" She was shaking. Ki wanted to put his arms around her but he didn't dare interrupt.

"It was as if—as if his grown body was a corpse. I could feel him. He was real."

Ki felt a chill and looked around nervously, wondering if Brother could appear in a temple.

"And I saw him following me up from the hole, too. That's when I fainted," she whispered, embarrassed. "Please, honored one, I have to understand. Everything she showed me seemed to be mixed up with Brother and how he and I are Skala, whatever that means."

"I don't know, Majesty, except that the link between you has not been severed yet. Put that aside if you can, and turn your thoughts to the throne. The queen is the land, as the Lightbearer told you. Your life is dedicated to the protection and preservation of your people, and you must be willing to sacrifice anything to do that, even if it means your own life."

Tamír frowned, tugging at one of her braids. "I'm supposed to fight Korin. But if the banner in my vision represented him, then I didn't know how! It was choking me. I was losing."

"But you saw no defeat."

"I didn't see anything. It just ended." She paused. "Well, it was choking me and I called on Illior to help me. Brother wouldn't; he just kept telling me I must avenge him."

"The vision ended when you called upon the Lightbearer?"

She nodded.

The priest pondered this. "You must keep this in your heart, Majesty. Illior guides your steps and keeps his hand above you."

"The Oracle called me a 'seed watered with blood.' She said she saw blood all around me, like a river. Am I to be like my uncle, for the sake of Skala? How can any good come out of evil?"

"You must find that out for yourself, when the time comes."

"What do I say to the people, when I go back to Atyion? They're all expecting some great pronouncement from Illior, like the one given to Queen Ghërilain. But I have nothing I'd want engraved in gold." She shook her head. "A river of blood."

Ralinus was quiet for a moment, then he leaned forward and placed a hand on her shoulder. "Blood is not only what's spilled but also what runs in your veins, Majesty. That same blood will live on in your children, as it lives in you, joining past and future. Is that not a river, too?

"Allow me to explain something very important to you. Lord Kirothieus, you are her good friend, so you must learn this as well, since she includes you in her confidence. What I tell you now, every priest of Illior knows. You, as queen, receive the revelations of the gods because you are strong and the chosen one. But what you reveal to your people should be no more, and no less, than what they would profit most by hearing."

Tamír exchanged a startled look with Ki. "Are you saying I should lie to them?"

"No, Majesty. You will tell them that Illior has confirmed your right to the crown 'by blood and trial.' You will warn them of the strife ahead, but you will also call upon them to lend you their strength to do the Lightbearer's will."

"And they don't need to know that I'm haunted by my dead brother?"

"That is no secret, Majesty. It is swiftly becoming a legend among the people, that you have a guardian spirit."

"A demon," Ki corrected.

The priest raised an eyebrow at him. "And what would it profit the people, to think their queen accursed? Let them weave your story for you, Tamír."

Tamír let go of Ki's hand and rose. "Thank you, honored one. You've helped me see more clearly."

"It is customary for the high priest to commit a vision to a scroll for you to carry back. I will have it ready for you in the morning."

As Ki walked out into the square with her he could tell that Tamír was still deeply troubled. She stood a long time by the spring, lost in thought. Ki waited silently, arms folded against the chill. The stars were so bright here that there were shadows on the ground.

"What do you make of it?" she asked at last.

"A worthy warrior knows the difference between good and evil, honor and dishonor." He stepped closer and carefully laid his hands on her shoulders. She didn't look up, but she didn't pull away, either. "You're the kindest, most honorable person I know. If Korin is too blind to see that, then it's his own weakness showing again. If you are Skala, then that's a good thing for everyone."

She sighed and covered one of his hands with her own. Her fingers were very cold.

Ki unclasped the brooch at his throat and draped his cloak around her shoulders, over her own.

Tamír gave him a wry smile. "You're as bad as Nari."

"She's not here, so it's up to me to look after you." He chafed her arms to warm her. "There, that's better."

She pulled away and just stood there, eyes downcast. "You—that is—I appreciate—" She faltered to a halt, and he suspected she was blushing.

There'd been too many of these moments of sudden shyness between them these past few months. She needed him. Not caring who might see, Ki pulled her into a rough hug.

Her cheek was cold and smooth against his. He tightened the embrace, wishing he could give her his warmth. It felt good, holding his friend like this again. Her hair was softer than he remembered, under his hand.

Tamír sighed and wrapped her arms around his waist. His heart swelled and tears stung his eyes. Swallowing hard, he whispered, "I'll always be here for you, Tob."

He'd hardly realized his mistake before she jerked away and strode back toward the guesthouse.

"Tamír! Tamír, I'm sorry. I forgot! It doesn't mean anything. Come back!"

The door slammed firmly behind her, leaving him

there in the cold starlight, confused by feelings he wasn't ready to claim and calling himself nine kinds of fool.

An ominous feeling weighed on Arkoniel's heart as he and Iya sat waiting in Tamír's little chamber. Iya would say nothing, and he was left to unhappy imaginings.

When she came in at last, the look on her face made his heart sink even further. Tamír glanced at Iya, then crossed her arms and fixed a hard look on Arkoniel. "I want you to tell me what really happened to my brother. What made him the way he is?"

And there it was, the question he'd dreaded for so long. Even before he opened his mouth, Arkoniel could feel the fragile new trust between them tearing like worn silk. How could he justify to her what had been done in the Lightbearer's name, when in his heart he'd never forgiven himself for his part in her misery?

Before he could find the words, a dank chill like marsh fog closed in around them. Brother appeared at Tamír's side, glaring at Iya. The demon looked very much as he had the few other times Arkoniel had seen him; a thin, evil, wraithlike mockery of Tobin, grown to young manhood. They looked much less alike now, and Arkoniel took strange comfort in that, though the anger in those eyes made them twins again.

"Well?" Tamír demanded. "If I am truly your queen, and not just a puppet you play with, then tell me the truth."

Iya still said nothing.

Arkoniel felt as if a part of him was dying as he forced the words out. "Your infant brother was sacrificed to protect you."

"Sacrificed? Murdered, you mean! That's why he became a demon?"

"Yes," said Iya. "What has he told you?"

"Nothing, except that *you* would tell me, Arkoniel. And the Oracle showed me—" She turned slowly back to Iya.

"You. 'Two children, one queen,' the Oracle said to you, and I saw the dead baby you held. You killed him!"

"I didn't take his life, but I was most certainly the instrument of his death. What you saw is what I was shown. You and your brother were still safe in your mother's womb then. But you were already the one ordained to save Skala. You had to be protected, especially from Niryn's magic. I could think of only one sure way to do that."

Brother crept toward Iya, and Arkoniel was horrified by the dark joy on that unnatural face.

Tamír stayed the demon with a look. "What *did* you do, Iya?"

Iya met her gaze levelly. "I found Lhel. I know the kind of magic her kind practices. Only a witch could accomplish what had to be done. So I brought her to Ero and into your mother's house the night you were born. You were the firstborn, Tamír, and you were beautiful. Perfect. You would have grown into a strong, dark-haired girl with too much of your mother's looks ever to be hidden away from prying eyes. While you lay in your nurse's arms, Lhel brought your brother from your mother's womb. She meant to smother him before he drew breath. That's the secret, you see, the thing she knew how to do. If that little body had remained empty of breath, there would have been no killing and this abomination you call Brother would never have been. But there was an interruption, and you know the rest." She shook her head sadly. "So it was necessary."

Tamír was trembling. "By the Four! That room, at the top of the stairs. He tried to show me—"

Brother pressed close to Tamír and whispered, "Sister, our father stood by and watched."

She recoiled from him so fast she slammed into the wall behind her. "No! Father would never do that. You're lying!"

"I wish he were," said Arkoniel. After all these years of

silence, the words finally tumbled out like water from a burst dam. "Your father didn't want to do such a thing, but he had no choice. It was to be a quick, merciful act. We promised him that, but we failed."

Tamír covered her face with shaking hands. "What happened?"

"Your uncle arrived with Niryn and a pack of swordsmen just as he was born," Arkoniel said softly. The memory had been burned into his mind, every detail knife-edge sharp, and with it all the horror of that night. "The noise startled Lhel, distracting her at the critical moment. The child drew breath and his spirit was sealed in flesh."

The demon's face twisted in a cold snarl. Arkoniel braced, expecting an attack, but to his amazement, Tamír turned to him and said something in a low voice. The demon remained at her side, his face resolving back into a blank mask, all but the eyes. The eyes still burned with hate and desire.

"Your mother was never meant to know," Iya told her. "I drugged her, to spare her that, but somehow she knew. It destroyed her."

Tamír wrapped her arms around her thin chest, looking as if she was in physical pain. "My brother. Mother— The Oracle was right again. I am 'the seed watered with blood.'"

Iya nodded sadly. "Yes, but not for spite or evil. You had to survive, and rule. To do that, you had to live and claim your true form. And so you have."

Tamír wiped a stray tear from her cheek and drew herself up. "So it was by your will that my brother died?"

"Yes."

"Lhel killed Brother and worked the magic, but it was you who made it happen?"

"I alone bear the responsibility. That's why he has always hated me so bitterly. I see it in him still, the desire for my death. Something holds him back. You, perhaps?" She bowed low, hand on her heart. "My work will be done,

Majesty, when the Sword of Ghërilain is in your hand. I ask for no mercy after that."

"And you, Arkoniel?" Tamír's eyes were almost pleading now. "You said you were there that night."

"He was only my pupil then. He had no say—" Iya began.

"I claim no absolution," said Arkoniel. "I knew the prophecy and I believed in it. I stood by while Lhel worked her magic."

"Yet Brother doesn't attack you. He hates you, but no more than most. Not the way he hates Iya."

"He wept for me," Brother whispered. "His tears fell on my grave and I tasted them."

"He cannot love," Iya said sadly. "He can only not hate. He doesn't hate you, Tamír, or Arkoniel. He didn't hate your mother, or Nari."

"Nari, too?" Tamír whispered as the grief sank deeper.

"Hated Father!" Brother snarled. "Hated Uncle! Mother hated and feared him! I knew her fear in the womb, and the night of my birth. She hates and fears him still. You forgot to hate, Sister, but we don't. Not ever."

"You wept over his grave?" Tamír's eyes were almost imploring now. "He was buried—But his bones were in Mother's doll."

"I buried him that night," Arkoniel replied sadly. "Sometime soon after, Lhel and your mother took him up again and put the bones in that doll. I suppose it was to control the spirit, or to keep him by your mother. She saw him as a living child."

"Yes. She saw him." Tamír drew a shaky breath. "Iya, you and Lhel are the ones who spilled my brother's blood?"

"Yes."

She nodded slowly, then, with tears spilling slowly down her cheeks, she said, "You are banished."

"You can't mean it!" gasped Arkoniel.

"I do." More tears fell, but her eyes blazed with an

anger he'd never seen before. "I have sworn before the people that anyone who spills the blood of my kin is my enemy. You knew that, and yet you said nothing. You, who murdered my brother! Destroyed my mother. My—my life!" She caught a sobbing breath. "My whole life—a lie! A river of blood. All those girls my uncle killed? Their blood is on my hands, too, because he was looking for me. Niryn—he was looking for me!"

"Yes." Iya still hadn't moved.

"Get out!" Tamír hissed, sounding like the demon in her anger. "You are banished from Skala forever. I never want to see either of you again!"

But Iya didn't move. "I will go, Tamír, but you must keep Arkoniel with you."

"You don't order me around anymore, wizard!"

Iya still did not move, but the air thickened around her and the room darkened. The hair on Arkoniel's arms prickled uncomfortably as her power filled the tiny chamber.

"I gave you my life, you foolish, ungrateful child!" Iya snapped. "Have you learned nothing? Seen *nothing* these past months? Perhaps I do not merit your gratitude, but I will *not* let you undo all I have wrought for you just because you don't like how the world works. Do you imagine I liked what I had to do? Well, I didn't! I hated it; but we don't choose our destinies, people like you or me, unless we turn coward and run away. Yes, I am responsible for all that has happened to you, but I have not one kernel of regret!

"Is one life, or a hundred, not worth the sacrifice, to lift the curse from the land? What else do you think you were born for? Go on, then. Stamp your foot and shout at me of murder and justice, but where would Skala be if Erius' line of monster-spawning sons still ruled? Do you think Korin is up there in Cirna, planning your coronation? Do you think he will welcome you with open arms if you go to him? It's time for you to stop being a child, Tamír of Ero, and be a queen!

"I will go, as you decree, but I will not allow you to put Arkoniel aside. He is touched by Illior, just as you are. But more than that, he has loved and served you since your birth, and would have stayed Lhel's hand if he could have. He must remain by your side to do the Lightbearer's will!"

"And what is that?" Tamír asked grudgingly. "I've survived. You've made me queen. What is there left for him to do?"

Iya folded her hands and the tension in the room lessened just a bit. "You need him, and you need the wizards he and I have gathered for you. That shining palace of wizards we told you of is not some idle pipe dream. It was a true vision, and it is as much a part of Skala's future strength as you are yourself. Do you imagine the other wizards will stay with you if you do this now? I promise you, most of them will not. It is only because of you that they have banded together, but they are free wizards, beholden to no one, not even you, and they will not serve you if they believe you are your uncle come again. It was Arkoniel and I who convinced them to go against their nature and become the Third Orëska. It is a more fragile confederation than you know, and it is Arkoniel's fate to nurture it. I saw that for myself the day I was shown your future. The two are intertwined."

Tamír stared at them for a moment, fists clenched at her sides. At last she nodded. "He stays. And I acknowledge what you have done for this land, Iya, you and all your kind. It is because of that that I spare your life. But I tell you this: If I lay eyes on you again after dawn, I will have you executed. For the good of the land, do not imagine that to be an idle threat."

"As you wish." Iya bowed and swept from the room without so much as a parting glance in Arkoniel's direction.

Stunned, he watched in horror as Brother smiled an evil smile and slowly faded away.

"Tamír, please, call him back. He'll kill her!"

"I've already told him not to, but that's all I can do. You and Lhel saw to that." She wiped her face on her sleeve, not looking at him. "Brother spoke for you. Because of that, I will let you remain in my court. But right now I—I—" Her voice broke. "Just get out!"

There was nothing he could do for her now. He made a hasty bow and hurried out. Lynx and Nikides were on guard at the door and had heard enough to eye him suspiciously.

"Where's Ki?" he asked.

"Outside, I think," said Lynx. "What the hell happened in there just now?"

Arkoniel didn't stay to answer. Iya's chamber was empty, and he found only Wythnir in his own.

"Master?"

"Go to bed, lad," he said as kindly as he could. "I'll be back later."

Hurrying outside, he spotted Ki leaning on the stele. "Tamír needs you."

To his amazement, Ki just shrugged. "I'm the last person she wants to see right now."

With a snarl of frustration, Arkoniel seized him by the collar and propelled him in the direction of the guesthouse. "She *does*. Go!"

Without waiting to see if Ki obeyed, he ran down to the stable.

It can't end like this! Not after all she's done!

Iya was there, saddling her horse.

"Wait!" he cried, stumbling through the muck. "It was the shock. She's upset. She can't really mean to banish you."

Iya slapped her horse's side and tightened the girth strap. "Of course she does, and so she must. Not because she is ungrateful, but because she is the queen, and must stand by her word."

"But—"

"I've always known this day would come, just not

when or what form it would take. To be honest, I'm relieved. I had assumed it would mean my death when she
learned the truth. Instead, I'm finally free." She touched a
gloved hand to his cheek. "Oh really now, Arkoniel. Tears
at your age?"

He hastily wiped his eyes on his sleeve but it was no
good. They kept coming. He clung to her hand, unable to
believe this was the last they would ever see of each other.
"This is wrong, Iya! What will I do without you?"

"You've done perfectly well without me these past few
years. Besides, it's the natural way of things. You're not my
apprentice anymore, Arkoniel. You are a strong and powerful wizard, with a mandate from the Lightbearer and
more ideas about magic than I've ever seen. You are too
modest, my dear, to realize what you've already accomplished, combining Lhel's magic with our own. Few would
risk such a thing, but you just forged ahead. I'm more
proud than I can say."

She blinked and turned back to adjusting her saddle.
"So, between your new Orëska and looking after our little
queen, I'm sure you'll be too busy to miss me very much.
Besides, we're both Guardians and that is not an easy path,
either."

"Guardians?" He scarcely thought of the bowl as more
than a piece of his usual baggage. Iya's use of the formal title sent an unpleasant chill through him, as he recalled the
prophecy old Ranai had passed on to him before she died,
the dream of the Guardian Hyradin: *And at last shall be
again the Guardian, whose portion is bitter, bitter as gall.*
He shivered again, feeling those words fulfilled for Iya.
"What does that have to do with any of this?"

"Perhaps nothing, perhaps everything. It's Illior's will
that you have the burden of both the bowl and the queen.
You are up to the task, you know. I never would have
given either of them into your keeping if I didn't believe
that."

"Will I ever see you again?"

She patted his arm. "I'm only banished, my dear, not dead. I'll send word."

"Brother will come after you. I think he followed you." Arkoniel searched the shadows nervously.

"I can handle him. I always have."

He watched forlornly as she led her horse out to the mounting block and climbed slowly into the saddle. "Your pack! Wait and I'll go fetch it. Tamír said you have until dawn."

"No need, Arkoniel. I didn't bring anything important." She reached for his hand again. "Promise me you'll stay. It was time she knew the truth, but now she must accept it and get on with things. Help her do that, Arkoniel. You may not believe it tonight, and perhaps she wouldn't either, but she does trust you. You, Tharin, and Ki are all she has left of anything like family. Love her as you always have and don't hold this against her."

He clung to her hand a moment longer, feeling a bit like Wythnir. "At least let me fetch you a cloak. It's cold."

"All right then, but hurry!"

Arkoniel ran back to the guesthouse and grabbed Iya's old traveling cloak from a peg by her door. He was gone no more than a few moments, but when he came back the square was empty. There was no sign of her, not even the sound of her horse's hooves. He ran down the track that led to the Keyhole, hoping to catch her. The whole valley was bright with starlight, but the road was empty in both directions.

He had no doubt she was there somewhere, but she'd always been adept at not being seen. She'd used the same magic the night they'd brought Lhel to the keep, but she'd never before used it to hide from him.

"Good luck!" he shouted at the empty road, standing there with her cloak knotted in his hands. His voice echoed hollowly across the pass. "I'll do all you said. I will! And—and thank you!" His voice failed him as fresh tears made the stars dance overhead. "I won't forget you," he whispered.

His only answer was the distant hunting cry of an owl.

Not caring what sentries there might be watching, he pressed his face into his beloved teacher's abandoned cloak and wept.

Chapter 34

Spurred by the fear and anger in Arkoniel's voice, Ki forgot his own trepidation and hurried to Tamír's chamber. Lynx and Nikides stood listening at the door with obvious concern.

"Now what's happened?" he whispered.

"She banished Mistress Iya, I think, and maybe Arkoniel," Lynx told him. "There was a lot of shouting and I swear the floor shook. Then we heard her yelling at them to get out—"

"Yes, I saw him just now. Arkoniel sent me."

"She doesn't want to see anyone. She gave orders," Nikides told him apologetically.

"She'll see me."

Lynx stepped back, motioning for Nikides to do the same. Ki nodded his thanks and lifted the latch.

Tamír sat on a low stool in front of the fire, arms locked tightly around her knees. Brother was crouched beside her, his face a mask of fury, and he was hissing angrily at her, too low for Ki to hear. The air was thick with menace. As he watched, Brother slowly reached out to her. Ki drew his blade and rushed the demon. "Don't touch her!"

Brother whirled and flew at him.

"No!" Tamír shouted.

Brother leered as he continued his rush, and Ki felt a deadly chill surround him. The demon disappeared. Ki's sword fell from numbed fingers and he fought to stay on his feet as a wave of weakness passed over him.

Tamír sprang to his side, gripping his arm to steady him. "Did he hurt you?"

"No, just gave me a scare."

"Good." She released him and sat down again, turning her face away. "Go away, Ki. I don't want to see anyone now."

Ki pulled another stool close to hers and sat down. "That's too bad, because I'm staying."

"Get out. That's an order."

Ki stubbornly folded his arms.

She glared at him, then gave up and buried her face in her hands. "Iya and Lhel killed my brother."

Somehow, that didn't surprise him. He kept quiet, waiting for her to go on.

"It's because of me that he is as he is now."

"It's not your fault. Bilairy's balls, Tamír, you were only a baby yourself! I'm sure they only did it because they had to."

"For Skala," she said, her voice heavy with grief.

"I won't say it was right, to use a baby so, but what if your uncle *had* found you and killed you? Where would Skala be then?"

"You sound just like them! I should have killed Iya for what she did. He was a prince of the blood. But—I couldn't!" Her shoulders shook. "I just banished her and now Brother is more hateful than ever, and I don't know how I'll ever look at Arkoniel again—and I was just starting to trust him again, and—" She curled forward in a knot of misery.

Ki forgot the earlier tension between them and pulled her into his arms again. She didn't weep, but her body was rigid and shaking. He stroked her hair again, and after a moment she relaxed just a little. Another moment and she put her arms around his waist and hid her face against his neck.

"Am I a monster, Ki? An unnatural thing?"

He tugged at a lock of her hair. "Don't be stupid."

She let out a choked laugh and sat up. "But you still see Tobin, don't you?"

She looked fragile again, the way she had that night before he left to fight. "I see my friend, who I've loved from the day we met."

"Loved. Like a brother," she said bitterly. "What does that make me now? Your sister?"

The pain in her eyes twisted his heart. *If not a sister, then what?* Fear and confusion still held his tongue, but he hadn't forgotten the look on her face when he'd called her by her boy's name tonight, or how it had felt when she'd smiled at that handsome Aurënfaie over supper. *Do I—? Could I—?*

Those dark eyes widened as he leaned forward and tentatively touched his mouth to hers, trying to give her what she needed.

Her lips trembled against his for an instant, then she turned her face away. "What are you doing? I don't need your pity, Ki."

"It's not." *Isn't it?* He hung his head. "I'm sorry."

She sighed and rested her face in her hands again. "I can't ask you to feel differently than you do."

That was the problem. He didn't know his own feelings. *She's a girl, damn it! You know how to please a girl!* He pulled her to her feet, wrapped an arm around her waist, and kissed her more decisively this time.

She didn't push him away, but her arms stayed at her sides, fists clenched. It wasn't like kissing a boy, exactly, but it wasn't a good kiss, either. There were tears and mistrust in her eyes when Ki released her.

"What are you going to do now, throw me on the bed?"

Defeated, he shook his head miserably. "I'm sorry."

"Stop saying that!"

"Damn it, Tamír, I'm trying!"

"I'm sorry it's such a chore!"

They glared at each other for an instant, then Ki turned and slammed out of the room, telling himself it was a strategic retreat.

Before he could escape, Lynx caught him by the arm and propelled him right back into the chamber. "Get back in there, you coward!"

His unbalanced forward rush caught her on her feet, and they tumbled together onto the bed. The ropes groaned under them as they struggled to get free of each other. Panting and blushing, they retreated to opposite ends.

"Lynx pushed me," Ki mumbled.

"I know." She pulled her disheveled skirts down over her knees.

An uncomfortable silence settled over them, broken only by the snapping of the fire. Ki could just imagine the others outside, ears pressed to the door. He started to apologize again, but she silenced him with a look.

After another excruciating moment she sighed and held out her hand. "You'll always be my best friend, Ki."

Ki clasped it and blurted out, "I *do* love you! I always will."

"But not as——?"

He looked down at their joined hands, searching his heart for some spark of desire. But he still couldn't imagine lying with her as he had with all those serving maids and scullery girls. It was as if some wizard had hexed him, sapping the heat from his loins. "I'd give everything I have to feel that way for you."

Her soft sob and the sight of the fresh tears sliding down her cheeks twisted Ki's heart again. Swallowing hard, he shifted over and pulled her close. This time she did cry.

"I'm cursed, Ki. Brother says so."

"Well, you don't want to believe anything he says. You know what a liar he is."

"You don't think I was wrong, to let Iya go, do you?"

"No. I think it would have been wrong to kill her."

Tamír sat up and wiped her nose on her sleeve, giving

him a trembling, shamefaced grin. "I really have turned into a woman, haven't I? I never used to cry like this."

"Don't let Una catch you talking like that."

She managed a weak smile. "Your friendship means more to me than anything. If that's all we ever have—"

"Don't say that." He looked earnestly into her sad eyes, wanting to cry himself. "You hold my heart. You always have and you always will."

Tamír let out a shaky sigh. "And you have mine."

"I know that, so don't—Well, don't give up on me yet, all right?"

She started to say something, then thought better of it. Instead, she sat back and wiped her face again. "I guess we'd better get some sleep."

"Do you want me to stay?"

She shook her head and Ki knew by the way she did not look at him that things had changed between them tonight in a way that neither of them could take back.

He ignored his friends' questioning looks as he went out. A room had been set aside for him just down the low stone corridor, but the thought of lying alone in the dark drove him in the opposite direction.

Tharin was still in the large room, playing bakshi with Aladar and Manies. Ki nodded in passing and went outside. He was halfway across the empty square when he heard the door behind him open and close. He turned, arms locked across his chest, and waited as Tharin joined him.

He didn't stop, just brushed Ki's arm and said, "Let's take a walk," then strolled off toward the trail that led to the Oracle's chamber.

They picked their way among the tumbled boulders and over the slick spots. Tharin seemed to be looking for something. It turned out to be a sheltered overhang above the trail. He settled there with his back to the rock face and motioned for Ki to sit beside him.

Ki pulled his knees up and wrapped his arms around

them, heart beating too fast as he waited for whatever Tharin had to say. "How much did you hear?"

"Bits and pieces. Iya's been sent away and Arkoniel may have gone with her. I haven't seen him since he sent you racing back in. What can you tell me?"

Ki poured it all out to him, about Iya and Brother and his own ham-handed failures at comfort. "I even tried to kiss her," he admitted miserably. "She wants me to be more than just her friend, Tharin."

"I know."

Ki stared at him in surprise.

Tharin smiled. "She told me, months back."

Ki felt his cheeks go hot in spite of the cold night air. "Why didn't you tell me?"

"To what end? I've got eyes, Ki."

"Do you want to smack me? I deserve it."

Instead Tharin just clapped him on the knee.

"What am I going to do?" He clutched his head and groaned. "I'm failing her when she needs me most."

"You can't change your heart, Ki, or order it, like a warrior into battle."

"People will still talk."

"There's no escaping that. People like to talk."

"They've always gossiped about us. Even when Tamír was a boy, they thought we were bedmates."

"It might have been easier now if you had been. But I figured out long since that you don't bed boys."

"So why can't I feel the way she wants me to now that she's a girl? Bilairy's balls, Tharin, I do love her, but when I think of lying with her, I just can't imagine it."

"You've been with other girls. Did you treat them badly?"

"What? Of course not!"

"Did you love any of them?"

"No, it was just a tumble."

"So you can't think of tumbling our Tamír?"

Ki cringed at the thought. "Of course not!"

He waited for Tharin to chastise him or at least give him some advice, but the man just jerked a thumb in the direction of the Oracle. "Have you thought of going down there yourself?"

"No, I don't go messing about with all that moon smoke and magic. Sakor is a damn sight cleaner to follow. You fight, and you live or die. No messing around with blood and ghosts."

Tharin stood and stretched. "Well, things change," he said quietly, then turned and gave Ki a look he couldn't quite interpret. "Sometimes you just have to be patient. Let's go back. It's cold."

Ki had to pass Tamír's door on the way to his own chamber, and endured Lynx's accusing look. Later, as he lay on his narrow bed, knowing sleep would be a stranger, he wished he had more faith in Tharin's words. Some things just couldn't be changed, no matter how much you wanted them to.

Chapter 35

Arkoniel spent the remainder of the night sitting on a stone by the road. Wrapped in Iya's cloak, he watched the stars wheel and fade.

The first hint of daylight was casting a pink tinge across the snow-capped peaks when he heard the sound of riders behind him.

It was the Aurënfaie, muffled in cloaks and wearing the plain white sen'gai they used for traveling.

"You're up early, wizard," Solun greeted him.

"So are you," replied Arkoniel, rising on stiff legs. "Are you leaving so soon?"

"I wanted to stay," Arengil said at once, looking a bit sulky. "Tamír offered me a place in the Companions."

"And me," said Corruth, looking no happier.

Sylmai gave them both a reproving look. "That is for your parents to say."

"You haven't seen much of Tamír," Arkoniel observed, concerned.

"We've seen enough," Solun assured him.

"Will Aurënen recognize her claim?"

"That is the decision for each of the clans to make, but I will urge Bôkthersa to accept Tamír as the true queen."

"I'll do the same in Gedre," said Sylmai.

"She means to declare war, you know."

"We will take that into consideration. Our ships are swift, should the need arise," Sylmai replied. "How will you get word to us?"

Arkoniel showed her the window spell. "If I can find

you, I can speak to you through this, but you must not touch it."

"Look for me in Gedre, then. Farewell, and good luck."

The others nodded to him and rode on, disappearing quickly into the morning mist. The Khatme, Arkoniel noted, had said nothing of support.

Unsettled, he walked slowly back up to the guest-house.

Tamír and the Companions were sitting around the main hearth with their breakfast. Neither she nor Ki looked rested, but at least they were sitting together. She glanced up as he came in, but didn't call him to join her. He wondered dully if she'd reconsidered his banishment. With an inward sigh, he went to the sideboard and helped himself to bread and cheese and went to his room.

The fire had gone out and the tiny cell was cold as a tomb. Wythnir was still asleep, curled up tightly under the blankets. Arkoniel placed a few logs on the hearth and cast a spell. He seldom wasted magic on anything as mundane as a morning fire, but he was too dispirited to make the effort with flint and tinder. The logs caught and a bright blaze flared up.

"Master?" Wythnir sat up, looking worried. "Did the queen really send Iya away?"

Arkoniel sat on the edge of the bed and handed him a bit of his breakfast. "Yes, but it's all right."

"Why did she do that?"

"I'll tell you another time. Eat. We're leaving soon."

Wythnir nibbled dutifully at the cheese.

Arkoniel was still wearing Iya's cloak. Her scent clung to the wool. That, and the worn old bag lying next to his bed, were all he had left of a lifetime together, it seemed.

Iya had been right, of course. Under normal circumstances he would have left her at the end of his training and gone his own way; but events had kept them together and, somehow, he'd always imagined that they would remain so, especially once they began gathering other wizards to them.

A small hand closed over his. "I'm sorry you're so sad, Master."

Arkoniel gathered him close and rested his face against the boy's hair. "Thank you. I'll miss her."

He couldn't find much of an appetite. As he threw his uneaten bread into the fire, Tamír slipped in without knocking.

"Good morning." He attempted a smile, but it did not come easily, not with his heart still aching at her treatment of Iya. "Wythnir, the queen and I must speak alone. Go finish your breakfast in the big room." The boy slid out of bed at once, still in his long shirt. Arkoniel wrapped him in Iya's cloak and let him go.

Tamír closed the door after him and leaned against it, arms folded tight across the front of her tunic. "I've sent Una and some riders to muster the southern holdings. I'm readying for war as soon as we reach Atyion."

"That's good."

She just stood there a moment, then sighed. "I'm not sorry, you know, about Iya. Brother wanted me to kill her. Sending her away—it was the best I could do."

"I know. She understood."

"But I guess—well, I'm glad you're still here, even if we can't be friends any longer."

Some part of him wanted to reassure her, but the words would not come. "Is that why you're here?"

"No. She said I had to keep you because of the vision you had here. I'd like to hear more about that."

"Ah. It was Iya who was given the vision of the white palace. But she saw me there. I was a very old man, with a young apprentice by my side. The great house was filled with wizards and wizard-born children, all gathered there to learn and share their power in safety, for the good of the land."

"Your Third Orëska."

"Yes."

"Where is it to be? In Atyion?"

"No. Iya said she saw a new, beautiful city on a high cliff overlooking the sea, above a deep harbor."

She looked up at that. "Then you think this city doesn't exist yet?"

"No. As I said, I was a very old man in her vision."

She looked disappointed.

"What is it, Tamír?"

She rubbed absently at the small scar on her chin. "I keep dreaming of being on cliffs, looking down on a deep harbor. It's somewhere on the western shore, but there's no city. I've seen it so often I feel like I've been there, but I don't know what it means. Sometimes there's a man in the distance, waving to me. I've never been able to make out who it is, but now I think maybe it's you. Ki's in the dream, too. I—" She broke off and looked away, lips pressed into a thin line. "Do you think Iya and I saw the same place?"

"Perhaps. Did you ask the Oracle about it?"

"I tried to, but got only the answer I told you of already. It wasn't much help, was it?"

"Perhaps more than you think. Iya had no idea what her vision meant at the time. Only now does it begin to make any sense. But it's encouraging if you and she saw the same place. I suspect it is."

"Do you hate me, for sending her away?"

"Of course not. I'll miss her, but I understand. Do you hate me?"

She laughed sadly. "No. I'm not even sure I hate her. It's Lhel who actually killed Brother, but I can't hate her at all! She was so good to me and helped me when I was all alone."

"She cares a great deal for you."

"I wonder when I'll see her again? Maybe we should go to the keep on the way home and look for her. Do you think she's still there?"

"I looked for her when I went to fetch your doll that night, but I couldn't find her. You know how she is."

"So, what was your vision, when you came here before?"

"I saw myself, holding a young, dark-haired child in my arms. Now I know that it was you."

He could see how her lips trembled as she whispered, "That's all?"

"Sometimes the Lightbearer can be very straightforward, Tamír." She looked so lost and young that he held out his hand. She hesitated, frowning, then came and sat stiffly beside him on the edge of the bed.

"I still feel like an imposter in this body, even after all these months."

"It hasn't been all that long, compared to your life before. And you've had so much to worry about, too. I'm sorry it's had to be this way."

She stared into the fire, blinking hard to keep from crying. At last she whispered, "I can't believe my father just stood by. How could he do that to his own child?"

"He didn't know the full extent of the plan until that night. If it's any comfort to you, he was devastated. I don't think he ever recovered. Illior knows, he had his punishment, watching what it did to your mother and you."

"You and Iya knew him well?"

"We had that honor. He was a great man, a kind man, and a warrior beyond compare. You're very much like him. You have all his boldness, and his great heart. I already see his wisdom in you, young as you are. But you have all your mother's best qualities, too, as she was before you were born." He touched the ring that bore her parents' paired likenesses. "I'm glad you found this. You possess all that was best in both of them and the Lightbearer did not choose you by chance. You are Illior's chosen one. Don't ever forget that, no matter what else happens. You will be the finest queen Skala has known since Ghërilain."

"I hope you're right," she said sadly, and took her leave.

Arkoniel sat for a while, staring into the fire. Relieved as he was at the accord that had survived between them, his heart still ached, both at the loss of Iya and at seeing how strong and fragile Tamír still was. A heavy burden lay on those narrow shoulders. He resolved to do a better job of helping her to bear it.

With that in mind, Arkoniel slipped out and made his way back to the Oracle's chamber. For the first time in his life, he went there alone, with his own questions firmly in mind.

The masked priests let him down and he found himself engulfed in the familiar darkness. He felt no fear this time, only resolve.

When his feet found the ground again he started off at once toward the soft glow nearby.

The woman sitting on the Oracle's stool might have been the same girl he'd spoken to. It was difficult to say, and no one but the high priest of Afra knew how the Oracles were chosen or how many there were at a given time. It wasn't always a girl or woman. He knew wizards who'd spoken with young men here. The only common factor seemed to be a touch of insanity or simplemindedness.

She shook back her tangled hair and gazed at him as he took his place on the stool facing her. Her eyes were already bright with the god's power, and her voice, when she spoke, held that strange timbre that was more than human.

"Welcome back, Arkoniel," she said, as if reading his thoughts. "You stand at the side of the queen. Well done."

"My task has only begun, hasn't it?"

"You did not need to come here to know that."

"No, but I want your guidance, great Illior. What must I do to help her?"

She waved a hand and the darkness beside them opened like a huge window. There was the city on the cliffs, full of great houses and wooded parks and broad streets. It was far larger than Ero and looked cleaner and more orderly. At its heart stood two palaces. One was low and forbidding, a fortress built into the curtain wall. The other was a huge, soaring, graceful four-sided tower, with thinner domed towers at each of the four points. This was guarded by nothing more than a single wall, and the land inside was planted with gardens. He could see people walking there, men and women and children, Skalan and 'faie, even centaurs.

"You must give her this."

"This is the new capital she must found?"

"Yes, and the Third Orëska will be the secret guardians."

"Guardians? I've been given that title already."

"You keep the bowl?"

"Yes!"

"Bury it deep in the heart of the heart. It is nothing to you, or to her."

"Then why must I keep it at all?" he asked, disappointed.

"Because you are the Guardian. By guarding it, you guard her and all of Skala and the world."

"Can't you tell me what it is?"

"It is nothing by itself, but part of a great evil."

"And this is what you would have me bury at the heart of Tamír's city? Something evil?"

"Can there be good, without the knowledge of evil, wizard? Can there be existence without balance?"

The vision of the city faded away, replaced by a large golden scale. In one pan lay the crown and sword of Skala. In the other lay a naked, dead infant: Brother. Arkoniel shivered and resisted the urge to look away. "Evil will always lie at the heart of all she accomplishes, then?"

"Evil is always with us. The balance is all."

"I think I must do great good, then, to keep your balance. That child's blood is on my hands, no matter what anyone says."

The chamber went very dark around them. Arkoniel felt the air thicken and the hair on the back of his neck stood up. Yet the Oracle only smiled and bowed her head. "You are not capable of doing otherwise, child of Illior. Your hands and heart are strong, and your eyes see clearly. You must see what others cannot allow themselves to accept and speak the truth."

A pair of naked lovers appeared on the floor between them, writhing in passion. It was Arkoniel, driving between Lhel's thighs as she clung to him. Her head was thrown back, her wild black hair spread around her ecstatic face. As he watched, his own face flushed and hot, she opened her eyes and looked directly at him. "You have my love always, Arkoniel. Never grieve for me."

The vision faded quickly. "Grieve?"

"You delved in her body, and she has left you pregnant with magic. Use it wisely and well."

"She's dead, isn't she?" Grief closed like a fist around his heart. "How? Can't you show me?"

The Oracle just looked at him with those shining eyes and said, "It was a willing death."

That took none of his pain away. All this time, he'd looked forward to going back and finding her waiting for him.

He pressed his face into his hands, tears hot behind his eyelids. "First Iya, and now her?"

"Both willing," whispered the Oracle.

"That's no comfort! What will I tell Tamír?"

"Tell her nothing. It serves no purpose now."

"Perhaps not." Arkoniel had long since grown used to carrying secrets and pain for the girl. Why should now be any different?

Chapter 36

Niryn returned from his afternoon stroll among the encampments to find Moriel and Mistress Tomara waiting for him in his private chamber. The woman held a small white bundle against her belly and she was positively beaming.

"She's with child at last, my lord!" She opened her bundle and displayed a collection of Nalia's linen undergarments.

Niryn eyed them closely. "Are you certain, woman?"

"Not a sign of blood these past two full moons, my lord, and she hasn't kept her breakfast down since the night of the floggings. I thought at first it was only her gentle spirit, but it's kept on. She's green as a marrow until noon and the heat makes her faint. I've been a midwife, as well as a lady's maid, these forty years and I know the signs."

"Well, that is happy news. King Korin will be delighted, I'm sure. You must come tomorrow and announce it before his court."

"You don't want to, my lord?"

"No, let's not spoil it for him. Let him think he's the first to know." He drew two gold sesters from the air with a conjurer's flourish and presented them to her. "For the king's sake?"

Tomara took the coins and winked at him. "As you say, my lord."

Tomara was as good as her word, and didn't so much as glance in the wizard's direction as she came to Korin the following morning as he held court.

He was in the midst of reports from his generals, but looked up in surprise to see her here at this hour. "Yes, what is it? Do you have word for me from your mistress?"

Tomara curtsied. "I do, Majesty. Her Highness bids me tell you that she is with child."

Korin stared at her a moment, then let out a happy whoop and pounded Alben and Urmanis on the back. "That's it! That's our sign. Master Porion, send out the word to all my generals. We march on Atyion at last!"

Men in the crowded hall began to shout and cheer. Niryn stepped to Korin's side.

"Are you certain the time is right?" he murmured, too low for anyone else to hear. "After all, she can't be more than a moon or two along. Wouldn't it be wiser to wait a little more, just to be safe?"

"Damn you, Niryn! You're worse than an old woman," Korin exclaimed, pulling away. "Do you hear that, my lords? My wizard thinks we should wait a month or two more. Why not say until next spring? No, the snows will come and the seas will be harsh. If we move now we may even catch them with their crops in the fields. What do you say, my lords? Haven't we waited long enough?"

Another thunderous cheer went up as Niryn hastily made Korin a chagrined bow. "You know best, I'm sure, Majesty. I worry only for your safety and your throne."

"My throne is in Ero!" Korin cried, drawing his sword and brandishing it. "And before the fall harvest is in, I will stand on the Palatine and claim it properly. On to Ero!"

The rest of the company took up the rallying cry, and soon it was passed from throat to throat out into the castle yards and beyond to the encampments.

Niryn exchanged a pleased look with Moriel. His little show had worked out well, and with the desired effect. No one could question that it had been the king's will to proceed, rather than his wizard's.

*   *   *

Nalia heard the shouting and hurried out onto the balcony to see if they were celebrating her news.

Korin's army was spread out on both sides of the fortress, a vast sea of tents and corrals. She could see runners fanning out, and men emerging from tents in their wake. She listened for a moment, trying to make out the chanted words. When she did, she felt a stab of pique.

"To Ero? Is that all this means to him?" She went back to her needlework.

Not long after, however, she heard Korin's familiar step on the tower stair.

He burst in, and for the first time since she'd met him, his dark eyes were alight with genuine joy. Tomara came in behind him and gave Nalia a happy wink over his shoulder.

"Is it true?" he asked, staring as if he'd never seen her before. "You carry my child?"

Our child! Nalia thought, but she smiled demurely and pressed a hand to her still-flat belly. "I do, my lord. By all the signs, I'm nearly two months gone. The child will be born in the spring."

"Oh, that's wondrous news!" Korin fell to his knees at her feet and put his hand over hers. "The drysians will watch over you. You'll want for nothing. You have only to ask and it's yours!"

Nalia stared down at him in amazement. He'd never spoken to her like this before—like she really was his wife. "Thank you, my lord. I would like more than anything to have more freedom. I'm so confined here. Couldn't I have a proper room down in the fortress?"

He nearly balked at that, but she'd chosen her moment well. "Of course. You'll have the brightest, most cheerful room in this benighted place. I'll have painters in to decorate it to your taste, and new tapestries—Oh, and I brought you this."

He took a silken pouch from his sleeve and laid it in her lap. Nalia untied the silk drawstring and a long strand of lustrous sea pearls cascaded out into her lap. "Thank you, my lord. They've very pretty!"

"They're said to bring luck to pregnant women and to keep the child safe in the waters of the womb. Wear them for me, won't you?"

A shadow fell across Nalia's heart as she dutifully put on the necklace. The pearls were beautiful, with a lovely pink luster, but the necklace was a talisman, not an ornament. "I will wear them, as you say, my lord. Thank you."

Korin smiled at her again. "My first wife craved plums and salted fish when she was pregnant. Have you had any urges? Can I send for anything special that you don't have?"

"Only more room to walk around," Nalia said, pressing her advantage.

"You shall have it, as soon as a room is prepared." He took her hands in his. "You won't always be shut up in this dreary place, I promise you. I march on Prince Tobin soon, to reclaim my city and my land. Our children will play in the gardens of the Palatine."

Ero! Nalia had always longed to go there, but Niryn would never hear of it. To see a great city at last, to be consort there . . . "That will be very nice, my lord."

"Have you swung the ring yet?"

"No, we thought you'd want to see, Majesty," Tomara lied, giving Nalia another wink. Of course they had, the moment Tomara had guessed that she'd kindled.

Pretending ignorance, Nalia lay back in her chair and handed Tomara the ring Korin had given her on their wedding day. Tomara took a length of red thread from her apron pocket and hung the ring on it, then dangled it over Nalia's lap. After a moment the ring began to move in tiny circles. These early motions meant nothing. If the midwife were a proper dowser, the ring would begin to swing back and forth for a boy child, or go in greater circles for a girl.

The ring made wide circles over her belly, just as it had the first time.

"A daughter for sure, Majesty," Tomara assured him.

"A girl. A little queen! That's good." His smile faltered a little as he placed the ring back on her finger.

He's worried that she'll look like me. Nalia pushed the hurtful thought away and squeezed his hand. She couldn't blame him, she supposed. Perhaps the child would favor him instead. His coloring would make for a pretty girl.

Korin surprised her again, raising her hand to his lips and kissing it. "Perhaps you can forgive me the difficult beginning we've had? With a child, and the throne secure, I will try to be a better husband to you. I swear by Dalna."

She had no words to describe how his kindness affected her, so she kissed his hand. "I will be a good mother to our children, my lord."

Perhaps, she thought, *I can come to love him, after all.*

Chapter 37

Ki hadn't been sorry to leave Afra. Far from helping Tamír, the Oracle seemed to have left her more troubled than ever. She was very quiet as they set out, and the treacherous going required too much attention for long conversations. Still, Ki sensed the deep sadness she carried.

He knew he couldn't lay all the blame on the Oracle. He'd failed her badly in his own clumsy way and left them both wounded. Wrapped alone in his blankets each night, he dreamed of their disastrous kisses and woke feeling tired and guilty.

On those rare occasions when his dream self managed to enjoy the kiss, he woke feeling even more confused. On those mornings, as he watched her washing her face in a stream and combing out her hair, he wished more than ever that things had stayed the same between them as when they were children together. There had been no shadow, no doubt between them. He could look at Tobin or touch him without all this turmoil inside. He didn't doubt the love between them, but it wasn't the kind of love Tamír wanted or deserved.

He kept all this locked away in his heart, knowing that she needed him strong and clearheaded, not moping around like some poetry-reading courtier. Despite his best efforts, the others had heard enough that night in the guesthouse to make them worry. No one asked Ki anything directly, but he often caught them watching him and Tamír.

*   *   *

Arkoniel was nearly as much a mystery as Tamír. No doubt he was still unhappy about Iya's banishment, yet he and Tamír seemed on closer terms than they had been in months. He rode beside her every day, talking of his wizards and their magic, and of the new capital Tamír was planning. She'd mentioned her dreams of a place on the western coast to Ki before, but something in her visions at Afra had caught her imagination and Arkoniel seemed eager to foster such plans, despite the obvious impediments.

Ki didn't care about the difficulties. He only knew that the sadness left her eyes when she spoke of it, planning ways to make it a grander place than Ero. She got the same look she used to while working on some new design for a ring or breastplate. She was always happiest when planning a new creation.

Arkoniel had traveled a great deal, and spoke of sewers and drainage as readily as he talked of magic. Saruel told her of Aurënfaie cities, and the innovations they used for ventilation and heat. The 'faie seemed particularly good at anything related to bathing. They devoted whole chambers to it, with channels for heated water and special raised tile floors that could be heated from underneath. Some of the larger houses had bathing pools large enough for a whole crowd to linger in. Apparently business was even conducted there.

"It sounds like your people spend more time bathing than anything else," Una noted with a grin.

"More than Skalans, certainly," Saruel replied wryly. "It's not only hygienic, but good for the spirit. When taken together with massage and the proper herbs, it is very healing, as well. In my experience, the 'faie not only smell better, but are a healthier people."

Nikides chuckled at that. "Are you saying that we stink?"

"I am merely stating a fact. When you come to build this new city of yours, Tamír, you might find it beneficial to provide proper bathing facilities for all, not only for your privileged classes. Send your builders to Bôkthersa to learn their methods. They are particularly good at such things."

"I wouldn't mind going there myself, if all of them look like that Solun and his cousin!" Una murmured, and more than one among the Companions nodded.

"Ah, yes." Saruel smiled. "Even among the 'faie, they are considered particularly beautiful."

"I'll have to make a point of visiting there," Tamír said with a little smile. "To learn of the baths, of course."

That earned an outright laugh from everyone. Everyone except Ki. He'd seen how interested she'd been in the handsome Aurënfaie. He'd tried to ignore it at the time, but to hear her joke of it, like this with all the others sent a fresh twinge of jealousy through him. He shook it off, but for the first time, he had to confront the fact that she must marry someone, and soon. He tried to imagine that and couldn't. All he could think of was the way she'd looked at Solun, and how it had made Ki want to drive the fellow and his pretty face from the room.

And yet I can't even kiss her? he thought in disgust. *What right do I have to be jealous?*

He had little to offer on the subject of architecture or hypocausts, but found his own imagination caught by the thought of seeing a new city take shape, especially one guided by Tamír's creative mind. She was already thinking about gardens and fountains, as well as defenses. A western capital made military sense, if they could overcome the trade route problem.

"There must be a way to make a good road through the mountains," he mused aloud as they made camp beside a river in the foothills their third day out. "I suppose it depends on where the city actually is, but there are roads already. I heard Corruth talking about the route they took to Afra. They sailed across from Gedre, but rode the rest of the way."

"There are several, but not ones suited to trade," Saruel replied. "And the passes are only open for a few months of the year. The Retha'noi still control some of the better ones, too, and do not welcome outsiders, 'faie or Tír. Anyone with goods to sell must go by boat. There are pirates on both seas: Zengati in the Osiat and brigands of all sorts among the islands of the Inner Sea. And, of course, the clans on the southern coast must go by way of the strait below Riga, a somewhat risky passage in the best of weather. But it's still safer than the overland route."

"It's no better for Skalan trade," said Tamír. "I don't suppose it would do to have a capital entirely isolated from the rest of the country."

Even as she said it, though, Ki could tell by the faraway look in her eyes that she was seeing it anyway, from the fancy sewer channels all the way up to the tall towers of Arkoniel's house of wizards.

"It would be shorter and safer to go around to the north, if the isthmus wasn't in the way," he noted.

"Well, until someone finds a way to move that, I'm afraid we're stuck with a long sail or bad roads." Laughing, Tamír turned to Arkoniel. "What do you say? Can your Third Orëska solve that problem for me with your magic?"

To Ki's surprise, and everyone else's, Arkoniel just looked rather thoughtful for a moment, then replied, "It's certainly worth considering."

Tamír was aware of how Ki was suffering, but there was nothing she could do to help him, or herself. As the days passed and they put the high mountains behind them, she tried to turn her thoughts to other things, but her nights were haunted.

"Where is your mother, Tamír?"

The Oracle's question had chilled her in that dark cavern, and those words followed her, stained even darker by what Iya had confessed. The Oracle had offered Tamír nothing but silence, yet in that silence she'd sensed expectation.

So, as she and her small entourage neared the crossroads that led to Alestun, she made up her mind. She had to screw her courage, reminding herself that no one but Arkoniel and Ki knew the shameful secret of Brother's death, or the angry presence in the tower.

"I want to stop at the keep for the night," she announced as they came in sight of the river road turn.

Tharin raised an eyebrow at that, and Ki gave her a questioning look but no one else seemed more than mildly surprised. "It's not far out of our way, and it will be better than an inn or sleeping in the open," she went on, making light of it.

"A day or two difference shouldn't matter," said Arkoniel. "It's nearly a year since you've visited there."

"I can't wait to see Nari's face when we ride over the bridge!" Ki exclaimed. "And you know Cook will make a fuss over not having enough food prepared."

The thought of something as familiar as being scolded by her old cook warmed Tamír, driving away some of her unease over the true task before her. Grinning, she replied, "Probably, but the surprise will be worth a cold supper. Come on, let's go give them a start!"

She and Ki kicked their horses into a gallop, laughing over their shoulders as the others lagged behind. Tharin soon caught up and there was no mistaking the challenge in his grin. The three of them led the pack, racing each other up the road and thundering by laden carts and startled villagers as they reached the meadows surrounding Alestun.

Tamír looked across the fields to the walled hamlet, standing on a bend of the river. She'd thought it was a city, the first time her father brought her to see it. It wasn't a completely happy memory; she'd foolishly tried to choose a doll for her name day treat, rather than a proper boy's toy, and her father been shamed before the whole marketplace. She understood better now why he'd reacted the way he did, but the memory still made her cringe after all these years.

She shook her head, letting the wind in her face scour away the bad feelings. He'd given her Gosie, her first horse that day, as well, and Tharin had given her that first wooden practice sword. All her early memories were like that, a mix of darkness and light, but the darkness always seemed so much greater. *Black makes white. Foul makes pure. Evil creates greatness,* the Oracle had said. That summed up her life.

They streaked through the forest and came out at last in the broad, steep meadow. On the rise above it, the old keep loomed against the mountains, its square tower pointing like a blunt finger at the sky. Her royal banner flew from a pole on the roof, but that wasn't what caught her eye.

The tower window that faced the road had lost one of its red-and-white-striped shutters. The other one, weathered and peeling, hung askew by one hinge. It was too easy to imagine she saw a pale face framed there.

Tamír looked away, slowing Midnight to a walk as she took in signs of life all around her.

The meadow had been mown and small haystacks dotted the slope. Sheep and goats grazed around them, cropping the new growth. There were wild geese and swans on the river, and a young servant boy fishing on the bank just below the plank bridge. He jumped up and stared at them as they approached, then bolted for the gate.

The barracks had a new roof, and the herb and flower beds she and Ki had helped Arkoniel plant beside it had been well tended and expanded. Bright flowers blossomed along the edges and there were rows of vegetables, too. Two young girls with baskets on their hips stepped around the corner of the barracks, then darted back out of sight as the boy had.

"Who are all these people?" asked Ki.

"New servants from the village," Arkoniel told him, catching up in time to overhear. "When I was here with the children, Cook needed more help. It appears she's hired a few more since I left."

"And Brother not here to scare them away," murmured Tamír. Then, whispering to the wizard, "Did my mother trouble them?"

"No," Arkoniel assured her. "I was the only one who ever saw her."

"Oh." Tamír glanced up again, and something else drew her attention: an expanse of blank wall where several windows should have been. "What happened there?"

"Oh that?" said Arkoniel. "I made a few changes a while back, to hide my presence. Don't worry, it's only magic. Nothing permanent."

They reined in at the front gate just as it swung open. Nari and Cook stood there, staring up at her with their hands pressed to their mouths. Nari was the first to recover.

Throwing her arms wide, she burst into happy tears and cried, "Oh, pets, come down for a hug!"

Tamír and Ki swung down from the saddle and she gathered them both into her arms at once. Tamír was amazed at how tiny Nari seemed. She was a head taller than her nurse now.

Nari rose on her toes and kissed them both soundly. "How you've grown this past year, the pair of you. And Ki with a bit of beard. And you, child!" She released Ki into Cook's waiting arms and took Tamír's face between her hands, no doubt searching for the boy she'd known. Tamír saw nothing but love and amazement in the woman's eyes. "Maker's Mercy, look at you, my darling girl! Slim as a wand and the image of your dear mother. Just as I always imagined."

"You recognize me?" Tamír blurted out, relieved. "I'm not so different?"

"Oh, pet!" She hugged Tamír again. "Boy or girl, you're the child I nursed at my breast and held in my arms. How would I not know you?"

Cook hugged her next, then held her at arm's length to look at her. "You've sprouted up like a weed, haven't you?" She kneaded Tamír's upper arm and shoulder. "Not an ounce of meat on either of you. Tharin, doesn't that aunt of yours feed them anything? And poor Master Arkoniel! You look like a scarecrow again, after I got you all fed up proper before. Come in, all of you. We've kept the house ready and the larder's full. None of you will go to bed hungry tonight, I promise you!"

Tamír strode up the worn stone stairs to the great hall. It was just as she remembered from her birthday visit, in good repair, but with a dusty, tarnished air about it. Even with the afternoon sun shining in through the open doors and windows, there were still shadows lurking in the corners and up in the carved rafters. There were good smells on the air, though: warm bread and apple pie and spices.

"You've been cooking. Did you know we were coming?"

"No, Majesty, though you might have sent someone ahead," Cook chided. "No, I've been trading with the town and making a bit of profit for you. I've laid down some good wines and the buttery's full. By the time your people are settled I'll have a proper spread on for you. Miko, go and start the fire for me, there's a good boy! Girls, you see to the linens."

The servants they'd seen by the bridge emerged from the shadows by the door and hurried off on their assigned tasks.

As Tamír headed for the stairs she heard Tyrien whisper to Lynx, "The queen grew up *here*?"

Smiling to herself, Tamír took the stairs two at a time, with Ki close behind. She wondered when she could steal away to find Lhel, or if the witch would even show herself. And if she did, then what would Tamír say to her now?

Their old room was neat and well aired as if they still lived there. There was the wardrobe Brother had tried to crush Iya with, and the carved clothes chest where Tamír had hidden the doll. She felt a familiar pang, looking at that wide bed with its faded hangings and thick coverlet. She caught a look of the same pain in Ki's face as he stepped next door to the toy room.

"The extra bed's still here," he called. "The Companions and I can use this room."

Tamír leaned in the doorway, looking at the toy city and the other bits and pieces of her childhood lying about. The only things missing were the old rag doll and Brother's sullen presence. Before Ki came to live with her, the demon had been her only playmate. She hadn't felt or seen Brother since Afra.

She went across the corridor and stood a moment in her father's room, trying to imagine she could still sense his spirit or catch his scent. But it was just a room, long abandoned.

Arkoniel paused in the doorway, with his traveling bundle in his arms. "I'll take my old room upstairs, if that's all right with you."

"Of course," she replied absently, thinking of a different room. She would visit that one later, and alone.

She lingered a moment longer, and Tharin quietly stepped in to join her. He had his saddlebags over one shoulder and looked slightly baffled.

"The guard will take the barracks. I still have my old room there, but—Well, perhaps you'd rather I take one of the guest chambers upstairs?"

"I'd be honored if you'd sleep in Father's room." Before he could object, she added, "I'd feel better, knowing you're so close by."

"As you wish." He set his bag down and looked around. "It's good to be back. You should come more often, when things settle down. I miss the hunting here."

She nodded, understanding all he couldn't say. "Me, too."

Chapter 38

Cook was as good as her word; the supper was ample and well received. Everyone gathered around one long table and the squires helped the serving girls carry the dishes back and forth from the kitchen.

Nari sat on Tamír's left and asked endless questions about her battles and Ero and all that was going on at Atyion in preparation to meet Korin, but not once did she ask about the change. She treated Tamír just as she had treated Tobin, not in the least troubled by the alteration. She didn't even forget and call her Tobin. Not once.

They sat around the fire with their wine afterward and told more stories of the fighting they'd seen. Then Tharin and the women began reminiscing about Tamír and Ki when they were children here, much to the amusement of the other Companions. Arkoniel joined in, embellishing with apparent relish on what a poor student Ki had been. There was no mention of the death and tragedy these walls had witnessed, but Tamír caught the younger squires glancing around nervously as night closed in.

"I've heard this keep is haunted," Lorin ventured at last. Nikides gave him a warning look and the boy shrank down on the bench, murmuring, "That's only what I heard."

With no proper entertainment, there was little to keep them up late. Tamír kissed Nari and Cook good night and sent her guardsmen off.

"It's time we got some sleep, eh?" Nikides said, gathering the others.

They said good night outside their rooms, but Ki lingered at her door. "I'll stay, if you want. No one here cares."

The temptation to say yes was so strong it took her breath away, but she shook her head. "No, better not."

"Good night, then." He turned for the door, but not before she caught the hurt look in his eyes.

It's for the best. This is my task. He can't help and it would only endanger him needlessly. It's for the best . . .

She kept telling herself that as she sat cross-legged on the bed, waiting for the others to settle next door.

Someone laughed. A low murmur of voices followed, and the sounds of a good-natured argument as the unlucky squires were relegated to the pallets on the floor. She heard the shuffle of feet, the creak of bed ropes, then a dwindling murmur.

Tamír waited a bit longer and wandered over to the window. The moon was bright over meadow and river. She rested her chin in her hands, thinking of all the times she'd played there with Ki, the snow soldiers they'd fought, the fishing and swimming, and just lying on their backs in the tall grass, finding shapes in the clouds.

Satisfied that all was quiet next door, she took her night lamp and stole from the room. There was no sound from Tharin's room, either, and no light beneath his door.

Upstairs a single lamp burned in a niche near Arkoniel's chamber. She tiptoed past, keeping her gaze fixed on the tower door. Only when her hand was on the tarnished latch did she recall it had been locked since her mother's death, the key long since thrown away. Brother had opened the door for her last time.

"Brother," she whispered. "Please?"

She pressed her ear to the door, listening for any sign of him. The wood was cold, much colder than it should have been on a summer night, even here.

Another memory stirred. She'd stood here before, imagining the bloody, angry ghost of her mother just on the other side, in a rising tide of blood. She looked down, but nothing crept out from beneath it but a big grey spider. She flinched as it scuttled across her bare foot.

"Tamír?"

She nearly dropped her lamp as she whirled around. Arkoniel caught it and placed it safely in a niche beside the door.

"Bilairy's *balls*! You scared the piss out of me!" she gasped.

"Sorry. I knew you'd come and thought you might need some help with that lock. And you'll need this, too."

He opened his left hand and light spilled out between his fingers from the small pebble glowing there.

She took the lightstone. It was cool as moonlight in her hand. "Less chance of me setting the place on fire with this, I guess."

"I should go with you."

"No. The Oracle said it's my burden. Stay here. I'll call out if I need you."

He pressed a palm to the door beside the lock and Tamír heard the wards grind and fall. She lifted the latch and pushed the door open with a squeal of rusty hinges. Cold air rushed out, smelling of dust and mice and the forest beyond the river.

They stepped into the little open space between the door and the base of the tower stairs and Arkoniel pushed the door to, leaving it open just a crack.

She climbed the stairs slowly, holding the lightstone up and steadying herself with one hand against the wall. The scabrous feel of lichen and bird droppings brought back more memories. She felt like a little child again, following her mother up these stairs for the first time.

I'm like these swallows, with my nest high above the keep.

The door at the top of the stairs stood wide, a gaping mouth of darkness. She could hear the breeze sighing in the room beyond, and the skitter of mice. It took all her courage to climb those last few stairs.

She paused in the doorway, clinging to the jamb as she

searched the deeper shadows beyond. "Mother, are you here? I've come home."

Ki had guessed what Tamír intended to do the moment they'd turned aside for the keep. During supper he'd seen how often her gaze strayed to the stairs. When she turned down his offer to stay with her that night, he knew for certain she meant to go to the tower alone.

Lying in bed beside Lynx, he listened until his ears rang, and heard the sound of her door quietly opening and the soft pad of bare feet passing his door.

She'd have asked me to come if she'd wanted me along. Tamír had always been close-mouthed about the ghosts who haunted this place, even with him. So he wrestled with himself, and tried to sleep, but every instinct said to follow her.

He'd lain down in his shirt and breeches. It was a simple matter to ease out of bed and step carefully around the squires on their pallets. He thought the others were all asleep, but as he opened the door to creep out, he glanced back and saw Lynx watching him.

Ki put a finger to his lips and closed the door softly behind him, wondering what his friend thought he was off to do. There was no help for that now.

There was no sign of Tamír. He crept up the stairs and paused, stealing a quick look down this corridor just in time to see Arkoniel slipping through the tower door.

That gave him pause. She'd left him behind, but asked the wizard to help? Ki shrugged off the hurt and stole down the corridor to the tower door. It was slightly ajar and he pushed it open.

Arkoniel was sitting on the bottom step, fidgeting with his wand. A lightstone glowed on the next step up.

Arkoniel gave a start when he saw Ki, then shook his head. "I might have known you'd show up," he whispered. "She insisted on going alone, but I don't like it. Stay here with me. She'll call if she needs me."

Ki joined him on the step. "Is her mother really up there?"

"Oh yes. Whether or not she chooses to show herself—"

He broke off, and they both looked up as they heard the faint sound of Tamír's voice. Ki broke out in gooseflesh, knowing what it meant. Tamír was talking with the dead.

Mother?"

There was no reply.

The room was just as Tamír remembered. Broken furniture, rotting bolts of cloth, and mice-chewed bales of stuffing wool still lay where Brother had thrown them. A table had been righted under the east window and the last of her mother's mouthless dolls sat there in a row, leaning awkwardly against each other like drunken men. Arkoniel had found her doll among them; she could see a gap where it had been.

She went to the table and picked one up. It was mildewed and discolored, but her mother's small, careful stitches were still visible in the seams. She held it up to her light, looking at the blank face. This one was still plump with wool, its limbs even and loose. It surprised her, how tempting it was to carry it away with her. In a way, she missed the misshapen doll she'd hidden for so long, though it had been a burden at the time. But it had also been a tie to her mother, and her past. She clutched this doll impulsively to her heart. How she'd wanted her mother to make one for her! Tears stung her eyes and she let them fall, mourning the childhood she'd been denied.

A soft sigh made the hair on her neck stand up. She turned and searched the room, clutching the doll and the lightstone.

The sigh came again, louder this time. Tamír squinted into the shadows by the western window—the window her mother had leaped from, that winter day. The one she'd tried to push Tamír out of.

Brother's not here to save me this time.

"Mother?" Tamír whispered again.

She heard the rustle of skirts, and another sigh, full of pain. Then, in the faintest of whispers, a ghostly voice murmured, *my child—*

Hope made the breath catch in Tamír's throat. She took a step closer. "Yes, it's me!"

Where is my child? Where? Where—

The brief stab of hope died, just as it always had. "Mother?"

Where is my son?

It was just like it had been on her mother's worst days. She wasn't even aware of Tamír, longing instead for the child she'd lost.

Tamír started to speak again, but a sharp crack startled her so badly she nearly dropped the lightstone. The shutters on the western window shook as if they'd been struck, then creaked slowly open, pushed by unseen hands.

Tamír clenched the doll and stood her ground, watching in mounting horror as a dark figure resolved from the shadows and lurched with slow, jerking steps to the window. Its face was turned away, as if watching the river below the window.

The ghostly woman wore a dark gown and was clutching something to her breast. She was of a height with Tamír and her shining black hair fell in loose disarray to her waist. Strands of it stirred around her, coiling lazily on the air. Framed against the night sky, she seemed as solid as a living person.

"Mo—mother? Look at me, Mother. I'm here. I've come to see you."

Where is my child? The whisper was more of a hiss this time.

Where is your mother? The Oracle's voice goaded her.

"I'm your daughter. I'm called Tamír. I was Tobin, but I'm Tamír now. Mother, look at me. Hear me!"

Daughter? The ghost turned slowly, still with that unnatural, jerking hesitation, as if she'd forgotten how a body moved. She was holding her old misshapen doll, or at least its ghost. Tamír held her breath as she caught sight of a pale cheek, a familiar profile. Then her mother was facing her, and the sight of her was like an eerie mirror.

The others were right after all, Tamír thought numbly, beyond fear as those eyes came to rest on her with something like recognition. In the months since the change, Tamír's face had altered subtly, not so much softening as shifting into more of a semblance of this dead woman's face. Tamír took a step toward her, vaguely aware that they were clutching their dolls the same way, in the crook of their left arm.

"Mother, it's me, your daughter," she tried again, searching for comprehension in that face.

Daughter?

"Yes! I've come to tell you that you have to go on, to the gate."

The ghost saw her now. *Daughter?*

Tamír moved the light to her left hand and reached out to her. Her mother mirrored her, reaching out to her. Their fingertips brushed and Tamír could feel them, solid as her own but deathly cold as Brother's.

Undeterred, she clasped that cold hand tight. "Mother, you must rest. You can't stay here anymore."

The woman came closer, staring at Tamír as if she was trying to understand who she was.

A tear tickled down Tamír's cheek. "Yes, it's me."

Suddenly the room was bright around them. Sunlight streamed in at all the windows, and the room was cozy and filled with color and the good smells of wood and sun-dried linen and candles. The hearth was filled with withered flowers and the chairs were upright beside it, their tapestry cushions whole and unblemished. Dolls littered the table, clean and dressed in little velvet outfits.

Her mama was alive, blue eyes warm with one of her rare smiles. "Have you learned your letters, Tobin?"

"Yes, Mama." Tamír was crying outright now. She dropped the doll and the lightstone and embraced her. It was strange, being tall enough to bury her face in that silky black hair, but she didn't question it, overcome by the light flower scent she remembered so well. "Oh Mother, I've come home to help you. I'm sorry I was gone so long. I tried to help Brother. I really did!"

Warm hands stroked her hair and back. "There, there, don't cry my darling. There's a good boy—"

Tamír froze. "No, Mother, I'm not a boy anymore—" She tried to pull back, but her mother held her tight.

"My sweet, dear boy. How I love you! I was so frightened when I couldn't find you."

Tamír began to struggle, and then they both went still as the sound of horsemen came to them from the road outside.

Ariani released her and ran to the east window. "He's found us!"

"Who? Who's found us?" Tamír whispered.

"My brother!" Ariani's eyes were wide with terror and black as Brother's as she rushed back to Tamír and grasped her arm in a painful grip. "He's coming! But he won't have us. No, he won't have us!"

And she pulled Tamír toward the west window.

Ki and Arkoniel had moved halfway up the stair, straining to make out what Tamír was saying. Suddenly they heard her call out to her mother, pleading with her about something.

Then the door at the top of the stairs slammed shut with a bang so loud that Ki missed his footing and tumbled backward into Arkoniel.

* * *

*T*amír knew beyond all doubt that she was fighting for her life, just as she had that other day. Her mother had been too strong for her then, and her ghost easily overpowered her now. Caught in that inexorable grip, Tamír was dragged across the floor toward the window as if she weighed no more than a child.

"No, Mother, no!" she pleaded, trying to break loose.

It was no use. The specter gave a last yank and Tamír found herself halfway out the window, teetering with her belly on the sill, only her bent knees keeping her from falling. It was night again. The river flowed black and the rocks it tumbled around looked silver and she was tilting farther and screaming and something dark was hurtling past her, dragging her down, a pale wraith with swirling skirts and wild black hair . . .

*K*i and Arkoniel tumbled over each other to the base of the stairs. Ki was up first and dashed back up, heedless of the bruises or the taste of blood in his mouth as he took the worn steps two and three at a time. He struck the door with his shoulder and wrenched at the latch, but someone or something was holding it shut from the other side. He could hear the sounds of a struggle, and Tamír's wordless cry of fear.

"Arkoniel, help!" Ki yelled, frantic. "Tamír, can you hear me?"

"Get back!" Arkoniel shouted.

Ki barely had time to duck before a wave of force swept over him, knocking the door off its hinges. Ki scrambled up again and bolted into the room. It was cold inside, and a foul, swampy odor hung in the air. A lightstone lay amid the wreckage on the floor, casting enough illumination to see the horrid, bloody figure at the west window trying to force Tamír out. All Ki could see of her were her flailing legs and bare feet. Even as Ki dashed to save her, the thing thrust her out over the sill.

It was a woman, that much he could tell in his headlong

rush. The form was pale and flickered like fox fire. Ki had an impression of writhing black hair and empty black eyes in a bone-pale face. Hands like claws clutched Tamír by the hair and tunic as it shoved her out even farther.

"No!" Ki reached Tamír just as she began to teeter over the brink. He lunged through the specter and felt an even denser chill, but his hands were strong and sure as he caught Tamír by one bare foot and hauled with all his might, roughly dragging her back to safety.

Tamír collapsed limply to the floor. Ki crouched over her, ready to fend off her mother's vengeful spirit with his bare hands if he had to, but there was no sign of her now.

He pulled Tamír farther from the window, then gently turned her over. Her eyes were closed and her face was horribly pale. Blood flowed from a deep cut across her chin, but she was breathing.

Arkoniel stumbled across the littered floor and fell to his knees beside them. "How is she?"

"I don't know."

Hands clawed at her back, then Tamír was flying backward again. Something struck her chin hard enough to stun her. The world spun—stars and river and rough stone walls and darkness.

Then she was lying in the dark, ruined room again and someone was holding her tight, so tight she couldn't breathe.

"Mother, no!" she screamed, struggling with what little strength she had left.

"No, Tamír, it's me! Open your eyes. Arkoniel, *do* something, for hell's sake!"

She heard a sharp crack and she was blinking in soft pale light. It was Ki holding her, his face etched with sorrow. Arkoniel stood just behind him, wand in hand, blood streaming from a cut on his forehead. A strange smell hung in the air, bitter like burned hair.

"Ki?" She tried in vain to comprehend what had just

happened. She felt chilled to the bone and her heart was pounding so hard it hurt.

"I have you, Tamír. I'm taking you out of here." He stroked her hair back with shaking fingers.

"My mother—"

"I saw her. I won't let her hurt you again. Come on!" He dragged her up and wrapped an arm around her waist.

Tamír found her feet and staggered with him for the door. Ki's arm was strong and sure around her, but she could still feel the icy grip of her mother's hands.

"Take her down to my room. I'm going to seal this door," Arkoniel said behind them.

Somehow Ki got her down the stairs without falling and hurried her into Arkoniel's chamber. Candles and lamps burned brightly there, casting a bright, comforting glow.

Ki lowered her into a chair by the empty hearth, then yanked a blanket from the bed and tucked it around her. Kneeling, he chafed her hands and wrists. "Say something, please!"

She blinked slowly. "I'm all right. She—she isn't here. I don't feel her anymore."

Ki glanced around and let out a shaky laugh. "That's good news. I don't *ever* want to see anything like that again." He used a corner of the blanket to dab at her chin. It hurt and she flinched away.

"Hold still," Ki said. "You're bleeding."

She touched her chin and felt warm, sticky wetness there. "The sill. I hit the sill. Just like before."

Ki gently pulled her fingers away. "Yes, just like before, only you're going to have a bigger scar this time."

Tamír clutched her forehead, feeling faint. "He—Brother? He pulled me back?"

"No, that was me. I heard you cry out, and got there just—" He was pressed close to her, his belly against her knees. He was shaking.

"By the Flame," he went on, his voice less steady now.

"She almost had you out, that horrible creature. It was worse than Brother—" He broke off again and wrapped his arms around her as if she could still fall.

"You pulled me back?" she whispered against his shoulder.

"Yes, but I almost lost you. Damn it, what were you thinking, going up alone?"

He was weeping! She hugged him, burying one hand in his hair. "Don't cry. You were there, Ki. You saved me. It's all right."

Concern for him swept away the last of her fear. She'd never heard Ki weep like this before. It shook his whole body and his grip on her was painfully tight again, but it felt good.

At last he sat back on his heels, wiping his face on his sleeve. "I'm sorry! I just—I thought—" Tamír saw real fear in his eyes. "I didn't think I was going to get to you in time, before she—" He grabbed her by the arms as fear gave way to anger. "Why, Tamír? What made you go up there alone?"

"The Oracle said—"

He shook her angrily. "That you ought to get yourself killed?"

"What did the Oracle say to you?" asked Arkoniel, coming in to join them. The bitter smell around him was stronger than it had been upstairs.

"She told me that my mother—how she is now—it's my burden. I thought that meant I was supposed to set her free. I thought if she saw me in my true form, it would—I don't know, that it would give her peace? But it didn't," she finished miserably. "It was just like that day Uncle came here."

"Then Nari was right." Arkoniel stroked Tamír's hair. "Why didn't you ever tell me?"

"I don't know. I guess I was ashamed."

"Of what?" asked Ki.

Tamír hung her head. They couldn't know what it had been like, to not be enough, to not be *seen*.

"Forgive me, Tamír. I should never have let you go alone." Arkoniel sighed. "You can't reason with a spirit like that, any more than you could with Brother."

"Then why did the Oracle tell her to do it?" Ki demanded.

"I can't imagine. Maybe Tamír misunderstood."

"I don't think so," Tamír whispered.

"Damn Illiorans!"

"You mustn't blaspheme, Ki," Arkoniel chided.

Ki stood up and wiped his face. "I'm staying with you, in case she comes back. Don't even try to talk me out of it. Can you walk?"

Tamír was too tired to pretend she didn't want that.

"Stay here," said Arkoniel. "I have protections on this room, and I'll keep watch outside. Rest well." He went out, closing the door behind him.

Tamír let Ki tuck her into Arkoniel's bed, and caught his hand when he was finished. "Sleep with me? I—I need you."

Ki climbed in under the covers with her and pulled her into his arms. She put an arm around his waist and relaxed against his shoulder. He stroked her hair for a few minutes, then she felt the warm press of lips against her forehead. She brought his hand to her lips and kissed him back.

"Thank you. I know this isn't—"

Lips against her own cut off the apology. Ki was kissing her, *really* kissing her. It lasted longer than any brotherly peck they'd shared before, and was far softer yet more decisive than his awkward attempt in Afra.

Even now, with Tamír safe in his arms, Ki kept reliving that awful moment when he was so certain he wasn't going to reach her in time. Over and over again, in his imagination, he felt what it would have been like if she'd died. His own tears earlier had shamed him, but this sudden impulsive kiss did not. He wanted to do it, and she was responding. So was his body.

Tamír. This is Tamír, not Tobin, he told himself, but he still couldn't quite believe what he was doing.

When it ended they stared at each other, wide-eyed and unsure, and she gave him a hesitant smile.

It did something to him Ki couldn't explain, and he kissed her again, lingering a little longer over it this time. His chin bumped the cut on hers and he tried to pull back, but the arm across his chest tightened and he felt her leaning into him. He buried his fingers in her hair, snagging a braid. She flinched as it pulled, then chuckled.

At the sound of it, he felt like something that had been dammed tight in his heart let go at last. He combed his fingers through her hair more confidently, then stroked his way down to her waist. She was still fully clothed, wearing the dress she'd put on for Nari at supper. The skirt had ridden up a little. He could feel her bare leg warm against his through his breeches. No, this wasn't any boy in his arms. It was Tamír, as warm and different from his own body as any girl he'd ever bedded. His heart beat faster as he deepened the kiss and felt her eager response.

Tamír felt the difference in Ki's touch and the unmistakable press of his arousal against her thigh. Unsure what she wanted or where this would lead, but determined nonetheless, she took his hand and pressed it to her left breast. He cupped it gently through her bodice, then tugged the lacings and chemise aside and slipped his fingers inside to caress her bare skin. Rough and warm, his fingertips found the scar between her breasts and traced it lightly, then brushed across a nipple. He'd never touched Tobin like that. It sent warmth spiraling down through her to blossom into a new sensation between her legs.

So this is what it's like? she thought as he kissed his way down to her throat and bit her gently on the side of the neck.

She caught her breath and her eyes widened as the feeling between her legs flared stronger. Just as before, she could still feel the phantom shape of her male body, but with something much deeper, in places only a woman had. If she had both bodies at once, male and female, then both were awakened by Ki's hands and lips against her skin.

It was too much, too unsettling, that dual sensation. She pulled back a little, heart pounding, her traitorous body at once yearning and afraid. "Ki, I don't know if I can—"

He withdrew his hand and stroked her cheek. He was breathless, too, but smiling. "It's all right. I'm not asking for that now."

That? Bilairy's balls, he thought I meant fucking! she realized with dismay. *Of course he did. That's what he does with girls.*

"Tamír?" He gently urged her head down on his chest and held her tight. "It's all right. I don't want to think about anything but you being here right now, alive and well. If you'd—died tonight, like that?" His voice went husky again. "I couldn't have stood it!" He fell silent a moment and his arms tightened around her. "I was never scared like this for you in battle. What do you suppose that means?"

She found his hand with her own and clasped it. "That no matter what, we're both still warriors, before all else?" Somehow, that was comforting. At least in this, she still knew who she was.

She could still feel the hardness against her thigh, but Ki seemed content just to lie next to her, as they used to. Without thinking, she shifted her leg a little to get a better sense of his body.

It's bigger than what I had, she thought, then froze as Ki let out a soft sigh and shifted a little against her.

Arkoniel sat in the doorway of his workroom, gaze fixed on the tower door, and wondered if he dared leave long enough to fetch Tharin. He ached here and there from his tumble down the stairs and his ears were still ringing from the spell he'd cast to seal the door.

No, he decided. He'd stay until dawn, then go down and make certain the others didn't worry at finding Tamír's bed empty.

And what will I do if Ariani does come looking for her child again?

It had been Ki who'd saved Tamír, not him. He'd only driven the ghost off after Ki had her safe.

Blessed Lightbearer, what was your purpose, putting that into her mind? You couldn't mean for her to die, so what was it you were trying to show her? Why open up those old wounds now?

His bruised limbs were beginning to stiffen. He stood and paced the corridor, pausing a moment outside the bedchamber door. All was quiet inside. He reached for the latch, thinking to check on them, then drew it back. He stood there a moment longer, debating, and cast a wizard eye instead.

Ki and Tamír were fast asleep, wrapped in each other's arms like lovers.

Lovers?

Arkoniel took a closer look. They were both still dressed as they had been, but he could make out the faint smiles they both wore in sleep. Ki had a smear of dried blood on his chin that matched nicely with the cut on Tamír's chin.

Arkoniel dispersed the spell and turned away smiling. *Not yet, but there's been a change. Perhaps some good will come out of this night, after all.*

Chapter 39

K i had intended to get Tamír downstairs to her own bed before anyone noticed they were gone, but instead he fell asleep, and woke just after dawn with Tamír still in his arms. She didn't stir when he tilted his head back to see if she was asleep.

Her face was half-hidden behind a fall of black hair. The cut on her chin was scabbed over, the area around it bruised and a little swollen. She'd have a new scar there, to show for last night's adventure.

Even in daylight, Ki felt a chill as he thought of the spirit haunting the tower room. He'd never met Ariani in life. Last night he'd seen no sign of the woman Arkoniel described, only a vengeful specter. He unconsciously tightened his arm around Tamír's shoulders.

"Ki?" She gazed sleepily at him for a moment, then gasped and sat up, taking in the fact that they were still in bed together. The lacings of her bodice were still undone, showing the swell of a breast.

Ki looked hastily away. "I'm sorry. I didn't mean to stay all night."

He started to untangle himself from the bedclothes, but the way she colored and looked away made him stop. He stroked the hair back from her cheek, then leaned in and kissed her on the mouth again, the way he had last night. He did it as much to reassure himself as her, and was glad it still felt right in daylight. Her hand came up to cradle his cheek and he felt her relax against him. Blue eyes met brown and widened in unspoken acknowledgment.

"I'm sorry about Afra," he said.

She closed a hand over his on the comforter. "I'm sorry about last night. I just hoped—Well, I suppose I'll have to try again. But I'm not sorry about—" She waved a hand at the rumpled bed.

"Neither am I. First decent night's sleep I've had in months."

She grinned, then threw back the covers and got up. Ki had another glimpse of those long bare legs before her skirt fell into place. She was still very slender and coltish, but those were girl's legs now, the muscle subtly rounder on the long bones, though just as taut. How could he not have seen it before?

She turned and caught him staring. "You look like you swallowed a fish bone."

Ki climbed out of bed and went to her, looking her over again, as if he'd never seen her properly before. She was just a handspan shorter than he was.

She raised an eyebrow. "Well?"

"Nari's right. You have gotten prettier."

"So have you." She licked her thumb and rubbed at the dried blood on his chin. Then she ran a finger over his sparse moustache. "This makes my lip itch when you kiss me."

"You're the queen. You can ban beards if you want."

She considered this, then kissed him again. "No, I think I might get used to it. We don't want anyone saying that all my court turned into girls along with me."

Ki nodded, then voiced the question hanging between them. "What now?"

She shrugged. "I can't take a consort until I'm sixteen, but that's scarcely two months away." She stopped, blushing hotly as she realized what she'd said. "Oh, Ki! I don't mean to—That is—"

He shrugged and scratched nervously at the back of his neck. Marriage was too big a thing to contemplate right now.

Her eyes still held a question. He took her face between his hands and kissed her again. It was chaste, as kisses went in his experience, but his body warmed to it and he could tell by the way her eyes fluttered closed that she felt it, too.

Before he could think of anything to say, Arkoniel knocked and came in. They jumped back from each other with a guilty start.

Arkoniel grinned. "Ah, good, you're awake. Nari was a bit frantic, finding your bed empty—"

Nari pushed past him and gave the two of them a narrow look. "What have you two been up to?"

"Nothing you need upset yourself over," Arkoniel assured her.

But Nari was still frowning. "It won't do, her getting a big belly so young. She hasn't the hips for it yet. You ought to know better, Ki, even if she doesn't!"

"I suppose you have a point," said Arkoniel, looking like he was trying not to laugh.

"I didn't do anything like that!" Ki objected.

"We didn't!" Tamír exclaimed, blushing scarlet.

Nari shook a finger at Tamír. "Well, see you don't, not before you know how to keep from catching. I don't suppose anyone's even shown you how to make a pessary yet?"

"There's been no need," said the wizard.

"Fools, the lot of you! Any girl who has her moon times ought to know that. Out, you men, and leave me to have a proper chat with my girl."

She all but pushed Ki and Arkoniel from the room and shut the door after them.

"I know what a pessary is!" Ki grumbled. His sisters and the servant women had sat around the fire, making the little hanks of wool and ribbon and soaking them in sweet oil. With the whole household sleeping all but on top of one another, there'd been no mystery as to their use either. If a girl didn't want a baby, she put one up her cunny before she bedded her man. The thought of Tamír in that light still left him feeling very odd. "I only kissed her. I wouldn't touch her like that!"

Arkoniel chuckled and said nothing.

Scowling, Ki folded his arms and settled himself to wait for Tamír.

She emerged at last, looking a bit pale. Nari leveled an accusing finger at Ki. "You just keep your trousers laced!"

"I will, damn it!" he called after her as she stomped off downstairs. "Tamír, are you all right?"

She still looked a little stunned. "Yes. But I think I'd rather go into battle naked than have a baby, if all Nari says is true." She shivered, then straightened up and glanced over at the tower door. "Is it locked?"

Arkoniel nodded. "I'll open it, if you like."

"I have to try one more time. You two can come up with me."

"Just try and stop us," Ki told her, not meaning it as a joke.

Arkoniel touched the door and it swung open. "Let me go first and remove the ward from the upper door."

Ki followed close behind Tamír as she climbed the stairs, and was surprised at how ordinary it all looked in daylight. Dust motes glinted in the shafts of early-morning light, and he could smell the sweetness of balsam on the breeze that stirred through the arrow slits.

More brightness greeted them as Arkoniel opened the door to Ariani's room, but Ki stayed close beside Tamír and scanned every corner suspiciously. The shutters on the west window were still open and Ki could hear the sound of the river below, and the calls of birds in the forest.

Tamír stood in the middle of the room and turned slowly around. "She's not here," she said at last, looking more forlorn than relieved.

"No," Arkoniel agreed. "I've felt her presence often at night, but never in daylight."

"I see Brother all the time, day or night."

"He's a different sort of spirit."

Tamír went to the window. Ki followed, unwilling to trust in Arkoniel's appraisal of ghosts. For all he knew, that bloodied nightmare could come rushing out of nowhere at any moment. Ghosts were always unlucky things, or so he'd been taught, and those who haunted Tamír gave truth to the saying.

"What do I do?" Tamír wondered aloud.

"Perhaps nothing," Arkoniel replied.

"Why did the Oracle send me back, then?"

"Some things can't be mended, Tamír."

"What about Lhel?" asked Ki. "We haven't even looked for her yet. She could always put Brother in his place. Come on, Tamír, let's ride up the road, like we used to."

Tamír brightened at once and made for the door. "Of course! I bet she's waiting for us, like always."

"Wait." Arkoniel called after them.

Ki turned to find Arkoniel regarding them sorrowfully.

"She's not here anymore."

"How do you know that?" asked Tamír. "You know how she is. If she doesn't want to be found, then you can't, and if she does, she's right there waiting for you, every time."

"I thought the same, until—" Arkoniel paused, and Ki read the truth in his face before he even said it. "She's dead, Tamír. The Oracle told me."

"Dead?" Tamír sank slowly to her knees among scattered bits of yellowed wool. "But how?"

"If I were to guess, I'd say Brother was responsible. I'm sorry. I should have told you, but you already had so much to contend with."

"Dead." Tamír shivered and buried her face in her hands. "Another one. More blood!"

Ki knelt and put an arm around her, blinking back tears of his own. "I thought—I thought she'd always be there waiting for us in that hollow tree of hers."

"So did I," Arkoniel agreed sadly.

Tamír raised a hand to the hidden scar on her chest. "I want to look for her. I want to bury her. It's only right."

"Have a bite to eat and change your clothes," Arkoniel advised.

Tamír nodded and turned to go.

"Hold on," said Ki. He ran his fingers through her disheveled hair. "That's better, eh?" he said, straightening his own rumpled tunic. "No sense giving them too much to gossip about."

That was easier said than done. As Tamír went to her chamber to change, she noticed Lynx and Nikides watching her from their open doorway. Tamír didn't think she or Ki gave anything away, but they took one look and turned away with knowing smiles.

"Damn it!" she muttered, mortified.

"I'll talk to them." Ki gave her a rueful look and went off to deal with their friends.

Tamír shook her head as she closed her own door, wondering what he'd say. She wasn't entirely sure herself what had happened between them, but she somehow felt lighter, and more hopeful, even with her sorrow over Lhel.

Whatever Ki told them, no one asked any questions.

As soon as they could slip away she, Ki, and Arkoniel set off up the old mountain road.

It would have been a pleasant ride if not for the sad knowledge they carried. The sun was bright and the forest showed early splashes of yellow and crimson.

Ki spotted the faint hint of a trail half a mile on from the keep. Leaving their horses tethered, they followed it on foot.

"It could just be a game trail," he noted.

"No, there's her mark," Arkoniel said, pointing out a faded, rust-colored mark on the white trunk of a birch. Looking closer, Ki saw that it was a handprint, much smaller than his own.

"That's from her hiding spell," Arkoniel explained, touching it sadly. "The power of it died with her."

The faded traces of more handprints guided them along a faint path winding through the trees and up a slope to the clearing.

At first glance nothing had changed. The deerskin flap still covered the low doorway at the base of the huge hollow oak. Beyond it, the spring roiled silently in its round pool.

As he approached the tree, however, Ki saw that the ashes in the fire pit were old, and her wooden drying racks were empty and in need of repair. Tamír pushed the deerskin aside and disappeared inside. Ki and Arkoniel followed.

Animals had been in here. Lhel's baskets were scattered and gnawed, the dried fruit and meat long gone. Her few implements still lay on low shelves, and her pallet of furs was undisturbed.

What remained of Lhel was there, as if she'd lain down to sleep and never wakened again. Animals and insects had done their work. The shapeless dress with its deer tooth beading was torn and pulled awry, exposing the bare bones beneath. Only her hair remained, a dark tumble of black curls framing the eyeless skull.

Arkoniel sank down with a groan and wept quietly. Tamír remained silent, shedding no tears. The empty look in her eyes as she silently turned and went outside troubled Ki.

He found her standing by the spring.

"She showed me my true face here," she whispered, staring down at her shifting reflection in the water. Ki was tempted to put an arm around her, but she stepped away, still lost and empty. "The ground is hard and we have nothing to dig with. We should have brought a spade."

There was nothing among Lhel's meager possessions that would serve, either. Arkoniel found her silver knife and needle and tucked them into his belt. The rest they left, and piled stones in front of the doorway, making her home her tomb. Arkoniel cast a spell on the stones so that they would not fall away.

Through it all Tamír did not weep. When they were finished with the stones she pressed a hand to the oak's gnarled trunk, as if communing with the spirit of the woman immured inside.

"There's nothing more to be done here," she said at last. "We'd better get on to Atyion."

Ki and the wizard exchanged a sad look and followed, letting her alone with her silent grief.

She's seen too much of death already, Ki thought. *And we still have a war ahead of us.*

Chapter 40

The pain of Lhel's death, compounded with the knowledge of the role she'd played in Brother's death, was too black and deep to give voice to. Tamír left those feelings behind with the witch's bones, taking away only a numb sense of shock and loss.

There was no reason to stay, and the keep was once again a place with too many bad memories. They left that same day.

Nari and Cook kissed her and Ki both over and over again, then wept in their aprons when they finally departed. As she rode along the river, Tamír turned and looked up at the tower window one last time. The broken shutter on the east window was still hanging by one twisted hinge. She saw no face in the opening, but she swore she felt eyes on her back until they rode into the cover of the trees.

I'm sorry, Mother. Perhaps another time.

Ki leaned over and touched her arm. "Let it go. You did what you could. Arkoniel's right. Some things can't be mended."

Perhaps he was right, but she still felt she'd failed.

They rode hard that day and slept wrapped in their cloaks that night. Lying there among the others, Tamír touched the bruise on her chin, letting her thoughts stray back to Ki and the way it had felt to kiss him and fall asleep in his arms.

He lay within arm's reach, but she couldn't touch him.

As she was about to turn over he opened his eyes and smiled.

It was almost as good as a kiss.

She wondered what they'd do when they were in the castle again, under so many watchful eyes.

When they were in half a day's ride of the town, Tamír sent Lynx and Tyrien ahead with news of her safe return. By the time they came in sight of Atyion early that evening, the city was brightly lit with torches and lanterns, and a great crowd had assembled along the main street, eager to hear the Oracle's words to their queen. Illardi met her on horseback at the town gate, dressed in the robe and chain of his office. Kaliya, head priestess of the Illioran temple of Atyion, and Imonus were with him.

"Majesty, did the Oracle speak to you?" Imonus inquired.

"Yes, she did," she replied, loud enough to be heard by those gathered around the small square there.

"If it please Your Majesty, will you share it with us, in the temple square?" asked Kaliya.

Tamír nodded and led her entourage toward the square of the Four. Illardi leaned closer in the saddle. "I have news for you, Majesty. That young fellow of Arkoniel's—Eyoli—he sent word a few days ago by pigeon from Cirna. Korin is preparing to move against you. It seems he finally got his new wife with child."

"Is he on the march?" asked Tharin.

"Not by today's report, but from what your wizards were able to show us of the encampments, they are nearly ready."

"I'll speak with Eyoli as soon as we're finished here," Arkoniel murmured.

Tamír's heart sank, though she was hardly surprised. "Give him my thanks. And send word to Gedre and Bôkthersa. The emissaries should be home by now, Lord Chancellor, and I'll speak with you and my generals—"

"Tomorrow's soon enough, Majesty. You're weary, I can tell. Rest tonight. I've already begun preparations."

People thronged the steps of the four temples, and more stood on the roofs, eager to hear the first official prophecy of her reign.

Still in the saddle, she took out the scroll Ralinus had given her. "These are the words of Illior, given to me by the Oracle of Afra."

She'd been amazed when she'd read it in Afra. She hadn't told Ralinus what the Oracle had actually said, word for word. Yet what he'd written was nearly the same.

"Hear the words of the Oracle, people of Skala." Her voice sounded thin and high in the open air, and it was a strain to speak so loudly but she pressed on. "'Hail, Queen Tamír, daughter of Ariani, daughter of Agnalain, trueborn scion of Skala's royal line. By blood you were protected and by blood will you rule. You are a seed, watered with blood, Tamír of Skala. By blood and trial, you will hold your throne. From the Usurper's hand you will wrest the Sword. Before you and behind you lies a river of blood, bearing Skala to the west. There will you build a new city, to my honor.'"

A stunned silence greeted her words.

"Prince Korin calls himself king in Cirna and is massing an army against me," she went on. "I've sent him messages, asking him to give up his claim and be honored as my kinsman. His only answer has been silence. Now I'm told that he means to march on Atyion with an army at his back. As much as it grieves me, I will heed the words of the Oracle, and the visions given to me. I am your queen, and I will put down this rebellion against the throne. Will you follow me?"

The people cheered and waved swords and colored banners in the air. The acclaim warmed her, lifting some of the darkness from her heart. Korin had made his decision.

Now she must act on hers, no matter how painful the outcome.

Her duty done, Tamír gave the scroll to Kaliya to be displayed in the temple and copied and read out across the land by heralds.

"That went well," Ki noted as they rode on for the castle.

"The people love you, and they'll fight to keep you," said Tharin.

Tamír said nothing, thinking of all the blood the Oracle had shown her. She could already feel it staining her hands.

They made their way through the barbican and found Lytia and most of the castle household waiting for her in the castle yard. "Welcome back, Majesty," Lytia greeted her as Tamír dismounted and stretched her stiffened legs.

"Thank you. I hope you didn't go to the trouble of a feast. I just want a bath and my bed."

Some of the other wizards and children were there, as well.

"Where is Mistress Iya?" asked Rala.

Tamír heard, and wondered what Arkoniel would tell them, and if they'd stay. For now, though, he evaded the questions as he drew them away, already asking for reports on Korin.

Tamír left him to it and strode up the steps, anxious to relax in private before the court duties descended on her. She hadn't missed those at all.

Lytia accompanied her and the Companions upstairs. As Tamír reached her chamber door, Lytia touched her sleeve and murmured, "A word in private, Majesty? It's rather important."

Tamír nodded for her to follow, leaving the others outside.

Baldus was curled up in a chair with Ringtail on his lap. He pushed the cat off and jumped up to bow.

"Welcome back, Queen Tamír! Shall I light the fire for you?"

"No, go tell the bath servants I want a tub. And make it a hot one!"

Baldus dashed out, happy to have his mistress back. Tamír wondered fleetingly what he did when she wasn't around to wait on. She unbuckled her sword and tossed it on the abandoned chair, then began struggling with the buckles on her breastplate. The cat wound around her ankles, purring roughly and nearly tripping her.

Lytia shooed him away and took over the task. Tamír pulled off her hauberk and draped it on its rack, then flopped back on the bed, unmindful of her dirty boots. Ringtail leaped onto the bed and curled up on her chest. "Bilairy's balls, that's better!" She ruffled his thick fur. "Now, what is it you wanted to tell me?"

"Majesty, some of the other Companions arrived in your absence. They've had a hard journey—"

"Una? Is she hurt?" Tamír sat up in alarm. Ringtail hissed and darted away.

"No Majesty. It's Lord Caliel, Lord Lutha, and his squire. I've settled them in one of the guesting chambers in this tower."

Tamír jumped to her feet again, happy beyond words at the news. "Thank the Four! Why weren't they down to greet me? The others will be thrilled to see them."

"I think perhaps you and Lord Ki might wish to see them alone first. There's someone else with them."

"Who?" she asked, already at the door.

The other Companions were waiting outside. Lytia glanced their way, then said softly, "I'll tell you on the way upstairs."

Puzzled, Tamír nodded. "Ki, you come with me. The rest of you wait here."

Lytia led the way to another corridor on the far side of the tower. Pausing a moment, she whispered, "The stranger with them? Well, he's apparently one of the hill folk, Majesty. Lord Lutha claims he's a witch."

"A witch?" Tamír exchanged a startled look with Ki.

"That's why I thought you should come up without too many other eyes," Lytia hastened to explain. "Please forgive me if I've done wrong letting such a creature in, but the others wouldn't be parted from him. I had to put them all under guard. Fortunately they came in at night, and only a few of the servants and guards saw them. None of them will talk. I have their oaths on it until you've had your say."

"Does this man admit to being a witch?" asked Tamír.

"Oh yes. He makes no secret of it. He was dreadfully filthy when they first arrived—well, they all were, poor lads—and he strikes me as a simpleminded fellow, but the others vouched for him and claim he helped them. They've been cruelly used."

"By whom?"

"They wouldn't say."

Four armed men were on guard outside the guest room, and old Vornus and Lyan were sitting on a bench just across from the door, wands across their knees, as if expecting trouble at any moment. They stood and bowed as she approached.

"Can you tell me what's going on?" Tamír asked them.

"We've been keeping watch on your unusual guest," Vornus replied. "Thus far he's behaved himself."

"We've felt no magic from him at all," Lyan added, tucking her wand up her sleeve. "Your people seem terrified, but I've sensed no harm in him."

"Thank you for your vigilance. Please continue to keep watch for now."

The guards stepped aside, and Tamír knocked at the door.

It swung open and there stood Lutha, barefoot and dressed in a long shirt over a pair of breeches. He was thin and pale, and his braids had been cut off, but the look on his face as he recognized Tamír was almost comical. Across the room, Caliel lay on his stomach on a large bed, with Barieus hunched over in a chair beside him. Both stared at her as if they'd seen a ghost.

Lutha gasped. "By the Four! Tobin?"

"It's Tamír, now," Ki told him.

A tense pause followed, then Lutha broke into a tearful grin. "So it's true! Bilairy's balls, we've been hearing rumors ever since we left Ero, but Korin wouldn't believe it." He wiped at his eyes. "I don't know what to say, except that I'm damn glad to see you both alive!"

"What happened to you?"

"Come in first and let the others see you properly."

He led the way to the bed, and Tamír noted how stiffly he moved, as if in pain.

Caliel pushed himself up with a grimace as she and Ki approached. Barieus rose slowly and gave her an uncertain smile, wonder and confusion warring in his eyes.

"Yes, it's Tobin," Ki assured him. "But she's Queen Tamír now."

Barieus looked from Tamír to Ki. "Have you two been fighting? Tamír—your chin? Ki, what happened to your cheek?"

"I fell, and Ki was bitten by a dragon. We both were, actually."

"A dragon?"

"Just a small one," Ki told him.

Lutha laughed. "We've missed a lot, it seems."

It was good to see him smile, but the way they all held themselves, together with Lytia's comment, sent a pang of foreboding through her. All three were missing their braids.

"How?" Caliel asked, staring at her in consternation. His handsome face was mottled with fading bruises, and his eyes were haunted.

With a sigh, Tamír quickly sketched out the details of the change and watched their eyes go wide.

"I know it sounds like something out of a bard's tale, but I saw her change with my own eyes, right here in Atyion, along with about a thousand other people," Ki told them.

"Now, tell me what happened to you three," Tamír urged.

Lutha and Barieus turned their backs and lifted their shirts. Caliel hesitated, then slowly did the same.

"Bilairy's balls!" gasped Ki.

Barieus' and Lutha's backs were crosshatched with half-healed lash marks, but Caliel must have been whipped raw. His skin was a mass of scabs and angry red scar tissue from neck to waist.

Tamír's throat went dry. "Korin?"

Lutha lowered his shirt and helped Caliel pull his back down. All of them looked ashamed as Lutha haltingly told Tamír of their time at Cirna and how her letter to Korin had been received.

"We'd only had the word of Niryn's spies about you, and we didn't trust them," Caliel explained. "I wanted to go see for myself, but Korin said no."

"And you went anyway," Tamír said.

Caliel nodded.

"Niryn had his spies watching us," Lutha said bitterly. "You remember Moriel, who wanted Ki's place as your squire so badly?"

"The Toad? Of course," muttered Ki. "Don't tell me he's still with Korin?"

"He's Niryn's hound now, and he watched every move we made for his master," Caliel said.

"Oh, my friends!" Tamír whispered, deeply touched by their faith in her. "So, what do you say, now that you've seen me?"

Caliel regarded her for a moment, and that haunted look returned. "Well, you don't seem mad. I'm still trying to figure out the rest of it." He looked to Ki. "I don't suppose you'd go along with this if it was necromancy?"

"No necromancy. Retha'noi binding," a low, amused voice broke in.

Tamír had been so alarmed by the condition of her friends that she'd forgotten all about the hill witch. As he rose from a pallet in the corner and came forward, she saw that he was dressed more like a Skalan peasant farmer, but there was no mistaking what he was.

"This is Mahti," said Lutha. "Before you get angry, you should know that he's the reason we got here at all."

"I'm not angry," Tamír murmured, studying the man with interest. He was small and dark like Lhel, with the same olive skin and long, black curls in wild disarray around his shoulders, and the same rough, stained bare feet. He wore a necklace and bracelets strung with animal teeth, and held a long, elaborately decorated horn of some sort.

He came closer and smiled broadly at her. "Lhel tell me come to you, girl who was boy. You know Lhel, yes?"

"Yes. When did you last see her?"

"Night before today. She says you come."

Ki frowned and stepped closer to Tamír. "That's not possible."

Mahti eyed Tamír knowingly. "*You* know dead not stop coming if they want. She tell me of your noro'shesh, too. You have eyes that see."

"He's talking ghosts?" muttered Barieus. "He never said anything about that to us. He just kept claiming he'd seen us in a vision or something and that he was supposed to come with us."

"You be scared." Mahti chuckled, then pointed to Tamír. "She not be scared."

"How did you first meet her?" Tamír asked.

"She come in vision. Dead when I know her."

"He never said anything about anyone named Lhel, either. Who is she?" asked Lutha.

"It's all right. I think I understand."

The witch nodded sadly. "Lhel is loving you. She tells all the time for me to come to you."

"Her ghost told you, you mean?" Ki asked.

Mahti nodded. "Her mari come to me when I make dream with oo'lu."

"That's what he calls that horn of his," said Barieus. "He does magic with it, like a wizard."

"Korin sent trackers and a wizard after us, but Mahti played that horn and not one of them saw us, though we were standing in plain sight in the road," Lutha explained.

"He's a good healer with it and his herbs, too. Good as a drysian," added Barieus. "And he knew a shortcut way through the mountains, too."

"I wouldn't have lived to get here if it wasn't for him," said Caliel. "Whatever else you might say of him, he took good care of us."

"Thank you for helping my friends, Mahti," Tamír said, holding out her hand. "I know how dangerous it is for you to come this far into our lands."

Mahti touched her hand lightly and chuckled again. "No danger for me. Mother Shek'met protect and Lhel be guide."

"Even so, I'll make certain you have safe passage back to your hills."

"I come to you, girl who was boy. I come to help."

"Help me do what?"

"I help as Lhel help. Maybe with your noro'shesh? That one still no sleep."

"No, he doesn't."

"What's he talking about?" asked Lutha.

Tamír shook her head wearily. "I suppose I'd better tell you everything."

She pulled a chair up by the bed, and Ki and Lutha sat carefully on the edge of the bed beside Caliel. As she told them what she knew, Mahti hunkered down on the floor and listened intently, his brow furrowed as he tried to follow her words.

"Your brother was killed so you could take his form?" Caliel said when she'd finished. "Isn't that necromancy?"

Mahti shook his head vehemently. "Lhel make mistake making baby die. Not should have—" He paused, searching for the word, then took a deep breath, pointing at his chest. "Lhel tells you this?"

"Lhel never told me how he died. I only heard the truth a few days ago, from some wizards who were there."

"Iya?" asked Caliel.

"Yes."

"Not breath. *First* breath. Brings mari into—" Mahti hesitated again, then pinched the skin on the back of his hand.

"Into the body?" asked Ki, touching his chest.

"Body? Yes. No breath in body, no life. No mari to be make like him. Bad thing. No breath for body, mari have no home."

"Mari must mean spirit," mused Ki.

"I mean no offense, Tob—Tamír, but perhaps he doesn't understand what necromancy is," Caliel warned. "Who else controls ghosts and demons, but a necromancer?"

"No necromancy!" Mahti insisted indignantly. "You Skalan, you no understand Retha'noi!" He held up the horn again. "No necromancy. Good magic. Help you, yes?"

"Yes," Caliel admitted.

"Why would he help us if he's evil, Cal?" Lutha insisted, and it sounded to Tamír like they'd had this debate before. "Tamír, couldn't that friend of yours, Mistress Iya, tell if he's that sort or not?"

"Iya isn't with me anymore, but I have others to advise me. Ki, send for Arkoniel. He knows more about Mahti's people than anyone else."

Caliel waited until Ki was gone, then said, "I should tell you, Tamír, that I am not here by my own will. When I tried to come to you before, it was to parley on Korin's behalf. He's my friend and my liege. The oath I swore to him as a Companion is one I won't break. I don't mean you any harm, but I won't dishonor myself by accepting your hospitality under false pretenses. I'm no spy, but I'm no turncoat, either."

"No, you're a damn fool!" Lutha growled. "Korin's the one who's mad. You saw it as clearly as I did, even before he had you flogged half to death." He turned to Tamír, eyes flashing with outrage. "He was going to hang us all! You can call me traitor if you want, but I'm here because I think Korin's wrong. I loved him, too, but he broke his oath to us and to Skala when he let himself become the puppet of a creature like Niryn. I can't dishonor my father's name any longer, serving in such a court."

"He's bespelled," Caliel muttered, resting his face in his hands.

Ki returned and settled on the bed again, looking at Caliel with concern.

"He's got Korin seeing traitors in every shadow," Lutha went on. "All anyone has to do is disagree with him and they're likely to end up at the end of a rope."

"How did you get away?" asked Ki.

"It was your spy, Tamír. A fellow calling himself Eyoli? I don't know how he managed it, but he got us out."

"He's a wizard," Ki told him.

"I thought it might be something like that."

"How is it in Cirna now?" Tamír asked.

"There's grumbling among the ranks. Some don't hold with Niryn's ways. Others are losing patience with Korin just sulking there in Cirna. He's sent some forces to put down nobles who've taken your side, but his generals want him to come after you."

"He is," Tamír told him. "I just had word of it."

Caliel looked up at that. "With respect, I don't want to be here for this. I'm sorry, Tamír. I can't be party to any talk against Korin. I—I should go back. Sakor knows, I don't want to fight against you, but my place is there."

"He'll hang you, sure as I'm sitting here!" Lutha exclaimed. "For hell's sake, we didn't drag you all the way here for you to just turn around and go looking for your death!" He turned to Tamír and Ki. "This is what he's been like. He won't listen to reason!"

"You should have left me, then," Caliel snapped.

"Maybe we should have!"

"Please, don't fight!" Tamír reached out and took Caliel's hand. He was trembling with emotion. "You're in no condition to go anywhere. Rest here until you're stronger. Honor the laws of hospitality, and I'll still call you friend."

"Of course. I give you my oath."

She turned to the witch, who'd been watching all this with evident interest. "And you. Will you swear by your great Mother to do no harm in my house, to any of my people?"

Mahti gripped his horn in both hands. "By the full moon of Mother Shek'met, and by the mari of Lhel, I come only to help you. I do no harm."

"I accept your pledge. You're under my protection. All of you are." She looked sadly at her friends. "I won't keep any of you here against your will, or expect you to serve me as you did Korin. As soon as you're strong enough to ride, I'll give you safe conduct anywhere you want to go."

"I don't think you've really changed at all, no matter what you're calling yourself," Lutha said, smiling. "If you'll have me, Queen Tamír, I'll serve you."

"And you, Barieus?"

"Yes." His fingers stole to the cropped hair at his temple as he added, "If you'll have me."

"Of course I will."

"What about you, Cal?" Ki asked.

Caliel only shrugged and looked away.

Arkoniel came in, then stopped dead as he caught sight of Mahti.

The witch eyed him with equal interest. "Oreskiri?"

"Retha'noi?"

Mahti nodded and touched his heart, then replied at length in his own language.

The two of them conversed for several minutes. Tamír recognized the word for "child" and Lhel's name but nothing else. Arkoniel nodded sadly at the mention of the dead woman, then continued with his questioning. He took Mahti's hand but the witch quickly pulled away and shook an accusing finger at him.

"What's he saying?" asked Tamír.

Arkoniel gave her a guilty nod. "My apologies. It was just something Lhel taught me, but it was rude."

Mahti nodded, then handed Arkoniel his oo'lu horn to examine.

Satisfied, he turned back to Tamír and the others. "He claims Lhel's spirit came to him in a vision, asking him to come and protect you. She's been his guide and led him to your friends as they made their way here."

"So he said. What do you think?"

"I can't imagine a hill witch coming all this way without good reason. They've never been the sort to send assassins. I must warn you, though, that he can kill with his magic and has done so, but only in self-defense, or so he claims. You must either take him at his word or send him away. I'd like to keep him among the wizards for now if you have no objection?"

"Very well. I'll come down when I'm done here."

Arkoniel held out his hand to Mahti. "Come, my friend. You and I have much to talk about."

"Lutha, you and Barieus are free to join the other Companions," said Tamír when they were gone.

"Who's left?" asked Lutha.

"Nikides—"

"Nik's alive?" Lutha exclaimed. "Thank Sakor! I thought I'd left him to die. Who else?"

"Just Lynx and Tanil. We have some new members, though."

"Tanil?" Caliel gasped.

"Can we see them now?" asked Barieus, brightening noticeably at the mention of Lynx.

"Of course. Ki, go fetch them, will you?"

"What about Tanil?" asked Ki.

"Him, too. I'll explain while you're gone."

Ki nodded and strode out.

"What about Tanil?" Caliel demanded.

"The Plenimarans weren't gentle with him." She told them all of it, wishing she could spare them the details, but it would be plain enough when they saw him.

Caliel groaned and closed his eyes.

"Oh, hell," Lutha muttered.

Ki soon returned with the other Companions. Nikides stopped just inside the doorway, staring at Lutha and Barieus.

"I—can you forgive me?" Lutha said at last, voice trembling with emotion.

Nikides burst into tears and embraced them both.

Lynx had his arm around Tanil and was speaking quietly to him. The moment the squire saw Caliel, however, he pulled away and ran to him.

"I've lost Korin!" he whispered, tears welling in his eyes as he knelt by the bed. "I don't know what to do, Cal. I can't find him!"

Caliel reached for his hand and touched the red, raised scars on his wrist. "You didn't lose him. We lost you. Korin's been very sad, thinking you were dead."

"Really?" He stood up at once, looking around the room. "Where is he?"

"He's at Cirna."

"I'll go saddle our horses!"

"No, not yet." Caliel drew him back.

"It's all right. I'm sure Korin won't mind," said Lynx. "He'll want you to look after Cal, won't he?"

"But—Mylirin?"

"He's dead," Caliel told him.

"Dead?" Tanil looked at him blankly for a moment, then buried his face in his hands and began to weep softly.

"He fell honorably." Caliel drew him down on the bed and held him. "Will you take his place as my squire until we go back to Korin?"

"I—I'm not worthy to be a Companion anymore."

"Of course you are. And you'll earn those braids back, as soon as we're both well again. Won't he, Tamír?"

"Yes. The healers did a fine job. For now, your duty is to Caliel."

Tanil wiped at his eyes. "I'm sorry about Mylirin, but I'm glad to see you again, Caliel. Korin will be so pleased that you weren't lost, too!"

Caliel shared a sad look with Tamír. For now, they would let Tanil cling to his hopes.

They talked for a while, catching up on both sides, then left Tanil with Caliel and went back to Nikides' room.

"Cal isn't going to change his mind, you know," Lutha told her as they made their way to the Companions' chamber. "If he hadn't been so badly hurt, he really would have gone back."

"He'll do what he must. I won't stop him."

Tharin was there with the young squires and clasped hands happily with Lutha and Barieus. Tamír stayed with them a little while longer, then rose to go. Ki rose to follow, but she smiled and motioned for him to stay.

She paused in the doorway, gladdened beyond words to see her friends together again. Even if Caliel couldn't join them, at least he was alive.

Chapter 41

Arkoniel took the hill witch down to his chamber by back passages and servants' stairs. The few people they met paid the stranger little mind, accustomed to Arkoniel bringing strays of all sorts into the castle.

His room was by far the most luxurious he'd ever had, with finely carved old furnishings and bright hangings. The rest of the wizards were housed in similar chambers on this small courtyard. Tamír, in keeping with her promise, had granted them a generous allowance from her treasury and given them space in the castle to train and teach.

Wythnir was where Arkoniel had left him, curled up in the deep embrasure of a window, watching the other children play outside in the twilight. He hopped down at once as Arkoniel and Mahti entered, staring up at Mahti with apparent interest and none of his usual shyness, much to Arkoniel's surprise.

"You're a witch, aren't you, just like Mistress Lhel? She told me that men could be witches, too."

Mahti smiled down at the boy. "Yes, keesa."

"She was very nice to us. She showed us how to find food in the forest and kept people from finding us."

"You be oreskiri, little one? I feel magic in you." Mahti squinted his eyes a little. "Ah, yes. Little piece Retha'noi magic here, too."

"Lhel taught the children and some of the older wizards a few small spells. I think you'll find most of my people more welcoming toward you, thanks to her."

"I make magic by this." He held the oo'lu out to Wythnir, encouraging the boy to hold it. Wythnir glanced at Arkoniel for reassurance, then accepted it, stooping a little under its weight.

"This little one does not fear me," Mahti remarked in his own language, watching Wythnir fit his small hand into the burned palm print near the oo'lu's end. "Maybe you and he can teach others not to fear my people and to share magic with us, as Lhel did."

"That would be a good thing for all. Tell me, where do you come from?"

"The western mountains. I would not have found my way here if not for Lhel and my visions."

"Very strange, indeed."

"You speak my language very well, Orëska. It's easier for me, and I can make myself clear."

"As you wish. Wythnir, go out and play with your friends while there's still some daylight. I'm sure they missed you while we were gone."

The child hesitated, then dropped his gaze and started for the door.

"He is frightened to be parted from you," Mahti observed. "Why not let him stay? He doesn't understand my language, does he? Even if he did, I have nothing to say that a child may not hear."

"Wythnir, you may stay if you like." Arkoniel seated himself by the hearth and Wythnir sat down at once by his feet, hands folded in his lap.

"He is obedient and intelligent, that child," Mahti said approvingly. "He will be a strong oreskiri, if you can heal the fear in him. He has been hurt deeply."

"It often happens to children born into poverty or ignorance with the power. He won't speak of his past, though, and the wizard who had him before doesn't seem to know much about him."

"You are good to him. He loves you as a father."

Arkoniel smiled. "It's best so, between master and apprentice. He's a very good boy."

Mahti settled on the floor facing them, his oo'lu across

his knees. "I saw you in my vision, Arkoniel. Lhel loved you in life, and loves you still. She shared much of her magic with you, so she must have trusted you, too."

"I'd like to think so."

"That is not against the ways of your people, to use our magic?"

"There are many who say so, but my teacher and I disagreed. Iya sought her out specifically because she could make the kind of binding spell that would protect Tamír. I remember that when we found her, she was not surprised to see us. She said she'd seen us in a vision, too."

"Yes. Her manner of hiding the girl was a harsh one, though. Your mistress, she understood that it would require the death of the boy child?"

"Those were desperate times, and she saw no other way. Lhel was good to Tamír, watching over her without our knowledge for some time."

"She was lonely, until you came to her bed. But you could not fill her belly."

"If it had been possible, I'd have gladly done that for her. It's different with your people, isn't it?"

Mahti chuckled. "I have many children, and all of them will be witches. It's how we keep our people strong in their mountains. We must be very strong, to still be alive after the southlanders drove us away."

"They fear your kind, and your magic. Neither our wizards nor our priests can kill so easily as you."

"Or heal as well," Mahti pointed out.

"So, why are you here? To finish Lhel's work?"

"The Mother marked me for long traveling." He stroked a hand down the length of his oo'lu to the black, hand-shaped mark near the end. "My first vision of my traveling time was of Lhel, standing with that girl, and you. That was in the quarter of melting snows, and all this time since, I've been coming to find you."

"I see. But why does your goddess want her witches to help us?"

Mahti gave him a wry smile. "For many years your people have treated my people like animals, hunting us down and chasing us away from our sacred places by the sea. I, too, have said often to the Mother, 'Why help our oppressors?' Her answer is this girl, and perhaps you yourself. You both honored Lhel, and were her friends. Tamír-Who-Was-A-Boy greeted me with an open hand, and made me welcome, even as I saw others in this great house make signs and spit on the floor. This queen of yours, she might make her people treat the Retha'noi better."

"I believe she will, if she can. She has a kind heart and yearns for peace."

"And you? You take our magic and do not call it necromancy. That boy upstairs was wrong. I know what necromancy is: an unclean magic. The Retha'noi are not an unclean people."

"Lhel taught me that." It still shamed him, how they'd underestimated the woman at first. "But it's difficult for most Skalans to perceive the difference, because you also use blood and control the dead."

"You can teach others the truth. I will help you if you will keep them from killing me first."

"I'll try. Now, about what you said to Tamír; can you make her demon twin go away?"

Mahti shrugged. "It wasn't my magic that made him, and he is more than just a ghost. Demon souls like those are difficult to make magic on. Sometimes it's better just to let them alone."

"Tamír is haunted by another ghost, that of her mother, who took her own life. She's very strong and very angry. She's one who can touch the living, and seeks to hurt them."

"Spirits like that are for women's magic to deal with. That's why your mistress sought out a woman witch rather than a man. We deal mostly with the living. Is the ghost in this house?"

"No. She haunts the place where she died."

Mahti shrugged. "That is her choice. I am here for the girl."

There was a knock at the door, and Tamír came in. "Pardon me for interrupting, Arkoniel, but Melissandra said you two were in here."

"Please, come in," said Arkoniel.

She sat down by Arkoniel and gazed at the witch a moment in silence. "Lhel came to you, as a ghost."

"Yes."

"She sent you specially to find me?"

Arkoniel translated that, and Mahti nodded.

"Why?"

Mahti glanced at Arkoniel, then shrugged. "To help you, so you not hurt Retha'noi."

"I have no intention of hurting your people, as long as they remain peaceful toward mine." She paused and her eyes grew sad. "Do you know how Lhel died?"

"She not tell me. But she is not angry spirit. Peaceful."

Tamír smiled a little at that. "I'm glad."

"We were just discussing what brought Mahti here," said Arkoniel. "He's from somewhere in the western mountains."

"West? How far west?"

"Almost to the Osiat, apparently."

She went to the witch and knelt in front of him. "I have visions, too, and dreams of the west. Can you help me with those?"

"I try. What you see?"

"Arkoniel, do you have anything to draw with?"

The wizard went to a table covered in magical paraphernalia and fished around in the mess until he found a lump of chalk. He guessed what she was thinking, but it seemed rather improbable.

Tamír cleared away some of the rushes strewn over the floor and began drawing on the stone paving beneath. "I see a place, and I know it's on the western coast below

Cirna. There's a deep harbor guarded by two islands, like this." She drew them. "And a very high cliff above it. That's where I'm standing in the dream. And if I look back, I can see open country and mountains in the distance."

"How far away mountains?" asked Mahti.

"I'm not sure. Maybe a day's ride?"

"And this?" He pointed to the blank floor beyond the little ovals she'd drawn for islands. "This is western sea?" Mahti stared down at the map, chewing at a hangnail. "I know this place."

"You can tell, just from this?" asked Arkoniel.

"I not lie. I have been to this place. I show."

He brought his fist up in front of his face, closed his eyes, and began to mutter to himself. Arkoniel felt the prickle of magic gathering even before the pattern of intricate black lines appeared on the witch's hands and face. He recognized the spell.

Mahti blew into his fist and made a ring with his thumb and forefinger. A disk of light took shape, and then grew as he framed it with his other hand and drew it larger, to the size of a platter. They could hear the call of seabirds through it and hear the wash of the tide.

"Master, he knows your window spell!" Wythnir exclaimed softly.

Through the window lay a view from atop a high cliff overlooking the sea just as Tamír had described. It was dark already here in Atyion, but there the setting sun still cast a coppery trail across the waves under a cloudy sky. The ground at the top of the cliff was broken and overgrown with long grass. Huge flocks of gulls sailed against the orange sky. Their cries filled Arkoniel's room. He half expected to smell the sea breeze and feel it against his face.

Mahti moved slightly and the view changed with dizzying swiftness, so that they were looking over the edge to a deep harbor far below.

"That's it!" Tamír exclaimed softly, and Arkoniel had to

catch her by the arm to keep her from leaning too close to the aperture. "Maybe this is why Lhel brought you to me, rather than someone else."

"*Remoni*, we call it," Mahti told her. "Mean 'good water.' Good to drink, out of the ground."

"Springs?"

Arkoniel interpreted and Mahti nodded. "Many springs. Much good water."

"Look, see how there's enough land at the base of the cliffs for a town?" said Tamír. "A citadel on the cliffs above would be impossible to attack the way Ero was. Where is this place, Mahti? Is it near Cirna?"

"I don't know your *seer-na*."

Arkoniel cast a window spell of his own, showing him the fortress at Cirna, on its narrow strip of ground.

"I know this place! I came close by it when I was looking for Caliel and his friends," he explained in his own language, leaving Arkoniel to translate for Tamír. "But I saw the great house in a vision, too. Caliel and the others came from there. There's evil living in that house, and great sadness, too."

"How far is Remoni from there?"

"Three, maybe four days' long walk? You southlanders don't go there, to Remoni. We still have sacred places by this sea. Boats come into the protected water behind the islands sometimes, when people come to fish, but no one lives there. Why does she want to go there?"

"What's he saying?" Tamír asked.

Arkoniel explained.

"It might be only two days, riding hard," she mused. "Tell him I'm going to build a new city there. Will he guide me?"

Arkoniel translated, but Mahti was rubbing his eyes now, as if they hurt him. "Need sleep. I go there." He pointed out the window at the garden. "Too many time in this house. Need sky, and the ground."

"But there's so much I want to know!"

"Let him rest a while," Arkoniel said, sensing that Mahti had some reason for not answering her. "You should rest, too, and be ready to speak with your generals."

As she turned to go, Mahti looked up and tapped himself on the chest. "You have pain. Here."

"Pain? No."

"Where Lhel make magic bind to you, there is pain," he insisted, looking at her very intently as his hand stole to his long horn again. "I make dream song for you. Take away some pain."

Tamír hastily shook her head. "No! It's healed. There's no pain."

Mahti frowned and went back to his language. "Oreskiri, tell her Lhel's magic is not broken yet. She had no witch to help her cut the spell. There are still threads that bind them. That is why her brother demon still comes to her."

"I'll try to explain to her," Arkoniel replied. "She doesn't trust magic very much, though. The only magic she knew as a child was hurtful or frightening. That fear still haunts her, even with everything else she's seen. She doesn't like it practiced on her, even for her benefit."

Mahti looked thoughtfully at Tamír, who was regarding him more warily. "She cannot be completely herself until she is freed of these last threads, but I will not without her consent."

"Give her time."

"What's he saying?" Tamír asked, looking from one to the other.

Arkoniel walked her out to the corridor. "You're still bound to Brother somehow."

"I figured that much out for myself."

"Mahti is quite concerned about it."

She stopped and folded her arms. "You trust him already?"

"I think so, yes."

For just an instant she looked unsure, as if there was

something she wanted to say, but instead, she just shook her head. "I've had enough of that magic. I'm a girl now. That's enough. I can deal with Brother."

Arkoniel sighed inwardly. Even if he could have forced her, he would not.

Returning to his room, he found Wythnir and Mahti sitting on the floor together. Wythnir had one hand extended, a silvery orb hovering over his open palm.

"Look what Master Mahti showed me how to do," the boy said, eyes fixed on the orb.

Arkoniel knelt beside them, caught between curiosity and protectiveness. "What is this?"

"Only water," Mahti assured him. "It's one of the first spells witch children learn, for fun."

Wythnir lost his grip on the spell and the orb of water fell, splattering his hand and knees.

Mahti ruffled his hair. "Good magic, little keesa. Something to teach your friends."

"May I, Master?"

"Tomorrow. It's time for you to go say good night to them. I must make our guest comfortable."

The moon was almost full. Mahti sat down on the damp grass near a rosebush, savoring its sweetness and the good smells of earth and air. Arkoniel had sent all the southlanders from the garden so he could be alone here under the sky. He was grateful for the solitude. Being confined in a room so far above the ground for so many days had been difficult. The unhappiness and fear of the three southlanders he'd cared for had filled the room like a fog.

Lutha and Barieus were happy now that they'd spoken to Tamír. He was glad for them; they'd treated him well from the first. The older one, Caliel, was darker in his mind, and not only because of his fear of Mahti. He carried a deep hurt in his soul. The betrayal of a friend was a bad wound to carry, and very hard to heal. Mahti had mended Caliel's bones and played the poisons away as they tried to gather, but his heart stayed dark. It was the same with the one named Tanil. Mahti saw at a glance what had been done to him. He wasn't sure even he could help that one.

And then there was Tamír. She was hurt very deeply, but she did not feel the wounds. When he'd looked at her from the corner of his eye, he could see the black tendrils still issuing from the place where Lhel had made her binding. Tamír's spirit was still bound to the noro'shesh, and that tie kept her from healing completely into her new form. She was a young woman, certainly, but some vestige of her old self held on. He could see it in the hollowness of her cheeks and the angular lines of her body.

He tilted his head back and filled his eyes with the white moon. "I have seen her now, Mother Shek'met. Did I come all this way just to finish the magic of Lhel and heal her? She does not want that. What must I do, so that I can go home again?"

Holding these questions in his mind, he raised the oo'lu to his lips and began the prayer song. The pregnant moon filled him and lent him her power.

Pictures began to form behind his eyelids and after a time his brows drew down in surprise. He played the song to its end, and when he was finished he looked up at the moon's pale face again and shook his head. "Your will is strange, Mother, but I will do my best."

What do you think of them, my girl and my oreskiri? Lhel whispered to him from the shadows.

"They miss you," he whispered back, and felt her sadness. "Do they hold you here?"

I stay for them. When all is finished, I will rest. You will do as the Mother has shown you?

"If I can, but our people will not welcome her."

"You must make them see her as I do."

"Will I see you anymore, now that I've found her?"

He felt an invisible caress, then she was gone.

A man stirred in the shadows by the courtyard door.

Arkoniel had come into the garden while he was dreaming. Without a word, the oreskiri disappeared back inside.

There was great pain there, too.

Mahti laid his horn aside and stretched out on the grass to sleep. He would do as the Mother required, then he would go home. It was tiring, being with these stubborn southlanders who would not ask for help when they needed it.

Arkoniel sat by his window, watching Mahti sleep. He looked very peaceful there on the bare ground, head pillowed on his arm.

Arkoniel's heart was in turmoil. He'd heard Lhel's voice, smelled her scent on the air. He understood why she had gone to Mahti, but why had she never come to him?

"Master?" Wythnir asked sleepily from his bed.

"It's all right, child. Go back to sleep."

Instead, he came to Arkoniel and climbed into his lap. Curling up there, he tucked his head under Arkoniel's chin.

"Don't be sad, Master," he murmured, already half-asleep. By the time Arkoniel recovered from his amazement the boy was fast asleep.

Touched by this innocent affection, Arkoniel sat there for some time, just holding him, the sleeping child's trust a reminder of the work that lay ahead.

Tamír found the reunited Companions in Nikides' chamber. Lutha and Barieus were stretched out on their bellies across the wide bed. Ki and Tharin sat on the edge beside them, and made room for Tamír between them. The rest were sprawled in chairs or on the floor. Ki was telling Lutha and Barieus about the dragon they'd seen in Afra. "Show them your mark," he said as Tamír came in.

She held out her finger.

"I wish we'd been with you," Barieus exclaimed enviously.

"Next time you will be," she promised. "Tell me more about Korin. Is there any chance he can be reasoned with?"

Lutha shook his head. "I don't think he can ever forgive you, Tamír."

"And now he'll have an heir," said Ki. "All the more reason for him to fight."

"Lady Nalia's with child? Well, I don't wonder," Lutha muttered, coloring a little. "Korin was trying hard enough. I guess it finally took."

"What do you know of her?" asked Tamír.

"Almost nothing, beyond what Korin said. He keeps her shut up in the tower most of the time. She was always pleasant to us when we did see her, though."

"Is it true she's ugly?" asked Ki.

"More like plain, with a big pink birthmark on her face and neck." Barieus traced a pattern on his own cheek. "Sort of like that one on your arm, Tamír."

"What else can you tell me, now that we're away from Cal?" she asked.

Lutha sighed. "Now I do feel like a spy. Korin's gathered a sizable force—riders, men-at-arms, some ships, mostly from the northern holdings and the mainland territories. He's sent out some raids against those loyal to you."

"I've been doing the same."

"I know," Lutha replied. "It galled him no end, along with the reports of your second victory against the Plenimarans. I don't know if it's Niryn's influence, or just Korin's own jealousy, but now that he is ready to move, I don't think he'll settle for anything less than an all-out fight."

"Then that's what he's going to get. We've only got a few good months left before winter closes in. Tharin, ask Lytia to have a complete inventory of supplies ready for my audience tomorrow morning. I need to know how long a siege we could withstand here, if it comes to that. Send out runners to all the camps and heralds to all the lords

who've gone back to their holdings north of here. I mean
to march as soon as possible."

"With your own Companions at your side," Ki said. "At
least those of us who are fit," he added with an apologetic
look at Lutha.

"We're fit enough!" Lutha assured him.

Looking around at the fierce smiling faces of her
friends, Tamír wondered how many more would be lost
before this was over?

Thoughts of war fled for a moment, however, as she and
Ki walked back to their rooms. Reaching his own door, Ki
paused, looking uncertain. Tamír realized he was waiting
for her to say where he would sleep.

She hesitated, too, all too aware of the guards posted
nearby.

Ki glanced their way and sighed. "Well, good night."

Later, as Tamír lay alone in her great bed with Ringtail
curled up and purring under her chin, she traced her lips
with a finger, remembering their kisses only a few nights
ago.

I'm queen. If I want to sleep with him, I can! she told
herself, but blushed at the thought. It had been easy when
they were both so scared, so far from court. Maybe Ki even
regretted it?

She shook off the thought, but a hint of doubt
remained. Now that they were back among the others, he
was acting as he always had.

And so am I. And this is no time to be thinking of love!
Nari's stern talk had given her other things to consider, too.
That sort of love led to babies if you weren't careful. Nari
had given her a jar of pessaries, just in case.

In case—

As much as she longed for Ki, the thought of actually
coupling scared her more than she liked to admit. If she

used this body like that, it was the final admission that she was a girl—no, a woman—in every sense.

All the same, the bed felt too big and lonely, especially knowing that Ki was so close by. She fingered the healing cut on her chin. She didn't mind if it left a scar. Every time she saw it in the mirror, it would remind her of him, and what it had felt like, lying beside him in their old bed at the keep. She traced slowly down her throat to her chest, thinking of his fingers taking the same path.

As her fingers brushed the scar, however, it brought back what the witch had said. What had he meant? The wound was healed. It didn't hurt at all.

She hugged the cat closer, wishing his soft fur was Ki's hair or skin. For the first time in her life, she wondered what it would be like between the two of them if she was an ordinary girl, with no dark secrets or great fate, and neither of them had ever seen Ero at all.

"If wishes were meat, then beggars would eat," she whispered into the darkness. She was what she was, and there was no changing that.

When she slept at last, however, it was not Ki she dreamed of, but battle. She saw that rocky place again, and Korin's red banner coming ever closer.

Chapter 42

Tamír rose early the next morning, better rested than she'd expected. Having finally accepted the path she must take, she was eager to move. If this was the only way she could meet with Korin, then so be it.

With Una still gone, she had the luxury of dressing herself, with only a little help from Baldus. She put on the necklace and bracelet the Aurënfaie had given her, and was combing her hair when Ki knocked. Baldus let him in. She turned with the comb in her hand to find him staring at her. "What's wrong?"

"Umm—nothing," he replied, going to the armor rack. "Do you want your cuirass?"

"Yes," she replied, puzzled at his odd demeanor.

He helped her into the burnished breastplate and fastened the buckles on the side.

"There. Do I look like a warrior queen?" Tamír asked them, wrapping her sword belt around her hips.

"You do."

There it was again, that strange look of uncertainty on Ki's face.

"Baldus, go and fetch the rest of the Companions and Lord Tharin. Tell them I'm ready for the audience."

The page ran off to carry out her order.

"Did Lutha and the others sleep well?" she asked.

"Yes."

"I don't suppose Caliel has changed his mind?"

"No. But Tanil is better than he has been. He slept with Cal last night and won't be parted from him. Caliel seems a little better, too."

"Perhaps there's hope for them both."

"I'm taking Lutha and Barieus to look for a swordsmith later. They're absolutely determined to ride with you." Ki reached behind her to free a lock of hair trapped under the cuirass, then ran a thumb lightly across the cut on her chin. "You're a sight, but it's healing."

They were standing very close, almost touching. On impulse, she touched the dragon bite on his cheek. "You, too."

"It doesn't hurt anymore." He kept his gaze on her chin, fingers just brushing her cheek. It sent a little shiver down her arms and Tamír caught her breath as the feelings that had awakened that night at the keep came flooding back—pleasure, and with it the confused sensation of having two bodies at once.

That didn't stop her from leaning closer and kissing Ki lightly on the mouth. He kissed her back very gently, cupping her cheek. Tamír slid her fingers into the warm, soft hair at the nape of his neck and her body went hot and cold at once. Emboldened, she put her arms around him but her cuirass knocked the wind out of him and made him laugh.

"Gently, Majesty! Your humble squire needs those ribs."

"My liegeman, Lord Kirothieus," she corrected with a chuckle, embracing him more gently, seeing her own wonder mirrored in the depths of his dark brown eyes. The ache between her legs grew stronger, and confusion began to give way to something else.

She was about to kiss him again but the sound of the door opening made them jump apart, blushing guiltily.

Nikides stood in the doorway, looking amused. "Tharin, Master Arkoniel, and the witch are here. Shall I send them in?"

"Of course." Tamír brushed her hair back, feeling to see if her cheeks were hot.

Ki retreated to the armor rack, trying to hide his own embarrassment as he pretended to check her mail.

Nikides' grin widened as he took his leave. Arkoniel took no notice of their state as he hurried in with a large scroll tucked under his arm, with the others close behind.

Mahti was dressed like a minor noble. His hair was combed and pulled back in a bushy queue and the barbaric jewelry was gone. He'd left his horn behind, as well, Tamír noted, guessing this was Arkoniel's doing. Mahti did not seem to be very pleased about it. He was not smiling.

"Mahti has something to tell you," said Arkoniel, looking rather excited.

"I have vision for you," the witch told her. "I show you a way to west."

"To that harbor, you mean? Remoni?" Tamír asked.

"You will be go west. My goddess says so."

"And you saw this road in a vision?"

He shook his head. "I know road. But the Mother say I bring you there." He looked even less happy now. "Is hidden way, forbid to those outside the people. This my help for you."

Baffled, Tamír gave Arkoniel and Tharin a questioning look. "That's all very interesting, but right now I'm more concerned with—"

"Ah, but I think this may be of use." Tharin took the scroll from Arkoniel and unrolled it on the bed. It was a map of northern Skala and the isthmus. "Korin will most likely come straight at you here by the coastal route. From what Lutha has said, he doesn't have enough ships to bring his whole army by sea. The route Mahti is talking about seems to go here, through the mountains." He traced a finger just south and west of Colath. "That would bring you out here, near your harbor. From there you're within easy striking distance to either cut Korin off on the isthmus, or come at him from behind as he heads east."

"It's a trail that the Retha'noi keep hidden with the same magic Lhel used to hide her camp," Arkoniel explained. "They have many villages along it, and won't welcome outsiders, but Mahti claims he can take you that way without harm."

Tamír stared down at the map, heart beating a little faster. Was this what the Oracle had tried to show her? Is this what all her dreams of the place had been leading to?

"Yes, I see," she said faintly. It felt like she'd been inhaling the Illiorans' smoke again.

"Are you all right?" Ki asked.

"Yes." She took a deep breath, wondering what was wrong with her. "I attack from the west, perhaps even surprise him if he thinks I'm still here readying for a siege."

She looked up at Mahti. "Why would you do this?"

"You will give word to make peace to the Retha'noi. You will not kill us again. We be free to leave mountains."

"I'll gladly try, but I can't promise to change things overnight. Arkoniel, make him understand. I want to do what he asks, but it won't be easy, changing people's minds."

"I told him that, but he's convinced you can help. A better understanding between our two peoples will work in your favor, too."

"It will be hard to bring supplies through the mountains," said Tharin. "This isn't a proper road."

"The Gedre could meet us with supplies," Arkoniel pointed out. "Their ships are swift. They could probably reach Remoni harbor by the time we do."

"Contact them at once," Tamír ordered. "And the Bôkthersans, too. Solun seemed eager to help."

"Didn't he, though?" muttered Ki.

Word of her plan spread quickly. The audience chamber was packed by the time Tamír entered. Her generals and their captains stood closest to the dais, but there were others, too—courtiers, common soldiers, townspeople—crowded in between the pillars, all talking excitedly.

She ascended the dais, and the Companions took their places behind her. Lutha and Barieus stood with them, pale but proud in their borrowed clothes.

Tamír drew her sword, feeling the momentous import of what she was about to do. "My lords, generals, and my good people, I come before you to formally declare that I, by the will of Illior, will march against Prince Korin to secure my throne and unite our divided land."

"Three cheers for our good queen!" Lord Jorvai shouted, raising his sword in the air.

The cry was taken up, and the cheering went on until Illardi banged the floor with his staff of office and got their attention again.

"Thank you. Let the heralds carry word across Skala. All who fight with me are my friends and true Skalans." She paused, then added, "And all who oppose me shall be called traitor and stripped of their lands. May Illior give us the strength to make our victory swift and the wisdom to be just. Lord Chancellor Illardi, I charge you now to oversee the levy of warriors and supplies. Steward Lytia, you will oversee the sutlers and baggage wagons. I mean to march before the week is out. All captains are to return to their companies and begin preparations at once."

Leaving the court to its excitement, Tamír retired to the map room with her generals and Companions. Arkoniel was waiting there with Mahti and his principal wizards, Saruel, Malkanus, Vornus, and Lyan.

The Companions took their places around the table, but Jorvai and some of the other nobles paused, eyeing the hill witch uneasily.

"What's the meaning of this, Majesty?" he asked.

"This man is responsible for the safe return of my friends, and he is under my protection. I've been aided by his kind before, and have come to respect their magic. I charge you all to do the same."

"With all due respect, Majesty, how do you know it's not some kind of trick?" Nyanis asked.

"I've read his heart," Arkoniel replied. "Some of the queen's other wizards have, as well. He speaks the truth, and was guided to Queen Tamír's aid by visions, just as we were."

"This man is a friend of the Crown," Tamír said firmly. "You will accept my judgment in this. I hereby declare peace between Skala and the hill people, the Retha'noi. From this day forth no Skalan will offer them any violence, unless attacked. That is my will."

There was some grumbling and wary looks, but everyone bowed in obedience.

"That's settled, then." Tamír proceeded to her plan to outflank Korin, using Arkoniel's map and several others spread out on the great table.

"I have spoken with the Khirnari of Gedre," Arkoniel told them. "He knows the harbor and will send supply ships and archers. He's also relayed word to Bôkthersa. With any luck, they'll be there to meet us."

"That will be a fine trick, if Korin isn't already halfway to Atyion by the time we get through," said Jorvai. "If he gets word that you've left here, he'll come for Atyion all the faster. The granaries and treasury would be fine plums for him if he could capture them, not to mention the castle itself. I daresay he's been stretched thin, holed up in Cirna all these months."

"It's true he needs gold," said Lutha.

"That's why I won't risk leaving Atyion undefended," Tamír replied. "I'm going to keep two battalions of the Atyion garrison here as a holding force. If Korin does come this far, he'll have to fight his way through. That will slow him long enough for me to catch up." Tamír ran a finger up the eastern coast. "The Atyion army can come at Korin from the south. I hope to draw him west instead, but he could divide and attack us on both coasts." She paused, turning to Tharin. "Lord Tharin, I name you as marshal of the eastern defenses. Arkoniel, choose among your wizards those who can best help him here."

Tharin's eyes widened, and she knew he was on the verge of arguing with her. Only the presence of the others stopped him, which is why she'd made up her mind to broach the subject here rather than in private. She put a hand on his shoulder. "You're an Atyion man. The warriors know and respect you."

"After Queen Tamír herself, there's no one else better respected among the ranks," Jorvai agreed.

"You also know the nobles who hold land between here and Cirna better than anyone else among my generals," Tamír added. "If you do march north, you might be able to raise more fighters as you go."

"As you wish, Majesty," Tharin said, though it was clear he was not at all happy.

"You're not breaking your oath to my father," she said gently. "He wanted you to protect me. At the moment, this is the best way you can do that."

"It's a risk, splitting your army. By all reports Korin outnumbers you nearly three to one," Nyanis pointed out.

"I can move faster with a smaller force. Mahti's route will save us days." She turned to the witch. "Can we take horses through there?"

"The way small in places. In other, hard walking up."

"The Retha'noi don't use horses. They carry everything on their backs," Arkoniel told her.

"Then we must do the same, and hope the 'faie arrive in good time." Tamír frowned down at the map for a moment, then looked up at her lords. "What do you advise?"

"I'd say rely on men-at-arms and archers, for the greater bulk of your force, Majesty," Kyman replied. "You'll want horses for reconnoitering, but the fewer we have to find forage for on the way, the better."

"You could also use what ships you have at Ero," Illardi suggested.

"They wouldn't reach us in time to do much good.

Keep them here and use them to defend Atyion and Ero. Illardi, you'll oversee the ships. Jorvai, Kyman, Nyanis: you are my marshals."

They spent the rest of the day forming their plans. Lytia's inventories were encouraging; even accounting for the provisioning of Tamír's army, it would still leave enough that it would take Korin months to starve them out. Two companies would remain in the garrison; two thousand foot and five hundred horse would go with Tharin. The rest, nearly ten thousand of the best foot, archers, and one hundred cavalry, would take the mountain route with Tamír, with Mahti as their guide.

Tamír and the Companions had just entered the hall for the evening meal when Baldus came pelting through the crowd toward her, dodging between startled servants and courtiers.

"Majesty!" he cried, waving a folded piece of parchment in his hand.

He came to a breathless stop before her and bowed quickly. "I found this—under your door. Lady Lytia said to bring it to you at once. He asked her for some clothes—Lord Caliel—"

"Hush." Tamír took the parchment and opened it, recognizing Caliel's elegant hand at once.

"He's gone, isn't he?" said Ki.

Tamír read the brief message through and handed it to him with a resigned sigh. "He's taking Tanil back to Korin. He wanted to be gone before he could hear our plans."

"Damn him!" Lutha cried, clenching his fists in frustration. "I should never have left him alone. We've got to go after him."

"No."

"What? But he's mad to go back!"

"I gave him my word, Lutha," she reminded him sadly. "It's his choice. I won't stop him."

Lutha stood a moment, a mute entreaty in his eyes, then stalked away with his head down.

"Tamír?" Barieus said, clearly torn between duty and his friend.

"Go on," Tamír said. "Don't let *him* do anything stupid."

When the war council was over, Arkoniel took Mahti back to the Orëska hall and gathered the others in the courtyard to make their own plans.

"Hain, Lord Malkanus, and Cerana, I ask you to ride with me. Melissandra, Saruel, Vornus, Lyan, and Kaulin—I give you charge of the castle and the rest of the wizards." He glanced over at the children, who were huddled together on the grass beside him. Wythnir gave him a heartbroken look. It pulled at Arkoniel's heart, but there was no help for it.

"I'm to stay behind, but *that* goes?" Kaulin demanded, jerking a thumb at Mahti, who sat on the grass near the children. "Is he one of us now?"

Arkoniel sighed inwardly. Kaulin was his least favorite among the wizards. "He was guided to Queen Tamír by visions, just like the rest of us. Whether it was by his own gods or ours, he is one of us for as long as he serves her. You were with us in the mountains; you know the debt we owe to Lhel. Honor her by honoring this man. We can no longer let ignorance divide us. However, Kaulin, if you wish to come with me, you are welcome." He looked around at the others. "All of you are here by choice. All of you are free as always to choose your own paths. I am master to no free wizard."

Kaulin backed down. "I'll go with you. I can do a bit of healing."

"I'd prefer to accompany you, as well," Saruel said.

"I'll take her place here," Cerana offered.

"Very well. Anyone else?"

"You've portioned us wisely, Arkoniel," Lyan replied.

"There are enough of us in both places to harm the enemy and protect the innocent."

"I agree," said Malkanus. "You have led us well, and you were the closest to Mistress Iya and shared her vision. I see no reason to change things now."

"I appreciate the fact that you are all still here and willing to support the queen."

"I suppose Iya had her reasons for leaving, but we'll surely miss her strength," Cerana sighed.

"Yes, we will," Arkoniel replied sadly. He'd told them simply that Iya had finished her part and gone away by her own choice. Tamír needed their loyalty, and those ties were still too tenuous to risk the full truth right now.

You forgot your sword, Cal," Tanil noted as they rode north along the high road in the waning dusk. He ducked his head, looking guilty. "I lost mine."

"It's all right. We don't need them," Caliel assured him.

Tanil had left Atyion willingly, eager to see Korin again. Thanks to Tamír's generosity, they both had decent clothing and a bit of gold, enough for a pair of horses and food enough for the journey.

"But what if we meet up with the Plenimarans again?"

"They're gone. Tamír drove them away."

"Who?"

"Tobin," Caliel amended.

"Oh—yes. I keep forgetting. I'm sorry." He was plucking at that severed braid again.

Caliel reached over and pulled his hand away. "It's all right, Tanil."

Tanil's body had recovered, but inside he was broken, leaving him vague and easily confused. Caliel had considered simply taking him away, disappearing, but he knew that Tanil would never cease longing for Korin if he did.

And where would I go that I could forget him?

Caliel didn't allow himself to dwell on what his own

welcome was likely to be at Cirna. He would take Tanil back to Korin, as a last act of duty and friendship.

No, he silently amended. *Let my last act be to kill Niryn, and set Korin free.*

Bilairy could have him after that, with no regrets.

Chapter 43

Nalia had seen very little of Korin since he'd learned of her pregnancy. He did not come to her bed at all any longer—a welcome respite—and spent each day planning and organizing for his war.

Nalia watched the activity in the encampments and the constant coming and goings in the fortress yards below from her balcony. The air was filled with the steady din of armorers and farriers, and the rumble of carts.

She was not forgotten, however. Korin sent her little gifts each day, and Tomara went to visit him each morning with word of Nalia's health. In those rare moments that he did come to her, he was kind and attentive. For the first time, Nalia actually looked forward to the sound of his step on the stairs.

Korin was not thinking of Nalia as he and his men rode down the switchback road to the harbor. Before he'd come to Cirna, it had been nothing but a tiny fishing village. Over the course of the summer it had been transformed. Rows of makeshift houses, crude taverns, and long barracks houses had sprung up on the steep slope that stretched between the cliffs and the shoreline.

A brisk sea breeze stirred through Korin's black curls, drying the sweat on his brow. Summer was waning day by day, but the skies were still clear. Duke Morus' ships rode at anchor in the deep harbor, joined now by more than a dozen others. There were thirty-three in all. Some were little more than large coasting vessels or fishing boats, but he had twenty fine strong carracks, capable of carrying a hundred men each.

As Korin reached the stone jetty, the stink of hot tar and fish mingled with the salt tang in the air. "I wish we could sail with them," he said over his shoulder to Alben and Urmanis. "They'll be in Ero in a few days' time while we're still plodding along on the road."

"Yes, but you'll command the larger force," Alben replied.

He and Urmanis were the last of Korin's original Companions, and the last of his friends. He'd also raised Moriel to Companion. As Niryn pointed out, the Toad had proven his worth these past months, and though Niryn had been loath to release him from his own service, he'd had to agree that there were few enough properly trained young men left to fill out the ranks. Alben had always spoken well of him, and Korin found himself wondering why he hadn't taken him on sooner.

Morus greeted him heartily. "Good morning, Majesty. How is your lady today?"

"She's very well, my lord," Korin replied, clasping hands with the man. "How is my navy?"

"We'll load up and set sail as soon as you pour the libation. With a good following wind, we should make harbor above Ero in three days' time and be ready to close the vise on Atyion as soon as you arrive."

Moriel smiled at that. "You'll catch Prince Tobin like a nut between two stones."

"Yes." Korin's heart felt like a lump of ice in his breast every time his cousin was mentioned. He'd never hated anyone the way he hated Tobin. He haunted Korin's dreams, a pale and taunting figure, twisted to a dark-eyed specter. Only last night Korin had dreamed of wrestling with him, each one trying to take the crown the other wore.

Tobin had fooled half the country with his mad claims and even had a few victories to impress them. Those galled

Korin, and jealousy ate at his heart. Now the little upstart had even stolen Caliel away. He would never forgive any of them.

Niryn spoke darkly of the wizards who were gathering to Tobin's court. Few had come to Cirna, and the handful of Harriers who'd come north were a worthless lot, as far as Korin was concerned, good for little more than burning their own kind and scaring the soldiers. If the rumors were to be believed, Tobin's had greater powers. By the Flame, how he hated that brat!

"Korin, are you unwell?" Urmanis whispered close to his ear.

Korin blinked and found Morus and the others staring at him. Alben had him by the elbow and Urmanis stood close on the other side, alarmed.

"What are you all staring at?" Korin covered his momentary lapse with a glare. In truth, he felt a bit dizzy, and his clenched hands ached to strike out at something. "Come, summon your men, Morus."

Morus gave the signal to one of his captains. The man raised a horn to his lips and blew the assembly call. Within moments other signalmen on the ships and up the hillside were echoing the call. Korin sat on a mooring post to wait, watching as rank upon rank of men poured out of the barracks and marched to the jetties. Longboats skimmed in over the smooth face of the harbor to meet them.

"Are you better?" Alben murmured, staying close to him and shielding him from the sight of the others.

"Yes, of course!" Korin snapped, then, with a sigh, "Was it a long one, this time?"

"Only a moment, but you looked ready to kill someone."

Korin rubbed at his eyes, trying to fend off the headache that was building behind them. "I'll be fine once we're on the march."

This time he would not show weakness or make mistakes. This time he would be his father's son.

Chapter 44

Korin came to Nalia the night before his departure, dressed in his armor and a fine silk tabard bearing the royal arms of Skala. Nalia had not seen him dressed so since that first night he'd come to her. He'd been haggard and dirty and covered in blood then, a terrifying stranger. Now he looked every inch a king, with a shining helmet banded in gold under his arm.

"I've come to bid you farewell," he said, taking his customary seat across from hers. "We leave at first light and I have much to do before then."

She wished he'd sit closer and take her hand again, but instead he sat stiffly in his chair. He'd never kissed her, either, except on the hand. Nalia's mind strayed for just a moment to memories of Niryn and the false passion they'd shared. She quickly willed such thoughts away, as if they could somehow harm her child.

As much as she'd feared pregnancy, she felt fiercely protective toward the tiny life growing inside her. She would not be like that other wife. She would keep the child in her womb and it would be born healthy and beautiful. Her long-dead rival had kindled only boys, or so Tomara said. Surely Illior would let a girl child live.

"I may be gone through the winter, if we have to lay siege," said Korin. "I'm sorry your new chamber isn't complete yet, but it will be very soon. And I'll make certain there is an even better one waiting for you in Ero. Will you write to me?"

"I will, my lord," Nalia promised. "I will tell you how your child grows."

Korin stood and took her hand. "I'll make offerings to Dalna and Astellus for your health and our child's."

Our child. Nalia smiled and touched her pearl necklace for luck. "As will I, my lord, and for you."

"Well, that's good then." He paused, then leaned down and gave her an awkward kiss on the forehead. "Goodbye, my lady."

"Farewell, my lord." Nalia stared after him in amazement as he went out. Yes, perhaps there was hope.

She went out to the balcony when he was gone, knowing that she wouldn't sleep. She kept her lonely vigil there, wrapped in a shawl against the damp. Tomara slept in an armchair, chin on her breast, snoring softly.

Nalia settled by the parapet, chin resting on her hands. On the plain to the south, columns were forming in dark, shifting squares and rectangles against the moonlit grass. Watch fires burned everywhere and she could see men passing in front of them, making the flames wink and twinkle in the distance like yellow stars.

𝕬s the first light of the misty false dawn brightened in the east, Korin's guard formed up in the yard below. When Korin mounted his tall grey horse, Nalia couldn't help a sigh. He looked so handsome, so dashing.

Perhaps it is only on account of the child that he's grown kinder, but I don't care. I'll bear him many children and bind his heart to me. He doesn't have to love me or think me beautiful, so long as he's kind. Without wanting to, she'd begun to hope.

Thinking that, she was surprised to hear the sound of footsteps on the stairs. She rose and stood in the balcony doorway, listening with mounting dread. She knew that light step.

Niryn entered and bowed to her. "Good morning, my dear. I thought I'd find you awake. I wanted to say my farewells."

He was dressed for traveling and looked almost as he

used to when he visited her in Ilear. She'd yearned for his arrivals then and thrilled at the sight of him. The memory made her ill now. He looked so ordinary. And how could she ever have thought that forked beard attractive? It looked like a serpent's tongue.

Tomara stirred, then rose to curtsy to him. "My lord. Shall I make you some tea?"

"Leave us. I want a moment with your mistress."

"Stay," Nalia commanded, but Tomara went out anyway, as if she hadn't heard.

Niryn closed the door after her and locked it. When he turned back to Nalia, his look was appraising, and there was the hint of a smile on his thin lips.

"My, my. Childbearing does agree with you. You have a certain glow about you now, just like those pearls your dear husband gave you. That was my suggestion, by the way. Poor Korin has rather a tragic history when it comes to getting heirs. Every care must be taken."

"Is it true, that all his other women miscarried monsters?"

"Yes, it is."

"What will become of my child, then? How will I protect her? Tomara said Illior's anger blighted those other babes."

"A most convenient explanation, and one I was more than happy to foster. The truth lies a bit closer to home, I'm afraid." He came to her and stroked her cheek with one gloved finger as Nalia stood frozen with loathing. "You needn't fear for your child, Nalia. She will be perfect." He paused, and then traced the birthmark that marred her cheek and weak chin. "Well, perhaps not perfect, but no monster."

Nalia recoiled. "It was you! You blighted those other babes."

"Those that needed blighting. Young girls often lose the first one, without any assistance. As for those others, it was a simple matter, really."

"You're the monster! Korin would burn you alive if he knew."

"Perhaps, but he never shall." The man's thin smile widened maliciously. "Who would tell him? You? Please, summon him now and try."

"That spell you put on me—"

"Still in force. I have you quite nicely surrounded with spells, all to keep you safe, my dear. You mustn't bother him with trifles when he has so many more important things to worry about. He's quite terrified of battle, you know."

"Liar!"

"I assure you, it's true. I had no hand in that; it's just his nature. He's served his purpose admirably with you, though. He always excelled at rutting."

"That's why you found me and kept me hidden away all those years," Nalia murmured.

"Of course." He went out onto the balcony, beckoning for her to follow. "Look out there," he said, gesturing grandly at the massed army. "That's my doing, as well. An army, ready to secure your husband's claim once and for all. And so they shall. His mad cousin hasn't half so many."

Nalia lingered in the doorway as Niryn leaned on the parapet.

"Korin *will* win? You've seen this?"

"That hardly matters now, does it?"

"What do you mean? How could it not matter?"

"It is not Korin I see in my visions, dear girl. It is the child in your womb. I misread them for a long time, and it cost me considerable effort, but now it's all come clear. The girl child I foresaw is your daughter. As it is, the people now must choose between a usurper king, damned by Illior, or a mad girl spawned of necromancy."

"Girl? Prince Tobin, you mean?"

"I'm not entirely sure what Tobin is, nor do I care. No one can contest the true blood and true form of your little daughter when she arrives. She is of the purest royal lineage."

"What about my husband?" Nalia asked again as cold fear crept over her. "How can you, of all people, call him usurper?"

"Because that's what he is. You know the prophecy as well as I do. Korin, and his father before him, were useful placeholders, nothing more. Skala must have her queen. We shall give them one."

"We?" Nalia whispered through lips suddenly gone dry.

Niryn leaned over, watching the activity below with evident amusement. "Look at them down there, bustling around with visions of victory. Korin thinks he'll rebuild Ero. Already he sees himself playing with his children there."

Nalia clung to the doorframe as her knees threatened to give out under her. "You—you think he's not coming back."

The sky was much brighter by now. She caught the sly, sidelong look he gave her.

"I have missed you, Nalia. Oh, I don't blame you for being angry with me, but appearances had to be maintained. Come now, you're not going to tell me you're in love with him? I know his heart, my dear. You're nothing to him but a pair of legs to lie between, a womb to fill."

"No!" Nalia covered her ears.

"Oh, he flatters himself that he has a warm heart. See how he's feathered your little nest up here. It was more for his conscience than your comfort, I assure you. We agreed, he and I, that you had just enough spirit to try and scamper away, given the chance, so it was better to keep you safely caged up here, like your pretty birds. Though he's never called you pretty."

"Stop it!" Nalia cried. Tears filled her eyes, blurring Niryn to a dark, menacing shape against the sky. "Why are you so cruel? He *does* care for me. He's come to care for me."

"You have come to care for him, you mean. Well, I shouldn't be surprised. You're young and romantic, and Korin's not a bad sort, in his way. But I'm sorry you've become attached to him. It will only make things worse in the end."

Nalia went colder still. "What are you saying?"

Nalia could hear Korin greeting his men and calling out orders. He sounded so happy.

"You should take a good look at him now, while you can, my dear."

"He's *not* coming back." Darkness threatened to close in around her.

"He's done his part, albeit unwillingly," Niryn mused. "Think how cozy it will be; you the mother of the infant monarch, and me, her Lord Protector."

Nalia stared at him in disbelief. Niryn was waving at someone below. Perhaps Korin had looked up and seen him.

She imagined Korin trusting Niryn, just as she had.

She imagined her life stretching out in front of her, a voiceless pawn in Niryn's game, silenced by his magic. And her child, her little unborn daughter, looking up into that false face. Would he someday seduce her, too?

Niryn was still leaning on the parapet, one hip hitched up on the edge as he waved and smiled that false, empty smile.

Rage too long banked flared in Nalia's wounded heart, catching like wildfire on the tinder of her pain and betrayal. It scalded away the numbing fear and drove her forward. Her hands seemed to move of their own accord as she rushed at Niryn and pushed with all her might.

For an instant they were face-to-face, almost close enough to kiss. That false smile was gone, replaced by a wide-eyed look of disbelief. He clawed the air, catching her by the sleeve as he tried in vain to pull himself back from the tipping point. But he was too heavy for her and instead dragged her over the edge with him.

Or nearly so. For an endless instant she hung over the edge, and saw Korin and his riders there below, their faces pale ovals with open mouths. She would land at Korin's feet. She and her child would die there in front of him.

Instead, something caught her and pulled her back from the brink. She had one last sight of Niryn's disbelieving face as he fell, then she tumbled back onto the balcony and lay there in a quivering heap, listening to Niryn's brief, truncated scream and the cries of those who saw him fall.

I have you quite nicely surrounded with spells, all to keep you safe, my dear.

Nalia let out a disbelieving laugh. Trembling, she rose unsteadily and peered back over the parapet.

Niryn lay sprawled like a child's rag doll on the paving stones. He'd landed facedown, so she could not see if that look of dismay was still there.

Korin looked up and saw her, then ran inside the keep.

Nalia staggered back into her room and collapsed on her bed. She would tell him the truth, spilling out every detail of the wizard's treachery against them. He would understand. She would see that fond smile again.

Moments later Korin burst in and found her lying there. "By the Four, Nalia, what have you done?"

Nalia tried tell him, but the words stuck in her throat, just as they had before. She clutched at her throat as the tears came. Tomara came in and ran to take her in her arms. Lord Alben was there, too, clutching Korin's arm, and Master Porion and others Nalia did not know. In the courtyard below someone was wailing. It sounded like a young man.

Nalia tried again to tell Korin the truth, but the horror in his eyes silenced her as harshly as the magic still stopping her tongue. At last she managed to whisper, "He fell."

"I—I saw—" Korin stammered, slowly shaking his head. "I saw you!"

"Close that door," Porion ordered, pointing beyond Nalia to the balcony door. "Close it and make it fast. Bar the windows, too!" Then he was pulling at Korin, drawing him away from her before she could find the words to make them understand.

He was evil! He was going to cast you aside as he did me! He was going to take your place!

The words would not come.

"I saw you," Korin gasped again, then turned and strode from the room. The others followed and Nalia heard Korin cry out angrily, "It's the madness. It's in the blood. Guard her! See that she does no harm to my child!"

Nalia collapsed sobbing in Tomara's arms and wept long after the sound of horses and trumpets had faded away outside. Korin was gone off to his war. He would never smile at her again, even if he did return.

I'm free of Niryn at last, though, she thought, consoling herself with that knowledge. *My child will never be tainted by his touch or that false smile!*

Chapter 45

The late-summer sky overhead was blue as Zengati lapis the day Tamír led her army forth from Atyion. In the vineyards that lined the road women were cutting heavy bunches of grapes into deep baskets. In the distant meadows hundred of fine young foals gamboled among the vast herds, and the fields of grain shone like gold.

Tharin rode beside her, not yet ready to bid her farewell.

Behind them ranks of men-at-arms, archers, and mounted fighters marched under her banner and those of more than a dozen noble houses from Ilear to Erind.

Others, who had been levied from the towns and farms, had only knives, sickles, or cudgels, but they held themselves as proudly as the lords who led them.

The Companions all wore long blue tabards with her coat of arms emblazoned on their chests, and the baldric of her house.

Lutha and Barieus rode proudly, if a bit uncomfortably, talking happily with Una, who'd returned the day before with several regiments from Ylani.

Mahti rode with the wizards for now, with his oo'lu across his back in place of a sword. Word of their strange guide had spread quickly, soldiers' gossip being what it was. Word of their queen's sudden affection for the hill folk spread like wildfire. There was muttering, but their lords and captains kept everyone in line.

At midafternoon Mahti pointed inland toward the mountains. "We go that way."

Tamír shaded her eyes. There was no road, only rolling fields, meadows, and wooded foothills beyond.

"I don't see any pass," said Ki.

"I know way," Mahti insisted.

"Very well, then. We'll go west." Tamír reined in to make her farewells to Tharin.

He gave her a sad smile as they clasped hands. "This time it's you riding away, rather than me."

"I remember how that felt, watching you and Father leave. We'll have some good tales to tell when we meet again."

"May you hold the Sword of Ghërilain before the snow flies." Raising his sword, he shouted, "For Skala and Tamír!"

The army took up the cheer, the words rolling back down the long line like a tide.

With a final wave, Tharin and his escort wheeled their horses and galloped back toward Atyion.

Tamír watched him go, then fixed her gaze on the mountains.

The following day brought them to the foothills, and the next to the forests that covered the foot of the range.

Late that afternoon, Mahti pointed out a game trail leading through a thick patch of wild currant bushes.

"Is that the start of your secret road?" asked Tamír.

"Soon come to," Mahti replied. He spoke rapidly to Arkoniel.

"We follow this trail for a day, then follow a stream up to a waterfall," Arkoniel told her. "The hidden trail starts just beyond it. He says the way is easier after that. We'll reach the first hill folk village within two days."

"I didn't realize there were any living so close."

"I not know these Retha'noi, but they see my oo'lu and know I be witch." He spoke to Arkoniel again, evidently wanting to be certain that Tamír understood what he said clearly.

Arkoniel listened, his face going very serious. "The moment you see any hill folk you must call an immediate halt and stay still. He'll go ahead and speak with them on our behalf. Otherwise, they're likely to attack."

Mahti disappeared into the underbrush for a moment. When he returned, he was wearing his own clothing and the animal-tooth necklace and bracelets. Climbing back onto his horse, he nodded to Tamír. "Now we go."

The forest closed in around them, tall firs that scented the air and choked out the undergrowth. They saw no one that day or the next. The terrain grew steeper, and the wooded hillsides were strewn with large rocks. Mahti led them to the stream he'd spoken of and reached the small waterfall that afternoon. The faint game track they'd been following seemed to end at the pool beneath it.

"Good water," Mahti told them.

Tamír called a halt, then dismounted with the others to fill her waterskin.

Mahti drank, then took his oo'lu from its sling and began to play. It was a short, hooting song, but when he was done Tamír saw a well-worn path leading away from the pool's edge that had not been there before. The trees on either side were marked with faded handprints like the markings she'd seen around Lhel's abandoned camp.

"Come!" Mahti set off briskly up the new trail. "You be in Retha'noi place. Keep promise."

As they made camp that night Arkoniel joined Tamír and the others around their fire.

"I've just spoken with Lyan. Korin's fleet tried to land at Ero. Tharin had word from the wizards and coastal lookouts that they were making for the port, and Illardi was waiting for them, with the wizards. He used the few ships you had there, setting them ablaze to trap Korin's ships. The flames spread, and our wizards used their own spells to help things along. All the enemy vessels were destroyed or captured."

"That's very good news!" Tamír exclaimed. "But no word of an attack by land?"

"Nevus is bringing a sizable army south. Tharin's already heading out to meet him."

"Sakor bring him luck," Ki said, casting a stick onto the fire.

Lying in her blankets that night, watching the branches sway against the stars, Tamír sent up a silent prayer of her own for Tharin, hoping that he wouldn't be taken from her, too.

The next day the way grew steeper, and there was still no sign of a village. Just before midday, however, Mahti raised a hand to halt the others.

"There." He pointed up at a jumble of fallen stones on the right.

Tamír signaled a halt. It took a moment to make out the man squatting on the highest rock. He was staring straight back at her and had an oo'lu pressed to his lips.

Mahti raised his own horn over his head and waited. After a moment the other man lowered his and shouted something to him.

"You stay," Mahti told her, then climbed nimbly up the rocks to join the stranger.

"We're not alone," Ki whispered.

"I see them." At least a dozen more Retha'noi were visible, watching them from either side of the divide. Some had bows, others long horns like Mahti's.

No one moved. Tamír clutched her reins, listening to the low murmur of the two witches talking. Now and then the stranger's voice rose angrily, but presently he and Mahti climbed down from the rocks and stood on the trail.

"He talk to you and oreskiri," Mahti called out to her. "Others stay."

"I don't like this," Ki muttered.

"Don't worry, I'll be with her," Arkoniel told him.

Tamír dismounted and gave her reins to Ki, then unbuckled her sword belt and handed that to him, too.

She and Arkoniel walked together toward the witches, hands outstretched to show they were unarmed.

This man was older than Mahti and missing most of his teeth. His witch marks showed clearly on his skin, warning that he had some sort of spell in place.

"This Sheksu," Mahti informed her. "I tell him you come to bring peace. He ask how."

"Arkoniel, tell him who I am, and that I will tell my people to stop their persecution, as long as the Retha'noi are peaceful toward us. Tell him we only wish to pass safely through his valley. We do not come to conquer or spy."

Arkoniel relayed this, and Sheksu asked a sharp question.

"He asks why he should believe a southlander girl who hasn't even known a man yet."

"How did he know that?" Tamír hissed, trying to cover her surprise. "Tell him I will swear by all my gods."

"I don't think that will convince him. Prick your finger and offer him a drop of blood. That will be proof that you aren't trying to hide anything from him. Use this." He took Lhel's needle from his purse.

Tamír pricked her forefinger and held it out to Sheksu. The witch caught the droplet and rubbed it between his thumb and finger. He shot a surprised look at Mahti and asked him something.

"He said you have two shadows," Arkoniel murmured.

"Brother?"

"Yes."

Sheksu and Mahti spoke again.

"He's explaining about Lhel," Arkoniel whispered.

"He say to see mark," Mahti said at last.

"The scar? I'll have to take off my armor. Tell him I need his word that this is not a trick."

"He say no trick, by Mother."

"Very well, then. Arkoniel, can you help me?"

The wizard managed to get one side of her cuirass undone and held it while she pulled off her tabard.

"What the hell are you doing?" Ki called, starting forward.

Sheksu raised a hand at Ki.

"Ki, stop! Stay where you are," Arkoniel ordered.

"Do as he says," Tamír told him calmly.

Ki stayed put, scowling. Behind him, the other Companions remained tense and alert.

Tamír took off her hauberk and pulled down the neck of the padded shirt and the linen undershirt underneath to show Sheksu the scar between her breasts. He ran a finger over the faded white stitch marks, then looked deeply into her eyes. He smelled of grease and rotten teeth, but his black eyes were sharp as a hawk's and just as wary.

"Tell him that Lhel helped me so that our people could make peace," Tamír said.

Sheksu stepped back, still eyeing her closely.

"It might help if Brother made an appearance," Arkoniel whispered.

"You know I can't make him come and go as I please—"

But suddenly Brother was there. It was only for an instant, long enough for him to let out a low, mocking hiss that stood the hair up on her neck and arms; but for that instant she thought she felt another presence with him, and the scent of freshly crushed leaves lingered on the air. She looked around quickly, hoping for a glimpse of Lhel, but there was only the feeling of her, and the scent.

Sheksu appeared satisfied as he spoke to Mahti and Arkoniel.

"He believes you, because no Orëska wizard could

make that kind of magic," said Arkoniel. "Brother just did you a great service."

"Not Brother. Lhel," she replied softly. "I wonder if he saw her."

"He see," Mahti told her. "She speak for you."

Sheksu spoke to Mahti again, gesturing at his people still standing overhead, then down the trail in the direction they meant to go.

"He say you can pass with your people, but you must go quick," Mahti explained. "He will send song about you to next village and they send to next. He say he not—" He frowned and looked to Arkoniel to clarify.

"You've been granted safe passage, and Sheksu will relay your story on, but he can't promise you will be welcome, only that he has spoken for you."

Sheksu said something else and Arkoniel bowed to him. "He was impressed that you offered your blood, and by what he read from it. He says you have favor with his goddess. If you keep your word, you should be safe."

"I am honored by his trust." She took a gold sester from her purse and presented it to him. The coin was stamped with Illior's crescent moon and the flame of Sakor. "Tell him that these are the symbols of my people. Tell him that I call him friend."

Sheksu accepted the coin and rubbed it between his fingers, then said something that sounded friendly.

"He is impressed," Arkoniel murmured. "Gold is very scarce here, and highly prized."

In return Sheksu gave her one of his bracelets, made with the teeth and claws of a bear.

"It will give you strength against your enemies and mark you as a friend of the hill folk," Arkoniel interpreted.

"Tell him I am honored to wear it."

Sheksu bade her farewell and quickly disappeared among the rocks.

"Go quick now," Mahti told her.

Tamír put her armor back on and strode back to the Companions.

"That seemed to go well," Ki murmured, handing her sword back to her.

"We're not over the mountains yet."

Chapter 46

Niryn's death and the manner of it cast a pall over Korin's heart. As he led his army east, he could not shake off a sense of foreboding.

Nalia had killed Niryn; of that he had no doubt, despite her stammering assertion that he had only fallen. "Are all the women of the royal line cursed with madness?" he'd ranted to Alben as Niryn's broken body was carried away. Moriel had followed the litter, wailing like a woman over his former master.

"Mad or not, she bears your child. What are you going to do with her?" Alben asked.

"Not just a child. A girl. A new queen. I've sworn before the altar of the Lightbearer that she will be my heir. Why am I still cursed?"

He'd questioned the priests about it before they marched, but there were no Illiorans left in Cirna, and the others were too frightened of him to offer anything more than hollow assurances. The Dalnan priest assured him that some women went mad while they were pregnant, but grew calm again after the birth, and gave him charms to heal her mind. Korin sent them up to the tower with Tomara.

Thoughts of Aliya and the monstrous thing she'd died giving birth to came to haunt his dreams again, as well. Sometimes he was back in that birthing chamber with her; other nights it was Nalia in the bed, her marred face twisted in agony as she pushed out another abomination.

Tanil and Caliel used to calm him after such nightmares.

Alben and Urmanis did their best, bringing him wine when they heard him wake.

And then there was Moriel. The farther Korin got from Cirna, the more he found himself wondering again why he'd finally agreed to give the Toad a commission, knowing he'd been Orun's creature and Niryn's lackey.

Despite all these concerns, he felt increasingly lighter as the days passed. He'd been lax with himself since Ero, he realized with some chagrin. He'd let sorrow and doubt unman him, and depended too much on Niryn. His body was still hard, his sword arm strong, but his spirit had grown weak with lack of use. These past months seemed very dark, as if the sun had never shone on the fortress.

He turned in the saddle and looked back over the thousands of men at his back.

"It's a brave sight, isn't it?" he said to Master Porion and the others, looking proudly at the ranks of cavalry and foot.

Thanks to Duke Wethring and Lord Nevus, almost every noble between there and Ilear was either with him, dead, or under edict of execution. He would deal with the latter as soon as he'd taken care of Tobin and seized Atyion.

Tobin. Korin's hands tightened on the reins. It was past time to be finished with him, once and for all.

Korin was too honorable in his own mind to recognize the jealousy that lay behind his anger—a bitter, corrosive undercurrent fed by the memory of his own failures, thrown into stark contrast by his little cousin's natural valor. No, he wouldn't allow himself to think of that. He'd put those days behind him, as errors of his youth. He would not falter this time.

They left the isthmus and struck north and east toward Colath. The rains came, but spirits remained high among the ranks, and the Companions, as well. In a few days they would be in sight of Atyion, within striking distance of all the fine resources there—horses and granaries, and the wealth of the treasuries. He'd had little more than promises to hold his lords; now they had great spoils nearly at hand. He would raze Atyion and use her great wealth to rebuild Ero in greater glory.

That afternoon, however, one of his advance scouts came riding back at a gallop on a lathered horse, with another rider close behind.

"Boraeus, isn't it?" Korin said, recognizing him as one of Niryn's chief spies.

"Majesty, I bring you word of Prince Tobin. He's on the march!"

"How many with him?"

"Five thousand, perhaps? I'm not sure. But he isn't coming along the coast. He's sending another force to meet you, under the command of Lord Tharin—"

"Tharin?" Porion murmured, frowning.

Alben chuckled. "So Tobin sends his nursemaid after us. He must have learned to wipe his own nose at last."

"Tharin served in your father's Companions, Majesty," Porion reminded him, shooting Alben a warning glance. "He was Duke Rhius' bravest captain. It won't do to underestimate him."

"It's only a feint, Majesty," the spy explained. "The prince is taking a secret route through the mountains, to outflank you from the west."

"We'll see about that," Korin growled.

He called a halt and summoned his other generals, then made the messenger repeat his news before them.

"That's excellent news! We'll overwhelm that paltry advance force like a storm tide and take the city in your name, Majesty!" Nevus exclaimed, eager to avenge his father's death.

Looking around, Korin read the same hungry, vengeful gleam in every eye. They were already counting the spoils.

Korin went very still inside as he listened to all their

arguments, and his mind grew ever clearer. "Lord Nevus, you will take five companies of cavalry and meet the eastern force. Catch them between Duke Morus' forces and crush them. Bring me Lord Tharin or his head."

"Majesty?"

"Atyion is nothing." Korin drew the Sword of Ghërilain and held it up. "There can only be one ruler of Skala, and that is the one who holds this sword! Pass the order; we march west to crush Prince Tobin and his army."

"You're dividing your force?" Porion asked quietly. "You may be dooming Morus' ships. There's no way to get word to them now."

Korin shrugged. "He'll have to fend for himself. When Tobin falls, Atyion will fall. That is my will and those are your orders. Send out scouting parties at once, north and south. I don't want them taking Cirna under our very nose. The consort must be protected at all costs. We'll be the ones to surprise the prince, my lords, and when we do, we will crush him and put an end to his pretense once and for all!"

The generals bowed deeply to him and rode off to pass on his orders.

"That was well done, Majesty," Moriel said, offering him his wineskin. "Lord Niryn would be proud to see you now."

Korin turned and brought the tip of his blade under Moriel's chin. The Toad went a shade paler and froze, staring at him with frightened eyes. The wineskin fell and splashed its contents on the trampled grass.

"If you wish to remain a Companion, you will not mention that creature to me again."

"As you say, Majesty," Moriel whispered.

Korin sheathed his sword and strode away, heedless of the resentful glare that followed him.

Porion noticed, though, and cuffed Moriel sharply on the ear. "Be thankful for the king's patience," he warned.

"Your master is dead, and I'd have drowned you years ago if it had been up to me."

Caliel had hoped to meet Korin on the road, but there was no sign of an army or its passing. They rode all the way to the isthmus road with no sign of him, and Caliel learned in the villages they passed that Korin had turned back and gone south to meet Tamír on the western coast.

They rode on for a few miles, and Caliel could see the marks of an army's passage in the trampled fields, churned roadways, and deep ruts from heavy wagons.

"Why did they go west?" Tanil asked. "There's nothing there."

"I don't know." He paused, and looked Tanil over. The boy was still a bit vague, but the closer they came to Korin, the happier he seemed.

He's in no condition to fight. I should take him to Cirna and leave him there somehow, to keep him safe. But the longing in Tanil's eyes as he looked west was like a mirror of Caliel's own heart. They were Korin's men. Their place was at his side, no matter what.

He forced a smile and nudged his horse into a walk. "Come on, then. Let's catch up with him."

"He'll be surprised to see us!" Tanil laughed.

Caliel nodded, wondering again what his reception would be.

Chapter 47

The last of the passage through the mountains took four long, tense days. The trail ran along the banks of rushing rivers and up through stony divides that opened into small green valleys where herds of goats and sheep grazed. There were signs of catamounts and bears, and at night lynxes screamed like dying women.

Only in the valleys could Tamír assemble all her force at once, rather than strung out like a broken necklace. Nikides rode back one day and reported that it took two hours for them to pass a given point.

Word of Tamír's approach preceded her, just as Sheksu had promised. Several times each day Mahti would disappear ahead of them, taking a side trail up to some hidden settlement. Those that were visible from the trail were made up of a few stone huts with roofs of stretched skins. The inhabitants either hid or fled, but there was smoke from abandoned cooking fires and flocks of goats or chickens wandering among the silent huts.

On Mahti's advice, Tamír left gifts by the trail at each village: coins, food, rope, small knives, and the like. Sometimes they also found baskets of food left for them—greasy smoked goat meat, foul-smelling cheeses, berries and mushrooms, and bits of crude jewelry.

"They hear good of you," Mahti informed her. "You take gift or give insult."

"We wouldn't want that," Nikides said, wrinkling his nose in distaste as he and Lorin inspected the contents of a basket.

"Don't be so squeamish," Ki laughed, gnawing at a bit

of leathery meat. Tamír took some, too. It reminded her of
the food Lhel had given them.

Now and then the local witch man or woman came
out to see them, but they were wary even of Mahti and
watched the intruders from a distance.

The weather closed in as they crossed a high pass and
started down for the western coast. Heavy clouds and fog
hung low over the narrow divide. Freshets trickled down
through the rocks and made the trail into a stream at times,
dangerous underfoot with shifting stones. The trees were
different here, the quakeleaf still green and the underbrush
thicker.

Rain came in gentle, persistent showers and soon
everyone was soaked to the skin. Tamír slept badly in the
scant shelter of a tree, huddled for warmth with Ki and
Una, and woke to find a pair of newts playing tag across
the toe of one sodden boot.

The next day they passed close to a large village and
saw three witches on a rise just above the trail: a woman
and two men with oo'lus at the ready.

Tamír reined her horse aside, accompanied by Mahti,
Arkoniel, and Ki.

"I know these," Mahti said. "I go."

"I'd like to speak with them."

Mahti called out to them, but they kept their distance
and made signs at him.

"No, they say they talk to me." He went forward alone.

"It's downright eerie," Ki muttered. "I get the feeling there are a lot of eyes watching us without our
knowing."

"They haven't attacked us, though."

Mahti returned a few moments later. "They not hear
of you. Afraid of so many and be angry that I be with
you. I tell them you—" He paused, and asked Arkoniel
something.

"They don't know what to make of an army passing through without attacking them," Arkoniel explained.

Mahti nodded as they set off again. "I tell them. Lhel tell, too. You go, and they send on song."

One of the witches began playing a low drone as they rode past.

"I wouldn't think people this far into the mountains had ever seen a Skalan," said Lynx, keeping an uneasy eye on the Retha'noi.

"No see, but hear of, like you hear of Retha'noi," said Mahti. "If keesa be—" He stopped again, shaking his head in frustration, and turned and said something to Arkoniel.

The wizard laughed. "If a child is naughty, the mother says, 'be good or the pale people will come for you in the night.' I told him Skalans tell their children the same thing of them."

"They see you have great people, but you not hurt or burn. They remember you."

"Could they hurt us if they wanted to?" asked Ki, also keeping a wary eye on the witches.

Mahti nodded emphatically.

*A*t last the trail led steadily downward, back into forests of fir and oak overhung with mist. On the afternoon of the fifth day they emerged from the low-hanging clouds and looked out over a descending expanse of forest and rolling grassland. In the distance Tamír saw the dark curve of the Osiat.

"We made it!" cried Nikides.

"Where's Remoni?" asked Tamír.

Mahti pointed straight ahead and her heart beat a little faster. A day's march at most, and she would see that harbor. In her dreams she and Ki had stood above it, a breath away from a kiss. She hadn't had that dream for some time now, not since Afra.

And we have kissed, she thought with an inward smile,

though there had been no time for such things in days. She wondered if the dream would be different now.

"You have good thought?"

Mahti stood by her horse, grinning up at her.

"Yes," she admitted.

"Look there." He pointed back the way they'd come and Tamír saw with a start that the brow of the ridge was lined with dark figures, perhaps hundreds, watching the long line of foot soldiers passing by.

"Your people safe, if you do not try come this way again," Mahti explained. "You make your fight and go to your own land by another trail. Southland trail."

"I understand. You're not leaving us yet, though? I don't know how to find Remoni."

"I take you, then I go home."

"That's all I ask."

Arkoniel's heart had also leaped at the sight of that distant coastline. If the visions were true—and if this campaign succeeded—he would soon reach the place where he would eventually end his days. It was a strange but exciting thought.

Once beyond the narrow confines of the mountain trail, the way became easier. The trail was well-worn and wide enough in places for two horses abreast.

The rain came and went, but there was wood to burn that night, letting the Skalans take more comfort than they'd had in days. While the others made a fire and prepared the evening meal, Arkoniel drew Tamír aside under an oak. Ki followed, sitting down close beside her.

Arkoniel tried not to smile. They both tried to hide it, but something had changed between them since that night at the keep. They didn't look at one another with the eyes of a friend anymore, and they imagined that no one else could see it.

"Arkoniel, have you found Korin?" she asked.

"That's what I'm about to ascertain. Will you let me cast the wizard eye on you both?"

"Yes," said Ki, clearly eager to try it.

Tamír was less enthused, as always. Arkoniel had always regretted how he'd clumsily scared her, the first time he'd tried this spell with her. Nevertheless, she gave him a terse nod.

Arkoniel cast the spell and focused his mind on likely routes. "Ah! There." He held out his hands to them.

Tamír reached for his hand, braced for the inevitable jolt of vertigo she experienced whenever he tried to show her something this way. It was no different this time. She squeezed her eyes closed as she felt herself swept up into the spell.

She saw a rolling expanse of countryside far below, and an army encamped beside a broad bay. A sea of watch fires stretched across the darkened plain. "So many!" she whispered. "And look at all those horses! Thousands. Can you tell how close he is to us?"

"That appears to be the Bay of Whales. Perhaps two days' march from where we're headed? Maybe less."

"He could have been in Atyion by now. Do you think he got word of my movements?"

"Yes, I'd say so. Let go for a moment. I'm going to widen the search."

Tamír opened her eyes to find Ki grinning at her.

"That was amazing!" he whispered, eyes shining.

"It has its uses," she admitted.

Arkoniel rubbed at his eyelids. "That spell does take an effort."

"Korin will have scouts out looking for us," said Ki. "Did you see any sign of them?"

The wizard gave him a wry look. "I was lucky to find an army."

"We don't need magic to tell us that," Tamír said.

"We'd better move on quickly, before he decides to come find me himself."

Far to the east, Tharin sat his horse, counting the banners of the force spread out across the plain before him. He had two thousand men at his back, but Nevus had at least twice that many. He'd caught them within a day's ride of Atyion two days earlier and had not been surprised when Nevus had refused any sort of terms short of battle.

Drawing his sword, Tharin held it high, and heard a thousand blades singing from their sheaths in answer, and the rattle of hundreds of quivers. Across the field, Nevus did the same.

"I'll see your body hung beside your father's," Tharin murmured, marking him. Rising in the saddle, he shouted, "For Tamír and Skala!"

His army gave back the cry and their voices rolled over the plain like a tide as they charged.

Tamír spent the next day riding back along the line with some of her Companions, to take stock of her warriors. Some had taken sick during the cold wet nights, and a few had been lost in falls along the high passes. There had been some blood feuds settled, and a handful of others had simply disappeared. There was grumbling about them having been taken by the hill folk, though desertion or mishap were more likely. Wineskins were empty, and rations were running low.

Tamír paused often to speak with captains and common soldiers, listening to their concerns, promising them battlefield spoils, and praising their endurance. In return, she was warmed by their loyalty and their determination to set things right. Some were a bit too eager, offering to bring her Korin's head on a pike.

"Bring him to me alive, and I'll pay his ransom in gold," she told them. "Willfully spill the blood of my kinsman and you'll have no reward from me."

"I bet Korin isn't making that distinction," Ki observed.

To which Tamír wearily replied, "I'm not Korin."

The air grew warmer the farther they got from the mountains. There was ample game, and archers were sent out to supplement their dwindling food supplies with venison, hare, and grouse. Her scouting parties found no signs of habitation.

They reached the coast late that afternoon, and Tamír savored the sweet salt air after so many days inland. The rocky coastline was deeply cut with steep-walled bays and inlets. The dark Osiat stretched away to the misty horizon, dotted with a scattering of islands.

Mahti turned north. Open grassland between forest and the sea spread on endlessly before them, flanked on the east by forest. Deer grazed in the meadows, and rabbits broke from cover before their horses.

The land rose, until they were high above the water on a grassy headland. Cresting a rise, Tamír caught her breath, recognizing the place even before Mahti pointed down and said, "Remoni."

"Yes!" There was the long, deep harbor, sheltered by the two unmistakable islands.

She dismounted and walked to the cliff edge. The water lay hundreds of feet below. In her dreams she'd seen her reflection there, but that had only been an illusion. In reality, there was a sizable expanse of level ground at the base of the cliffs, just the place for a harbor town and jetties. The trick would be to make a passable road up to a citadel on the heights.

Ki joined her. "You really dreamed this?"

"So often I lost count," she replied. If there hadn't been so many eyes on them, she would have kissed him, just to make certain Ki didn't disappear and she didn't wake up.

"Welcome to your new city, Majesty," said Arkoniel. "It needs a bit of work, though. I haven't seen a decent tavern anywhere."

Lynx stood shading his eyes against the slanting light as she stared down at the harbor. "Uh—Tamír? Where are the 'faie ships?"

In her excitement at finding the place, she'd over-looked that important detail. The harbor below was empty.

They made camp there, setting out pickets to the north and east. As Mahti had promised, there were a number of good springs, and ample wood for a while.

It was several hours before the entire column caught up, and stragglers continued to drift in for hours.

"My people are exhausted, Majesty," Kyman reported.

Jorvai and Nyanis reported the same when they arrived.

"Tell them they've earned a rest," Tamír replied.

After a meager supper of stale bread, hard cheese, and a handful of wizened berries from the hill folk, she and Ki walked among the campfires, listening to the soldiers brag of battles to come. Those who had fresh meat shared it with them, and in return she asked their names and where they hailed from. Spirits were high, and word of her vision of Remoni had gotten around during the march. The soldiers were taking it as a lucky sign that such a place actually existed and their queen had led them to it.

The waning moon was high in the cloud-wracked sky as they started back for her tent. A fire was burning brightly and her friends sat around it. Still hidden in darkness, she paused, committing the sight of their smiling, laughing faces to memory once again. She'd seen the size of Korin's force; in a few days' time they might have little to smile about.

"Come on," Ki murmured, slipping an arm around her shoulders. "I think Nik might have a little wine left."

He did, and the warmth of it lifted her spirits. They might be hungry and footsore and damp, but they were here.

She was about to turn in for the night when she heard the low, throbbing drone of Mahti's horn somewhere nearby.

"Now what's he up to?" Lutha wondered aloud.

Following the sound, they found the witch sitting on a rock overlooking the sea, eyes closed as he made his strange music. Tamír approached quietly. The song was filled with strange ups and downs, croaks and vibrations that reminded her of animal sounds, all strung together on an endless stream of breath. It blended with the cries of night birds and the distant yelp of a fox, and the voices of her army, laughter, singing, and the occasional angry shout or curse, but she didn't feel magic in it. Relaxing for the first time in days, she leaned her shoulder against Ki's and gazed out at the moon-washed sea. She could almost feel herself out there, bobbing on the waves like a leaf. She was nearly asleep on her feet when the song ended.

"What was that?" Ki asked softly.

Mahti stood up. "Farewell song. I bring you to Remoni. I go home now." He paused, looking at Tamír. "I make a healing for you, before I go."

"I told you before, I don't need any healing. I wish you'd stay with us, though. We'll soon need your skills."

"I not make to fight as you do." Mahti gazed at her, his dark eyes thoughtful. "I dream of Lhel again. She say don't forget your noro'shesh."

Tamír knew that word meant Brother. "I won't. I'll never forget her, either. Tell her?"

"She know." He took up his little bundle and walked with them back to the fire to say his good-byes to Arkoniel and the others.

Lutha and Barieus clasped hands with him.

"We owe you our lives," Lutha said. "I hope we meet again."

"You be good guides. Bring me to girl who was boy, just as I say. Bring her to my people. You are friends of Retha'noi." He turned to Arkoniel and spoke to him in his own tongue. The wizard bowed and said something in return.

Mahti shouldered his horn and then sniffed the breeze. "More rain come." As he walked away, his feet made no sound on the dry grass and the shadows between the campfires soon swallowed him up as if he'd never been there at all.

Chapter 48

Korin dreamed of Tobin nearly every night, and the dreams were much the same. He might be walking through the great hall at Cirna, or in the palace gardens of Ero, and he would spy a familiar figure ahead of him. Each time, Tobin turned to smile tauntingly at him, then ran away. Furious, Korin would draw his sword and run after him, but could never catch up. Sometimes the dream seemed to go on for hours and he would wake tense and sweating, hand clenched around an imaginary hilt.

The dream was different this time, though. He was riding along the edge of a high cliff, and Tobin was waiting for him in the distance. He didn't run when Korin spurred his horse forward, just stood there, laughing.

Laughing at him.

Korin?"

Korin started awake and found Urmanis bending over him. It was still dark. The watch fire outside cast long shadows up the walls of his tent. "What is it?" he rasped.

"One of the southern scouting parties found Tobin."

Korin stared at him for a moment, wondering if he was still dreaming.

"Are you awake, Kor? I said we found Tobin! He's about a day's march south."

"On the coast?" Korin murmured.

"Yes." The other man gave him an odd look as he handed him a cup of watered wine.

It was a vision, he thought, downing the morning draft. He threw off the blankets and reached his boots.

"He came through the mountains, just as we were told," Urmanis went on, handing Korin a tunic. "If he tries to march on Cirna, we can easily cut him off here."

Glancing out through the open flap, Korin saw that it was close to dawn. Porion and the Companions stood waiting.

Korin joined them. "We aren't going to sit waiting for him any longer. Garol, have the trumpeters raise the camp. Prepare to march."

The squire sprinted away.

"Moriel, summon my nobles."

"At once, Majesty!" The Toad hurried off.

Korin downed the last of the wine and handed the cup back to Urmanis. "Where are the scouts who found him?"

"Here, Majesty." Porion presented a blond, bearded man. "Captain Esmen, Majesty, of Duke Wethring's house."

The man saluted Korin. "My riders and I spotted a large force on the coast yesterday, just before sundown. I went forward myself and spied on the pickets as soon as it was dark. It's definitely Prince Tobin. Or Queen Tamír, as we heard him called," he added with a smirk.

Wethring and the other nobles joined them, and Korin had the scout repeat his news. "How large a force does he have?"

"I can't be sure, Majesty, but I'd say considerably less than yours. It's mostly men-at-arms, not much in the way of cavalry. Perhaps two hundred horse?"

"Did you see any standards?"

"Only Prince Tobin's, Majesty, but the men I heard talking mentioned Lord Jorvai. I also heard them complaining of being hungry. I didn't see any sign of a baggage train."

"That would explain how he got across the mountains so quickly," said Porion. "He was foolish to come with so little support, though."

"We're well supplied and rested," Korin mused with

satisfaction. "We'll press our advantage. Assemble my cavalry and signal for a quick march."

Captain Esmen bowed again. "Begging your pardon, Majesty, but I've more to tell. There was mention of wizards, too."

"I see. Anything else?"

"No, Majesty, but some of my men stayed behind to bring word if he starts north."

"Well done. Lord Alben, see that this man is rewarded."

"Will you send a herald ahead, King Korin?" asked Wethring.

Korin smiled darkly. "The sight of my standard is all the warning my cousin will get from me."

Mahti had been right about the weather. Misty rain rolled in off the sea during the night, damping the watch fires and soaking the already exhausted soldiers. Barieus had been coughing all evening, though he was doing his best to hide it.

"Sleep in my tent tonight," Tamír told him. "That's an order. I need you fit tomorrow."

"Thanks," he rasped, stifling another cough behind his hand. Lutha gave him a worried look. "Take my blankets. I won't need them on watch."

"You should get what rest you can, too," Ki told Tamír.

"I will. But not just yet. I need to speak with Arkoniel."

"I know where he is."

He lit a torch and led her back to the cliffs. Arkoniel was there with Saruel, kneeling beside his own small fire. They were both hollow-eyed from casting seeking spells, and as Tamír approached, she saw Arkoniel cough raggedly against his arm.

"You're ill, too?" she asked, concerned.

"No, it's just the damp," he replied, though she suspected he was lying.

"Any sign of the 'faie yet?" asked Ki.

"I'm afraid not."

"It's the beginning of the stormy season on this sea," said Saruel. "They could have been blown off course."

"What about Tharin?" asked Tamír.

Arkoniel sighed and shook his head. "There is no siege at Atyion. That's all I can tell you. Lyan has sent no word."

With nothing to do now but wait, Tamír let Ki lead her back to her tent and attempted to catch a few hours' rest. Her damp clothes and Barieus' intermittent coughing prevented deep sleep. She dozed fitfully and rose before dawn to find the world shrouded in fog. The rain was still falling, cold and persistent. Lorin and Tyrien were on watch outside, huddled under their cloaks as they fed wood to the smoking fire.

Tamír walked away to relieve her bladder. She still missed being able to simply open her trousers. As it was, the fog spared her the necessity of going very far.

The world was all grey and black around her. She could make out the edge of the cliff, and the dark shapes of men and horses, but it was indistinct, like the landscape of a dream. She could hear people grumbling, talking, and coughing as they stirred around their fires. Three muffled figures stood at the edge of the cliff.

"Be careful of your footing," one of them warned, as she went to join them.

Arkoniel and Lord Malkanus both had their eyes closed, lost in some spell. Kaulin stood with them, holding each by the elbow.

"Has he been at it all night?" Tamír asked quietly.

Kaulin nodded.

"Any sign?" She could already guess the answer.

Lord Malkanus opened his eyes. "I'm sorry, Majesty, but I still don't see any sign of ships. It is very foggy, though, and it's a very large sea."

"That doesn't mean they're not out there somewhere." Arkoniel sighed, opening his eyes. "Not that it matters now. Korin is breaking camp. I cast a window spell earlier.

I still can't focus it on Korin, but I was able to find his generals. There's talk of moving south. I suspect he knows you're close by, to be moving so suddenly."

Tamír rubbed a hand over her face and back through her dirty hair, trying to ignore the empty rumbling in her belly. "Then we don't have long."

She walked back to the tent, where her marshals and the others were waiting. Ki handed her a roasted grouse, still hot on the stick it had been cooked on. "A gift from one of the Colath men."

Tamír pulled off a bit of the breast meat and handed it back. "Share it around. My lords, Korin is coming, and he's only a day or so away. I say we choose the ground and be ready when he gets here rather than going on to meet him. Nyanis, Arkoniel, and the Companions will ride with me. The rest of you rouse your companies and spread the word. And warn them to keep away from the cliffs until this damn fog lifts! I can't spare anyone to mishap."

The rain slowed to a drizzle as they rode north and the breeze picked up, pulling the fog to tatters around them.

"Korin has numbers on his side, and a large force of cavalry. We must find a way to cut down his advantage," Tamír mused, eyeing the countryside as they went.

"Your greatest strength is in your archers," Nyanis noted.

"What if Master Arkoniel cast a window spell and you shot at Korin through it, like you did with the Plenimarans?" asked Hylia.

Tamír frowned at the young squire. "That would be dishonorable. He and I are kin and warriors, and we'll meet as warriors on the field."

"Forgive me, Majesty," Hylia replied, reddening. "I spoke without thinking."

The ground fell away beyond their camp, and the forest closed in on the cliffs, leaving a space of open ground less than half a mile wide between trees and the sea. Farther on, the ground rose sharply beyond a little stream.

Tamír dismounted there and let her horse drink. The ground underfoot was soft. She jumped the stream and walked around on the far side, stamping her feet. "It's boggy over here. If Korin's cavalry comes galloping down, they're likely to find poor footing."

She crossed back and mounted again, then galloped up the hill with Ki and Nyanis to survey the view from the crest. The ground beyond the hill was firm and dry for as far as she could see. The forest was not so close here. From this direction the field grew narrower the farther down one went.

"If he charges from here, it'll be like peas into a funnel," she mused. "A broad line would end up bunched and crowded in on itself unless Korin narrows his ranks."

"If you were marching from the north, this would look like a good place to take a stand," Nyanis said. "You'd have the high ground."

"That's best for defense, though. We need to bring them down to us."

"Korin won't think anything of charging foot soldiers," said Ki. "There's a good chance he could break our lines, too, if he has as many people as you say, Arkoniel."

"That's just what he'll think," said Tamír, already seeing it in her mind's eye. "What we need is a herald, and a hedgehog."

Chapter 49

Cutting west to the Osiat coast under a grey sky, Korin turned south with his cavalry, leaving the foot with orders to catch up quickly.

Keeping the sea in sight, they rode hard all day, passing through open grasslands and skirting deep forest.

"Rich-looking country," Porion remarked as they stopped to water their horses at a river ford.

But Korin had no eye for bottomland or timber stands. His gaze was fixed on the distance, already seeing in his mind's eye the apparition of his cousin. After all the months of uncertainty and delay, it was almost beyond comprehension that he would finally face Tobin and decide the fate of Skala, once and for all.

It was midafternoon before the first of the scouts returned with word of Tobin's army.

"They've moved north a few miles, Majesty, and seem to be anticipating your arrival," the rider informed him.

"That will be his wizards' work," said Alben.

Korin nodded grimly. How was it that Niryn and his ilk had never been of such use?

They were about to set off again when Korin heard a rider coming up from the rear at a punishing gallop. The man hailed him and reined in.

"Majesty, two riders have been captured at the end of the column. One of them claims to be your friend, Lord Caliel."

"Caliel!" For a moment Korin could hardly get his breath. Caliel, here? He saw his own amazement on the faces of the remaining Companions, all but Moriel, who looked disconcerted.

"He begs your indulgence to see him and the man he brought you," the messenger said.

"Bring them to me at once!" Korin ordered, wondering what could have possibly brought Cal back. He paced restlessly as he waited, fists clenched behind his back while Alben and the others watched in silence. Was this some trick of Tobin's, sending the man back to spy? What could he hope to gain this late in the game? Korin could not imagine why else Caliel would risk execution to return. Revenge, perhaps? But that was simply suicidal, given the circumstances.

Presently an armed escort arrived and Korin made out Caliel in their midst, riding with his hands bound before him. Someone else rode beside him. As they came closer, Korin let out a shocked gasp as his heart turned over in his breast. "Tanil?"

The escort halted and four men brought the prisoners down from the saddle and marched them to where Korin and the others stood staring. Caliel met his gaze levelly and fell to one knee before him.

Tanil was pale and thin. He looked terribly confused, but broke into a beautiful smile as he caught sight of Korin and attempted to come to him, only to be restrained.

"My lord, I found you!" he called, struggling weakly. "Prince Korin, it's me! Forgive me—I got lost, but Cal brought me back!"

"Release him!" Korin ordered. Tanil ran to him and fell on his knees, clasping Korin's boot with his bound hands. Korin loosed the rope and wrapped his arms awkwardly around the boy's shaking shoulders. Tanil was laughing and sobbing at the same time, babbling apologies over and over again.

Korin looked past him to find Caliel watching with a sad smile. He was filthy and pale, too, and looked on the verge of collapse, but he was *smiling*.

"What are you doing here?" Korin asked, still not quite master of his voice.

"I found him in Atyion. He wouldn't rest until he came back to you, so I brought him."

Korin freed himself from Tanil's embrace and walked over to him, drawing his sword as he went.

Caliel didn't flinch or show the least fear, just kept his gaze fixed on Korin.

"Did Tobin send you?"

"No, but she honorably let us go, even knowing that it was back to you."

Korin leveled the blade under Caliel's chin. "You will not speak of him like that to me, do you understand?"

"As you wish, my lord."

Korin lowered the tip of his blade a few inches. "Why did you come back, Cal? You're still under the order of execution."

"Then kill me. I've done what I came to do. Just— please, be kind to Tanil. He's suffered enough, for the love of you." His voice was hoarse and hollow by the time he finished, and he was wavering on his knees. Korin thought of the flogging he'd endured and wondered how he'd survived at all. It hadn't mattered much at the time. Now he felt the first stirrings of shame.

"Untie him," he ordered.

"But Majesty—"

"I said untie him!" Korin barked. "Bring food and wine for them, and decent clothing."

Caliel rubbed his wrists as he was released, but stayed kneeling. "I don't expect anything, Korin. I only wanted to bring him back."

"Knowing that I would hang you?"

Caliel shrugged.

"Who is your allegiance to, Cal?"

"Do you still doubt me?"

"Where are the others?"

"They stayed in Atyion."

"But not you?"

Caliel fixed him with that direct gaze again. "How could I?"

Korin stood a moment, wrestling with his own heart. Niryn's accusations against Caliel seemed so hollow now. How had he believed such things of his friend?

"Do you swear yourself to me? Will you follow me and accept my course?"

"I always have, Majesty. I always will."

How can you forgive me? Korin wondered, astonished. He held out his hand and drew Caliel to his feet, then caught him as the other man's knees buckled under him. He felt thin and frail through his tunic, and Korin heard his muffled groan of pain as Korin's hands grasped at his back. The tufts of Cal's severed braids mocked him.

"I'm sorry," Korin whispered, so only Caliel could hear. "So sorry."

"Don't!" Caliel's hands tightened on Korin's shoulders. "Forgive me for giving you reason to doubt me."

"It's forgotten." Then, to those who stood staring at the spectacle he was making of himself, he said gruffly, "Lord Caliel has redeemed himself. He and Tanil are Companions once more. Alben, Urmanis, see to your brothers. Make them comfortable and find them arms."

The others gently helped Caliel to a seat by the stream. Tanil stayed by Korin, but his eyes kept straying back to Caliel. Moriel hovered near them, and Korin saw the look of naked hatred Caliel gave him, and the one he got in return. "Moriel!" he snapped. "You go see to the horses."

Chapter 50

Tamír had worked everyone tirelessly since dawn, preparing for Korin's arrival, and Ki stayed close by her side. The fog lifted by midday, but the clouds hung low and rain blew in off the water all that day, keeping clothing damp and making the fires smoke and die. The archers looked to their bows, tightening slack strings and rubbing them well with wax.

The entire army moved north, massing at the edge of the open ground she'd chosen. Ki and several of Nyanis' best archers took their bows up to the crest of the hill and let fly toward their own side of the field, arching some and sending others straight on to test the range. The other Companions carefully marked where the shafts landed and Tamír planned their lines.

"Korin's had the same lessons we did," Ki fretted as he rejoined her. "Don't you think he'll wonder why you're ceding him the advantage?"

Tamír shrugged. "We'll take our position and stay here until he comes to us."

Gathering her commanders by the stream, she took up a long stick and began scratching her plan into the soft ground. "We must draw him."

She set sappers to work their mattocks, digging trenches and holes to founder charging horses, while others cut small ditches along the stream to spread the water and make the ground softer. The archers went into the forest to fashion stakes.

As the morning passed and afternoon came on, Ki noticed how often Tamír looked south, watching for the lookouts she'd left behind at Remoni. There was still no word of the 'faie.

They were talking with the sappers, when some of the men behind them let out a shout and pointed up the hill. Ki caught a glimpse of a horseman before the intruder wheeled and galloped back out of sight.

"That'll be one of Korin's scouts," said Ki.

"Shall we go after him, Majesty?" Nyanis called.

Tamír grinned. "No, let him go. He's spared me the trouble of sending a messenger. Nikides, fetch your pen and call for a herald. Lutha, you and Barieus ride back to the lookouts. And tell Arkoniel I want to speak with him."

"They've done well," Ki murmured, watching the pair swing up into the saddle and gallop off. Lutha had let Ki see the stripes on his back that morning. They were healing well enough, but a few of the deeper cuts had pulled open and bled on the long hard journey over the mountains. Barieus wasn't faring any better. Both were wiry and stubborn as ever, though, and would have taken another flogging rather than utter a complaint.

Tamír followed them with her eyes, too. "Korin is a fool."

The sun was sinking behind the clouds when Korin neared Tobin's line. Caliel was still weak, but had insisted on riding with him. Tanil, though left a bit simpleminded by what the Plenimarans had done to him, was just as stubborn.

Korin called a halt and rode ahead with Wethring and his guard to assess the ground.

Topping a rise, he saw Tobin's army encamped a mile or so on, between the cliffs and the forest.

"So many," he muttered, trying to estimate the numbers with her. It was difficult in the waning light, with them all bunched together like that, but it was a larger force than he'd expected.

"Not many horse, though," said Porion. "If you claim this high ground, you have the advantage."

Tamír, look there," Arkoniel said, pointing toward the hill again.

Even through the rain, Tamír knew Korin by the way he sat his horse, as much as by the standard flapping in the breeze behind him. She recognized Caliel beside him, too. Without thinking, she raised a hand to wave to them. She knew Korin wouldn't see her, on foot among the others, but she still felt a pang when he wheeled his horse and disappeared over the crest of the hill. She closed her eyes as a tumult of conflicting emotions threatened to overwhelm her. Sorrow and guilt struck deep as memories of all those happy years together flooded back. That it should come to this!

A warm hand found hers and she looked up to find Arkoniel close beside her, shielding her from the eyes of the others.

"Steady, Majesty," he whispered, giving her an understanding smile. She felt strength return to her, though she couldn't be sure if it was his magic doing it or his friendship.

"Yes. Thank you." She squared her shoulders and waved the herald over. "My cousin the prince has arrived. Carry your message and return with his reply."

Korin and his generals sat their horses at the forest's edge, looking out at his cavalry spread across the grassy plain above the sea. Beyond them, lightning forked down from the lowering clouds over the water. A moment later the distant rumble of thunder rolled in.

"This is no sort of weather to be fighting in, with night coming on," Porion advised.

"You're right. Give the order to make camp."

Out of the gathering murk, a lone rider dressed in the blue-and-white coat of a herald appeared, holding his white baton aloft. Alben and Moriel rode out to meet him and escorted him to Korin.

The herald dismounted and bowed deeply to Korin. "I bring a letter from Queen Tamír of Skala, to her beloved cousin, Korin of Ero."

Korin scowled down at him. "What does the false queen have to say?"

The herald drew a letter from his coat. "'To my cousin, Korin, from Tamír, daughter of Ariani, of the true line of Skala. Cousin, I stand ready to do battle with you, but know that I make you this last offer of amnesty. Put aside your anger and your arms. Give up your claim to the throne and let us be friends again. You have my most sacred oath, by Sakor, Illior, and all the Four, that you, your lady wife, and the child she bears will be held in proper honor among my court, as Royal Kin. The nobles who follow you will be granted clemency, and retain both lands and titles. I call upon you, cousin, to put aside your unlawful claim and let there be peace between us.'"

The herald offered him the letter. Korin snatched it away, holding a corner of his cloak over it to shield it from the rain. It was Tobin's hand, and his seal. He looked to Caliel, expecting some comment, but his friend just looked away, saying nothing.

Korin shook his head and let the parchment fall. "Take back this answer, herald. Tell my cousin I will meet him tomorrow at first light at the point of my sword. All who fight in his name will be branded as traitors and forfeit all lands, titles, and their lives. No quarter will be given. Tell him also that I come without wizards. If he is honorable, he will not employ his own against me. Finally, give him my thanks for allowing Lord Caliel and my squire to return to me. They fight at my side. Tell him this message comes from King Korin of Skala, son of Erius, grandson of Agnalain."

The herald repeated the message and took his leave. Korin pulled his cloak tighter around him and turned to Porion. "Pass the order to set up tents and serve hot food. We'll rest dry tonight."

Tamír assembled her marshals and captains before her tent to hear Korin's reply. Everyone was silent for a moment when he'd finished.

"Cal's in no shape to fight!" Lutha fretted. "And Tanil? What's he thinking?"

"It's out of our hands." Tamír sighed, equally dismayed at the thought of meeting them in battle. "I wish now I'd locked them up in Atyion until this was over."

"You wouldn't have been doing either of them any favor," Lynx replied. "They're where they wanted to be. The rest is with Sakor."

"Do you believe what he says, about having no wizards with him?" she asked Arkoniel. "I can't imagine him leaving Niryn behind."

"We've seen no sign of him, or any magic around Korin, beyond the wards Niryn has had on him all these months," Arkoniel replied. "Wait! Surely you don't mean to honor his condition?"

"I do."

"Tamír, no! You're already outnumbered—"

"How much could you really do?" she asked, looking around at the wizards. "I haven't forgotten what you did for me at the gates of Ero, but you told me yourself that it took all your combined strength for one great assault. I saw how it exhausted you."

"But a focused attack, as we did during the second raid?"

"Are you offering to assassinate Korin on the field for me?" She shook her head at their silence. "No. I won't win the crown that way. You wizards have been a great help to me already. Without you, I would not be here. But Illior chose me, a warrior. I'll meet Korin honorably, and win or lose honorably. I owe the gods and Skala that, to wipe clean the sins of my uncle."

"And if he is lying about having wizards?" Arkoniel demanded.

"Then the dishonor is on his head and you can do as you like." She took his hand. "In all the dreams and visions I've had, my friend, I have not seen magic giving me victory. 'By blood and trial,' the Oracle said. Korin and I grew up together as warriors. It's only right that we settle this our way."

Tamír drew her sword and held it up before the others. "I mean to trade this blade for the Sword of Ghërilain tomorrow. Herald, tell Prince Korin that I will meet him at dawn and prove my claim."

The man bowed and strode off for his horse.

Tamír looked around at the others again. "Tell my people to rest if they can and to make offerings to Sakor and Illior."

As they saluted and went their separate ways, she leaned over to Ki and muttered, "And pray to Astellus to bring us those damn Gedre ships!"

Saruel and Malkanus drew Arkoniel away from the watch fire to speak privately.

"You don't really mean for us to stand idly by, do you?" the Khatme asked in disbelief.

"You heard what she said. We serve at the queen's pleasure. I can't thwart her in this, no matter how I feel. The Third Orëska must have her trust. We can't use magic against Korin."

"Unless he does so against Tamír. That's how I understood her," said Malkanus.

"Perhaps," Arkoniel agreed. "But even so, as she pointed out, we don't have the power to do more than cause a momentary disruption."

"Speak for yourself," Saruel muttered darkly.

The foot and baggage train arrived at nightfall, and Korin ordered wine to be distributed among the men.

He feasted with his generals and Companions that night around a warm fire, sharing bread brought down from the north and roasted venison and grouse as they laid out their strategy.

"It's as we thought," Porion told him. "Tobin lacks a decent cavalry. With your stronger force, you should be able to break their lines and overwhelm them."

"We'll scatter them like a flock of chickens," Alben vowed, saluting Korin with his mazer.

Korin took a long sip from his own, trying to numb the fear lurking deep in his heart. It had been the same in Ero, but he'd imagined that somehow this time would be different. It wasn't. His bowels went loose at the thought of charging down that hill, and he kept both hands tight around his mazer when he wasn't drinking, to quell the tremor there. Now that the moment was at hand, memories of his shameful failures ate at him, threatening to unman him once again. The bold certainty of Tobin's message had scorched his pride.

For the first time in a very long time, he could not drive away the memory of that night in Ero, when his father, lying wounded as the battle worsened, had called on Tobin, not his own son—put his confidence in that raw boy rather than him. That had been the proof of what Korin had always suspected, and his father's cold refusal to give him command when Tobin was gone had set the seal on his shame for all to see.

His father had died, the best generals had fallen, and there had been nothing left to do but put his trust in Niryn and flee, leaving Tobin to triumph once again.

Once he might have confided his thoughts to Caliel, but his friend was silent and pale, and Korin had seen genuine pain in his eyes as Tobin's message was given.

As they retired for the night, he paused, drawing Caliel away from the others. "Niryn wasn't completely wrong about you, was he? You still love Tobin."

Caliel nodded slowly. "But my love for you is greater."

"And if you meet him on the field?"

"I will fight for you against anyone," Caliel replied, and Korin heard the truth in his voice. It cut like a knife with the memory of Cal's bloody back.

He retired with only Tanil for company, and the boy fell into an exhausted sleep almost at once. Korin wondered how he could convince him to stay behind tomorrow. He was in no condition to fight.

The only comfort left to him was wine. Only that took the shame and fear away, or at least drowned them in numbing warmth. He would not allow himself to be drunk, though. He was an experienced enough drinker to know how much it took to keep the fear at bay.

Chapter 51

Tamír and her army spent an uneasy night on the plain. Fog rolled in off the sea again, so thick it blotted out the moon and made it hard to see from one watch fire to another. Eyoli crept down through the forest from Korin's camp, having survived among the army long enough to travel back with them. He brought not only dire confirmation of the numbers on Korin's side but word that Caliel and Tanil both planned to fight.

"Tanil can't be strong enough yet," Ki muttered.

But Lutha exchanged a sad, knowing look with Tamír. Only death would keep Tanil from Korin's side now.

Rolled in her damp blankets, Tamír tossed fitfully, caught in vague dreams of the rocky place in her vision. It was foggy there, too, and she could make out dark forms moving around her, but not who they were. She woke with a start and tried to sit up, only to find Brother straddling her, holding her down with one icy hand wrapped around her throat.

Sister, he hissed, leering down into her face. *My sister with a true name*. The pressure on her throat increased. *You who would not avenge me.*

"I sent her away!" Tamír gasped.

Through a haze of dancing colored stars she saw that he was naked, gaunt, and dirty, his hair a tangled mass around his face. The scar on his chest was still an open wound. She could feel the cold blood dripping on her belly, soaking through her shirt to chill her skin.

He ran an icy finger over the scar on her chest. *I will be with you today. I will not be denied.*

He disappeared and she struggled up, gasping for breath and shaking all over. "No!" she croaked, rubbing her throat. "I'll fight my own battles, damn you."

A shadow crossed the tent flap and Ki ducked in. "Did you call?"

"No, just—just a bad dream," she whispered.

He knelt beside her and stroked the hair back from her brow. "Are you coming down sick? There's fever in the camp."

"No, it's just this damn fog. I hope it clears for tomorrow." She hesitated, then confessed, "Brother was here."

"What did he want?"

"The same. And he said he'd be with me today."

"He's helped you before."

She gave him a sour look. "When it suited him. I don't want his help. This is my battle."

"Do you think he might go after Korin, like he did Lord Orun?"

Tamír searched the shadows for the demon. The memory of Orun's death still sickened her.

"Korin is Erius' son, after all, and he's in your place."

"He didn't have anything to do with what happened to Brother and me." She threw back the blankets and reached for her sweat-stained tunic. "I might as well get up. Do you want to sleep for a while?"

"I couldn't if I tried. I managed to find this, though." He pulled a slack wineskin from his belt and shook it, sloshing the scant contents. "It's wretched stuff, but it'll warm you."

She took a long pull and grimaced. It had been too long in the skin, but it dulled the hunger pangs a little.

She went to the open flap and gazed out at the sea of watch fires beyond. "We have to win, Ki. I wore them out, trekking over the mountains, and now they've all got empty bellies. By the Flame, I hope I didn't make a mistake, dragging them here."

He stood just behind her, looking over her shoulder. "Korin may have more men, but we have more to lose. Every man and woman out there tonight knows we have to win or die trying." He grinned again. "And I know which I'd prefer."

Tamír turned, pushed him a step back into the tent, and kissed him awkwardly on his unshaven cheek. His skin was rough, and left the taste of salt on her lips. "Don't die. That's my order to you."

She tightened her arms around his waist as their lips met again, overcome by pleasurable warmth that had nothing to do with bad wine. It almost felt natural now, kissing him.

"I hear and obey, Majesty," he replied softly, "as long as you promise to do the same." He stepped back and gave her a little push toward the door. "Come sit by the fire. You'll only brood in here."

Most of the Companions were sharing cloaks with their squires to keep warm. She longed to do the same, and would not have thought twice about it in times past. Still warm from his kiss, she felt too self-conscious in front of the others.

Hain, Lord Malkanus, and Eyoli were with them.

"Where are the others?" she asked.

"Kaulin is working with the healers," Eyoli replied. "Arkoniel and Saruel are still looking for signs of the Aurënfaie ships."

Barieus was dozing on Lutha's shoulder. He stirred, then let out a hoarse cough and sat up, blinking like an owl.

"Are you feverish?" asked Tamír.

"No," Barieus replied a bit too quickly, and then coughed again.

"There's a grippe spreading among the ranks," said Nikides. "The few drysians we have are hard-pressed."

"I've heard muttering that it's some illness put on us by the hill folk," Una said.

"Typical!" scoffed Ki.

Tamír looked out at the watch fires again. *Too many nights in the rain and too little food. If we lose tomorrow, we may not be strong enough to fight again.*

A freshening breeze signaled the coming dawn, but the sun stayed hidden behind banks of dark clouds.

Tamír gathered her wizards, marshals, and their captains and made a final sacrifice. Arkoniel joined them. There was still no sign of the 'faie.

Everyone sprinkled the dregs of their wineskins on the ground and threw wax horses and other offerings into the fire. Tamír added a handful of owl feathers and a large packet of incense Imonus had given her.

"Illior, if it is your will that I rule, give us victory today," she prayed, as the sweet smoke billowed up.

When the prayers were finished, Tamír looked around at their haggard faces. Some of these, like Duke Nyanis and the Alestun men, had known her since childhood. Others, like Grannia, had followed her for a few short months, but in every face she saw the same determination.

"Don't you fret, Majesty," Jorvai said, misreading her concern. "We know the ground, and you've got the gods on your side."

"With your permission, Majesty, my wizards and I have prepared a few spells to help protect you today," said Arkoniel. "That is, if you don't think it will be breaking your word to Korin."

"I promised not to use magic directly against him. I don't think this counts, do you? Go on."

The wizards went to each marshal and Companion, casting spells to secure their armor and quell the hunger gnawing at every belly. They did the same for the captains.

Arkoniel came to Tamír and raised his wand, but she shook her head. "I have all the protection I need. Save your strength for the others."

"As you wish."

Tamír turned to her marshals. "It's time."

"Give us the order, Majesty," Nyanis said.

"Give no quarter unless they surrender outright. Victory or death, my lords!"

Manies loosed her banner and shook it out to catch the breeze as the cry was taken up. Her trumpeter gave a short, muted call and the signal went out to all the others.

Arkoniel embraced her, then held her at arm's length, as if he wanted to memorize her face. "This is the moment you were born for. Illior's luck be with you, and Sakor's fire."

"Don't look so grim," she chided. "If the gods truly want a queen, then what is there to fear?"

"What indeed?" Arkoniel said, trying to smile.

Ki embraced him next and whispered, "If things go wrong, I don't give a shit for Korin and his honor. You *do* something!"

Torn, Arkoniel could only hug him back.

Like a great beast waking, Tamír's army coalesced and moved up to their initial positions, the ranks bristling with spears and pole arms. No one spoke, but the clink and rustle of armor, the rattle of thousands of shafts in hundreds of quivers, and the step of thousands of feet on damp grass filled the air.

Tamír and the Companions shouldered their shields and bows and walked up to the center of the forward line. Their horses were left behind with the young boys of the camp; they would fight on foot at first.

The fog slunk around their feet in tattered shreds as the two main wings formed up. It hung in the nearby trees like smoke as the standards were unfurled on their long poles.

Tamír and her guard had the center, with a company of Atyion archers on either side and three companies of men-at-arms just behind. Kyman had the left flank, with the cliff on their left. Nyanis' wing stretched to the trees. Both wings had blocks of archers on the outside and men-at-arms toward the center, bracketing Tamír's archers. Jorvai's fighters formed the reserve wing, to the rear, but his archers would send their shafts over the heads of those in front of them.

Each marshal had his banner, and each captain. Once battle was joined, each company would rally to their own standard, to move as one in the inevitable noise and confusion.

Tamír's front line was just out of bowshot range of the hill. They could hear the sounds of Korin's army approaching.

"Archers. Set stakes," she ordered, and the captains passed it on down both sides of the line.

Half the archers in each company set their pointed stakes into the ground at an angle facing the enemy. It formed the "hedgehog," a widely spaced hedge of sharp points hidden among their ranks like quills in fur.

They were still busy putting the last deadly touches to the points when a cry went up from the rear ranks.

"We're being flanked! Tell the queen, we're being outflanked!"

"Hold your positions," Tamír shouted, then started for the rear.

"Damn it, he must have moved people through the forest," Ki said, following as Tamír shouldered her way back through the lines.

The mist had thinned. They could see the dark mass of an army approaching, preceded by four riders coming on at a gallop.

"Could be heralds," said Ki. He and Lutha stepped in front of her to cover her with their shields nonetheless.

As the riders drew closer, however, she recognized the

foremost. It was Arkoniel, and he was waving and shouting. She didn't recognize the others, but saw that they were armed.

"Let them come," she ordered, seeing that some of the archers were nocking shafts to their strings.

"They've arrived!" Arkoniel shouted, reining in. "The Aurënfaie. They're here!"

The other riders with him swept off their helms. It was Solun of Bôkthersa and Arengil, together with an older man.

The stranger bowed in the saddle. "Greetings, Queen Tamír. I am Hiril í Saris, of Gedre. I have command of the Gedre archers."

"I have a company from Bôkthersa. Forgive us for coming so late," said Solun. "The Gedre ships stopped for us, then we had foul weather on the crossing."

"It threw us off course. We landed down the coast from your harbor yesterday," Hiril explained.

"We've brought you food and wine, and two hundred archers from each clan," said Arengil. He took a small scroll from inside his tabard and handed it down to her with a proud grin. "And I have the permission of my father and mother to become a Companion, Queen Tamír, if you'll still have me?"

"Gladly, but for today, I think it would be better if you stand with your own people."

Arengil looked a bit crestfallen at that, but he pressed his hand to his heart, Skalan style.

Tamír quickly explained her plan to Solun and Hiril and had them position their archers in the center of the third rank.

As she and the Companions returned to their position on the front line, the sound of a great commotion came from the hill. Korin's men were beating their shields and shouting war cries as they advanced to their places. It was a daunting sound, and grew louder as the first ranks appeared out of the morning mist.

"Answer them back!" Tamír shouted. Ki and the others drew their swords and beat them against their shields, shouting, "For Skala and Queen Tamír!"

The battle cry spread through the ranks in a deafening roar that continued as Korin's army massed above them.

When the shouting died away the two armies stood facing each other at last. Korin's banner was at the forefront of his line and Tamír could see his red tabard.

"Isn't that Duke Ursaris' banner over there?" said Ki. "The one you sent packing?"

"Yes," Lutha replied. "There's Lord Wethring's banner, on the left. That's Duke Syrus and his archers on the right. Korin's sure to rely mostly on horse, though, and his men-at-arms, since he has the most of those."

"Where's General Rheynaris?" asked Ki.

"He fell at Ero. Caliel said that none of these others are near the tactician he was."

"That's good news for us, then."

"He still has Master Porion," Barieus pointed out.

"Bilairy's balls, I hope none of us will have to face him!" Barieus murmured, speaking for all of them.

"Shit," Lutha muttered, still staring up the hill.

"What is it?" Tamír asked.

"On Korin's right. Don't you see them?"

Tamír shaded her eyes and looked. "Shit!"

Even at this distance, she recognized the golden-haired rider.

It was Caliel. And there, between him and Korin, was Tanil.

"Lutha, you and Barieus have my leave not to fight him, or Tanil," Tamír told them. "I won't ask that of you."

Lutha shook his head grimly. "We'll do what we must, when the time comes."

Korin's herald cantered down to the base of the hill, and Tamír's went out to meet him. They spoke briefly, exchanging intentions, then rode back to their lines.

"King Korin requires that you surrender or fight, Majesty. I gave him the same message to carry back as you instructed."

Tamír had expected nothing less. "You may withdraw."

"Illior give you victory, Majesty." The herald saluted her and rode off down the line. Heralds were sacred in battle, as well, and would observe the combat and carry word of the outcome.

Caliel sat his borrowed horse in his ill-fitting armor, his torn back sore under the rough shirt he'd been given. He cared nothing for the discomfort, though, as he gazed down at the opposing line with a heavy heart. He found Tamír at the center, just as he'd expected, and on foot. There were Ki and Lynx, too. Hoping against hope, he searched the other faces close to her, and his heart sank as he found Lutha.

Closing his eyes, he sent up a silent prayer to Sakor, *Keep me from them on the field.*

He owed Korin his loyalty, but he owed Lutha and Barieus his life, and Tanil owed his to Tamír, though he still did not grasp that they were facing her. Korin had tried to leave him behind with the baggage train, and even considered tying him up, but Tanil had wept and pleaded, thinking it was because he'd been disgraced.

"Let him come," Caliel said at last. "He's strong enough to fight. And if he falls? That's kinder than leaving him as he is now. At least he'll die a man again."

Looking at Tanil now, he knew Korin had been right to agree. He looked more alert and alive than he had since Caliel had found him again.

As he watched Tamír's banner fluttering below, however, his own doubts warred with duty, making him vaguely ill. Korin would not hear the truth about Tamír, and Caliel's oath kept him silent. *But what if she is a true queen?* His conscience spoke with Lutha's voice. *What does it mean for us if we go against the true queen?*

He looked at Korin again and sighed. No, he'd made his choice. He would stand by it, come what may.

Standing at Tamír's right hand, Ki's heart swelled as he looked around. Lynx, Una, Nikides, and their squires formed a square around them, every one of them fearless and ready. He saw the same determination in the faces of the soldiers. Grannia and the women of her guard gazed fiercely up at the other army—an army they would not have been welcome in. He wondered where Tharin was, and if he'd been victorious. Only the thought of Caliel and Porion in that other line gave him pause, but he pushed regret aside. They'd all made their choices.

A hush fell over the field. He could hear men talking in Korin's ranks, the sound of coughing from their own. The rising sun was a faint white disk behind the clouds. In the forest, birds were waking up, their songs mixing with the measured sigh of the sea against the cliffs. It was strangely peaceful.

An hour passed, then two as Tamír and Korin waited for the other to make the first move. In his lessons on battle, their old teacher Raven had said that this was one of the hardest parts of a battle, the waiting. Ki had to agree. The day was turning heavy, making him sweat in his damp clothing. His empty belly rumbled under his belt and his throat felt sore.

Another hour passed, and the two sides began to trade taunts. But Tamír stood silently, gaze fixed on Korin, who'd dismounted to consult with some of his generals.

Nyanis walked up the line to join them. "He's not going to move."

"Then we'll just have to make him," Tamír replied. "Ready your archers. Grannia, pass the word down to Kyman's wing."

The shout went down the line, and was answered by

the rattle of quivers being made ready. Ki unshouldered his and set an arrow to the shaft.

Tamír drew her sword and held it up, shouting, "Archers forward!"

The entire front line rippled as the archers ran to close the margin of flight with the enemy line. The rear ranks had moved up, too, keeping the stakes hidden.

The archers let fly, aiming high and sending a deadly hail of arrows down on the heads and upraised shields of Korin's line. The enemy's taunts turned to curses and cries of pain, mingled with the screams of wounded horses.

Tamír stood with her standard-bearer as the Companions and archers loosed shaft after shaft. Arrows fell like dark rain and continued for several minutes, as the archers loosed at will, then retreated to their original positions.

On the hill, horses were rearing and bolting. Korin's banner wavered but did not fall. The line remained firm and, just as she'd hoped, the first attack began.

Korin saw Tobin advance on foot. That blue banner mocked him as he huddled under his shield and Caliel's, fending off the whistling onslaught of arrows. Three struck his shield, jolting his arm, and another glanced off his mail-covered thigh.

Porion's horse and Garol's were hit and threw them. Urmanis threw out his shield arm to protect his fallen squire, then tumbled backward out of the saddle with an arrow jutting from his throat. Garol crawled to him, and held him as he clawed at the shaft.

"Get him to the rear," Korin ordered, wondering if this, too, was a bad omen. *Another taken from me!*

"Look, Majesty, they've fallen back," said Ursaris. "You must answer with a charge before they shoot again. Now's your moment, Majesty!"

Korin drew his sword and brandished it, signaling Syrus and Wethring's cavalry to charge from the wings.

With blood-chilling war cries, they booted their horses and flew down the hill, bearing down like a great wave on Tobin's line. The front line of men-at-arms followed at a run.

"Look, they're already breaking!" Alben whooped as Tobin's smaller force immediately pulled back.

But the ranks didn't break and run, they only fell back to expose a bristling hedge of angled stakes that the charging riders saw too late. Meanwhile, another thick volley of arrows rose from the rear, falling with deadly certainty among the charging riders. Men were knocked from the saddle or went down with their horses. Others in the forward ranks, unable to halt in time, were thrown as their mounts impaled themselves on the stakes, or reared and bolted. Others foundered inexplicably or fell over the downed ones and were trampled by those still charging.

The charge held, even so, and clashed against Tobin's front line. The center bowed and Korin had a moment's hope as Tobin's standard veered wildly. But her line held and surged forward again, catching Korin's cavalry between the press of his own men-at-arms as their line caught up. Boxed in between the forest, cliffs, and Tobin's strong line, his own fighters were packed tight as a cork in a bottle. Another volley of arrows rose from Tobin's rear ranks, arching over Tobin's line to rain death among Korin's stymied forces.

Just as Tamír had hoped, Korin's advance force was crowded together as they charged, and their headlong rush made it impossible for the frontmost to avoid the stakes, mud, and holes they'd prepared to catch them. As the Aurënfaie archers loosed their second volley, the carnage increased and the air was filled with the screams of wounded horses and the cries of their riders. It did not stop the charge, only slowed it a little and created confusion.

"Defend the queen!" Ki yelled, and the Companions closed in around her as enemy riders came on.

Her archers dropped their bows and fought with swords or the mallets they'd used to drive the stakes. The blocks of men-at-arms surged forward, unseating riders with their pole arms or pulling them from the saddle to be dispatched with swords and clubs. Already at a disadvantage, Korin's own charging line of foot caught his riders even tighter.

"For Skala!" Tamír cried, rushing into the fray.

There was no question of holding back. Ki kept close to Tamír as he met the enemy with drawn sword.

It was like hacking at a wall of flesh, and for a while it seemed they were going to be driven back. The clamor of battle was deafening.

Tamír stood fast, yelling encouragement and urging them all forward as she laid about with her sword. Her blade caught the light with a red gleam. Trapped in the press, her standard-bearer fell, but Hylia caught the pole as it wavered, and held it high.

It seemed to go on forever; but at last the enemy fell back, making a ragged retreat across the stream, leaving hundreds of their own dead or dying on the trampled ground. Aurënfaie arrows followed them, slaughtering the hindmost as they tried to scale the hill again.

Korin cursed aloud as his advance line fell into confusion and retreated. Tobin's banner still held fast, and he was certain he could see Tobin still boldly at the fore.

"Damn him!" he snarled, furious. "Porion, have the charge sounded again. And this time I will lead! We'll strike them before they can regroup. Wethring, I want a flanking force sent through the forest to engage the rear lines."

"Majesty, at least wait until the others have come

back," Porion urged quietly. "Otherwise, you'll be riding down your own men!"

Gritting his teeth, Korin lowered his sword, aware of the many eyes upon him. As he waited, the fear came back, gnawing at him as he surveyed the dead littering the field.

No, I won't fail this time, he swore silently. *By the Sword of Ghërilain and my father's name, I will act as a king today!*

He glanced sidelong at Caliel, who sat on his horse so calmly beside him, watching the field with impassive eyes.

Korin drew strength from his friend's presence. *I will not shame myself before you.*

As soon as Korin's first wave retreated Tamír sent people out to collect the wounded and carry them back behind their lines. By her order, enemy wounded were to be treated with the same courtesy rather than being dispatched on the field, unless they appeared to be mortally wounded.

She remained in position, already bloody and winded. The Companions were equally bloody, but it was all the enemy's so far rather than their own.

Nikides gave her a wry grin as he wiped his face on the sleeve of his tabard and only succeeded in making both bloodier. Gone was the soft, shy boy he'd been. After days of hard marching and rough living, he was as unshaven and dirty as any of the others, and looked proud of himself.

"You don't need to find yourself an new chronicler just yet," he observed, chuckling.

"See that I don't." She was more concerned with Lutha and Barieus. They were both pale under their helms.

"Don't worry about us," Lutha told her. "We mean to get our own back on Korin today."

The mist had burned off, and the rain was clearing. The sun stood at noon. Ki handed her a waterskin and she drank deeply as she stood watching Korin consult with his nobles. Just then there was a stir among the soldiers behind her. Arengil pushed through, his arms filled with cheese and sausages.

"Our baggage train caught up at last," he told her, handing her a sausage. "Hiril took the liberty of having food distributed after he learned how hungry you've been."

Tamír bit into the sausage with a grateful groan. It was tough and spicy. Her mouth watered so hard it hurt.

"Now I'm even more glad you showed up!" Ki exclaimed around a mouthful of cheese. "I was afraid we'd be eating horse meat tonight. I don't suppose you brought any wine?"

"That, too." Arengil pulled a clay flask from his belt and handed it to him. Ki took a pull and passed it to Tamír.

She took a sip and handed it on to Lynx. "Bilairy's balls, that's good!"

All around them her people were laughing and cheering as the provisions were passed through the ranks.

Their respite was a short one. Trumpets sounded from Korin's side of the field and she saw that he was massing for another charge.

Tamír and the Companions sent for horses and she called up what cavalry she had, placing them at the center and setting deep ranks of archers to either side of them.

Korin was no fool. Having been caught on the quills of her hedgehog once already, he angled his new assault against their right flank, skirting the forest to come at them from the side. Reaching the stream, some of the horses foundered in the soft ground and holes, as Tamír had hoped, but not enough to make a difference.

"Kyman isn't turning!" Ki shouted, looking back to see the old general's line advancing parallel to the cliffs.

Korin's line was bowing. Those riders closest to the forest's edge had rougher ground and did not come on as fast as the outer end of the line. Kyman was making for the laggards, putting himself in danger of being pushed back to the cliff.

Tamír marked Korin's standard as he rode down the hill and led her cavalry to engage him. As the two forces closed she spotted him, mounted and closely surrounded by his guard. Caliel and Alben were still with him, and someone else wearing the baldric of a King's Companion.

"That's Moriel!" Lutha shouted.

"So he got his wish as last," said Ki. "Let's see how he likes the duty."

"Please, Tamír, leave the Toad to me if we get close enough," Lutha asked. "I have a score to settle."

"If it's Sakor's will, he's yours," Tamír replied.

Ki had to kick his horse hard to keep up with Tamír as she charged. On foot it had been easy to stay with her. This time Korin was leading the charge and Tamír was bent on reaching him. As usual, it was up to Ki and the rest of the Companions to keep up as the battle lust took her. Lynx was riding on her left with Una. Nikides and Lutha were on Ki's side, grinning grimly under their steel helmets.

The two lines collided like waves, each one stemming the other's momentum. One moment they were in a rough formation, the next it was chaos.

The foot soldiers came boiling in behind the horses soon enough, too, thrusting at the riders with pikes and spears. Ki saw a spearman making for Tamír, meaning to come up under her guard. He kicked his horse forward and rode the man down, then cut down two more who sprang forward to drag him from his horse. When he looked up again arrows were raining down on Korin's massed ranks. Judging by the arc, the Aurënfaie were shooting over their heads. Praying that they could tell friend from foe, he urged his horse on.

*   *   *

Korin had assumed Tamír's line would angle out to meet him, but the far wing stayed back, not letting themselves be drawn. Instead, they waited, and came out at his center like a clenched fist, forcing part of his cavalry to turn and meet them.

Korin pressed on, keeping Tobin's banner in sight. His cousin was mounted this time, and seemed to be trying to reach him, too.

Always in the lead, aren't you?

The two armies surged back and forth, churning the soft wet ground to a deadly slick mess for man and horse. Korin rode with sword drawn, but he was hemmed in by his guard, unable to do more at the moment than yell commands.

In the distance he could hear a new outcry as Wethring's flanking force burst from the trees behind Tobin's line. Just as he'd hoped, those lines had to turn to meet the raiders, thus dividing Tobin's force as his had been.

Even so, Tobin's front line held and Korin found himself being pressed back toward the forest.

Arkoniel and the others had stationed themselves just behind the Aurënfaie, mounted and ready to act if things took a dire turn. Saruel had been the first to notice the riders in the woods.

"Look there!" she shouted in her own language. "Solun, Hiril, turn. You must turn to meet them!"

The Bôkthersan ranks were closest to the forest and they sent a deadly flight of arrows into the pack of riders as they burst from the cover of the trees. They continued to shoot as the horsemen bore down on them.

Hiril and the Gedre were farther back, and had more time to brace as Solun's men took the brunt of the charge.

"Are we really going to just sit and watch?" Malkanus cried out in frustration.

"We gave Tamír our word," Arkoniel replied, not liking it any better than the others.

"Only not to work magic against Korin's army," Saruel said. She closed her eyes, muttered a spell, and clapped her hands. Across the field, the trees at the edge of the forest where riders were still emerging burst into flame. Wildfire flames licked up ancient trunks, spread down branches, and leaped to neighboring boughs.

From where Arkoniel was sitting, it did not appear that men or horses were catching fire, but beasts maddened by the heat and smoke threw their riders, or bore them into the midst of the Aurënfaie as they tried to flee. Arkoniel sent a wizard eye beyond the flames and saw many more riders trying to control their mounts and find a way around the spreading blaze.

"If she takes me to task over this, shall I tell her you attacked the trees?"

"We had no treaty with the forest," Saruel replied serenely.

Any semblance of order was gone as the battle devolved into a close melee. Still mounted, Korin could see Tobin's standard a few hundred tantalizing yards away, beyond a solid press of men and horses.

Fighting his way forward, he caught a glimpse of Tobin's helmet in the chaos, and a few moments later, his face. Tobin was on foot now and making straight for Korin, his face twisted in that same taunting smile Korin had seen in his dreams.

"There!" Korin yelled to Caliel and the others. "Prince Tobin! We must reach him!"

"Where, my lord?" Caliel called back.

Korin looked back, but there was no sign of him. Tobin's standard was some way off, swaying over the press near the standard of Lord Nyanis. In the distance beyond, white smoke was billowing up against the sky, shot through with red sparks.

"They've set fire to the woods!" Porion shouted.

"Korin, look out!" Caliel cried.

Korin turned in time to see a woman with a spear breaking through his guard and coming at him on the left. He tried to rein his horse around to meet her, but the damn beast chose that moment to step in a hole. The horse lurched under him and went down, throwing Korin at the woman's feet. She thrust at him, but Caliel caught her at the back of the neck with a downward sword stroke, killing her with a blow that took her head half-off. Blood burst from the wound, drenching Korin's face.

Caliel dismounted and pulled him to his feet, then turned to fend off the enemy. "Are you hurt, Kor?"

"No!" Korin quickly wiped the blood from his eyes. In the distance he could see Ursaris still mounted, trying to reach him but stymied by the crush of fighting. As Korin watched, a pikeman caught the man in the chest and he disappeared from sight.

Strangely, now that Korin was in the thick of the battle, his fear had disappeared completely. He'd held it at bay during the charge, but faced with all-out fighting, long years of training took over, and he found himself easily cutting down one foe after another.

Another woman wearing the colors of Atyion came at him, screaming a battle cry as she swung her sword. He lunged forward and caught her under the chin with the point of his blade. As she fell he caught sight of movement just behind her and saw Tobin again, this time no more than a few yards away. He glared at Korin and disappeared.

"There!" Korin cried, trying again to follow.

"What are you talking about?" Caliel cried.

Suddenly another storm of arrows hissed down on them again. Mago screamed and fell, clawing at a feathered shaft protruding from his chest. Alben seized him by the arm, trying to cover them both under his upraised shield. An arrow took him through the thigh, piercing the front of his hauberk, and he staggered. Korin reached down and snapped off the long end of the shaft. It was fletched with three vanes rather than four.

"Aurënfaie. That must be the reinforcements we saw. Alben, can you stand?"

"Yes. It's not deep." But he remained kneeling by Mago, holding his squire's hand as the young man writhed in pain and the battle surged around them. Bloody foam flecked Mago's lips and his breathing was labored and desperate. Air and blood bubbled from the sucking wound in his chest.

There was no question of getting him off the field, and if they left him, he would surely be trampled. With a sob, Alben stood and dispatched his squire mercifully with his sword. Korin turned his face away, wondering if he'd have to do the same before this day was over. Tanil was still beside him, wild-eyed and bloody. His mind might be weak, but his arm was not. He'd fought well.

The battle raged on as the afternoon lengthened. It was impossible to tell where Korin's other generals were, except when he got a glimpse of them or their colors.

Tobin's standard appeared and disappeared like a tantalizing apparition, and so did the young prince. Korin would make for him, only to look over his shoulder and find Tobin had somehow gotten away through the press. It was maddening how fast he moved.

"I want his head!" Korin yelled, catching another glimpse of him near the distant tree line. "After him! He's making for the forest."

Tamír tried to reach Korin but, try as she might, she couldn't fight her way through the throng to his standard. Every time she got close it seemed to melt away.

"Korin's outflanked us!" Lynx shouted to her. "And he's set fire to the woods."

Tamír glanced back and saw her rearmost line being

split and smoke rising in the distance. "There's no help for it. Keep pressing Korin!"

"Damn it, wait for the rest of us!" Ki yelled, hacking down a swordsman who'd lunged on Tamír's right.

The Aurënfaie had turned to meet the horsemen who'd outflanked them. That left Tamír with her guard and Nyanis' wing, while Kyman held off another regiment near the middle of the field.

On foot again, she stumbled over bodies, some dead, others crying out in agony as the battle raged back and forth over them. Those who couldn't drag themselves away were trampled into the mud.

She and the rest of her guard were covered in blood and mire, impossible to tell if they were wounded or not. Nik appeared to be favoring his left arm, Lynx had a cut across his nose, and Barieus was staggering, but they stayed close around her, fighting fiercely. Her own arm was growing heavy and her throat burned with thirst.

The fighting was so thick that it was often difficult to know what part of the field they were on. As the afternoon drew on and the sky began to take on a golden tint, she found herself with one foot in the muddy, blood-tinged water of the stream. The dark line of the forest loomed ahead of her, and suddenly she saw Korin's banner again, not twenty yards away.

"Ki, look! He's going into the trees there!"

"Thinks he can hide, does he?" Ki snarled.

"To me!" Tamír shouted, brandishing her sword to show the way. "We'll capture him in the woods and put an end to this."

Chapter 52

Korin reached the edge of the forest and paused just inside the trees, heart pounding in his ears. He could smell smoke, but the flames were still far off.

"Korin, what are you doing?" Caliel panted, wiping blood and sweat from his face as he caught up.

"You can't leave the field now!" Porion exclaimed in dismay as the rest of Korin's guard and a score of men-at-arms gathered around to protect him.

"I'm not. I saw Tobin go in here."

"Are you sure, Majesty?" Porion asked doubtfully.

Korin caught a flash of blue and white through the trees. "There! See? Come on!"

It was an old forest, with towering firs and little undergrowth. The ground was covered in fallen needles and carpets of soft green moss and mushrooms. Fallen trees lay everywhere, some with needles or leaves clinging to their branches, others weathered silver, shining in the green dusk like the bleached bones of fallen giants.

The fighting had already spilled into the woods, but it was scattered, with small groups battling among the trees. Their cries and curses rang out from all directions.

With Tanil and Caliel at his side, he ran after the banner, leaving the others to follow, leaping over logs and rocks and stumbling over the uneven ground. Korin wrinkled his nose as he ran; the air smelled of death and rot. A sickly odor seemed to enfold him as he pursued the shadowy figure ahead of him.

It was impossible to tell how many were with Tobin, but it didn't appear that he had a large force.

He's running away! Korin thought with grim satisfaction. He would redeem his own honor with Tobin's shame.

Ki imagined enemy archers behind every tree as he ran with Tamír. It was much darker under the trees. The afternoon was waning and rain began to spatter down through the branches again.

"I'm not sure this is wise," Nikides panted.

"He can't lead a whole army through here," Tamír replied, pausing to get her bearings.

"Maybe he's running away again," Ki offered.

"I don't think so." Tamír strode off again.

"At least let me go back for more people, Majesty," Una gasped, holding her side.

"Maybe you're—" Tamír froze, staring at something deeper in the woods.

"What?" Ki tried to make out what had caught her attention.

"I see him," she whispered.

"Korin?"

"No. Brother."

The demon was just visible through the trees, and he was waving to her. In the heat of battle, she'd forgotten all about him, but here he was and there was no mistaking his intent. He wanted her to follow him.

Ki caught her arm as she started off. "I don't see anything."

"He's there," she replied.

"It could be one of his tricks!"

"I know." But she followed anyway. *You are Skala, and Skala is you. You are your brother, and he is you.*

Sword in hand, she broke into a run. Ki cursed aloud as he and the others raced to follow.

Korin burst into the clearing and stopped short. Tobin was there waiting for him, sitting on a large stone, face partially hidden by the cheek guards of his helm. It made no sense. He was all alone, without a guard in sight. They must have fallen behind somehow. Korin could hear the crackle of twigs and hushed voices coming from beyond the trees nearby.

Korin ducked back behind a large tree in case there were archers waiting. "Cousin, have you come to surrender?" he called out.

Tobin raised his hands, showing that they were empty. Too easy.

"He looks no more like a girl than you do," Alben scoffed.

"Korin, something's not right," Caliel warned, frowning at the silent figure.

Tobin stood slowly and took a step toward Korin. "Hello, cousin."

The pure malice in that voice shocked Korin. It didn't sound like Tobin; the voice was lower, and hoarse. He could hear the creak and rasp of armor as Tobin undid the chinstrap of his helm and lifted it off.

Korin had never seen such naked hatred on his cousin's face, or seen him so haggard and pale. His eyes were sunken and looked dark, almost black. This was the Tobin he'd seen in dreams.

Caliel gripped him by the arm. "Kor, that's not—"

Before he could say more, the ambushers burst from the trees at the far side of the clearing and Korin heard a familiar voice shouting, "Tamír, come back!"

Ki and Lutha broke from the trees, hard on the heels of someone wearing Tobin's tabard and helm.

"What in the name of Bilairy is it?" Porion gasped, catching a glimpse of the face under the helm.

It was Caliel who replied. "*That* is Tamír."

"Look, it's Tobin. And there's Ki!" Tanil started forward, waving happily to them. "Where have you been?"

Korin caught him by the arm. "No, they're our enemy now."

Tanil's eyes clouded with confusion. "No, those are your Companions."

"Oh gods," Korin groaned softly. "Cal, how can I——?"

"Tanil, look at me," Caliel said, letting his sword fall. As the squire turned, Caliel punched him hard in the chin, and the boy dropped at his feet without a sound.

Damnation!" Ki exclaimed, racing forward to get in front of Tamír. Lutha and Lynx did the same, shielding her from attack. Korin was standing there in plain sight with Porion and Cal at the far edge of the clearing, well within bow-shot. Ki caught glimpses of movement all through the trees on that side.

Tamír paid them no mind, staring instead at Brother, who was dressed in her clothes and armor. "You!"

The demon turned slightly to leer at Tamír. As always, the light struck him wrong, not touching him as it did the living. His black hair gave back no sheen. Ki swallowed hard, recalling what the Oracle had told Tamír in Afra. Something about her being him and him being her. They'd never looked less alike.

"What sort of trick is this?" Korin called. "Have you brought your necromancers after all?"

Brother slowly began to advance on Korin, hissing, "Son of Erius, I am not Tobin and I am not Tamír."

"He's going after him!" Ki whispered. If Brother killed Korin, this would all end.

"Brother, stop!" Tamír shouted. "Don't touch him. I for-bid you!"

To Ki's amazement, Brother halted and glared back at her.

"This is my fight! Go away," Tamír ordered, as she used to when they were all children.

Brother curled his lip at her, but faded away.

"What sort of trick is this?" Korin demanded.

"It's me, Kor," Tamír called back. "That was my brother,

or would have been. He was killed to protect me from your father."

"No!"

"It's a trick, just as Lord Niryn said," Moriel scoffed.

"You're wrong, Toad," Lutha shouted back.

"You!" Moriel's shock was almost comical.

"You should know better about necromancy than anyone, after being Niryn's lapdog. Where is your master, anyway? I'm surprised he's let you off the lead, you ass-licker!"

Moriel's expression was poisonous. "He wasn't wrong about you was he, traitor?"

Ki glanced away and locked eyes with Caliel. He gave Ki a slight nod of acknowledgment. "Damn it," Ki muttered, waving to him.

"Who are you really?" Korin demanded. "Show your face if you dare!"

Tamír pulled off her helmet and pulled back her mail coif. "It's me, Kor, as I was meant to be. Caliel can vouch for me. Just ask him. We don't have to fight anymore. Talk with me. Let me show you the proof—"

"Liar!" Korin spat back, but Ki thought he sounded uncertain.

"I must be queen, Korin, but you're still my kin. Fighting you is like fighting my own brother. Please, we can make peace here, once and for all. I swear on my honor that you'll have your rightful place at my side. I'll grant amnesty to all who've backed you."

"Honor?" Alben jeered. "What's the word of an oath breaker worth?"

Ki clutched his sword as more swordsmen stepped from the trees behind Korin. "What the hell are you thinking, Tamír, just standing here like this? We're outnumbered three to one at least!"

"He'll listen to me, now that he's seen the truth," she replied softly. "He has to!"

*   *   *

Still rocked by the sight of the demon, Korin stared at this girl who claimed to be his cousin. "Tobin?" he whispered, warring against the evidence of his own eyes.

Her sudden, unexpected smile—Tobin's smile—nearly undid him. "I'm Tamír, just as I wrote you. Lutha said you got my letter."

"Lies!"

"No, Kor. Tobin was the lie. I am Ariani's daughter. I swear it by the Flame and the Four."

Korin could hardly breathe.

Nothing but a boy in a dress, Niryn's voice whispered in his mind. Korin wanted to cling to that belief now as a sick feeling of certainty swept over him. If Tobin—if *she*—spoke the truth, then Caliel had been right all along. Niryn *had* lied to him and manipulated him. Cal had been ready to hang to make Korin see sense, and he'd nearly killed him for it.

"We can be friends again," Tobin said.

"A trick!" Moriel insisted.

A trick! A trick! A trick! Niryn's cold voice whispered in his memory.

Majesty, where are you?"

Tamír could hear Nyanis shouting in the distance behind them, louder than the sounds of battle still coming from the field.

"Here!" Una called back.

There were voices calling to Korin as well, and Tamír could hear others coming to reinforce him. There was going to be a bloody fight here unless she could make Korin believe her.

She kept her eyes fixed on him, like a hawk she was trying to tame. She knew him so well; she could see the way he was struggling with himself. Hope made her catch her breath.

By blood and trial, you must hold your throne. From the Usurper's hand you will wrest the Sword.

No! she thought. *It doesn't have to be like that! I can make him listen! Brother brought us together so we could settle this.* Smiling again, she held out her hand.

Korin, strike. You have the greater force," Porion urged. "Strike now!"

"Yes! We can crush Tobin once and for all," Alben whispered.

Caliel touched Korin's arm, saying nothing, but his eyes were pleading.

Tamír dropped her helmet and pushed past Ki and Lynx. "It can end now, Korin," she said, still holding out her hand to him. "Give me the Sword of Ghërilain and—"

Give me the Sword—

Korin went cold all over. He'd spoken those same words to his father, that night in Ero, and still burned with shame at the memory of how his father's hands had tightened on the hilt and his eyes had gone hard. *Only one hand wields the Sword of Ghërilain. While I have breath in my body, I am still king. Be content with proving yourself worthy of it.*

Korin's hand clenched around the hilt as all the old rage and guilt and sorrow came rushing back, drowning doubt, drowning love. "No, *I* am king!"

Tamír saw the fatal shift. She had just enough time to scoop up her fallen helmet and jam it back on before Korin's men rushed her band. Only Korin hung back, and Caliel with him.

Tamír was not surprised to find herself facing Alben in the midst of the fray. There had never been much friendship between them, and she saw none in his eyes now as he closed with her. He'd always been a fierce match and Tamír was hard put to hold her own against him. She pressed him grimly, seeing no hint of remorse in his eyes as they slashed at each other.

The clearing was full of fighters now, leaving little room for fancy maneuvering. They hacked at one another like woodchoppers. At some point a dagger appeared in Alben's left hand and he tried to stab her in the ribs as they locked hilts. Her mail held off the point, and she elbowed him hard in the face, breaking his nose. He staggered back, and she drove her knee into his groin, sending him to the ground.

"Tamír, behind you!" Ki yelled, fending off a man wielding a cudgel.

Tamír ducked as she turned and narrowly missed being struck in the head by Moriel.

"Demon bitch!" He kicked her hard in the knee to unbalance her and raised his blade to strike again.

Snarling in pain, Tamír staggered and brought the tip of her blade up to catch him in the throat as he came on, but Moriel sidestepped her awkward attempt.

Lutha appeared out of the chaos and sprang at Moriel, grappling with him and knocking him away from Tamír.

She left him to it and looked around for Alben, but instead found herself facing Caliel. He had his sword up, ready for an attack, but he didn't move.

"I don't want your blood, Cal."

"I don't want yours," he replied, and she heard the pain behind the words as he raised his sword to strike.

Tamír raised her own to block it, but before their blades could meet she saw a blur of motion from the left and the flash of steel. Caliel's helmet flew off and, empty-eyed, he crumpled to the ground. Nikides stood over him, clutching his bloody blade in both hands, chest heaving. "Tamír, behind you!"

Not knowing if Cal was alive or dead, she whirled and caught the blade of a tall warrior. As she held him, Ki lunged under the man's guard and stabbed him in the throat.

Ki pressed his back to hers, panting raggedly and clutching his sword in both hands. "Are you hurt?"

"Not yet." She put weight on her knee where Moriel had kicked her to make sure it wouldn't fail her. "Where's Korin?"

"I don't see him."

This way, Sister, Brother hissed in her ear. She turned and caught a glimpse of Korin's banner near the edge of the clearing.

A spearman thrust at her, only to fall dead where he stood, with Brother gloating over him.

"This is my fight!" Tamír shouted at him, even as she rushed to take advantage of the opening he'd made for her.

Shoulder to shoulder, she and Ki fought their way toward the banner.

Korin saw Caliel fall under Nikides' blade.

"Traitor! I'll kill you!" Before he could reach him, however, a young squire wearing Tobin's baldric lunged out of the press and blocked his way. He knocked the boy's sword from his hands with a single swing, then ran him through. Nikides screamed and flew at him, but Porion stepped in and drove him back.

Korin was about to help when he saw a crowned helm above the fray mere yards away.

"Tobin's mine!" Korin shouted. Ki tried to intervene but Porion threw himself between them, catching Ki's blade with his own.

Korin lunged at Tobin with all his might, fueled by his rekindled sense of betrayal. Face-to-face with her at last, he saw what looked like genuine sorrow in her eyes, but she did not hesitate.

Ki tried to keep Tamír in sight out of the corner of his eye as he faced Master Porion. "I don't want to fight you," he blurted out, keeping his guard up.

"Nor I you, lad, but here we are," Porion replied. "Come on, and let's see how well you learned your lessons."

* * *

*T*amír had fought against Korin only once before, that day he'd let her fight out her anger at having to flog Ki. Older and stronger, he'd been more than a match for her then. She'd grown stronger since, but he was still a dangerous opponent. The ferocity of his attack was stunning.

He rained down blow upon blow, forcing her to parry and retreat. They whirled around each other, striking and grappling, until they were almost in the trees. He drove her back again into a stand of tall ferns. The green smell of them rose around them as they crushed them underfoot, and she could hear the sound of flowing water close behind her.

"Tamír!" Ki shouted, farther away.

"Here—" she began, but Korin pushed her back again and she missed her footing, catching her heel on something and falling backward.

The ground was not where she'd expected it to be. She tumbled over the edge of a small gully behind the ferns and rolled down a rocky slope, dashing her left elbow painfully against a rock as she fell and losing her sword somewhere along the way. She came to rest in cold mud at the edge of a stream. It must be the same stream that ran across the battlefield, she realized, getting her bearings.

She staggered up, cradling her bruised arm and looking around for her sword. It was halfway up the steep bank, caught on an exposed tree root. She started up after it, then froze as she took in her surroundings. It looked almost exactly like the place in her vision.

The banner? Where is the banner?

Instead, Korin came bounding over the edge after her with murder in his eyes. Her sword was too far away to reach before he was on her.

"Illior!" she cried, drawing her knife and bracing to meet him.

"Tamír!" Ki leaped into view, white-faced and covered in blood. He sprang down the slope and tackled Korin before he could reach her. They tumbled together, landing in the mud a few yards away with Ki on the bottom.

"Get your sword!" Ki yelled, wrestling with Korin.

Tamír scrambled up the gully and grabbed her blade. As she turned back, she was horrified to see Korin rise suddenly and strike at Ki as he struggled on the ground. It was a shameful act.

"You coward!" she screamed. She had to reach Ki, help him, but it was like being trapped in a nightmare. She slipped and slid over the rocks, making straight for them, but she just couldn't seem to move fast enough.

Korin brought his sword down on Ki's arm as he tried to raise his blade to fend him off. She heard the sickening snap of bone and Ki's snarl of pain. He tried to roll out from under Korin but the prince lunged after him and brought his sword down against the side of Ki's helmet. Ki collapsed on his side in the mud and Korin grasped his sword in both hands and thrust it down into Ki's side through the gap in his cuirass.

"Bastard!" Tamír shrieked. Grief and fury propelled her the last few yards to close with Korin. She struck him hard across the shoulders, driving him back from Ki's body. He leaped away and whirled to face her. There was fresh blood on his blade, mingling with the rain.

Ki's blood.

With a scream of rage, she flew at Korin, driving him back with savage swings, away from Ki's motionless body.

They splashed across the stream, and onto higher ground. Korin fought hard, cursing her as he parried every swing. Their two blades clashed and rang, echoing loudly in the gully. She struck him in the side, denting his steel cuirass. He answered her with a glancing blow to the head that knocked her helmet off. There'd been no time to fasten the strap.

She fell back, hoping to retrieve it. Korin laughed and pressed the advantage, driving her back to the stream, where Ki lay clawing weakly at the ground.

She turned and jumped back, hoping to draw Korin away from him again. "Get up, Ki! Get your sword!"

With a sneer, Korin left off his attack and turned to Ki, raising his blade again for the killing blow.

She sprang at him with a despairing cry and felt Brother's dead chill close in around her.

It felt as if the demon crawled inside her own skin, filling her with the strength of his own unimaginable hatred. It drew her lips back from her teeth in a snarl and tore an unearthly cry from her throat. With the clarity of the demon's rage, she spotted the gap in the hauberk under Korin's raised arm and made a long, unerring lunge.

The tip of her blade found its mark. Korin's blood soaked like a blossoming red flower through shirt and mail.

He twisted away before she could plunge it in deeply enough, and whirled to attack her again, both of them stumbling over Ki. Korin was coughing blood as he lashed out at her, and his swings grew wilder as he kept up a staggering fight.

From the Usurper's hand you will wrest the Sword.

"Yield!" she cried, catching his blade on her own and holding him, hilt to hilt.

"Never!" Korin gasped, spewing blood.

They pulled free of each other and she felt another surge of Brother's cold hatred rush through her as she caught sight of Ki again. He lay very still now, and the mud around him was stained red.

This time she welcomed Brother's strength. It joined with her own pent-up rage over all they'd lost or been denied: Ki, her mother's love, a living brother, her father's kindness, her very identity—all sacrificed to bring her to this moment.

"Damn you!" she screamed, flying at Korin again, battering him down, pushing him back. A red haze filled her eyes. "Damn all of you for stealing our *lives*!"

Korin struck her on the left shoulder, blade catching

on the leather strap of her cuirass. She barely felt it as she used the force of the blow to duck and whirl around, catching Korin behind the knees with her foot.

Korin staggered, dropping his guard as he fought to keep his balance. Still bent low, Tamír swung her sword up with all her might and felt Brother's hand on hers, gripping her sword's hilt as she caught Korin across the throat, just under the chin, burying the edge of her blade there.

Korin gave a strangled cry, and hot blood spurted out, nearly blinding her. She pulled the blade free and quickly wiped a hand across her eyes.

Korin stood very still, staring at her in disbelief. He tried to speak, but only bloody foam found its way past his lips. His breath made a horrible wet wheezing sound through the gaping wound across his throat. His chest heaved again and he collapsed backward among the rocks. Blood still pulsed from the wound in slow spurts and ran down between the stones.

A river of blood.

Tamír strode over to him, blade poised for the final stroke.

Korin stared up at her. His rage was gone, replaced by an expression of terrible sorrow. Still clutching his sword, he mouthed a single silent word: *Cousin.*

Tamír's own sword slipped unnoticed from her fingers as she watched the life fade from those dark eyes. A last, strangled breath and he was gone, hand still locked around the hilt of the great sword.

Brother had deserted her, and the horror of the battle rolled over her. "Oh hell. Oh, Korin!" In death, he looked again like the boy she'd played and sparred and gotten drunk with, lying there broken and bloody in the mud.

The sounds of battle were still raging beyond the gully, and she could hear her friends frantically calling for her and Ki.

Ki!

"Here!" she tried to tell them, but it came out a choked

whisper. Weeping, she stumbled back to where Ki lay and fell to her knees beside him. His tabard was soaked with blood and his broken arm was twisted awkwardly under his body. She found the buckle of his dented helm and pulled it free, then felt vainly for signs of a heartbeat. His soft brown hair was sodden with blood on the side Korin had struck.

She gently lifted his limp body into her arms, clasping his good hand and cradling his head against her chest. "Oh no. No, please, not him too!"

His blood soaked through her tabard and gummed her fingers to his. So much blood.

"Is this what you wanted?" she cried out to Illior. "Is this what it takes to give Skala a queen?"

Something struck her shoulder and splashed into the water beside her. Looking down, she let out a strangled cry.

It was Korin's head.

Brother loomed over her, looking stronger and more solid than he ever had. He held the bloody Sword of Ghërilain in his right hand, and as she watched, he raised his left and licked the blood that covered his fingers like it was honey.

He tossed the sword down beside her, then with a chilling smile, stroked her cheeks, painting them with more of Korin's blood. *Thank you, Sister.*

She shrank from his icy touch, clutching Ki closer. "It's over. You've had your vengeance. I don't ever want to see you again! Never!"

Brother was still smiling as he reached toward Ki.

"Don't you touch him!" she cried, shielding him from the demon with her own body.

Save your tears, Sister. He still lives.

"What?" She pressed a finger to the side of Ki's neck, searching frantically for a pulse again. She found the faintest flutter just under his jaw.

"Tamír, where are you?" That was Lynx, sounding frantic.

"Here!" she shouted back, finding her voice.

"Tamír!" Arkoniel appeared at the top of the bank. He took in the scene at a glance and plunged down to join her.

"He's alive," Tamír cried. "Find a healer!"

Arkoniel touched Ki's forehead and frowned. "I will, but you must go and end this battle."

It was like tearing out her own heart to relinquish Ki into Arkoniel's arms but somehow she did it.

Staggering to her feet, she picked up Ghërilain's sword. The hilt was sticky with gore, but it fit her hand as if it had been made for her.

She'd held it once before, the night of her first feast with her uncle. The worn gold dragons set in raised relief on the sides of the curved quillons were crusted in blood now, and so were the gold-wrapped ivory hilt and the carved ruby seal on the pommel. The Royal Seal. Her seal now—a dragon bearing Sakor's Flame in a crescent moon on its back. Sakor and Illior united.

You are Skala.

She bent and grasped Korin's head by the hair and picked it up, too, feeling the lingering warmth of his scalp against the backs of her fingers.

"Care for Ki, Arkoniel. Don't let him die."

Bearing her grisly trophies, she gave Ki one last anguished look, then climbed up the bank to carry out the Lightbearer's will.

Chapter 53

Daylight was nearly gone and the rain was pelting down in earnest when Tamír emerged from the gully. The fighting was nearly over here. Porion lay dead in the trampled ferns. A little way off Moriel sprawled in a pool of blood, with Lutha's poniard in his neck.

She found Cal by his hair. He was lying facedown where he'd fallen and Nikides was sitting beside him, clutching a shoulder wound and weeping. Una was holding Hylia, whose arm appeared to be broken.

Companion against Companion. Skalan against Skalan.

Lynx, as usual, was still on his feet, and Tyrien, too. They were the first to see her and what she carried.

"Korin is dead!" Lynx shouted.

Everything seemed to stop completely for a moment. The last of Korin's men fell back and stared at her, then ran away into the trees, leaving their fallen comrades behind.

Nikides staggered up to meet her. His eyes went wide as he saw what she carried.

"I killed him. The blood is on my hands." Her voice sounded distant in her ears, like someone else speaking. She felt numb all over, too exhausted to grieve or feel victory. She set off in the direction of the battlefield, dimly aware of others falling in behind them.

"Are you wounded?" Nikides asked, concerned.

"No, but Ki's—" *No, don't think of that now.* "Arkoniel's with him. How are the rest?"

"Lorin's dead." Nikides swallowed hard, collecting himself. "Hylia has a broken arm. The rest of us have only minor wounds."

"And the others? Caliel?"

"He's alive. I—I turned my blade at the last moment. I'm sorry, I just couldn't—"

"It's all right, Nik. You did well. Make sure he and any others are brought to the camp."

But still he stayed by her side, looking at her very oddly. "Are you certain you're not hurt?"

"Do as I say!" It took all her concentration to keep putting one foot in front of the other. Nikides fell back, presumably to follow her order; but Lynx, Tyrien, and Una closed around her as she reached the edge of the trees.

The battlefield was a scene of carnage. Dead warriors and horses lay everywhere, the bodies piled on top of one another three deep in places. So many had fallen at the stream that the water was pooling red behind them, dammed with corpses.

There were still scattered groups fighting on. Some of Korin's forces had withdrawn up the hill. Others were wandering among the dead.

Tamír looked around in dismay, still clutching the head.

Malkanus was suddenly at her side, though she hadn't noticed the wizard's approach. "Allow me, Majesty." He walked a little way apart from the others and raised his wand. A terrific roar like thunder rolled across the field with such force that men fell to their knees and covered their heads.

In a voice that seemed as loud as the thunder, Malkanus cried, "Attend Queen Tamír!"

It worked. Suddenly hundreds of faces turned her way. Tamír strode farther out from the trees and held up the Sword and Korin's head. "Prince Korin is dead!" she shouted, her voice thin by comparison. "Let the fighting cease!"

The cry was passed across the field. The last of Korin's

warriors made a disorderly retreat to the base of the hill beyond the stream. The only banner still visible among their
disordered ranks was Wethring's.

"Lynx, take some men and bring out Korin's body,"
she ordered. "I want it treated with respect. Make a litter
and cover the body, then bring it back to our camp. Tell
the drysians I need it prepared for burning. Nik, you see to
Lorin's remains. We must take him back to his father. And
someone find me a herald!"

"Here, Majesty."

She held out Korin's head. "Show this to Lord
Wethring and declare that the day is ours, then bring it
back to my camp. I require all nobles to present themselves to me at once or be declared traitors."

The herald wrapped the head in a corner of his cloak
and hurried away.

Freed of that burden, Tamír wiped the Sword of
Ghërilain on the hem of her filthy tabard and slid it into her
scabbard, then walked back to the clearing.

Ki had been carried up from the gully. Arkoniel sat on
the ground under a large tree, holding the younger man's
head in his lap as Caliel tried to staunch the wound in his
side.

She was amazed to see Cal conscious. His hands
shook as he held the cloth, and tears were streaming down
his cheeks.

Tamír knelt beside them and reached out hesitantly to
touch Ki's muddy face. "Will he live?"

"I don't know," Arkoniel told her.

The wizard's quiet words struck harder than any blow
Korin had dealt her.

If he dies—

She bit her lip, unable to finish such a thought.
Leaning down, she kissed Ki on the forehead and whispered, "You gave me your word."

"Majesty?" Caliel said softly.

Unable to look at him yet, she asked, "Where is Tanil?"

"In the trees, just over there. Alive, I think."

"You should go to him. Give him the news."

"Thank you." He rose to go.

Looking up, she searched his face, but still found only sorrow there. "You're both welcome in my camp."

More tears slid slowly down Caliel's cheeks, carving pale trails through the blood and grime as he made her an unsteady bow.

"For what it's worth, Cal, I'm sorry. I didn't want to fight him."

"I know that." He stumbled off toward the trees.

She turned to find Arkoniel watching her, looking sadder than she'd ever seen.

Litters for the dead and wounded were hastily made up from saplings and cloaks. Korin's body was carried out first, with Ki's litter just behind. Tamír walked beside Ki, stealing glances down at him to see the labored rise and fall of his chest all the way back to camp. She wanted to sob and scream and hold Ki tight to keep him from leaving her. Instead, she had to hold her head high and return the salutes of the men and women they passed.

Warriors from both sides were moving among the dead, claiming fallen friends or stripping the enemy. Ravens had already arrived, drawn by the smell of death. Flocks of them massed in the trees, filling the air with their hoarse, hungry cries as they waited their turn.

At the camp Ki was carried into her tent and given over to the care of the drysians. Tamír watched them anxiously through the open flap as she waited for Korin's lords to surrender.

Korin's body lay under a cloak on a makeshift catafalque nearby, with Porion and the other fallen Companions beside him. Her Companions kept silent vigil over them, all except Nikides and Tanil.

Nik, in spite of his own grief and his wound, had

stepped in and was seeing to the necessary details, sending off heralds to carry word of the victory and Korin's death, and seeing that messenger birds were let loose to carry the news quickly to Atyion. Tamír was grateful, as always, for his competence and foresight.

Tanil crouched on the ground by his fallen lord, sobbing inconsolably under his cloak, and would not be moved. He could not grasp what had happened, and perhaps that was for the best. Caliel knelt with him, sword planted before him, keeping the vigil with him. He'd already reported seeing Urmanis, Garol, and Mago fall earlier in the day. There'd been no sign of Alben among the living or the dead.

Messengers arrived from her own side with word that Jorvai had suffered an arrow wound to the chest; but Kyman and Nyanis arrived soon after, unhurt. Korin's baggage train had been captured, yielding much-needed food and tents. That, together with the supplies the Aurënfaie had brought, would be sufficient to make camp here until the wounded could be safely moved.

Arengil brought news that the Aurënfaie had killed all the horsemen Korin had sent to flank them and suffered no losses of their own. Solun and Hiril soon followed, bearing the captured standards. Tamír listened with half an ear. Inside the tent Ki remained motionless and the drysians looked concerned.

Wethring and a few of the remaining nobles arrived under a flag of truce. Tamír stood and drew the Sword, holding it up before her. The herald had brought Korin's head back and placed it carefully under the cloak with the body.

Kneeling, Wethring humbly bowed his head. "The day is yours, Majesty."

"By the will of Illior," she replied.

He looked up, studying her face.

"Do you believe what your eyes show you?" she demanded.

"Yes, Majesty."

"Will you swear fealty to me?"

He blinked in surprise. "I will if you will accept me."

"You were loyal to Korin. Show me the same loyalty, and I will confirm your title and lands, in return for the blood fee."

"You shall have both, Majesty. I swear it by the Four and vouch for all those who've followed my banner."

"Where is Nevus, son of Solari?"

"He went east, to Atyion."

"Have you had word back from him?"

"No, Majesty."

"I see. And Lord Alben? Did he fall today?"

"No one has seen him, Majesty."

"What of Lord Niryn?"

"Dead, Majesty, at Cirna."

"Did Korin kill him?" Lutha asked, overhearing.

"No, he fell from Lady Nalia's tower."

"He fell?" Tamír let out a short, mirthless laugh. It was a ridiculous death for someone so feared. "Well, that's one bit of good news, then."

"Do I have your leave to burn our dead?"

"Of course."

Wethring cast a sad look at the draped form beside them. "And Korin?"

"He's my kin. I will see that he's properly burned and his ashes gathered for his wife. Send your army back to their homes and attend me in Atyion in a month's time."

Wethring stood and gave her another deep bow. "I hear and obey, merciful Queen."

"I'm not quite done with you yet. What are the defenses at Cirna? What provisions did Korin make for Lady Nalia?"

"The fortress garrison was left behind. They're mostly Niryn's Harriers now, and a few wizards."

"Will she stand against me?"

"Lady Nalia?" Wethring smiled and shook his head. "She wouldn't have the first idea how, Majesty."

Lutha had been listening intently and he stepped forward now. "He's right, Tamír. She's been sheltered and kept locked away. The nobles who know Korin's court know that. She's helpless there now. With your permission, I'd like to take a force north immediately to protect her."

"You should bring her here and keep her close," Arkoniel advised. "You can't risk her and the child becoming pawns to be used against you."

Lutha went down on one knee before her. "Please, Tamír. She's never done anyone any harm."

Tamír sensed more than mere courtesy behind his interest in Lady Nalia. "Of course. She knows you. It's best if you are my emissary. Make her understand that she is under my protection, not being arrested. But you'll need warriors to take the fortress."

"I'll go, with your consent," said Nyanis.

Tamír nodded gratefully. She trusted all her nobles, but Nyanis most of all. "Capture the place and leave a garrison. Lutha, bring her here."

"I'll guard her with my life," Lutha vowed.

"Arkoniel, you and your people go, too, and deal with Niryn's wizards."

"I will be certain we do, Majesty."

"Show them no more mercy than they showed to those they burned."

"We will go, as well, and destroy the blasphemers," Solun said.

"And my people," said Hiril.

"Thank you. Go now. Take what supplies you need and ride hard."

Lutha and the others saluted and hurried off to make ready. Arengil moved to follow as the others started away, but Tamír called him back. "Do you still wish to be a Companion?"

"Of course!" the young Gedre exclaimed.

"Then stay." She rose to go to Ki but noticed that Arkoniel had lingered behind.

"The others can deal with Niryn's people if you'd rather I stay?"

"There's no one I trust more than you," she told him, and saw the color come to his cheeks. "I know that you will do what is best and protect her for me, no matter what. You understand better than anyone else why I will not have innocent blood spilled in my name."

"That means more to me than I can say," he replied, his voice rough with emotion. "I will keep an eye on you here and return at once if you need me."

"I'll be fine. Go on now." With that, she ducked through the low doorway of the tent and pulled the flap down.

The air inside was heavy with the smell of the drysians' herbs. Kaulin was sitting with Ki.

Ki's arm had been set and wrapped securely in rags and a cut-down boot top. His chest and head were wrapped in ragged bandages. His face was still and white under the streaks of mud and blood.

"Has he woken yet?"

"No," Kaulin replied. "The sword thrust missed his lung. It's the blow to his head that's bad."

"I'd like to be alone with him."

"As you wish, Majesty."

Sitting down beside Ki, she took his left hand in hers. His breathing was almost imperceptible. Leaning over him, she whispered, "It's all over, Ki. We won. But I don't know what I'll do if you die!" Thunder rumbled in the distance as she pressed his cold fingers to her cheek. "Even if you never want to be my consort—" The blessed numbness she'd clung to was slipping away and the tears came.

"Please, Ki! Don't go!"

Chapter 54

K i was lost, and chilled to the bone.

Scattered images flashed behind his eyes. *She's in danger! I'm not going to get there in time.*

A starlit window and flailing legs—

Tamír unarmed, under Korin's shining blade—

Too far! Can't reach—

No!

The blackness took him before he could reach her, and the pain. So much pain.

Drifting, alone in the darkness, he thought he heard distant voices calling to him. *Tamír?*

No, she's dead—I failed and she's dead—

Then let me die, too.

Such pain.

Am I dead?

No, not yet, child.

Lhel? Where are you? I can't see!

You must be strong. She needs you.

Lhel? I've missed you!

I've missed you, too, child. But you must think of Tamír, now.

Panic shot through him. *I'm sorry. I let her die!*

A small, rough hand closed hard around his. *Open your eyes, child.*

Suddenly Ki could see. He was standing beside Lhel in the tent. Rain was drumming down on the canvas and dripping through all around them. And Tamír was there, asleep on the ground next to a pallet, where someone else lay.

She's alive! But she looks so sad. Did we lose the battle?

No, you won. Look closer.

Tamír, we won! he cried, trying to touch her shoulder. But he couldn't. He couldn't feel his hand at all. As he bent closer to her, he saw dried tears on her cheeks, and the face of the person she was sleeping beside.

That's me. He could see his own pale face, and the thin crescents of white under his parted lashes. *I am dead!*

No, but you aren't alive either, Lhel replied.

You're waiting. Brother appeared beside Tamír, gazing up at Ki with less hostility than usual. *You're waiting as I wait, between life and death. We're both still bound.*

Look closer, Lhel whispered. *Look at her heart, and yours.*

Squinting, Ki could just make out something that looked like a thin, gnarled black root stretching from Brother's chest to Tamír's. No, not a root, but a wizened birthing cord.

Looking down, he saw another cord between him and his own body, and one that stretched from his body to Tamír, but these were silvery and bright. Other strands, less bright, radiated out and disappeared in all directions. One dark one stretched from Tamír's chest across the tent to the open flap. Korin stood out there, gazing in with a lost expression.

What's he doing here?

She killed me, Korin whispered, and Ki felt fear as that empty dark gaze turned to him. *False friend!*

Don't let him trouble you, child. He has no claim on you. Lhel touched the silver cord joining Ki to Tamír. *This one is very strong, stronger than your own life cord.*

I can't die! I can't leave her! She needs me.

You saved her life today. I foresaw that the first time we met, and more. She will be very sad if you die. Her belly may never swell. Your people need the children you and she will give them. If I help you live, will you love her?

Looking down at his own still face, Ki saw tears well out from under his lashes and trickle slowly down his cheeks. *I do love her! Help me, please!*

But even as he said it, he felt the cord joining his spirit to his body pull painfully at his chest and grow thin. He was floating above himself, looking down at Tamír. Even in sleep she held his hand tightly, as if she could hold him back from death.

Please, he whispered. *I want to stay!*

Hold on, Lhel whispered.

Keesa, wake up."

"Lhel?" Tamír sat up, startled.

It was still dark in the tent, and rain was pounding on the canvas. A sudden flash of lightning turned the darkness grey. It was Mahti leaning over her, not Lhel. A clap of thunder shook the ground. Something struck her cheek; water was dripping from the witch's hair. He had just come in from the storm.

"Mahti? You came back!"

"Hush, keesa." The witch pointed to Ki. "He very weak. You must let me play healing for him. His *mari* try to go."

Tamír tightened her hold on Ki's cold hand and nodded. "Do whatever you can."

Another flash of lightning lit the tent and thunder shook the ground, as if the world were falling down around them.

Mahti sat as far from Ki as the cramped quarters allowed, back pressed to the sodden canvas behind him. He put the oo'lu to his lips, resting the mouth of it next to Ki's side, and began the spell song.

The boy's spirit was already out of the body. Mahti could sense it hovering nearby. He could see Lhel and Brother, and the sad spirit lurking outside in the rain; but Ki was caught between life and death, so Mahti could not see him clearly. There was no need for the lifting out song, but he knew he must work quickly to heal the body enough to hold the spirit in before it was lost.

Sojourn's deep voice filled Mahti's head and chest as he played, gathering the necessary power. When it was strong enough, he sent the song out to the floating spirit, wrapping him in binding song to keep him from flying away. Then he wove the voices of night herons and frogs to wash the dark blood away from inside the boy's head. It was a bad wound, that one, but Mahti had wrestled with them before. It took time, but he finally felt some of the pain flow away.

He played into the body next, leaving the arm bones to knit on their own and concentrating on the deep sword wound in his side. He used the song of bears to take the heat from it; there was good magic at work already, from the other healers. Mahti touched it with his song and approved. This would heal well if Ki lived.

He played through the rest of the body, finding little that needed his attention. Ki was young and strong and wanted to live.

The head wound was still fighting him, though, so Mahti increased the power of the song to drive the dark threat from it. It took a long time, but when he finished the heron song a third time, the pain was nearly gone and Ki's face was more peaceful. Mahti blinked the sweat from his eyes and gently coaxed the spirit back into the flesh. It went willingly, like a loon diving under the water after a fish.

When he was done only the sound of the rain and thunder filled the tent, and the tense breathing of the girl and her oreskiri as they stared anxiously at the boy, waiting.

Ki?" Tamír stroked the dirty, blood-stiff hair back from his bandaged forehead and caught her breath as his eyelids fluttered.

"Ki, open your eyes!" she whispered.

"Tob?" he mumbled. He opened his eyes very slowly,

not focusing on anything. His right pupil was larger than the left.

"Thank the Light!" Tears crept down her cheeks unnoticed as she leaned closer. "How do you feel?"

"Hurts. My arm . . . head." He looked blearily at nothing. "Gone?"

"Who's gone?"

His eyes finally found her, though they were still very vague. "I—I thought—I don't know." He closed his eyes again and tears welled under his lashes. "I killed Master Porion."

"Don't think of that now."

"Keep him awake," Mahti told her. "He will—" He mimed vomiting. "Not sleep until sun goes down again."

With help from Mahti, Tamír got Ki propped up with his head on a pack. He began to retch almost at once. She snatched up a discarded helmet and held it under his chin as Ki brought up what little he'd had to eat.

"Rest," Mahti told Ki as he slumped limply back in Tamír's arms. "You heal now."

"How can I thank you?" asked Tamír.

"Keep promise," Mahti replied. "And let me play healing for you. Lhel say."

"I keep telling you, I don't need it."

Mahti grasped her by the knee, dark eyes suddenly intimidating. "You don't know. *I* know! Lhel know." He reached down and cupped her roughly between the legs. "You still tie to demon *here*."

Tamír knocked his hand away angrily, but even as she did, she felt again the strong, disconcerting sensation of having two bodies at once, her own and Tobin's.

"This end magic," Mahti promised, as if he understood. "Make you clean."

Clean. Yes, she wanted that. Suppressing a shiver of apprehension, she nodded. "What do you want me to do?"

Mahti shifted, letting the mouth of his oo'lu rest near her leg. "Just sit."

Closing his eyes, he began a deep, throbbing drone. Tamír tensed, expecting the fire that had burned away her other body.

But it wasn't like that at all, this time.

Lhel sat close beside Mahti, whispering in his ear, showing him what to look for. It was a woman's spell he was undoing, and he had to be careful not to damage what should remain.

Brother hunkered down beside Tamír, staring not at the girl, but at Lhel.

Mahti started to play a water song, but the tune changed. He knew this song; it had been the first one he'd played on Sojourn. Now it showed him the thick, gnarled birthing cord that joined brother and sister. It showed him the phantom shape of the boy's body that still clung to the girl like shreds of a snake's cast off skin. The wasted shape of a penis still rested between her thighs. His song made the last of the ghost body fall away, leaving only living flesh.

Snakeskin song, that's what he would call this one should he ever need it again. He silently thanked Lhel for it.

The birthing cord that joined her to her brother was tough as an old root, but the song burned through it, too. It fell away like ashes between them.

You go now, he whispered in his mind to Brother.

From the corner of his eye he saw Lhel rise and take the trembling demon boy by the hand. *Child, let go of this life that was never yours. Go and rest for the next.*

She embraced the pale figure. He clung to her for a moment, like a living boy, then disappeared with a sigh.

Well done, Lhel whispered. *They are both free.*

But Mahti saw another dark cord joining Tamír to a ghost outside. He played the knife song and freed the dark-eyed dead man, so he could go on to peace, too.

There was another very old cord from her heart that

stretched far, far away. He touched it with his mind. An angry, confused spirit lurked at the end of this one. *Mother.*

Cut that one, too, whispered Lhel.

Mahti did, and heard a brief, distant wail.

There were many other cords around her, as there were around all people. Some were good. Some were harmful. The one between Tamír and the boy in her arms was the strongest, bright as lightning.

Lhel touched it and smiled. This one needed none of Mahti's spells.

Satisfied with the girl's heart, he played to draw the pain from her wounds, then turned his attention to the red night flower of her womb. Lhel's binding magic had not reached so deep there. Despite her narrow hips and small breasts, the womb was well knit, a fertile cradle waiting to be filled. Mahti played his spell instead into the bony yoke of her pelvis, so that it might let the babies out more easily in the years to come.

It was only when he'd finished that he noticed that Lhel was gone.

*T*amír was surprised at how comforting Mahti's strange music was. Instead of the cold, crawling feeling she'd experienced with Niryn, or the dizzying effect of Arkoniel's sighting spells, she felt nothing but a gentle warmth. When he finished she sighed and opened her eyes, feeling more rested than she had in days.

"That's all?"

"Yes. Now you only you," Mahti replied, patting her knee.

"How do you feel?" Ki rasped, squinting up at her as if he expected her to look different somehow.

She was very still for a moment, her gaze turned inward. There was a difference, but one she had no words for yet. "Thank you," she whispered at last. "I owe you so much."

"Keep promise and remember Lhel and me." Giving her a last fond smile, Mahti rose and left the tent.

Alone with Ki again, she brought the fingers of his good hand to her lips and kissed him as fresh tears stung behind her eyelids. "You almost broke your promise to me, you bastard," she managed at last.

"I did? No!" Ki laughed softly. He was quiet for a few moments, unfocused eyes fixed somewhere in the shadows above. She was afraid he was drifting into sleep but suddenly his hand tightened painfully around hers. "Korin! I couldn't get to you!"

"You did, Ki, and he nearly killed you."

"No . . . I saw . . ." He closed his eyes and grimaced. "Bilairy's balls!"

"What?"

"Failed you—when it counted most!"

"No." She held him closer. "He would have had me if not for you."

"Couldn't let him . . ." Ki shivered against her. "Couldn't. But what—?" His eyes drifted closed for a moment, then opened very wide. "*You* killed him?"

"Yes."

Ki was silent for a moment, and she saw his gaze stray to the open flap of the tent again. "I wanted to spare you that."

"It's better this way. I see that now. It was our fight."

Ki sighed, and the confusion came back.

"Ki? Don't go to sleep. You have to stay awake."

His eyes were open, but she could tell his mind was wandering. Fearful of letting him fall asleep, she babbled on for hours about nothing—what they would do when they visited the keep again, horses, anything she could think of to keep his eyes open.

He didn't respond at all for a while, but presently she saw the glimmer of tears in his eyes, and pain as he focused on her again. "I can't—stop seeing him going for you. Saw you fall. I couldn't get to you—"

"But you did!" Leaning down carefully, she pressed her lips to his and felt them trembling. "You did, Ki. You almost died for me. He—" She swallowed hard as her voice failed. "You were right about Korin, all along."

"Sorry," he mumbled. "You loved him."

"I love *you,* Ki! If he'd killed you, I wouldn't have wanted to live."

Ki's fingers tightened on hers again. "Know the feeling."

She took an unsteady breath and smiled. "You called me 'Tob' when you woke up."

He let out a faint laugh. "Knock on the head. Scrambled my brains."

She hesitated, then asked softly, "Am I Tamír to you now?"

Ki studied her face in the dim light, then gave her a sleepy smile. "You'll always be both, deep down. But it's Tamír I see, and Tamír I kiss."

A weight lifted from Tamír's heart, not only from the words, but the warmth in his voice and eyes. "I don't ever want to be without you!" The words tumbled out in a rush, and she couldn't hold them back. "I *hate* having you sleep in other rooms, and feeling bad every time I touch you. I hate not knowing what we are to each other anymore. I—"

Ki squeezed her hand again. "Guess I better marry you and clear things up, eh?"

Tamír stared at him. "You're delirious!"

The smile turned to a grin. "Maybe, but I know what I'm saying. Will you have me?"

A heady mix of joy and fear made her feel faint. "But what about—" She couldn't bring herself to say it. "With me?"

"We'll manage. What do you say? Will the Queen of Skala take a grass knight son of a horse thief for her consort?"

She let out a shaky laugh. "You, and no other. Not ever."

"Good. Then it's settled."

Tamír shifted her back more comfortably against the pack, with Ki's head resting on her chest. It felt good, just as it used to, and yet different, too.

"Yes," she whispered. "It's settled."

Mahti paused near the edge of the forest, looking back at the scattered fires and the distant glow inside the tent. Beyond lay the battlefield, where the spirits of the newly dead writhed and twisted like wisps of fog the rain could not dispel.

"Why, Great Mother, should we help such a people?" he whispered, shaking his head. But there was no answer for him, and no companion, either. Lhel was gone as surely as the demon spirit was gone. He wondered if he would meet her again, in the eyes of a child?

Gaining the cover of the trees a thought struck him and he stopped again and ran his hands carefully over the length of his oo'lu. It was still sound, with no sign of any cracking.

He smiled wryly as he shouldered it and continued toward the mountains. His journeying was not over yet. He didn't mind, really. It was a good, strong horn. He only wondered who his new guide would be.

Chapter 55

Tamír held Ki all night and kept him awake talking of the battle and her plans for a new city. They both shyly avoided the understanding they'd arrived at. It was too new, too fragile to dwell on with so much still before them. Watching Ki retch into a helmet was not conducive to such thoughts, either. His right cheek and eye were badly bruised, and his eye had swollen shut.

By dawn he was exhausted and uncomfortable but more alert. The rain had let up and they could hear people moving about outside, and the moans of the wounded. The smell of rank smoke came to them on the breeze, carried from the first of the pyres.

Lynx brought them breakfast—bread and a bit of good lamb stew sent up by the captain of one of the Gedre ships. He also had a healing tonic for Ki. He helped him drink it, then grinned. "You look like hell."

Ki tried to scowl, grimaced in pain instead, and held up the middle finger of his good hand.

Lynx chuckled. "You *are* feeling better."

"How are the others?" Tamír asked as she traded spoonfuls of the stew with Ki.

"Well enough. We've got pyres ready for Korin and the others. They're eager to see you both, if you're up to it."

The tent wasn't large enough for everyone, so Tamír stepped outside to make room. Lynx came out, too, and stood quietly by as she stretched the stiffness from her back. Tents had sprung up overnight, and more were being set up. The drysians were at work among the hundreds of wounded still in the open, and in the distance columns of black smoke rose against the morning sky. Several large pyres stood a little way off near the cliff edge. One was decorated with Korin's banner and shield.

The clouds were shredding away in long tatters that promised better weather, and the dark blue sea was flecked with white.

"Looks like we finally get to dry out," she murmured.

"A good thing, too. I've got moss on my ass." Lynx gave her a sidelong glance and she caught his slight smile. "Are you two going to make an announcement or wait until we get back to Atyion?"

"You heard?" She could feel her cheeks going warm.

"No, but I've got eyes. Nik and I have had bets on it since we left Alestun. So it's true? Ki finally came around?"

"You could say that."

"About time, too."

Her gaze strayed to the shrouded bodies still lying nearby. Tanil and Caliel were still there, keeping watch. "Don't say anything yet. Korin should have proper mourning. He was a prince, after all."

"And a friend." Lynx's voice dropped to a hoarse whisper and he looked away. "If I hadn't gone with you that night—"

"I am glad you ended up on my side. Are you?"

"I suppose I am." He sighed and glanced back at Caliel and Tanil. "It'll be harder for them."

They burned Korin and the others that afternoon, with all the Companions as honor guard. Ki insisted on being carried out, and kept watch with them from a litter until his strength gave out. Caliel stood dry-eyed; Tanil was calm, but stunned.

Tamír and the others cut their horses' manes and cast the strands on the pyres. Tamír cast in a lock of her own hair for Korin, Porion, and Lorin.

The fires burned all day and through most of the night, and when the ashes had cooled they were gathered in clay vessels to be carried away to the families of the dead. Tamír took Korin's into her tent.

In answer to the question that had hung unanswered between her and Ki, and perhaps the whole camp by now, she spread her bedroll by his that night, and slept at his side, holding his hand.

Chapter 56

Nalia woke in darkness to shouting and the sounds of horses in the courtyard below. For one startled instant she thought she must be dreaming of the night Korin first arrived.

Trembling, she sent Tomara off for news, then threw on a dressing gown and hurried out to the balcony. There were only a handful of riders there. She could not make out what was being said, but it did not sound like victory. When Tomara still did not return, she dressed quickly and sat down by the fire, toying nervously with the strand of pearls on her breast.

Her fears were confirmed. The door burst open and Lord Alben staggered in, leaning heavily on Tomara. His face and clothes were bloody, and his hair was tangled around his pale face.

"Tomara, fetch Lord Alben water, and wine! My lord, sit, please."

Alben collapsed into the armchair and for a time they could get no sense out of him. Tomara bathed his face in rosewater to revive him while Nalia hovered anxiously, wringing her hands.

At last Alben recovered enough to speak. "Majesty!" he gasped, and his sudden tears confirmed their worst imaginings. "The king is dead!"

"We're lost!" Tomara wailed. "Oh, my lady, what will become of you?"

Nalia sank down on a stool beside the distraught man, feeling faint and numb all at once. "When, my lord? How did he die?"

"Two—no, it's three days now, at the hand of the traitor Tobin. I came away at once to warn you." He clutched her hand more tightly. "You're in danger here. You must flee!"

"Dead." Nalia could scarcely get her breath. *I have no husband now, my child no father* . . .

"You must come with me," Alben insisted. "I will protect you."

"Would you?" First Niryn, who'd betrayed her, then Korin, who could not love her, and now this man, who'd never had a kind word for her before? Who'd snickered openly about her homely face? He would be her Protector? Tomara was already flying around the room, throwing open the clothes chests and pulling out garments to pack.

"Highness?" Alben was waiting for her answer.

She looked up at him, into those dark eyes full of panic, and something else. Something she recognized all too well. She withdrew her hand from his and stood up. "Thank you for your gracious offer, Lord Alben, but I must decline."

"Are you mad? Tobin and her army are on my heels!"

"Her? Then it was true, all along?"

"I saw her with my own eyes."

Another lie, Niryn?

"Lady, listen to him! You must escape, and you cannot take to the roads alone!" Tomara begged.

"No." Nalia replied firmly. "I thank you for your offer, my lord, but I see no advantage in it. I will remain here and take my chances with this queen, whatever she is. If you would help me, take command of the garrison and see to the defenses. Go and make whatever preparations you think best."

"It's the shock, my lord," said Tomara. "Let her rest and think on it. Come back in the morning."

"He may do as he likes, but my answer will be the same," said Nalia.

"As you wish, Highness." Alben bowed and took his leave.

"Oh, my poor lady! A widow before you're a mother!" Tomara sobbed, embracing her.

Nalia did weep then, as the reality of her situation sank in. She wept for Korin, but her sorrow was mingled with guilt. Her hope of his love had been short-lived, and she'd dashed it with her own hand when she'd killed Niryn. She wanted to mourn her husband, but instead she could only imagine what a lifetime of his coldness and duty would have been like.

Whatever comes, at least I'm spared that.

Nalia dried her eyes and went back to her bed. She fell asleep searching for the proper sorrow in her heart but could not find it.

When she woke again the sun was high and all was quiet outside. She sent Tomara off for their breakfast. She had no proper widow's weeds, so instead she put on her finest gown—the one she'd meant to wear for Korin on his return.

Tomara came back empty-handed and frantic. "They're gone!"

"Who?"

"All of them!" the woman wailed. "Lord Alben, the soldiers, everyone, except for a few servants. What are we to do?"

Nalia went to the tower door. For the first time, there was no one there to stop her from leaving. A feeling of dreamlike unreality came over her as she descended the stairs with only Tomara to attend her. Together they passed through the deserted corridors to the great hall.

There was no one in sight but Korin's abandoned hounds. They trotted up to her, whining and wagging their tails. Nalia went out into the courtyard and found the northern gate ajar. For the first time since the nightmare of her captivity began, she passed through and walked down the road a little way, marveling at her own freedom.

"We must run away," Tomara urged. "Come down to

the village with me. I have people there. They'll hide you, get you away in a fishing boat—"

"And go where?" Nalia wondered, gazing up at the sky. It looked as empty as she felt. "I have no one in the world now. Do what you like, but I'll stay."

Nalia retreated to her tower. No longer her prison, it was the only place in this great fortress that she had ever called her own.

Early that evening a shout came from the lookout on the south wall. Through the gathering dusk Nalia could make out a dark mass of riders on the road, coming on at a gallop. She could not guess their number for the great cloud of dust that hung over them, but she could see the dull glint of helms and spearpoints.

Fear gripped her then, as the reality of her own helpless state sank in.

There's no help for it now, she told herself. She smoothed her hair and gown and descended to the great hall to meet her fate.

Tomara clung close beside her as she ascended the dais and for the first time, sat in the chair that had been Korin's. Presently a stableboy came running in. "It's a herald, my lady, and Lord Lutha! Shall I let them in?"

"Lord Lutha?" What could this mean? "Yes, bring them to me."

Lutha and Nyanis had been prepared for resistance, not to find the fortress abandoned and the gate open to them. Arkoniel was equally suspicious, but there'd been no sign of ambush. The soldiers and the wizards were simply gone.

A frightened boy greeted them from the walls and returned with word that Lady Nalia welcomed them.

Lutha left Nyanis and the Aurënfaie, taking only

Arkoniel and the herald with him into the echoing court-yard. There too, it was eerily deserted.

Nalia was waiting for them in the great hall, seated on the dais in Korin's place. Tomara was her only attendant.

Nalia gave him an uncertain smile. "I am glad to see you alive, my lord, but it appears you have changed your allegiance. Word of the king's death has already reached us here. Lord Alben brought word, before he fled."

"Korin died bravely," Lutha told her. Tamír had told him no more than that before he left. "Queen Tamír sent me to you at once, to ensure your safety, and to tell you that you have nothing to fear from her if you do not stand against her claim."

"I see." She glanced at Arkoniel. "And who are you?"

"Master Arkoniel, wizard and friend of Queen Tamír." Seeing her eyes widen at that, he added quickly, "Highness, I have come only to protect you."

Lutha wished there was something more he could say or do to reassure her, but knew she had good cause to be wary.

Nonetheless, she maintained her dignity and turned to the herald. "What is your message?"

"Queen Tamír of Skala sends her respects to her kinswoman, Princess Nalia, widow of Prince Korin. It is with great sorrow that she sends word of Prince Korin's death. She offers you and your unborn child her royal protection."

"Yet she sends an army with the message." Nalia sat very straight, gripping the arms of her chair.

"Queen Tamír assumed Korin had left you better protected. She did not expect you to be deserted," Lutha replied, trying not to let his anger show.

She waved a hand around. "As you can see, my court has diminished considerably."

"We were told that Lord Niryn died," said Arkoniel.

Nalia lifted her chin a little. "Yes. Lord Lutha, at whose hand did my husband die?"

"He and Queen Tamír met in single combat. She offered parley, but he would not have it. They fought, and he fell."

"And you wear the queen's colors now."

"Tamír, who was Prince Tobin, is my friend. She took us all in after we escaped from here. Barieus and I serve with her Companions. She sent me ahead, thinking a familiar face might reassure you. She pledges by the Four that she means no harm to you or your child. It's the truth, I swear."

"And what of Lord Caliel?"

"He went back to Korin and fought beside him."

"Is he dead?"

"No, only wounded."

"I am glad to hear it. And now what? What is to become of me and my child?"

"I'm to conduct you back to her camp. As a kinswoman, Highness, not as a prisoner."

Nalia laughed softly at that, but still looked sad. "It seems I have no choice but to accept her hospitality."

Here I am again, thought Nalia, watching the activity of the newcomers from her balcony later that night. *At least this time it's by my own choice.*

As much as she wanted to trust Lord Lutha, she dreaded the morrow. "Please, Dalna!" she whispered, pressing her hands over the slight swell below her bodice. "Let my child be spared. She's all I have."

Tomara had gone down for news, but came hurrying back, her face white with fear. "It's that wizard, my lady! He asks to come to you. What shall we do?"

"Let him in." Nalia stood by the hearth, bracing herself against the mantelpiece. Was this to be her answer? Would he quietly kill her or blight her child after all?

Master Arkoniel did not look very threatening. He was younger than Niryn and had a friendly, open face. She saw none of Niryn's cunning in this one, but she had been fooled before.

He bowed, then remained standing. "Highness, forgive my intrusion. Lutha and the others told me something of your treatment here, enough for me to guess that you are a woman who has been grievously wronged. Niryn was a vile creature, and many of your husband's less noble actions must be laid at that villain's feet."

"I would like to believe that," Nalia murmured.

They stood a moment longer like that, sizing each other up, then he smiled again. "I think you could do with a nice cup of tea. If you show me where the makings are, I'll brew it."

Astonished and wary, Nalia watched closely as the man warmed the pot and measured out the leaves. Did he mean to poison her? She saw no sign of it, and when it was steeped he poured for both of them and took a long sip. She took a hesitant sip of her own.

"Is it to your liking, Highness? My mistress taught me to make it rather strong."

"Your mistress?" she asked, wondering if he meant a lover.

"The wizard who was my teacher," he explained.

"Ah."

They fell silent again, but presently he set his cup aside and gazed at her thoughtfully.

"Did you kill Niryn?"

"I did. Does that shock you?"

"Not really. I know what the man was capable of, and if I'm not mistaken, so do you."

Nalia shivered and said nothing.

"I sense something of his foul taint lingering on you, my lady. If you would allow me, I can remove it."

Nalia gripped her cup tightly, torn between revulsion at the thought of any vestige of Niryn, and fear of trickery.

"By my hands and heart and eyes, lady. I would never

hurt you, or the child," Arkoniel said, guessing her thoughts once again.

Nalia struggled with herself a little longer, but when he did not press her, she finally nodded. If he was going to betray her with that kindly manner and reassuring words, better to know it at once and be done with it.

Arkoniel drew out a slender crystal wand and held it between his palms as he closed his eyes. "Ah yes, there it is," he said after a moment. He rested a hand on her head and Nalia felt a tingling warmth course through her body. It felt nothing like Niryn's magic; this was like sunlight compared to frost.

"You are free, my lady," he told her, returning to the other chair.

Nalia wondered how to test it. Not knowing what else to do, she blurted out, "Niryn seduced me."

"Ah, I see." The wizard did not appear shocked by the news, only sad. "Well, he has no more hold on you. As long as you are under Queen Tamír's protection, I will see to it that no one abuses you so again. You have my oath on that."

Tears sprang to her eyes. "Why are you doing this? Why does Tamír send such people to me when I bear the child of her rival?"

"Because she knows what it is to suffer, and because she loved Korin very much, even at the end when he had no love left for her. When you meet her, you will see for yourself." He rose and bowed. "Rest well tonight, dear lady. You have nothing more to fear."

Nalia sat by the fire for a long time after he left, caught between sorrow and hope.

Chapter 57

Lutha returned with Lady Nalia a week later. In keeping with her status, Tamír sat on a cloak-draped stool outside her tent with her nobles around her and her army massed in two large squares, forming an avenue through the great camp. Ki was on his feet again, and in his proper place at her side, still impressively bruised and wearing his arm in a sling.

Caliel had politely refused the baldric she'd offered him, and no more had to be spoken between them. He stood apart with some of the nobles, Tanil close beside him, as always. The two were inseparable.

As the returning force approached, Tamír was surprised to see that their number had greatly increased. The mystery was solved when Lutha and Nyanis rode up with a third rider between them.

"Tharin!" Throwing dignity to the wind, Tamír jumped to her feet and ran to meet him.

Tharin swung down from the saddle and caught her in his arms with a stifled grunt.

"Are you wounded?" she asked, backing up again to search him for blood.

"It's nothing serious," he assured her. "Lord Nevus gave us a good fight before I killed him. It was the same day we got word of your victory here." He looked down at the Sword hanging at her side, and touched the hilt reverently. "At last, it hangs at the side of a true queen."

Ki limped over to join them, and Tharin laughed at the sight of him as they clasped hands. "Looks like you have a few tales to tell, yourself."

"More than you know," he replied with a pained smile.

"I'm glad to see you, Tharin, but what are you doing here?" asked Tamír, walking him back to her makeshift throne.

"After we routed Nevus and burned the ships Korin sent, I pushed north, thinking I'd meet you coming the other way. We reached the isthmus in time to meet with Lutha and Nyanis and I decided to carry word to you myself. Atyion is secure and the last of the northern lords are declaring their loyalty in very loud voices. I only had to kill a few on the way. Ki, your brother sends his regards. Rilmar held out under siege and your family is well."

When the Companions and her generals had greeted the others, Lutha sent a messenger back to summon Nalia.

Nalia arrived, mounted on a fine white horse and escorted by Arkoniel and the two Aurënfaie commanders. Tamír recognized her at once from Lutha's description. She was indeed homely, and the wine-colored stain was pronounced, but Tamír also saw the mix of fear and gentle dignity in her eyes and bearing.

Arkoniel helped her dismount and gave her his arm as he escorted her to Tamír. "Queen Tamír, allow me to present Lady Nalia, Prince Korin's wife."

"Your Majesty." Nalia made Tamír a deep curtsy and remained on one knee before her, trembling.

Tamír's heart went out to her at once. Rising, she took the young woman's hand and drew her to her feet. "Welcome, cousin. It grieves me to meet you at last under such sad circumstances." She motioned to Lynx and he stepped forward with the jar containing Korin's ashes. Nalia looked at a loss and did not move to take them. Instead, she clasped her hands over her heart and gave Tamír an imploring look.

"Lord Lutha and Master Arkoniel have been most kind to me and have given me many assurances, but I must hear it from your own lips. What are your intentions toward my child?"

"You are pregnant, then?" Nalia was still very slender.

"Yes, Majesty. The baby will be born in the spring."

"You are Royal Kin, and your child shares my blood. If you will give me your oath to uphold my right to the throne and put aside all claims of your own, then you will be welcome in my court and given titles and lands in keeping with your station."

"You have my oath, with all my heart!" Nalia exclaimed softly. "I know nothing of court life, and ask nothing but to live in peace."

"I wish the same for you, cousin. Lord Caliel, Lord Tanil, step forward."

Caliel gave her a questioning look, but did as she asked, drawing Tanil along by the arm. "My lords, will you become the liegemen of Lady Nalia, and protect her and her child as long as they are in need of you?"

"We will, Majesty," Caliel replied as understanding dawned. "You are most kind."

"That's settled, then," Tamír said. "You see, my lady, you are not without friends at my court. Lord Lutha also holds you in high esteem. I hope you will call him friend, as well."

Nalia curtsied again, her eyes bright with tears. "Thank you, Majesty. I hope—" She paused and Tamír saw how her gaze strayed to the funeral jar. "I hope one day I may understand, Majesty."

"I hope so, too. Tomorrow we will start the march back to Atyion. Dine with me tonight and rest well."

Tamír made her farewells to the Aurënfaie that evening, exchanged oaths and treaties with them before her nobles and wizards. After they'd taken their leave, she saw Nalia to her tent, then turned with Ki for their own. Arkoniel took note of the arrangement but only smiled.

While the rest of the army made ready to march the next morning, Arkoniel and Tamír rode back to the cliffs above the harbor. Reining in, they gazed out across the water in silence. They could just make out the sails of the Gedre ships in the distance, speeding homeward under a clear sky.

"It's not a bad configuration for a seaport, if you mean to trade mostly with the 'faie," Arkoniel noted. "What about the rest of Skala?"

"I'll find a way," she mused. "It will be harder for the Plenimarans to surprise us here. I've been scouting while you were gone. Mahti was right. There's good water, and good soil, too, and plenty of stone and forest for building." She looked around, eyes shining with anticipation. "I can already see it, Arkoniel! It will be better than Ero ever was."

"A great, shining city, with a castle of wizards at its heart," Arkoniel murmured, smiling.

As a child, Tamír had thought him very homely and awkward, and often rather foolish. She saw him with different eyes now, or perhaps he'd changed as much as she had. "You'll help me build it, won't you?"

"Of course." He glanced at her and smiled as he added, "Majesty."

Arkoniel could already see the walls rising, too, and already imagined the safe haven they would create for all the wandering wizards, and all the lost children like Wythnir and the others. He felt the weight of the travel-stained bag against his knee, still hanging from his saddlebow as it had from Iya's. He would make a safe place for that burden, too. He didn't mind it so much now. Still dangerous and baffling, the ugly, evil bowl joined him to Iya and the Guardians who'd come before—and to all who would come after, too. Perhaps Wythnir had come to him for that purpose, to be the next Guardian?

"I will serve you always, Tamír, daughter of Ariani," he murmured. "I will give you wizards the like of which the Three Lands have never seen."

"I know." She went quiet again and he sensed she was

working up to something. "Ki and I are going to be married."

He chuckled at her shyness. "I should certainly hope so. Lhel would be so disappointed if you didn't."

"She knew?"

"She saw it even when you were children. She liked him very much. Even Iya had to admit that he was more than he seemed at first." He paused and chuckled softly. "Turnips, vipers, and moles."

"What?"

"Oh, just something she said. Ki was the only boy she thought worthy of you."

"I never have understood her." She trailed off, and he guessed that she was uncomfortable speaking of Iya to him.

"It's all right, Tamír."

"Is it?"

"Yes."

She gave him a grateful smile. "I dreamed of this place so often. Ki was with me and I'd try to kiss him, but I always fell over the cliff or woke up before I could. Visions are odd things, aren't they?"

"They are indeed. The gods show us a possible future, but nothing is ever fixed. It's up to us to grasp those dreams and shape them. There's always a choice to be made."

"If that's true, then I could have chosen to run away, couldn't I? There were so many times when I thought of it."

"Perhaps the Lightbearer chose you because you wouldn't."

She stared thoughtfully out over the sea for some time, then nodded. "I think you're right."

She looked around one last time, and Arkoniel saw the future in those blue eyes before she laughed and kicked her horse into a gallop.

Arkoniel laughed too, long and gladly, and followed her, as he always would.

Epilogue

Only sheep wander the Palatine now, and even Atyion has faded. Remoni became Rhíminee to suit Skalan tongues, but the meaning remains the same. Good water. Rhíminee, the life spring of Skala's golden age.

'We wizards are stones in a river's course, watching the rush of life whirl past.'

I think of your words often, Iya, as I walk the streets of Tamír's shining city. From my balcony I can still trace the walls she laid out that year, with a spring at its center. The old city lies like the yolk in an egg surrounded by the additions of her successors. I know it would please her to see the building continue. That was her true calling, after all, even more than warrior or queen.

To the north, where Cirna fortress stood, lies the great canal we hewed for her, the first gift of the Third Orëska to the new capital. Her statue still guards it, carved when she was older. How often I've gazed up into that solemn face; but in my heart she will always be sixteen, standing with Ki in a swirl of bright autumn leaves as they declare their union before the people, with all their friends around them.

Tamír and Ki. Queen and Consort. Fast friends and peerless warriors until the end. The two of you are forever entwined in my heart. Your descendents are strong and beautiful and honor-

able. I still catch glimpses of you both in eyes of darkest blue or brown.

Rhíminee has forgotten the others—Tharin, the Companions, Niryn. Rhius and Ariani. Erius and Korin are shadowed names in the lineage, a cautionary tale. Even you, Tamír—Tamír the Great, they call you now—you are only a half-told tale. Just as well. Brother and Tobin are the twin darknesses at the heart of the pearl; it's only the luster that matters.

An infant's brief cry still haunts my dreams, but the last echoes will die with me. What Tamír built lives on, and carries her love and the love of those who stood by her into the future.

—From a document fragment, discovered by the Guardian Nysander, in the east tower of the Orëska House

Afterword

Some of you observant readers, having just turned the last page, may well be asking yourselves, "But what about that wretched bowl Iya made such a fuss over? What was that all about?"

Arkoniel couldn't have told you that, because he never knew. Instead he kept it safe, as he'd been charged, and let the knowledge of it fade away with the years. He was a Guardian, after all, but not the last. What the bowl really is and what became of it is someone else's tale to tell, long after the time of this trilogy.

You will find those answers in two of my other books, *Luck in the Shadows* and *Stalking Darkness*. I hope you enjoy the quest!

LF
January 19, 2006
East Aurora, New York